Readers love
SUSAN LAINE

Haunted Heart

"This is another must read, must own book by an author who seems to understand the healing power of love and forgiveness. I definitely believe that Ms. Laine is an automatic read, every book leaves me wanting to read more."

—Sensual Reads

"The words sweet and endearing sum up the story for *Haunted Heart* by Susan Laine. It has a wonderful storyline with fantastic characters and it's very easy to lose yourself within the story of this book."

—Top 2 Bottom Reviews

Devil's Own

"The romance is sweet and sexy, Niall and Gus are a great couple and I look forward to more books in this series."

—Love Bytes

"Susan Laine gives the reader so many wonderful elements to enjoy in this story… The Wheel continues to turn and more stories will come. I can't wait to see what happens next!"

—Scattered Thoughts and Rogue Words

"This is a fantastic installment to this series and I just found myself learning more and more of the mysteries of the occult."

—Multitasking Mommas Book Reviews

Sensible Commitments

"This is a sweet wrap up to the Senses and Sensations series… a very nice way to give closure to some wonderful characters."

—Hearts on Fire

By SUSAN LAINE

Falling for Rain
Haunted Heart
Sage Advice
The Sensualist & the Untouched
Two Tickets to Paradise (Dreamspinner Anthology)
The Witching Hour

ISLESHIRE CHRONICLES
Lofty Dreams of Earthbound Men
Wishing Wings

LIFTING THE VEIL
Book One: The Wolfing Way
Book Two: Genie's Wish
Book Three: Hunter's Moon
Book Four: Love of the Wild
Monsters Under the Bed

SECOND CHANCES
Accidental Chemistry
Twice by Chance

SENSES AND SENSATIONS
Love in Plain Sight
A Luminous Touch
Sensible Commitments
Sounds of Love
The Sweetest Scent

THE WHEEL MYSTERIES
Book One: Sparks and Drops
Book Two: Devil's Own

Published by DREAMSPINNER PRESS
http://www.dreamspinnerpress.com

THE SENSUALIST
THE & Untouched

SUSAN LAINE

Dreamspinner Press

Published by
DREAMSPINNER PRESS

5032 Capital Circle SW, Suite 2, PMB# 279, Tallahassee, FL 32305-7886 USA
http://www.dreamspinnerpress.com/

The Sensualist & the Untouched
© 2014 Susan Laine.

Cover Art
© 2014 Bree Archer.
http://www.breearcher.com
Cover content is for illustrative purposes only and any person depicted on the cover is a model.

ISBN: 978-1-63216-500-8
Digital ISBN: 978-1-63216-501-5
Library of Congress Control Number: 2014945924
First Edition December 2014

Printed in the United States of America
∞
This paper meets the requirements of
ANSI/NISO Z39.48-1992 (Permanence of Paper).

I dedicate this tale of falling in love to anyone wishing to love and be loved. May hope fly with swift wings.

CHAPTER 1

"I'M THIRTY-THREE, and I'm a frigid virgin."

For admitting *that* wretched truth out loud, Corey didn't expect any prizes, but dammit, some acknowledgment would have been nice. But the curvaceous brunette in the tight burgundy business dress and black high heels expressed no emotions on her subtly made-up face.

Then again, Adelaide Kingsley *was* a renowned psychologist of the rich and famous, trained to maintain a neutral facade, to show no startled reactions. Or maybe some other adult virgin had already shocked her with their tale of woe, Corey mused sardonically.

"You feel these are a problem for you, Mr. Paige?" she asked with a flat voice.

Corey shrugged, feigning indifference while looking out the skyscraper window, where the Manhattan skyline was cast under an iron-colored, cloudy sky. "Isn't determining that *your* job?"

"You pointed out three things," she remarked, scribbling into the iPad on her lap. To Corey she looked far too overtly sexy to be a professional. Yet, she had been recommended to him. A psychologist who specialized in sex disorders. Apparently, lifelong celibacy was among them. "Your age, your physiological condition, and your sexual inexperience."

Since she added nothing else, Corey assumed reasonably that Adelaide was expecting him to fill in the blanks. He sighed. "I'm not over the hill yet. I'm still young. That's fine."

Adelaide quirked a smile. "Go on." She was a tough nut to crack. Corey couldn't read her very well, just a hint here and there, uncertain and rife with multiple interpretations.

Corey resisted the urge to roll his eyes or grit his teeth. "I've never been diagnosed as frigid. But I know I am." Adelaide cocked her head, always waiting it seemed. Corey stared out the window, where the glass was gathering droplets and wet striations from the drizzle that had begun. "When I look at people, I... I feel nothing. Not for women, not for men." He huffed out, angry. "And no, not for kids, farmyard animals, or corpses, either."

Adelaide wrote on her high-tech notebook, her gaze quickly reverting back to her client. "I'm glad to hear that."

"Why? Wouldn't sexual perversions be right up your alley? Your bread and butter, so to speak?" Corey knew he was being pissy, but he didn't care. He didn't want to be here—yet he knew he needed to be. For nearly twenty years now, he should have been accumulating a vast array of sexual experiences like everyone else, but... he had none. Not a single kiss, not even a hug. A few pats on the back didn't qualify.

And that did piss him off, so he should probably apologize to the woman trying to help him.

But she spoke first, calm as ever. "Tell me about your frigidity, Mr. Paige."

Corey closed his eyes briefly, inhaling. "I'm logically aware that you, for example, are a beautiful woman. But I feel nothing when I look at you. It's as if... you're made of paper, two-dimensional, with no depth at all. You barely register as human to me."

"Please, go on." Her look was focused, pensive, even a bit intense.

Looks like I got her attention now. "It's the same with everyone. And no, it's not just about being able to read signals and interpret another's attention or attraction. I can see the signs in others. Sometimes even directed at me. But... I feel nothing for them. I don't want to know them, I don't want to kiss them, touch them, be naked with them. None of that."

Adelaide remained quiet for a time, as if scrutinizing him. He feared what kind of mental illness she would diagnose. Suddenly she smiled softly. "I imagine there have been quite a few different diagnoses on the table with other doctors."

Corey scoffed. "Lucky guess."

She chuckled in response. "Well, right off the bat I'm ruling out dissociative identity disorders."

Corey let out a sigh from somewhere deep inside him. He'd never had memory lapses or suffered major emotional trauma. Hearing the confirmation by a specialist was comforting.

"I was, however, considering schizoid personality disorder," she went on. "This is characterized by disinterest in social relationships." Corey swallowed nervously. "A person with this disorder is socially and emotionally distant, fearful of close interactions with other people, has a limited range of emotional expression, and his thinking process is distorted, all of which is apparent in speech and behavior." She offered a reassuring smile. "And these qualities I have not observed in you. You have excellent social skills and mature use of speech patterns, and you express your emotions freely, such as your nervousness right now. You do not fear relationships as much as you claim you feel nothing."

"So… I don't have that?" Relief once again washed over Corey like spring rain.

Adelaide shook her head, seeming pensive. "No, I don't think so. Another possibility is avoidant personality disorder, which is characterized by feelings of inadequacy, avoidance of activities that require interpersonal interaction, and hypersensitivity to negative evaluation. Also not a psychological disorder that would match with your condition." She stopped for a moment, as if lost in thought, but her gaze remained deeply focused. "Your medical records suggest you've had the typical physical causes for your possible condition checked?"

"You mean stuff like erectile dysfunction, low testosterone levels, diabetes, strokes, nerve damage, circulation problems, kidney problems, etcetera, etcetera?" Corey nodded. "Yeah. I have a full physical every year. Last one was four months ago. I'm in my prime."

"With your permission, I'd like to go over the findings of your last checkup, just in case." Corey nodded his acquiescence. Adelaide continued coolly, "You mentioned me, a woman. Have you considered the possibility you're gay?"

Corey snorted. "Yes, of course. Did you not hear me? I feel nothing for *anyone*. That includes men *and* women."

"You say you feel nothing. Yet you sound frustrated, nervous, agitated."

"I don't like talking about this." Wasn't that self-evident? Geesh!

"Why?" she pressed, her tone neither lowering nor rising.

Corey let out a mirthless chuckle and waved his hands with an irritated gesture. "'Cause it's embarrassing."

"What is?"

Corey stared at her then. Was she deaf? "Um, all of it? Being over thirty and a virgin? Being frigid, with no concept of sexual attraction? Having to talk to a complete stranger about all this? You gonna ask me about my mother next?"

"Do you want to talk about your mother?"

Corey reined in his temper. "Do you always answer a question with a question?"

Adelaide smiled. Corey couldn't read the gesture. Was it condescending or pitying or simply kind? "When you look at people around you, on the street, in a café, what are you thinking then? What goes through your mind?"

Corey frowned. "Think about? Nothing."

Adelaide leaned forward. "You said you're logically aware I'm a beautiful woman. Do you make similar observations about other people?"

The question actually made Corey stop. "I… I can tell if someone's hot or not."

"You focus on their physical attributes? Their looks?"

Corey fidgeted on the couch, uncomfortable. "I can't read their minds, if that's what you're asking."

"What about gauging their moods?"

Corey shrugged, calming. "Yeah, I guess I can do that. I mean, I can tell if a person is happy or sad or angry, stuff like that." He looked at the woman sharply. "If I weren't able to do that, would that make me a… a sociopath, or something? Not recognizing affect?"

Adelaide actually chuckled at that, leaning back again, relaxed. "How antisocial do you feel, Mr. Paige?"

"Not homicidal, if that helps." Corey smirked saying that, and Adelaide laughed.

"Good to hear."

Though Doctor Kingsley asked insightful, almost intrusive personal questions, Corey appreciated the fact that she kept the tone light. She wasn't forcing the situation, so Corey didn't feel trapped.

Still, Adelaide sat in the armchair, legs crossed, her gaze poignant but distant too, as if she were a faraway star, bright enough to catch one's eye but not enough to take up all of a person's attention. She was a hunter, Corey reflected, always skulking downwind.

"So, we've established you make instinctive observations about people. You yourself used the word logical. What kind of rational thought processes go through your mind when looking at people?"

Corey thought back to some of his most recent encounters. "Like I said, they feel like… pictures of people. Unreal." He frowned and huffed. "No, that's not right. I mean, I do know they're real. I don't think I'm dreaming or hallucinating. People just don't… feel like…." He didn't know how to finish the thought. It was difficult putting his feelings into words.

"Do you have friends, Mr. Paige?"

The sudden question scrambled Corey's train of thought. "What? Yeah, sure. I have friends. My apartment is right next door to a place shared by three other guys. We hang out."

"Are they your friends or casual acquaintances?"

"Both?"

"Are you asking me or telling me?"

Corey shifted on the couch by the window. "Look, I'm not a total loner, okay? I have people around me, in my life."

"People. Your friends?" Corey nodded. "You care for them?"

"Yeah, of course."

"Men? Women?"

"I have both male and female friends. Mostly male, I think."

"Do you feel attracted to any of them?"

"What? No!"

"But you have friendly feelings toward them?"

"Yes." God, why did he have to keep repeating all this shit? Corey was reaching the conclusion he should never have come here.

"Good." Adelaide smiled in a reassuring manner, as though Corey had done something right without realizing it. "The clinical definition of frigidity is a lack of sexual desire and desire for sexual activity. It is not, however, an absence of emotions. Do you see the distinction?"

Corey did. "Yeah. I am able to have feelings for people, like my friends. But not… the other kind. Wanting."

She nodded, acknowledging the statement. "Laypeople often get that confused."

"So you were testing me?" Corey should have felt indignant, but he didn't.

Adelaide nodded slightly. "You came in here for your first consultation. Then you said nothing for five minutes. Finally, the first thing you say is you're a thirtysomething frigid virgin. Yes, naturally I check what you mean by using those terms."

"Okay, I get it." Corey shook his head, chuckling, part resigned, part… whatever. "By virgin, in case that's your next inquiry, I mean I haven't done anything with a man or a woman. No sex of any kind, no foreplay, no making out. I have never even kissed anybody. And the only people who have ever touched me are my parents and a few of my friends, briefly, like on the shoulder."

"You've never wanted to kiss anyone?"

"No." Corey shook his head and knew it was the truth.

"Have you ever thought about it? Rationally, I mean. Imagined it?"

"Yeah, sure." Corey worried his bottom lip, his gaze all over the place, not settling on anything particular. "I see, um… lips, and I think, uh… they're full and luscious and…." He closed his eyes, defeated, when even seeing it through his mind's eye did nothing for him.

"Are you able to physically become aroused?" Adelaide cut in when Corey fell silent.

"Like get an erection?" He didn't blush since the topic was addressed so clinically. "I wake up hard."

"Do you masturbate?"

"Yeah, sometimes. In the morning 'cause I'm already…." He hung his head, eyes out of sight, and chewed on the inside of his cheek. "But it doesn't feel…. I mean, my head is sort of blank, you know."

"You have no sexual fantasies?"

Corey exhaled deeply, feeling weary. He hated being like this, as if the whole world was in color, but he was seeing everything in black and white, with no texture or shades, as if stuck in bubble wrap. *The bubble boy.*

"Um, kind of. I can get off." He decided to be clinical. "I ejaculate fine."

"Can you give me an example of a fantasy?"

Corey hesitated, for the first time wondering what Adelaide would think about his mindset. "I don't see any faces. They're obscure, a beige veil. No one specific. Ever."

"Bodies?"

"Yeah, they're clear." He chuckled dryly. "I know what you're gonna ask. Some are women, some are men. When I come... it's usually to images of men."

"Does the idea of possibly being gay bother you?"

Corey laughed at the ridiculous notion. "I don't care. Sex is sex. Isn't that what they say? It's all good—if you're getting some." He grew serious when Adelaide said nothing and just watched him with those neutral eyes. "My parents.... You know my family's rich, right? Not quite American aristocracy, but pretty damn close. Anyway, they have their, um, parties. They both have affairs." He saw the glint in Adelaide's eyes, and he put up his hand to stop her speaking. "I didn't tell you about that so you could draw some weird conclusions about it. My point is they've both had sex with women *and* men. So... am I afraid of their reaction if I turn out to be gay? Fuck that. To be honest, they're more concerned about me *not* having sex than the alternative. Hell, at this point I think they'd be exalted if I came down with an STD or something."

Adelaide was quiet for a moment, but her gaze never left him. "Can you give me a few details of your fantasies?"

Corey shrugged, waving his hand dismissively. "They're not that elaborate. Just, uh, a few hard bodies. Not much more."

"Are you an onlooker or a participant?"

Corey frowned. He hadn't expected that, though he should have. He licked his lips, suddenly dry, as discomfort and unease made him squirm. "Um, it varies," he replied vaguely. As expected, she waited him out. "I guess I look, mostly."

It was funny, but saying that out loud, he all of a sudden realized even in his head he didn't get close to people, who were faceless, nameless hard bodies without personalities, without words, without a single touch of reality. *I'm so fucking screwed up in the head.*

That's when Adelaide tapping her pen on the iPad caught his attention. "Through media and pop culture, society has become highly sexualized. Mr. Paige, you are not the first or the last to become distanced from the real world, from real people. Tell me. Do you watch porn?"

"Online, sometimes. Gay and straight, masturbation and orgies. Anything." He huffed, bored. "It's... unsatisfying." Then he chuckled, very amused. "Then again, so is everything else."

"Do you know what asexuality is, Mr. Paige?"

Corey closed his eyes, sighing. He had known they would come to this. Previous shrinks had mentioned it too. "Yeah. Lack of sexual attraction for members of either sex. Lack of interest in sex altogether."

Adelaide smiled in that quirky, mysterious way again. "I take it other mental health professionals have offered asexuality as a reason for your condition?" Reluctantly Corey nodded, gritting his teeth. "But you didn't say to me that you're an asexual virgin. You said frigid."

"So?" Corey licked his lips, nervous, practically barking the word out.

"You make the distinction in your head? When you look at yourself rationally, the word you associate with yourself is frigid, not asexual?"

Corey looked away, not wanting to show Adelaide how much he sort of wished he were frigid instead of asexual. The former could be worked on, cured even, while the latter... well, that was a permanent state of being, natural, a quality from birth. "I guess...."

That was when Corey noticed Adelaide jotting something down. A quirky smile lifted one corner of her lips. Then she rose from the chair, elegantly, like a cat, and walked to her desk. She rummaged through the top drawer and pulled out a calling card. First she stared at it, deep in thought. Then she came over to sit next to Corey on the couch.

"I would like to try something unorthodox with you, Mr. Paige," she said, toying with the calling card between her fingers. Corey swallowed, wondering what this was all about. "There is someone I'd like you to meet. For, uh, a consultation, if you will. If you agree, I will make all the necessary arrangements and call you with the time and place of your next session. How does that sound?"

Corey stared at her, leery. "Odd and suspicious."

Adelaide smiled. "Consider it an exercise in trust and a leap of faith."

Corey was torn between his many doubts and his many wishes. In the end, he was tired of being apart from the world and the people in it, walking through it all like a shadow, untouched.

"Okay. Sure. Why not?"

Chapter 2

"This has got to be the wrong address...," Corey mumbled to himself for the *n*th time.

He was escorted to a fancy elevator, where one of the receptionists—in a luxurious uniform, no less—walked in with him, held the doors open, turned the key to allow the top button to be pushed, and then exited with a polite smile, leaving him alone. It seemed the penthouse of one New York's high-class skyscrapers was Corey's destination for today.

Corey studied his surroundings unsteadily. Everything in the building screamed opulence, including the interior of the elevator. The image in the polished steel doors of a man with gray eyes, salt-and-pepper hair in unruly spikes, a five o'clock shadow on a chiseled jaw, raggedy jeans, white T-shirt, and leather jacket looked out of place—a bad-boy biker entering Buckingham Palace. Yet this was where Adelaide had directed him.

When the light ping indicated he had reached the penthouse, the doors opened. A girl of Asian descent—best described as petite and wearing a pink corset, the tiniest panties, silk stockings, and not much else—stood there in wait.

"Mr. Paige?"

Corey was wary. "Yes?"

"Please, follow me." She pivoted gracefully on her super high heels and walked to the end of the hallway. A set of uninspiring white double doors confused Corey. He'd been to his share of upscale apartments, but this seemed oddly low-key.

The girl pushed the door open and walked into a room that had to take up at least three floors. A glass dome formed most of the ceiling of the cavernous space dominated by white leather couches, a glass coffee table, and white wood bookshelves—though they held antiques and glass artifacts instead of literature. The space was more than neutral; it was bare and bleak.

The room was also empty of occupants. A wide doorway to the right led them to an open kitchen, dining room, and lounge, with no walls between the separate spaces.

There, by another glass coffee table and three divans, sat a man. His posture was lazy and sprawling, Corey guessed, though he could only see the man from the back. He had reddish-blond hair, more the former, in tastefully mussed-up curls. His skin was flawless and very white, as though he didn't venture outside much. He wore an expensive business suit. Well, at least the jacket was tailor-made. Corey wasn't able to see more than that.

But the man was inconsequential at the moment because Corey's gaze was drawn to the pet the man was feeding. A half purr, half growl emerged from the black panther, sleek and at rest, with a steel-and-diamond collar around its neck. Its round green eyes turned to Corey, who swallowed with instinctive fear.

"Hush, my pet," the man crooned soothingly. "Another visitor. We get plenty of those, don't we? And do we eat them all?" He chuckled wickedly. "Well, some we do."

Corey frowned. He had a strong suspicion the man was giving him a show. But before he could interject even the smallest of thoughts, the man spoke.

"Melon balls."

Well, that was a surprising non sequitur. "Pardon me?"

The man simply popped another globe of green fruit in his mouth and chewed it slowly.

Corey glanced over his shoulder to ask for some guidance, but the petite girl was gone. It was just him and the mystery man. Unaccustomed to waiting, Corey walked to the couch and sat down opposite his host.

Up close, the man was silky smooth in appearance, groomed to perfection. His hair had been styled to appear casual, his nails were manicured, and his shirt with a cravat—unexpected, to be sure—didn't have a single stain or wrinkle on it. He was petite, delicate, and short, probably at least three inches shorter than Corey. He wasn't buff or bulky—not like Corey, who was muscular and athletic—but lean and lithe to the point of skinny, almost pixie-like. Some of his gestures were theatrical, even a bit effeminate. The very definition of an upper-crust twink.

Corey frowned. Who was this guy? And why had Adelaide directed Corey to him?

A white ceramic bowl half-full of melon balls sat on the coffee table, and Corey snatched one up.

A sudden slap on his hand made him grunt and jump, startled.

One green eye, one blue, both beautified with eyeliner, eye shadow, and mascara, met his, merciless. "Ask for them." His low voice was indeed a bit effeminate, but also commanding, expecting obedience. "Ask politely."

Corey dropped the melon ball, pulled his hand away, and lifted his chin in defiance. "I'm not really in the mood for melon balls."

The man quirked an amused eyebrow. "Or any other kinds of balls."

Corey's cheeks heated, but his dry mouth rendered him speechless. Either Adelaide had told this man about his possible homosexuality, or he was a good interpreter of people.

Those different-colored, predatory eyes studied him languidly. The man picked up another melon ball and put it in his mouth, making an obscene display of it. The smile on his lips told Corey the guy knew exactly the kind of reaction he was stirring in his guest. Or, more to the point in Corey's case, instilling in his head but not his body.

"My name—" He paused to lick the stickiness off his lips in an act of pure lewdness. "—is Lucian. Lucian Allard. At your service."

Corey cleared his throat, trying to control his temper. "I'm—"

"I know who you are." Lucian gave Corey a leisurely once-over, as real as a touch, giving Corey goose bumps. "Adelaide gave me a mystery." Then he chuckled dryly, rolling his eyes. "Well, that's at least what I was hoping for. How sad to be so disappointed. For you, Mr. Paige, are no mystery whatsoever."

Corey knew when he was being insulted. "In that case I'll be on my way." He stood to leave.

"And here I thought you wanted to sample my balls." Lucian was staring at the bowl of melon bits, but Corey was certain that wasn't what he had meant. "Adelaide didn't tell me much about you, other than your name. How old are you?"

Hesitating between simply walking away, indignant, and staying, Corey munched on the inside of his cheek, frowning. "Thirty-three. How old are you?"

Lucian laughed. It was a high-pitched sound, and yet it carried a seductiveness Corey was sure he didn't like. "As old as the sun and the moon and the stars." He waved a delicate, bony hand about impatiently. "Sit, sit. Stop hovering."

With a deep exhale, Corey gathered his patience, controlled his temper, and sat back down. "Why did Adelaide recommend I meet with you?"

Lucian took a sip from his champagne flute. Corey contained his grimace. It wasn't even ten in the morning yet, for fuck's sake. Far too early for bubbly.

"I offend you," Lucian remarked, putting down his glass, not once looking his guest in the eye.

"I'm not sure what you mean by—"

"Don't be so bourgeois, darling. I imagine I offend your delicate sensibilities in more ways than one. Be crass, be honest." He smiled in an annoyingly smug way that made Corey want to punch him.

"I'm not fond of spending time with alcoholics." Corey tried for a neutral tone.

Lucian chuckled. "How very pedestrian." Corey looked away, biting his lower lip, so he wouldn't say anything back. That seemed to amuse Lucian more. "Oh, my dear, how you tickle my funny bone."

Corey bit his lip harder. God, how that man made everything sound absolutely rude and obscene. "So glad I could provide you with some asinine amusement."

Lucian laughed harder this time, with his head thrown back, exposing the long, thin, pale column of his neck. He had the smallest Adam's apple Corey had ever seen on a guy, almost nonexistent.

"Speaking of asses...." Yup, Corey had expected that segue, so he plastered a polite smile on his face and waited. "How about you get yours off the couch and come help me in the kitchen? I'm making roasted beef tenderloin with sherry vinaigrette and watercress." He jumped off his seat and headed for the open kitchen behind the island.

Dumbfounded, Corey blinked hard and then followed his host to stand by the island's marble counter, feeling more than a little lost. Thankfully the panther remained in place, resting on the floor by the couch, its diamond collar attached to a metal post Corey hadn't paid attention to until then. With one last wary glance at the elegant beast, Corey refocused on Lucian.

"I don't know much about cooking," he confessed. He contemplated sitting on one of the bar stools.

"I adore food," Lucian said, smacking his lips with an exaggerated show of hunger. "Then again, I adore a multitude of sinful pleasures. Of the mouth, among other orifices." He perused Corey's body with careful scrutiny, and Corey had to lock his knees to prevent himself from squirming. "What do you do for pleasure, Mr. Paige?"

That felt like a very intimate and personal question, Corey thought, unwilling to give an immediate, honest reply. "Are you a shrink?"

Those mesmerizing eyes widened with surprise and then crinkled at the corners with amusement. "Do I look like a psychiatrist? My, I must recheck my wardrobe." He took off his suit jacket and practically tore off his cravat, tossing them carelessly onto a barstool. He popped open a couple of shirt buttons, exposing delicate clavicles and the top of a flat, hairless chest that for some reason made Corey nervous.

Aggravated by this mystery of a host, Corey asked, "What do you do, then?"

Lucian cocked his head, frowning as if puzzled. "Do?"

"You know, for a living?"

"Oh." Lucian turned back to the stove and stirred something out of sight. "Nothing. I'm what you might call independently wealthy."

"Uh-huh." It wasn't like Corey should judge. After all, so was he, by virtue of birth into the right family. Well, a rich family, not one for hugging or closeness, at least not in public and rarely in private either. "Business or inherited?"

"Bit of both." Lucian glanced at him over his shoulder, grinning. "You too, I take it?"

Corey shrugged, as if he didn't care. But he did. Unfortunately, his parents didn't, not much, not enough. Was that why he was such a coldhearted person? Or to be more accurate, a man with a cold libido?

"Why did Adelaide send me to you? If you're not a shrink, that is."

With a chuckle Lucian turned to face Corey and held a wooden ladle with brown sauce on it. Blowing gently he stepped forward and offered Corey a taste. "What do you think?"

Even while opening his mouth and accepting the delicious offering, Corey was aware Lucian's words had multiple interpretations. "Sweeter than I expected."

Lucian wrinkled his nose. "It's the sherry. A bit tart for my typical tastes." He winked and then went back to his cooking.

Lucian had a variety of facets, Corey concluded, wondering for the nth time which—if any—was his truest aspect. Or were they all mere showy facades? Different from the earlier domineering dilettante, Lucian was now the playful, boyish chef, more real, and Corey actually liked this one a bit. Definitely more than the previous version.

"So, tell me what troubles you—in three sentences, or less." Lucian's tone was neutral, giving Corey the same anxious feeling he'd had with Adelaide.

Well, what the hell, right? "I'm frigid and a virgin."

The vigorous motion of Lucian's stirring hand stopped instantly.

Lucian's head was cocked to the side, as if to hear better. Corey would have wished to see the man's revealing expression right then instead of the back of his head. "Repeat, please."

Corey held back a sigh. "I'm frigid and a virgin." Then he added with a growl, "There's nothing wrong with being a virgin. It's nothing to gawk at. Everybody starts out that way."

Lucian whirled around, suddenly whimsical and impish, his arms crossed over his chest, mischief gleaming in his eyes. "How could I possibly be gawking at you with my back turned?" He rolled his eyes, but his smile never left. "Since you've been so direct with me... I'm a hedonist and a total slut."

Corey let out a snort, unable to help it. "Uh-huh." Was that the reason Adelaide had put the two of them together? So Lucian could introduce Corey to wild orgies or uninhibited and promiscuous sexual exploits? Total opposites attract?

"What I find interesting is that your first reaction was defending your inexperience rather than your lack of desire for experience," Lucian remarked slyly.

Corey looked down at the counter, embarrassed. Sometimes it was easier to speak with a stranger about things that ailed you, but not always. Certainly not with people like Lucian, who were impossible to read accurately unless they wanted you to.

"In this day and age, being frigid is a mere sexual challenge for other people. Being a virgin means you're defective somehow or a freak." He scoffed with disdain at the prejudice and hypocrisy people showed. "I mean, on the one hand, one should remain chaste and well-mannered until the age of twenty-one, but on the other hand, if one is still a virgin by the time college enrollment comes up, then there's something wrong."

Lucian said nothing, simply stared at Corey mysteriously. "No worries. I can help you with both."

"How?" Corey chuckled sarcastically. "By throwing me an orgy?"

Lucian joined in the laugh, cocky. "Oh, I think I can do *much* better than that."

Chapter 3

"Do I make you nervous, darling, or horny?" Lucian asked, watching the young man before him.

Corey was bigger than Lucian in every way, probably in masculine endowments as well. He wore casual but trendy clothes, as though he rebelled or was uncomfortable with the wealth he undoubtedly possessed. He must have shaved in the morning, but he already had stubble. Corey's big eyes were steely gray, his lips were only two shades above his peachy skin tone—his nipples would probably be the same—and his features were handsome but unremarkable. Yes, they were chiseled and raw, but did they reveal anything of significance about his character? No.

Lucian let himself revel in the mystery—wrapped within a self-evident package.

Corey shifted his weight from one foot to the other, grimacing and fidgeting. "Why do I feel like I'm in a bad parody of *Austin Powers*?"

Lucian chuckled. "I don't know. Why do you?"

"It was a rhetorical question," Corey grunted and then promptly plopped his ass down on one of the barstools, looking deflated and resigned—but with a hint of anger as well. "Didn't Adelaide tell you anything about me?"

"She warned me the first thing to come out of your mouth would be a lie." Amused, Lucian watched as suspicion rose in Corey's eyes. "I interpret that to mean you being frigid."

There was a visible tick in Corey's jaw. "Why would anyone in their right mind lie about something like that?"

Lucian shrugged. "I imagine there are a lot of reasons why people wouldn't want to have sex with anyone. You do know what asexuality means?" Corey snorted, rolling his eyes derisively. "So would I be safe in assuming you're feeling a lack of sexual desire as opposed to simply abstaining from sexual activity?"

Corey closed his eyes for a while, as if willing himself to remain patient. "Of course. I'm not celibate. I have a dysfunction. And FYI, we've covered this, Adelaide and me."

Lucian smiled, waggling his eyebrows. "Do I look like our lovely shrink lady? Am I psychically linked to her? No, so you have to tell me more."

"I thought you said I was no mystery to you." Corey smirked upon saying that, rubbing it in.

Lucian laughed, not hurt in the slightest. "I can read some things about you, it's true. Your virginity isn't written on your forehead, contrary to what you may think."

Corey's smirk faded. "Things like what?"

"Are you fearing transparency? You shouldn't. After all, the sooner I figure you out, the sooner I fix you, and you can go home."

Corey's jaw dropped. "Fix me? Is that why I'm here?"

Lucian cocked his hip, expressing an inner flare for the dramatic like a proper queen. "But of course, darling. You see, some are truly asexual, a lasting condition of feeling no sexual attraction, or even an orientation. But you, Corey... you are *not* like that."

A blinding fury darkened Corey's handsome features. "Oh, is that so?" His voice had gone low and dangerous, dripping with sarcasm.

"Some asexual people do engage in sex to procreate, others do it to please their—"

"Why even talk about asexuality if you think it doesn't apply to me?"

"You'd rather call yourself frigid than asexual? I know asexuality is a relative new topic in the public sphere, but it still carries a more neutral connotation than frigidity." When Corey just stared at Lucian, obviously surprised, Lucian gave a smirk of his own. "I may not be a shrink, but I do know more than my fair share of psychology."

Corey frowned angrily and swallowed hard. "What can you see when you look at me?"

Lucian approached his guest from the other side of the island, leaning on it to face Corey closer than ever before. "Cold, hard truth? Your clothes are new and high quality, but you wear them with disdain, with purposeful rips and tears in them, uncaring if there are stains or blemishes. So... you're rich, but you resent it, yet you know in your heart you can't do much without money. You speak of frigidity as though it were natural for you, as though you grew up believing it, and yet your only piece of jewelry is a family signet ring, so... you hate your parents for neglecting you, but you can't let go of your deep-seated need for family. You might say you have friends, but you see them as fair-weather friends, nothing more. You're high-strung and stressed beneath a calm, casual facade. Your nervous habits include biting your fingernails, grinding your teeth in your sleep, and you'll probably develop an ulcer before you turn thirty-five. Your cuticles look horrible, my dear, in desperate need of a manicure. Your incessant frown and shifting jaw suggest you have a headache, induced by grinding your teeth at night. And the way you're slightly hunched, your hand rubbing over your belly once in a while, subconsciously, tells me you're a stomach worrier. You feel stress in your belly, tightening in knots, a constant dull ache." He waited briefly before adding, "Do correct me if I'm wrong on any account."

Corey's hands balled into fists as he blinked, obviously infuriated with the direction the conversation was taking—even if he had been the one to ask. "What kind of role do *you* play in these mind games? Do you go around revealing embarrassing secrets to the world? Or are you the discreet blackmailer type?"

The vehement attack on Lucian's character wasn't a surprise to him. Many reacted like this. Offense was the best defense. "If you'd like, Corey, we can sign a confidentiality agreement. It wouldn't be my first time. In essence, it would state that nothing you divulged to me could be discussed with anyone else. A legally binding contract, effective immediately."

Once again Lucian had clearly managed to shock Corey into silence and awe. He kind of liked this stupefied expression on his guest's face. "Really?"

"Absolutely." Lucian snapped his fingers. The pretty Asian girl reappeared at the door, as if conjured out of thin air, and presented Lucian with a bundle of papers. Lucian took them, rifled through them, and then handed out several for Corey. The girl gave Corey a pen.

"You had these ready?" Corey asked, suspicion tinting his tone.

Lucian smirked. His guest's reaction amused him. "Of course. You're not the first to step over my threshold for private counsel."

Harrumphing, Corey read the papers carefully before signing. "I'd like copies of these for my personal files."

"Of course. Amaya will have them ready when you depart." Lucian nodded to the Japanese girl, a friend and employee of the trusted variety. He knew she would do as she was told. She might be wearing only sexy undergarments, but she had a business degree from Dartmouth and a legal degree from Harvard. The fact that she was also a professional Dominatrix was neither here nor there. Lucian gave her the stack of papers back, and Corey handed her the ones he had signed. Then she bowed, pivoted, and vanished again.

"You really have done this sort of thing before," Corey remarked, suspicion in his eyes only slightly lessened as they flashed intently. "Funny. At first you were acting like a pretentious prick."

"Acting?" To show he was kidding, Lucian burst into giggles that hinted at his boyish nature. Then he sobered up. "That was my number one lesson, Corey. That first impressions aren't always the right ones. Neither are initial conclusions."

"You mean me being frigid?"

"Yes." Lucian studied Corey meticulously. "I do not play mind games. That is the one thing you need to know about me. You accused me of being duplicitous. What it was, however, was your interpretations of my behavior, more telling of you than me."

"I'm not two-faced," Corey denied vehemently.

"There you go again," Lucian reproached softly. "What I meant was how we all wear many masks, for the public, for friends, even for ourselves. We all play a variety of roles based on the current social situation—or loneliness. We adapt to our surroundings and the people around us."

"Psych 101, I get it." Corey sighed, using his stubbly fingernails to draw meaningless patterns on the counter. "I'm not expecting you to solve all my problems for me. I'm gonna pull my own weight. But I don't wanna play games."

"Sounds reasonable, if a bit boring." Lucian smirked when Corey glared at him. "What I demand, however, is complete and total honesty and transparency from you."

Corey chuckled. "I thought you could read me like a book—even if I lied."

Lucian liked the self-confidence Corey displayed when he was relaxed. Unfortunately, that condition wouldn't last long, not with what Lucian had in store for the man. "I'm going to take you on a journey. Be your guide. You will have to tell me how you feel at all times. Mind you, I will sometimes ignore your requests, but I still want the truth from you."

"Likewise." Corey expected tit-for-tat, and Lucian was on board. "For example, what was the point with the melon balls and your attitude when I arrived?"

Lucian smiled. "Simple. I wanted to see your reaction to an authority figure, especially one who is smaller than you, and how you react to deliberate provocation."

Corey frowned, his fingers brushing his temple, where the tightness was undoubtedly giving him a stress headache. "You mean you wanted to see if I acted violently or bullied you."

Lucian shrugged. "I have been bullied before. I had a horrible time in school."

Corey's eyes flashed with a hard glint. "I'm *not* like that."

"That's good to know." Lucian swiveled around to try the food again. Soon they would be ready to dine. "I'm going to ask you questions, and you're going to answer. That is how I will decide how to best proceed with you. Does that sound like a plan you can agree to?"

"I guess." Corey sounded reserved, and Lucian could relate.

"Let's start with an easy one. What do you think about when you kiss?"

"I've never kissed anyone," Corey admitted, embarrassment coloring his words.

Lucian wasn't deterred. "How close have you come? I mean, physically close?" Over his shoulder, he saw Corey grimace. "Tell me what went through your mind just now."

Corey closed his eyes, his cheeks pinked, and a low, resigned exhale came out of him. "When I think about kissing a guy, all I see is the... um, the ick factor."

Puzzled, Lucian faced the man, more intrigued than before. Corey looked positively ashamed, red-faced.

"I think about stupid things," Corey explained, "like... his breath smells funny. He should trim his nose hair. Gross, is that a pimple? Is that a piece of rancid meat dangling between his teeth? What if I kiss him, and it's dislodged, and I swallow it?" He shuddered violently, a disgusted look on his face. "And it's no better with women, like... I don't want to kiss lipstick. God, she's wearing a lot of perfume, I'm gonna sneeze. If I lick it off her skin, will I get nauseous? Man, she's got a lot of face powder on. What's that sticky stuff in her hair?"

At that point Corey seemed to run out of steam, and he quieted. His looked defeated and deflated again, like he had no reason to expect things to improve. "Stupid stuff like that. I can't... I can't shake those thoughts away. I can't shut my brain down enough to… to get close enough to tell if I'm wrong."

Lucian sympathized, worrying his lower lip and wondering how to proceed. "Have you tried closing your eyes?"

Corey scoffed loudly and waved a dismissive hand about. "That won't exactly turn my other senses off, now will it?"

"No, I suppose not." Lucian turned back to the food preparation, mulling over what he had heard.

"I'm beyond help, aren't I?"

Immediately Lucian whipped around, infuriated by the hollow misery in Corey's voice. "No one is. Ever. Stop that. Right now." He actually waved a spatula in his hand at his guest. "Don't make me spank you."

Corey blinked. Then the corners of his lips turned up, and he let out a chuckle. "Should I salute you next?"

Lucian laughed. "If you like. With any appendage you like."

"So, what are you going to do with me?" Corey asked after the silence had lasted for a few minutes, with Lucian busy by the stove. "And no, that's not sexual innuendo."

"Too bad." Lucian felt light and bubbly. Relaxed, Corey was fun company. But he also knew the guy needed help, so he grew serious. "After we enjoy our dinner and a show, we are going to visit my favorite after-hours hangout, Boudoir of Bondage."

Lucian didn't need to see Corey's confused frown to hear it in his voice. "The what?"

"You'll see." Lucian glanced over his shoulder to wink at his dumbfounded guest.

"Wait. A dinner *and* a show…? Sounds an awful lot like a date." Corey's bafflement continued, and Lucian suppressed a wicked giggle.

"Hate to sound like a broken record but…. You'll see." And he left it at that.

CHAPTER 4

THE ROASTED beef tenderloin with sherry vinaigrette, watercress, and red rice tasted heavenly, if Lucian said so himself. He and his guest, Corey the frigid virgin, ate in front of the floor-to-ceiling windows of the penthouse suite, sitting at a glass dining table with crystal glasses and fine china. Corey appeared to be used to settings such as this, though he didn't seem all that fond of it.

"How's the food and the wine?" Lucian asked politely.

Corey shrugged at first but then seemed to rethink the gesture and changed it to a courteous smile. "Fine." His gaze flicked over at Lucian. "You're a chef?"

"No." Lucian grabbed the wine bottle. "More wine?" Corey shook his head and covered his wine glass with his hand. "Dessert?" Lucian asked. "Or are you ready to take a journey to sensuality?"

Corey frowned, and his jaw moved; apparently he was grinding his teeth again. God, but this man needed to relax and unwind in the worst way.

"I've traveled all around the world, so whatever you throw at me, I can handle it," Corey said.

His brave, if somewhat foolhardy, words made Lucian smile. "Oh, I won't be throwing anything *at* you. But I will throw you into the deep end of the pool. Paddle or drown." He quirked an eyebrow, questioning his guest's resolve. "Ready?"

There was a minor nervous tic in Corey's jaw, but he nodded silently.

BOUDOIR OF Bondage was a privately owned, top-of-the-line, exclusive club for sexual connoisseurs. It catered to a privileged, though not necessarily entitled, clientele, much like Lucian, who could traipse down richly decorated, thickly carpeted, and dimly lit halls, belonging to that sensual sphere, shadowing their masked guides to rooms where magic happened.

Today was no different. Outside, in the so-called real world, it was barely past noon, but here it was a perpetual evening of delights.

Next to Lucian walked Corey, whose back was ramrod straight and expression that of a constipated statue. "How are you feeling, Mr. Paige?"

Corey started. He glanced at Lucian. His gray eyes grew wide but then quickly narrowed in wariness. "Fine." He studied his environment clinically. "I can't hear anything. Is the place typically empty this time of day?"

Lucian smiled and shook his head. "By no means. Boudoir is open twenty-four/seven. But the rooms are soundproof."

Corey sneered. "So, this is a common brothel?"

Lucian took the derision in stride. "I don't hear that word much these days. How nice of you to keep vocabulary traditions alive." His smirk was intended to infuriate Corey into revealing more of his emotional landscape, and he wasn't disappointed when Corey grimaced at the remark, his teeth flashing in the low lighting.

"What the fuck ever." Corey clearly wasn't in the mood to be toyed with.

Unlike other sex clubs in New York or on the East Coast, the Boudoir was a curious mix of classy and seedy, while others were only the latter. Sure, the place had low lighting, and red velvet abounded, but genuine erotic masterpieces hung on the walls, antique vases stood on small tables, and every visitor had a personal escort showing them around. No lurid music came through the speakers, no sounds of whips or chains echoed, and the only odors floating around were mildly sweet-scented or neutral.

When their escort arrived at a closed, thick wooden door and stopped there, Lucian inquired, "Has the room been set to my earlier specifications?"

Their guide, a young man in an impeccable and expensive business suit, only nodded with a bow of his head. He gave Lucian the door key and left quietly, a dignified expression on his handsome face.

Lucian turned the key in the lock, opened the door, and beckoned Corey enter with a swish of his hand. With an eye roll and an impatient pout on his lips, Corey walked into the room, and Lucian followed, then closed and bolted the door from the inside.

The room was bare of decor, containing nothing but a sleek black metal table large enough for two, plus a pair of stuffed red velvet chairs. The walls were so dark brown they appeared black, and red velvet curtains hung here and there as if camouflaging doors or windows. Lucian motioned for Corey to sit.

A perplexed frown marred Corey's forehead, but he did as instructed. He sat down and fidgeted as if uncomfortable with not only the chair, but the whole situation.

Keeping the man off-kilter was the point because that way his emotional reactions would ring true and uninhibited, Lucian knew, and he took the opposite seat.

Corey sat slightly sideways, crossed one leg over the other, and placed his hands in his lap, his gaze firmly fixed on Lucian, more suspicious than wary, but that too. "What are we doing here?"

"You went to school in New York?" Lucian asked, mimicking Corey's position.

Corey shook his head, looking as if he were bored out of his skull. His sigh suggested the same. "No. Yale. And before you ask, I studied architecture."

"You're an architect?" Lucian was surprised to hear that—and yet he wasn't. The Paige family was wealthy and renowned, so it made sense for Corey to rebel against academic prospects like business. But Lucian hadn't figured architecture would be Corey's main interest, expecting art or theater or music, those programs that were guaranteed to piss off parents with high aspirations for their children.

Corey looked down at his hands, giving nothing away with his blank look but revealing plenty with his fidgeting fingers and tapping feet. "No. Just what I studied."

That sounded more promising. "And your minor was…?"

"I had several. Humanities, psychology, anthropology, the classics."

Lucian smiled. Corey exposed much of his true and hidden nature with those choices. How he sought to understand the human condition— and himself. How these disciplines across the board opened up fundamental truths of humans throughout history, spanning cultural and geopolitical lines, from global states of affairs to the intricacies of the mind of a single person.

In essence, Corey had been seeking answers. Had he found any?

"Why architecture?"

Corey closed his eyes as if praying for patience. His lips thinned into a white line as he replied, "I was bored."

Well, that was a lie, Lucian concluded. "You get to break rule number two once, but no more. For your information, that was one. Break it again, and we're done."

Corey's eyes flicked back up to meet Lucian's. He all but snarled. "What's rule number two?"

"No lying."

Corey scoffed. "What's rule number one? You're always right?"

"Rule number one: Most of the time I ask the questions, not you." Lucian didn't smile. He was serious and emphatic. He could do nothing for a person who offered no information or who frequently lied. Not fertile ground to grow a seed into a forest. "I told you that before we left the penthouse."

Corey rubbed his temple, the strain in his jaw and muscles evident.

Lucian empathized. "Your stress level seems to be through the roof. Do you take antianxiety medication?"

Corey's eyes flashed intently. "No."

"You'll shatter your teeth, burn a hole through your intestines, and have a severe panic attack before you turn thirty-five. Stress can kill you, you know. Take some deep breaths and try to relax."

"Thanks, doc." Corey snorted scornfully. "What school did *you* go to?"

"Stanford, Princeton, and Harvard. Graduated all three before I turned twenty-one."

At that, Corey's eyes got big. He blinked in disbelief, and then blinked some more. "You're kidding." Lucian shook his head, saying nothing. "What do you do again?"

Lucian smiled softly, understanding coloring his voice. "Like you, I have a great deal of higher education, degrees, and diplomas under my belt, but they do not amount to a career, nor do they define me as a person. I was always good at school, excelling in each endeavor I took it upon myself to complete. But, as I said, school credits tell you nothing substantial about me."

Corey cocked his head to the side, as if trying to solve a puzzle. "Earlier you said that you're a hedonist."

"And a slut too. Let's not forget that." Lucian offered his guest a boyish grin and was rewarded with a quirk of Corey's lips. "But in short, I have spent my educational past learning about humanity, about other people. As a hedonist, I myself am the subject of my study. I experiment and focus on my own responses to sensual experiences, be they pleasurable or painful. It's not the end of the path that matters, but the journey, as cliché as that sounds."

Corey seemed to process the statement for an inordinate amount of time. "Aha. And *this* place comes into it how exactly?"

"Oh, no. You misunderstand. I have already been through this place on my path. This time, however, this establishment serves *you*." Lucian kept a neutral expression, not wanting Corey to get scared and run away. Of course, getting angry was the more likely reaction from someone like Corey.

"Or services me, eh?" Corey kept a mocking smile on his lips, but Lucian recognized the skepticism underneath the surface.

Lucian shook his head. "There'll be none of that for you. Not today. Maybe never." He looked around, familiar with the setting and what was about to transpire. "But you are right in one respect. Your path does begin here today. Right now."

As his voice still echoed in the room, the lights went out, drowning the small, intimate space in total blackness.

Showtime.

CHAPTER 5

AT FIRST Corey panicked. His imagination provided horrid scenarios of gang rapes and spiky whips and hot chains and anal probing and…. But Lucian's voice calmed him.

"You have nothing to fear, Corey. The door is locked. No one can enter. It's just the two of us in here. Nothing and no one will harm you here."

Corey swallowed down his anxieties. He readjusted his posture on the chair to a more relaxed one. Still, he never fully let go. "What's the meaning of this? I told you I didn't want to play games."

"No games. I promise." Corey heard the smile in Lucian's voice, the soothing lilt of his tone, the composed serenity of it. His body and mind both responded, uncoiling some of his knotted nerves. "This is our first session."

Corey centered his attention on the sound of his host's voice, as it was the only focal point in the dark. "Like a therapy session?"

"Yes."

Corey couldn't help but chuckle, baffled. "Am I supposed to expose my deepest and darkest secrets now? Is the absence of light somehow supposed to cure me?"

Surprisingly Lucian laughed. It wasn't a mean noise but simply highly amused. "No and no. Let's call this step one on our path to your sensuality."

Corey was confused, and that was getting annoying. He didn't appreciate being toyed with. "I don't get it. I don't get any of this." It didn't help that the space around him was categorized by the absence of everything suggestive of its existence: no smells, no sounds, no sights. If the place had been cleaned or sullied, no odors of detergents or bodily fluids could be detected. As Corey had walked down the labyrinthine hallways, he had noticed the lack of noise coming from any of the rooms. And the metaphorical black veil now covering his eyes did him no favors either.

"Be patient," Lucian said encouragingly. "I told you I could help you. Did you think it would happen in one sitting?"

"I'm not that much of an idiot."

Lucian chuckled, the sweet sound awfully sensual in the blackness where Corey could not see. "No, Mr. Paige. I don't think you're a fool at all."

The unexpected compliment threw Corey into silence. The truth was he usually had a good sense about things, people, and situations. He knew what to expect of any given scenario. But this was new. Not the dark room, of course, but everything it entailed and what it could lead to.

"So… when do we begin?" Corey asked, controlling his nerves once again.

"We already have," Lucian replied enigmatically. He was smiling too. Corey heard it.

But then, his eyesight veiled, he heard something that didn't quite fit.

Raindrops sprinkling on a rooftop, soft and mellow.

Corey frowned even though Lucian obviously couldn't see it. "Is it raining outside?" Dark clouds had been billowing in the sky when he left his penthouse apartment, but there had been no moisture in the air. The city was dry as a summer heat wave approached.

"Is it?" Lucian sounded amused.

Corey wondered what was so funny about rain. The whole situation seemed theatrical and began to feel more and more like a game, only Corey didn't know the players, the board, or the rules. Frustration made him fidgety.

"Are the ventilation shafts echoing the—"

"Do not seek rationalities here, Corey. Focus on sensations and reactions. Let yourself feel what is happening rather than trying to solve a riddle."

Feel what? Corey was utterly lost and confused. "It's just the rain." That was probably one of the dumbest things he had ever said since stating the obvious wasn't his style. Or at least it hadn't been before meeting this curious creature inhabiting the room with him.

Lucian chuckled, his voice the only anchor to the real world for Corey. "There is no *just*. Not here. Not ever. Corey, let go of your expectations and preconceptions. Tell me what you're hearing."

Having to explain his befuddled thoughts to Lucian was by far one of the strangest and hardest things Corey ever had to do. How could he make sense of what he was hearing if he was supposed to be solely feeling?

"Rain. It's raining."

"Have you ever stopped to listen to the rain? To really listen? To allow yourself to truly hear?" Was Lucian's voice receding? It was as if he were moving farther away.

Corey swallowed down his sigh but rolled his eyes in the safety of the darkness. "No. I don't see the point."

"What do you think about when you contemplate rain?"

"I don't spend a lot of time thinking about stuff like rain. Not at all, in fact."

It was then that Corey realized the mild shower had escalated into a gushing rainstorm, silence drowned under the wash of running water. And the downpour was landing on water, the melodic splashing surprisingly sweet.

A memory long past sprung up in Corey's muddy mind, of the seaside house where his parents took him as a child. He recalled the ocean, the calm horizon, the lapping waves, the wet striations of precipitation on the large windows of the porch.

Corey gasped. It had been ages since he had reminisced about times gone by, and it wasn't a wholly pleasant experience.

But before he could shove the spiritual souvenirs back into the attic of his brain, Lucian asked, "What came over you, Corey?"

"Nothing." Corey dismissed the memory and the idea of speaking about it, curt and rude in his response. Lucian remained silent in the dark, and Corey found it almost felt like he was speaking to himself. Was this therapy? Was this the reason Adelaide sent him here to this odd man? "A childhood memory is all." Even as he said it, he knew Lucian would latch on to it, dragging the whole story out of him, kicking and screaming.

Because of that notion, Corey was shocked when Lucian spoke, quietly and reverently. "When I was a child, I lived in France and Italy and Greece. My parents had money, and they were bitten by the traveling bug. My boyhood summers were spent in a lavish, sprawling mansion in Italy. Like a babe lost in a wood, I lingered in the halls and chambers, stairs and alcoves, traversing a maze of rooms and people. I was surrounded by adults who barely noticed my existence."

Corey didn't know what to say. That surely didn't sound like an ideal childhood. "I'm sorry."

"No, don't be." Lucian's voice was gentle and whispery, happy and rueful, all at the same time. "I learned a lot by being there. The world adults inhabit, from my perspective back then, was so curious and bewildering and… and one I could not wait to explore."

As Lucian paused, Corey acknowledged yet another morphing of noise as the rain turned into waves crashing on a shore, a soothing sound, repeating patterns of ebb and flow. But as Corey listened, leaning against the backrest of his chair, he observed how much the waves resembled breaths, rising and falling in an endless cycle. It was the baseline of life—and love.

Corey found himself smiling in the dark.

"Corey?" Lucian's voice was enticing as well as amused, as though the man had seen Corey's reaction and now awaited an explanation.

"Just a positive association, that's all," he replied casually.

"There is no *just*, remember?" The soft scolding was playful.

Corey actually chuckled. He heard the increased pace and thunder of the waves only an impending gale could produce. A hurricane was rising. "This is about sex."

"Oh?" Lucian's tone rose at the end, but Corey could have sworn he was not at all surprised at the mental connection.

"The waves. The natural rhythm of breath and heartbeats. The rising tide and swelling rumble of a sexual furor. This is meant to show me how natural erotica and sensuality are." Corey was proud of his deduction, having figured out the purpose of this exercise.

"And what lead you to that conclusion?" Lucian asked, sounding pleased.

Corey opened his mouth to reply that he had inferred it from the setting, the man opposite him, and all that. But, in the end, he had to admit it had been the sporadic memories and impressions elicited by the sounds that had guided him toward a conclusion, one born of emotions, not reason.

"Hearing."

"Hearing?" Lucian whispered in query.

"Listening," Corey corrected, amused and feeling a bit ridiculous.

Lucian said nothing. And that was fine because Corey had a feeling his answer had been the right one. That, however, didn't really show Corey what the ultimate point of this exercise was. So, he had learned something. Was he cured? No.

"What turns you on?" Lucian asked suddenly.

Corey struggled to comprehend the way Lucian's mind worked, but he had a hard time following his train of thought. Besides, he should have known the answer by now. "Nothing. That's kind of the basic nature of frigidity."

"Do you have an erection when you wake up?"

"Morning wood? Yeah, sure. But getting rid of it doesn't give me pleasure or—"

"Do you get an erection in the shower? Many men jerk off in the shower."

At that moment Corey wished he *were* in the shower. Not so he could beat his meat but because then the noise would silence the inane questions coming from Lucian. "Yeah, I guess. Sometimes. Rarely."

That's when he realized what Lucian was after. The sound of rain *and* the shower. A physical sensation, droplets on his skin, something other than his own hand touching him—and he could get an erection.

Then he frowned. "It's not the water that makes me hard, you know."

"But it enhances the sensual experience, yes?"

Corey had to give Lucian that since it was sort of true. He'd just never thought about it in those terms before. Then again, as Lucian had remarked, there was no *just*; only more excuses.

Hesitantly, he replied, "Maybe…." He couldn't be sure. Was this a first step toward fathoming he wasn't a total basket case and toward healing? At least the association of the rush of water and the rush of passion between human beings wasn't a total loss, Corey concluded. Any thought that brought him closer to feeling free in his body had to be considered a win.

Hmm, maybe Lucian had his uses after all.

Waves were no longer washing. Instead, a slow musical piece played, hovering in the room from speakers Corey could not see in the dark. Was Lucian controlling the audio play somehow? It was very possible, he surmised.

Then he recognized the score and snorted. "'Boléro'?"

Everyone knew the orchestral piece of music by Ravel. The repeating rhythmic pattern starts soft and quiet, *pianissimo*, and rises steadily toward a powerful crescendo of all instruments, played *fortissimo*, or as loud as possible. The fifteen-minute composition had become a household name when its connection to having sex had been established decades ago.

But at the moment, all Corey heard was a cliché.

"You don't like the melody?" Lucian asked, his tone still lacking any annoyance.

Corey snorted. "It's ridiculous and corny. I mean... you're using it as a yet another reference to sex, aren't you? A pretty blatant one at that."

"No." Lucian's denial held no emotional overtones at all, as if he didn't personally care either way. That puzzled Corey even more. "Did you know the composition 'Boléro' was designed for ballet? With dancers in mind?"

"Yeah, I must have heard that somewhere. So what?"

"Do you dance?"

As far as segues went, this one threw Corey for a loop, yet another one straight down the rabbit hole. "Um... sure, I guess. In clubs. You?" He longed to turn the spotlight off himself and onto someone else. Lucian would do in a pinch.

"Yes, the ballet." Lucian didn't sound proud or ashamed admitting that. It was merely one additional piece of information on a list that didn't seem to hold any emotional context. Corey began to wonder what, if anything, touched this man to the core. "Long ago. These days, yes, mostly in clubs. Plus the occasional fundraiser or a cocktail party, in a fancy ballroom dressed in my finest."

Funny how Lucian sounded as though he was joking. The darkness surrounding them started to irk Corey since he couldn't see the gestures and expressions of the man he was supposed to be conversing with.

"So, you picked this piece to talk about dancing, not sex?"

"Are they mutually exclusive?" This time Lucian was definitely laughing at him.

Corey suppressed a sigh. "No. Dancing can be very sexy."

"Erotically charged movements." Lucian paused, and Corey was of two minds whether to interrupt him. But Lucian decided faster. "But you, Corey, if you have never been touched by a woman or a man in an erotic, sensual, or sexual way, that means you've gone to nightclubs to dance by yourself. In the throng of wildly writhing bodies, how on earth did you manage to stave off all those potential lovers and one-night stands?"

"You mean how did I manage to get out with my virtue intact?" Corey mocked.

"You consider sex to be the opposite of virtue?"

Corey couldn't believe what he was hearing, although he had fallen right into that one. "Do you always answer a question with a question?"

"I'm the one asking questions today, remember?" Lucian was teasing, Corey could tell from his light tone.

Corey decided to throw the man a bone—and a brainteaser. "Are you saying one can't dance alone in a crowded night club and be sensual? Does sensuality require a partner at all times? 'Cause, you know, men and women alike do jerk—er, masturbate—and mostly without an audience. That's erotic, isn't it? Even though you're all by your lonesome."

Lucian chuckled in a seductive, dangerous manner. "Your words suggest you went to the club to dance—and to masturbate in public, where you risk others seeing you indulge yourself even if that is not your intention. Does that make you an exhibitionist? Hmm, something to consider."

That argument caught Corey off guard. He actually had to stop and consider the insane possibility. Was that why he went to those places alone? Not to seek a connection, per se, but to be seen as an object of desire, sexualized and explicit? The mere notion was mad. He wasn't like that. Right?

Dancing by himself, was it stress relief, was it physical release, or was it an exercise in creating erotic tension out of thin air?

Perhaps. Corey frowned. When he danced, he felt an uncoiling of inner knots and a loosening of nerves. And... he felt beautiful, desirable, coveted.

But... was it crass, was it tawdry, was it vulgar? Was he at heart those things?

How could he be when he hadn't even rationally recognized what he was doing?

The memories flooded his mind. The blast of bass, thudding and echoing in his chest; the bright, flashing lights that blinded him as effectively as the darkness around him now; the press of hot bodies brushing against him, not touching him on purpose, barely even aware of his presence as their skins grazed; the sultry, torrid promises made in a sexualized venue, where nights of quick pleasure were bought and sold with kisses and fucks....

Corey's head was swimming. Therapy with Adelaide had never been like this.

CHAPTER 6

A GENTLE hand landed on his shoulder comfortingly. "It's all right, Corey. This is all a lot to take in. Here, take this."

In the dark Lucian handed Corey a glass of water, and greedily, Corey drank it down to the last drop. "Thanks," Corey said hoarsely, coughing a bit. He sensed Lucian retreating back to his seat. "You move well in the dark. You've done this before." It wasn't a question.

Lucian chuckled. "As a matter of fact, no. Never quite like this."

"Am I your first frigid man?" Corey wondered briefly if that were true. Statistically he couldn't be the only one in town.

"You're not my first enigma" was Lucian's cryptic reply. That seemed so like Lucian that it made Corey laugh. "You want to dance, Corey? No one would see. Not even me."

Corey bristled. "I happen to be a good dancer." Then he cleared his throat. "Not that that's the point or anything."

Lucian let out a merry sound. "I'd love to dance with you. I bet you lead very well. I must confess the notion of your hand on the small of my back is enthralling."

Corey swallowed nervously in the blackness. He wasn't sure what it was about the idea of dancing with Lucian that made him anxious and jumpy. His confused mind still reeled and refused to provide him with clear-cut answers. And his body was so deep into the land of confusion, Corey wondered if it would ever get unlost again.

The rising pace of the "Boléro" changed to a new piece then. A lone saxophone began to play, a blues tune so soft and melancholy it stirred something in Corey's chest. A heavy weight shifted, an ever-present reminder of the pain he carried. And yet, the notes of the sax held a certain erotic charge that tingled on the edges of Corey's awareness and in his gut, this time showing him how a single instrument could depict his condition so accurately. The sad longing for sensuality.

Would it be so bad if I danced with Lucian?

Corey threw caution to the wind. "We can try that. One dance."

Lucian let out a surprised, gleeful gasp. "Really?" Corey heard chair legs scrape on the floor as the man rose and then soft footfalls as he approached. "Take my hand."

Corey knew that if Lucian had used an endearment right then, he would have changed his mind so fast his head would have been left spinning like in those old time cartoons. But Lucian's voice sounded gentle and kind and even somewhat yearning, so Corey stood up and fumbled to find his host's hand in the dark.

How Corey wished he could have felt passionate sparks and colorful fireworks as their hands touched. Alas, all he felt was a hand smaller than his own with delicate bone structure, long, svelte fingers, soft skin that carried the scent of passion fruit, and the feel of luxuriously manicured nails.

That last bit had Corey postulating the possibility of Lucian's pedicured toenails.

And *that* thought brought all kinds of crazy ideas and images into Corey's head. In his mind's eye, he pictured Lucian before him—naked as the day he was born. Would his skin be alabaster white or tanned golden brown? Would his muscles be ripped, hard, and well defined or more sinewy, hidden, and soft? Would he have lots of body hair or none at all? Would he have a washboard stomach or one flat and silky to touch? Would his cock be gargantuan to defy the stereotype of small men, or would it be fitting his stature, all pink and beautiful? Would he be cut or uncut?

Corey was sweating bullets by the time he managed to gain control over his wayward mind. Thank goodness it was still pitch-black, so he could focus on being close to Lucian in a dance.

On instinct, though he had never danced with anyone before, only by himself, Corey rested his right hand on the small of Lucian's back and pulled him closer. But he kept a discreet distance so their bodies didn't more than brush. Lucian began to sway ever so slightly, as if barely moving at all. Sometimes his whole body shifted, at other times only his hips. Corey felt the slow spins and steps with ease, puzzled at how natural it seemed.

That was when Lucian began to speak, his tone, as usual, subtle and soft, unimposing. "The full spectrum of sexuality's audible world is vast and timeless. The beating of primitive drums, the pop song melodies riddled with sexual imagery, the roar of an animal's mating call, the ebb and flow of the tide. How reminiscent they are of our primal instinct to connect with another human being, regardless of gender. Don't you agree?"

It wasn't always easy for Corey to comprehend the ulterior motives behind Lucian's speeches. What could one answer to a question like that? "Yeah...?"

Lucian chuckled as he moved his left hand from Corey's arm to his shoulder and from there onto his nape, carding his fingers through Corey's hair. "You don't have to say that just to please me, you know."

"I didn't." Corey realized he hadn't, in actuality. "I said it 'cause I didn't *dis*agree."

"Ah. A careful distinction." The minor lilt in Lucian's voice suggested he might have been playfully mocking.

Corey sighed. As alien a feeling as it was to hold this man, or any person, in his arms, he still found it oddly comforting too. The physical closeness, of course, did not imply emotional or spiritual intimacy. Yet, Corey couldn't deny that the feel of a man wasn't without its effects. In fact, his body did feel things. A warmth spread through him, as if via osmosis, through contact with this man's skin against his. The kindling sensation wasn't one of sexual desire, Corey could tell, but it might have been the beginning of a friendship, a spark of an amiable fire.

He kind of liked the idea. Corey knew lots of people. He had acquaintances. But he had no real friends, no confidants, no bosom buddies. Even the guys who lived on the same floor as he were simply people who lived under the same roof and hung out occasionally. Corey knew the basics about them but not their inner truths, their secrets, or their hearts.

"What's going on in that busy brain of yours?" Lucian asked in a teasing tone.

Corey tensed. He wasn't ready to admit his ponderings out loud. "I just... I fail to see the benefits of this... whatever this is."

"Are you afraid of the dark? Or yourself in the dark?"

Corey scoffed. "You see? I mean, what the hell kind of question is that? None of this makes any sense!"

"Do you wish to stop?" Lucian halted his dance movements, waiting for an answer.

Corey was glad he couldn't see Lucian's expression. But, if he was truly honest with himself, he sort of also wished he could. "I don't know. Maybe." He exhaled sharply, vexed. "I just feel like you're playing some kind of game, and I'm in the dark. Pun intended."

Lucian started dancing again, leading, and Corey followed, purely on instinct, not wanting to get trampled on or fall on his ass.

"I've said it before, Corey," Lucian said. "I do not play mind games. Besides, it is I who is in the dark. I don't know you, and yet I'm supposed to help you."

"But you keep asking things that don't make any real sense!" Corey cut in, frustrated.

"Maybe not for you," Lucian replied, patient as ever. "Every person is layered. With some, what you see is pretty much what you get. You, however, are not like that. My questions may seem crazy and pointless to you, but they reveal hidden facets about your true essence."

"Oh, and another thing? People don't normally talk like that." Corey sneered but tried to hide it in a cough because he didn't really want to hurt Lucian's feelings.

"Like what?" Lucian seemed deeply perplexed by the observation, and Corey needed to see the guy's face to determine what was happening.

"So... so formal and... pompous. A bit." Suddenly his cheeks burned in the dark as shame washed over him. The man was only trying to help, and Corey was giving him shit. "Forget it. I'm sorry. I didn't mean it."

"It's all right. I'm not easily offended." Lucian sounded neutral and unaffected, but Corey couldn't trust it, not without seeing the truth on his face. "Corey, I may not be a licensed sex therapist like Adelaide Kingsley, but I really am only trying to help. My questions may sound weird and perverse, but your situation is, shall we say, unique."

"I'm not the only frigid—" Corey defended himself.

"No, you're not. But I also don't think you are frigid."

Corey didn't know how to respond to that. He had used that term to describe his case for so long, he believed it. And consequently, every shrink he'd ever seen had agreed with the same assessment. Even though secretly Corey wished someone would disagree.

Now someone did. And Corey had no idea how to react.

If I'm not in fact frigid, what am I?

"All right, then," Lucian said, kind patience rising back to his tone. "I see the teacher and/or psychologist role is not working. What a shame. I sometimes think I could have made a good one."

"Which one?" Corey asked, baffled.

"Either one." Lucian moved his right hand from Corey's hand up his arm to grip his shoulder and then wind around his neck. This brought their bodies into direct, intermittent full-body contact. Corey gulped down his nervousness as best he could.

"So," Corey started to speak, just to break the silence—even though there was sexy music in the air. "When we first met, you played the part of the rich dilettante and then the boyish chef buddy. And now the shrink with a hint of the seducer. Do you always do role-playing with people you've never met before?"

Surprisingly Lucian laughed, though not meanly. "What a peculiar observation. I'm sure you've read your psych 101 and know that people always play roles, based on individual social situations and the company they keep. Sometimes a person even acts with himself. It happens." He let out a sigh, apparently for no reason. "But for the time being, I'm trying to ascertain what, eh, role *you* play."

Corey blinked in the dark. "*Me?*"

"Yes. For one, are you a leader or a follower?" Lucian's question only stupefied Corey more. "By the way you dance, I'd say you're most definitely a leader."

"You mean… the man…?"

"Good heavens, no!" Lucian chuckled. "I'm not speaking of gender designations. In some aspects of sex, the roles are clearly defined. BDSM, for example, with the roles of master and slave set before the sex even begins. Most virgins tend to be followers, seeking experience from an expert, from a well-informed and well-endowed lover."

"I see." Corey tried not to bristle since Lucian surely hadn't meant his comments as suggesting Corey was so new that he was ignorant of all things sexual. But it was hard not taking it personally. "What does it say about me that I search for counsel from a shrink instead of practical knowledge from a modern-day Casanova?"

Lucian chuckled, clearly preening. "Who says you haven't?"

At that, Corey actually had to join in on the laugh.

"You didn't answer me," Lucian prodded gently, his tone light and carefree, coaxing Corey into revealing anything. Well, almost anything. "Does it frighten you to confront yourself in the dark?"

Corey shook his head before he realized, stupidly, that Lucian couldn't see him do so. "No. I'm not afraid of being a sexual freak. Being a frigid virginal freak is worse. In the light or in the dark."

"Many people in the world, all ages and genders, are virgins. Everyone starts out that way, as you yourself said. There's nothing inherently wrong with that." Lucian's rational reminder didn't improve Corey's mood one damn bit.

"Duh." Corey rolled his eyes and let his sardonic attitude come through loud and clear. "It carries a strong social stigma, you know, especially once you've passed your midtwenties or so."

"Is that why you always seem to say frigid first? To offer it as an explanation of why you're still a virgin?"

"It *is* an explanation, not an excuse," Corey interjected, stiffening.

"All right, let's drop that for now." Lucian inched even closer to Corey, practically skintight, as they rocked in place, quietly and reverently, dancing to the lonely, erotic sound of the saxophone. "Tell me. Do you like dancing? Like this?"

"I guess." Corey shrugged. "I mean, I'm not hating it." He was somewhat surprised he actually meant it. Whether he liked Lucian or not, Corey did like holding Lucian close. Well, closer than normal. In fact, he had never danced this way with anyone, letting Lucian past the invisible barrier of his personal space, which surely was wider than with other, more normal people.

Lucian rested his head on Corey's shoulder. "Oh, such a ringing endorsement." Corey could feel the smile on Lucian's face as he spoke. It was evident in his voice.

"Give me a break. This is my first slow dance, okay?" But Corey wasn't angry when he said it. He was growing accustomed to Lucian and his quirks, be they words or deeds.

"Did you never slow dance at your boarding school functions or at the cocktail parties at your house?" Lucian sounded actually curious.

Corey shrugged. "I always managed to avoid it somehow. I had a plethora of excuses at the ready. You wouldn't believe how many times an imaginary corn saved me from a rumba with an overeager heiress."

Lucian's soft laugh made Corey sort of warm and tingly. And the sensation of Lucian's head pressed against his shoulder, his breath on Corey's neck, that didn't exactly turn his stomach either. But was it good? Corey analyzed his body's responses as best he could.

But he soon came to realize he was taking stock of Lucian in his arms. Warmth, slight pressure born of weight, fruit-scented cologne, slim-fit dress shirt with a luxurious high thread count and mother-of-pearl buttons, tight Gucci pants for that expensive casual look, those golden-red locks that softened his delicate, pixie-like features. Corey considered the possibility that Lucian might break if rough sex was ever on the table with his lovers.

The sudden, red-hot flash of jealousy surprised Corey to the core.

"What's wrong?" Lucian's sotto voce voice queried when Corey stopped dancing, causing them both to stand immobile, holding on to one another like in a still-life photo.

Corey swallowed, buying time to find the right answer. But he was too confused inside to come up with anything rational. It was mere hours since he had met this oddity among men, so Corey couldn't possibly have gotten so invested in this that his emotions demanded Lucian's sole and full attention. He licked his dry lips, nervous again.

"I'm...," Corey stuttered, cutting himself off before he made a fool of himself. He told himself this was nothing but the unintentional influence of the unprecedented setting, the dark room, and a seducer extraordinaire. Yes, that was it surely. A sexually charged atmosphere, something out of Corey's realm of experiences.

"A brand-new soundtrack." Lucian sounded so unaffected in the blackness that Corey nearly hated the man for his indifference. Was he so used to situations like this that he was immune to the physical and emotional effects? Corey wasn't sure he wanted to know the answer.

Exasperated, Corey demanded, "What's that supposed to—"

The jazzy notes of the saxophone ceased.

In their place echoed a rhythmic squeak of... mattress springs...?

CHAPTER 7

"WHAT THE hell?" Corey's outburst was understandable, he believed, as he stood in a dark room, all but embracing a very unusual man, and listening to the intimate sounds of undeniable sex. Those noises could be nothing else.

"Yes. Even a virgin can recognize that, I'm sure." Lucian seemed amused, but Corey saw little humor in the situation, eavesdropping on a sensitive moment. Unless it was a porn soundtrack....

He sighed, relieved when he made the connection to Lucian's words about a brand-new soundtrack. "I can't believe you. Do you really think listening to that will make me, um...."

"Aroused? Hot? Horny? Randy?" Lucian was helpful only to the point when he started chuckling. But then, while Corey was busy blushing in the darkness, Lucian grew serious. "Are you embarrassed hearing these sounds? The dip in the bed, the rustling of sheets, the sighs emanating from willing bodies coming together, the hiss of skins touching, the slapping of sweat-soaked skin on sweat-soaked skin, the cadence of lovemaking?"

Corey tried to stifle the riled groan but was unsuccessful. "No, of course not. One can hear that stuff everywhere, the radio, TV, Internet, even fucking commercials."

"Sex has been cheapened by making it so accessible to the public? Demystified?"

"Yeah, maybe. Don't you think so?" Corey was curious to hear the answer.

"No." Lucian's reply was emphatic, unhesitant. "I think two people, or more if need be, can bring mysticism back to sex with ease. If they so choose."

"Oh? How?"

"Two ways. First, finding a new lover to satisfy that need to experience some*one* new when some*thing* new is no longer an option."

"Sounds like you speak from personal experience."

Lucian was quiet for a moment, too long for comfort, and Corey regretted asking. "In this day and age, yes, I suppose that's true. Anyway, the second option is to understand that no two lovemaking sessions with the same person are the same. There is always a novelty to learn about the one you're with, be it for the second or two-hundredth time." He sounded melancholy and full of longing in the blackness. "A fundamental truth about sex. Yet most people choose to ignore it, impatient and bored too easily, dismissing the potential for more."

Corey had to ask; he simply had to. "You practice what you preach?"

Lucian let out a mirthless chuckle, a mere shadow of his past merriment. "If I had a true love at my side and a stable relationship, I dare to say I would be a very different person. To offer you a reply, the answer is no. I preach and teach, hoping other people learn from my mistakes. You make room for a loving person in all aspects of your life. That should be everyone's goal. A lonely life is a cold one, an icy coating around a dying heart."

A poetic response, to be sure, Corey thought. Did the wealthy playboy regret living a fast life with disposable lovers? Maybe that, like any kind of lifestyle, grew old after a while. Not having experienced sexuality in any meaningful way, Corey wasn't sure if he could relate.

Even though he himself was a playboy too, with money and toys to play with, but with few important ambitions. And the sexual playground was not one he had played on.

"Are you, um, trying to change your life, then?" Corey asked carefully.

Corey could hear the smile in Lucian's voice. "I'm here with you, aren't I?"

Mystified by the response, spoken as though it should be self-evident, Corey was more confused than ever.

"In fact, to tempt you further," Lucian said with a husky, seductive tone. "I think I'm going to give some homework. Yes, that sounds good."

Befuddled, Corey had to shake his head. "Homework…?"

"Yes. On your way home tonight, I want you to stop on occasion and listen to sexual signals around you, whatever they may be. A couple walking past you, whispering; a sultry kiss on a street corner; a tender good-bye at the end of a date next to a waiting cab; lovers holding hands; looks and laughter and closeness. That sort of thing. The everyday mysteries of love."

Corey had no clue as to how to do any of those things, how to spot them, let alone listen for any hidden subtext.

But for the moment, he didn't get the chance to contemplate the mystery because he began to hear voices whispering, yearning in the dark. Low sighs, sharp whimpers, husky moans. They drifted through the air.

He flushed with heat. Yet he wasn't sure if the reaction was born of embarrassment or arousal. Instead, he stood in place with Lucian, listening, unsure but riveted.

What became apparent right off the bat was that the two people engaged in a sensual act were both men. One was older, Corey imagined, with a deep, rumbling voice filled with grunts and "oh yeahs," while the other was younger, showing his youthful exuberance with high-pitched cries and soft begging that almost resembled lamenting. With a drawl, the first man kept praising his lover's beauty and sounds, while the second pleaded the stronger man to show his prowess by fucking him relentlessly and roughly. The occasional low chuckle and tender query continuing demonstrated the two had made love before and were knowledgeable with each other.

Corey's ears burned with listening to the intimate scene. Outside the dark cocoon he and Lucian inhabited, a slow, sensual game was being played. Daring, dirty words echoed amid the scuffle of sheets and the headboard banging against the wall. The passion and frenzy exalted their private session, offering glimpses of lingering pleasures, of secluded bedrooms and gentle whispers.

The sounds were all but alien to Corey in their lack of inhibitions, and yet shockingly familiar in some timeless sense he could not quite fathom or rationalize. Corey felt weird in his body, as though he were caught in a trap with fires burning around him, all but licking his skin. His clothes were glued to his skin with sweat born of a kind of sensual heat he had not known before.

Was this… lust…?

But, though his groin tingled and ignited, his cock didn't really react. Corey's cock was less than half-hard, and he was sure even that was more because of Lucian in his arms than the hot sounds he was listening to.

"Corey, tell me what you're feeling," Lucian urged softly, quietly entreating.

Without being logically aware of it, the truth was the cadence of Lucian's voice was much more erotic for Corey than the recorded lovemaking of strangers he could not see.

"You want a clinical interpretation?" Corey asked, guarded. His hands still rested on Lucian's hips, as if unwilling to let go, though they weren't dancing anymore. He should let go, he told himself. Yet his hands didn't budge an inch.

Lucian snorted. "No."

"I... I feel like... like it's wrong for us to listen to them, even if it is just a recording. We're trespassing on intimate parts of their lives, things we shouldn't be privy to. No one should." He paused, adding hesitantly, "Unless they're into exhibitionism or some such."

"That explanation would justify this eavesdropping?" Lucian sounded amused.

Corey was ruffled by Lucian's casual dismissal of his concerns. "I don't like spying on people. It's unethical and immoral."

Lucian feigned shock. "Hmm, both of those? Goodness gracious."

"No one talks like that anymore. If they ever did at any time or place in the course of recorded history. Jesus fucking Christ."

"Blasphemer." Lucian chuckled, and Corey swallowed down his indignation. "Cursing is all right, then, but spying is not?" Corey scoffed, about to go into a rant, when Lucian continued, "What if I told you those men do not mind we're their audience? That they get turned on by the knowledge their lovemaking has interested parties listening?"

At that remark Corey had to pause to consider the ramifications of Lucian's allegation. It would surely simplify matters. "Are you going to tell me that, or is this just a thought experiment or a test of my character?"

Before Lucian could answer, caught in a fit of giggles, the sounds of sex faded briefly as one of the men said, "They sound so formal, stiff, and defensive. Are they arguing or flirting? I can't tell."

The other man grunted, clearly displeased by the interruption. "Does it matter? Their business is their own. Now c'mere and kiss me." Wet smooches became audible, and then the steady tempo of a rocking bed resumed.

Corey cocked his head in the dark, baffled. "This is a... a recording.... Isn't it?"

Lucian giggled some more, and a horrible feeling sank into Corey at the exact same moment one of the lovers tittered. "Aww, he's so cute when he's flustered. Wish I could see him for myself."

Corey's mind reeled. He was completely taken aback by the revelation.

Lucian confirmed Corey's fears. "No. This is a live show. Right on the other side of the wall. Almost within reach." He must have leaned closer because although he whispered, Corey heard him fine. "We could join them if you like. A visual session. Or physical, if you so choose."

With a fury he hadn't experienced in ages, Corey shoved Lucian out of his arms. He realized while they had heard the lovers, the pair had also heard *them*. Corey's private business out there without his permission. Anger and disgust made him act violently.

An act he immediately regretted but wouldn't allow himself to vocalize.

Corey heard Lucian stumble and then fall to the floor, but he didn't care. "Turn on the fucking lights. This freak show is over." Immediately low lights by the walls illuminated the lonely room. He saw Lucian lying in a heap on the floor, unmoving, trepidation coloring his expression. Pointing a finger at him, Corey growled, "You had no right to talk about my personal matters to strangers. You betrayed my trust. I don't ever want to see or hear from you again!"

As he stormed out of the room, he resisted the urge to call Lucian names, like pervert or freak or plain old asshole. He should never have come, should never have trusted the man, a total unprofessional weirdo.

Corey made his way out of the private club, fuming. Adelaide Kingsley had steered him wrong, and now he was lost. It was bad enough that Lucian felt like someone Corey could confide in. But everything that had happened today proved to Corey he should try to solve his own problems, without odd outsiders who didn't understand him or give a shit about important things like privileged information.

Only... he felt like Lucian actually got him. In a weird, baffling sort of way.

And wasn't that the most depressing thought of all. As he hailed a cab and tumbled in, Corey felt the start of a migraine and groaned in pain, rubbing his taut temple muscles. The knot in his stomach tightened, adding to the overall hum of torment running through his body. It was high time to conceal himself in the cocoon of his bedroom, under heavy sheets, and let the world fade into nothingness.

Now that sounded like a plan.

CHAPTER 8

"YOU HAVE a guest waiting here to see you, Lucian." Amaya was neutral as she spoke, as cool and composed as ever. Few people could pull off that act while dressed in silk stockings, a corset, silk panties, and high heels.

Lucian perked up from his seat on the couch where he'd been moping for a week, glum and miserable. "Corey Paige?" He could barely contain his excitement at the prospect of seeing Corey again. He knew he had made a miscalculation in his dealings with Corey, but he had also, apparently wrongly, assumed the man would forgive him and, perhaps, be willing to try again.

"No. Randolph Paige."

Lucian frowned. Corey's father? What was he doing here? "Send him in." As Amaya walked off to bring the guest in from the foyer to the sitting room, Lucian got up, smoothed over his rumpled clothes, and groomed himself with a couple of fingers, carding through his unruly curls.

He went over in his head what he knew about Randolph Paige, the rich, influential newspaper and communications magnate. The self-made man owned three major newspapers in the country, one right here in New York, and he was among the few who had successfully made the transition from print to digital. Plus, he was the CEO of two international communications technology corporations, with rumors of hostile takeovers, mergers, and government contracts for satellites. In short, Randolph Paige was a shrewd businessman who could sniff profits in the wind and knew when to take risks to get at them.

"This way, please. Would you care for a drink, Mr. Paige?" Amaya asked.

The man she escorted into the room was noticeably shorter than his son. His brown hair and trimmed beard showed a considerable amount of silver. His stature was refined, and his business suit with a silk tie was immaculate and clearly expensive. He had crinkles around his mouth, but not his gray eyes, which suggested he habitually grimaced rather than smiled.

"Mr. Allard?" Randolph Paige asked when he saw Lucian.

Not quite hurrying but not exactly dillydallying either, Lucian made his way to the man and shook his hand. "Mr. Paige. To what do I owe this pleasure?"

"Mr. Allard, I—" He cut off his speech abruptly, glaring at Amaya, dismayed. Lucian waved her off quickly, not wanting to aggravate the man who clearly had a chip on his shoulder.

Amaya was one of Lucian's success stories. Growing up in a conservative Japanese family, she had been repressed for so long that the first time she orgasmed, she'd blacked out due to the intensity of the experience. Now she was an experienced Dominatrix and at ease dressed in sensual attire. In essence, with Lucian she had found freedom of self-expression, and Lucian was very proud of her.

Once Amaya was gone, Randolph turned back to Lucian. "I won't waste either of our time, so I'll be brief. Whatever it is you are... doing with my son, it will stop here and now."

Lucian betrayed no emotion. He had calculated roughly four possible reasons why the man had come to see him, and this demand was at the top of the list. Did Randolph spy on his son? Maybe.

"I'm not doing anything with Corey, Mr. Paige."

The denial was like pushing the button of an apocalypse machine. Randolph's face grew taut and his skin red with anger. "Perhaps you didn't hear me, or perhaps you misunderstood, Mr. Allard. You are to have no further contact, of any kind, with my son."

"With all due respect, Mr. Paige, you do not control my social calendar, nor do you have any say in how I conduct my affairs." Lucian might have been petite for a man, but he wasn't one to be taken lightly. He had several kinds of power behind his fragile appearance.

Upset and reddening, Randolph growled, "Corey is not a toy for your depraved games, Mr. Allard, which are well-known. Or should I say notorious?" Lucian had a reputation among the higher rungs of society, one filled with rumors of orgies and pleasure-enhancing drugs and so on. This time it was a hindrance, not an asset.

Lucian was impressed Randolph was so protective of his son, but he also had to conclude Randolph took his fatherly duties a bit too seriously.

After all, nothing happened with Corey. Then again, Randolph wasn't aware of that fact.

"What you are doing now with my son, Mr. Allard, is in bad taste, ruining the reputation of a good man." Randolph spat his words, showing his disgust without knowing any of the facts of the case. "You belittle a worthy man with your shameful behavior. You disgrace Corey, and others I'm sure, without a moment's thought to the ramifications of your—"

"I thank you, Mr. Paige, for your unsolicited counsel. Now I must ask you to go. I'm positive you would not allow such disrespect aimed at you in your own home. Please, leave." With a quirk of his eyebrow, Lucian gestured toward the staircase that led to the front door. He could not use his hands because they were behind his back, shaking with barely held restraint. This man didn't understand what was going on, and yet he presumed to pass judgment. Lucian had no patience or tolerance for such people.

Randolph's face resembled a storm cloud brewing. "I'm warning you, deviant. Stay away from my son, or I will show you how far my sphere of influence extends."

Lucian's lips curled up in a half grin, though he felt nothing like smiling. "My family are academics, politicians, diplomats. I dare say their sphere of influence, as you call it, supersedes yours, which is built solely on currency." *And bribes.* But he left that part out. He glanced at Amaya, who now stood on the threshold with a calm, expectant look. "Amaya, please show Mr. Paige out."

Lucian turned his back on the odious man, sauntered to the floor-to-ceiling windows with a view over Manhattan, and stared out, waiting for silence. It came when the front door closed with a slam as Randolph Paige departed. The windowpanes didn't rattle, not this high up.

"Lucian?" Amaya was in the room but not close, Lucian could tell from the echo of her voice. "Why didn't you tell him Corey doesn't want to have anything to do with you anymore?"

Lucian let out a mirthless chuckle. "Yes, the esteemed Randolph Paige would have stopped and left, then, happy with the end result." He lifted his chin defiantly, his eyes narrowing in concentration. "No one tells me what to do under my own roof."

Amaya said nothing for a time. Then she asked, "A drink?"

Lucian smiled. The case was concluded.

Well, at least with her. Corey Paige was another matter entirely.

THE GRANDFATHER clock was chiming midnight when Amaya knocked on Lucian's study door, even though it was open. "You have a guest waiting here to see you, Lucian," she said, mirroring the earlier encounter with Randolph Paige.

Lucian frowned and sighed. "It's late. Tell whoever it is to come back tomorrow—"

"Am I disturbing you?" Corey asked, barging in past Amaya, who didn't even try to stop him from entering. She smiled in that cunning way she had when she believed she knew better than Lucian what was best. Since she was privy to pretty much every detail of Lucian's private life and had unconventional work hours, Amaya was right about that. On occasion, at least.

"Do you care?" Lucian asked, nodding at Amaya to leave. She followed suit with a slight bow. Lucian leaned back in his comfy office chair, the leather creaking sharply.

Corey shrugged as if he didn't, but his expression was taut, pent-up with emotions. That didn't bode well. "I'd leave if you were...." It sounded as though he had intended a rude remark but thought better of it, letting his voice fade. He cleared his throat, his brow creased, while his gaze roamed along the bookcases of Lucian's study.

"Something wrong?" Lucian prompted gently.

Corey bit his lower lip and kept clenching and unclenching his fists at his sides. "Did my father pay you a visit today?"

Lucian saw no reason to prevaricate. "Yes."

Corey gritted his teeth, if the chewing motions of his jaw were any indication. "What did he say?"

"He suggested I should disassociate myself from you," Lucian offered formally. "Only he used slightly different terminology."

"Bastard!" Corey hit his thighs with his fists, so angry he was shaking.

"Would I be correct in assuming the two of you keep tabs on each other's activities?"

Corey scoffed, still avoiding eye contact. "That's the polite way of putting it." Finally he looked up at Lucian, surprisingly apologetic. "I'm sorry about that. He shouldn't have approached you at all. To be honest, I'm shocked he did."

Lucian chuckled a bit. "I dare say my reputation had something to do with that."

"Aha. So he assumed you were corrupting me?"

"Words like depravity and sexual deviant were thrown around."

Corey's eyes flashed intently. "He called you—"

"Implied." Lucian exhaled, finding serenity in the situation. "He's very protective of you. I found that a bit overdone but basically a nice sentiment." He met Corey's gaze head-on, with determination. "Does he know you're a…?"

"A virgin or frigid?" Corey moved on to inspect a couple of rare first editions on the shelf, touching the spines but not taking them out. Lucian figured he needed something to do with his nervous hands. "I don't know." He shrugged, but it was far from a casual gesture. It was a strong tell. Before Lucian could comment, Corey continued, "He can be such a hypocrite. I mean, he and Mom, the things they've done would send normal folk scurrying up the hill to get away. He's had his orgies and swinger parties and weekend revelries." Corey rubbed his forehead, looking tired and disappointed. Suddenly a soft chuckle escaped his throat, as if a surprise even to him. "I honestly don't get what my dad's problem is! He's never given a rat's ass about my love life, or lack thereof, and now he's all weirded out when I seek help for it? Fucking asshole!"

"Perhaps his reckless past weighs on him, and he does not wish you to make the same mistakes," Lucian offered in a conciliatory manner.

Corey laughed, tossing his head back. "That's ridiculous! My dad with a single regret? Not a fucking chance! That would mean he'd have to admit to himself and others he's capable of making mistakes. And Dad's never been wrong a day in his life."

With a silenced sigh, Lucian got up from his chair and walked to where Corey stood, his hand gripping the bookshelf white-knuckled, as if attached to an anchor. "Whether he's wrong or not, that seems very much like his problem to deal with. The question here is, what are you going to do about it?"

Corey made eye contact, his gaze fierce. "What do you mean?"

Lucian smiled amiably. "I don't mean to ask if you're going to kick his ass, probably because I don't think you would. Are you going to tell him you've already decided not to continue working with me?"

Corey grimaced. "Why didn't *you* tell him that?"

"I do not care for people threatening me in my own place."

Corey worried his lower lip, a suspicious look on his face. "That the only reason?"

This was an opening, Lucian realized, and he spoke the truth. "I'd love to continue the process we've begun. But that's up to you." When Corey didn't respond immediately, only stared at him, Lucian went on to say, "I wish to apologize for not warning you about the fact that the listening to sexual intimacy back at the club went both ways."

Corey sneered, but it seemed halfhearted. "Later, when I wasn't as angry anymore... I kind of figured you did it to provoke an emotional reaction, and maybe a physical one too. I mean, that's what the whole night was about, wasn't it?"

Lucian nodded. "Sort of, yes. Your reactions to sensual stimuli are indeed the goal of this whole process."

Corey looked at his feet, hesitant. "I get it. I do. It's just...."

Lucian hurried to say, "Yes, I understand. Now, after the fact, I realize it must have seemed as though we were making fun of you. I assure you that we were not. That was never my objective, never my intention. I apologize for that. Sincerely."

Corey nodded slowly and then appeared both appeased and amused. "You know, I still think people don't talk like you do."

Lucian offered a self-deprecating grin. "I'm the product of my upbringing. My parents come from scholastic backgrounds, from academia and diplomacy. As such, they instilled the same formality of behavior and speech patterns in me. I apologize if that offends you."

Corey returned the smile, warmth creeping back into his demeanor. "It doesn't. I guess I just can't help noticing it." All of a sudden, his smile turned impish and wicked. "In fact, I kind of like listening to your voice. It's so collected and smooth. Honeyed. Like you're trying to lull me into a *true* sense of security."

Lucian chuckled. "Honeyed? I don't think anyone's ever described my voice as such. How sweet."

Then, in the blink of an eye, Corey grew serious, sheepish even. "I'm sorry I shoved you. I didn't mean to hurt you. I'm really sorry. I'm not normally—"

Lucian waved a hand dismissively between them. "It's all right. I understand why you did it. We're fine." He paused. "I hope."

Corey let out a breath as if he'd been holding it and looked relieved. "Yeah. We're good."

"I'm glad you haven't formed too low an opinion of me." Lucian felt he had neglected his duties as a host, so he sprang into action, gesturing toward the liquor cabinet. "Would you like a drink?"

"No thanks." Corey glanced around briefly. He took notice of the armchair tucked in the corner where two cats lay tangled in each other, both purring away, a sweet, low cadence to the sound they made. Chuckling, he pointed at the cats. "What are those hairballs?"

Lucian rolled his eyes. "I will have you know my felines are very clean with their fur. The red one is called Oscar, the black one Casanova."

Corey quirked an eyebrow, bemused. "A womanizer in history and a, uh… what?"

"Cas does have a taste for the ladies, I admit. Oscar has not made up his mind when it comes to forming new attachments. And if you must know, his name derives from Oscar Wilde." Then Lucian burst into a hearty laughter. "But true to their feline selves, great lovers of people they are *not*!"

Chuckling, Corey nodded before settling his gaze back onto Lucian and again growing serious. "Listen. What I'd like is for us to have another session. If that's okay with you."

It was Lucian's turn to be hesitant. "Are you sure? Because it would seem we have a few trust issues to—"

"If you say right now that you have my best interest at heart and that you won't divulge any more personal information about me to anyone, not even in the name of this healing process, then I will take a leap of faith and trust you." Corey sounded adamant and resolved.

Lucian had to give it to Corey, who had obviously felt betrayed, and yet he found it in his heart to try again. "I promise."

Corey was silent for a moment, inspecting Lucian's face, perhaps searching for signs of dishonesty. Finally he seemed satisfied with the results. "Tell me something true about yourself. Anything."

The man was still unsure, Lucian concluded. "Like you, I was young when I diagnosed myself when it came to my approach to sex. From the empirical evidence, namely having lots of sex with lots of people, I deduced I was hypersexual."

Corey frowned, seemingly surprised. "Really?"

"Yes. Only… as I grew older, I came to realize I was not. I was in fact sexually fluid. I got aroused with both genders. Or all genders, as the case is these days. Well, to be exact and honest, I *am* predominantly gay. I don't engage in heterosexual acts anymore, not the way I did back when I was a perpetually horny adolescent. I suppose I simply find men more, shall we say, palatable. Women no longer do it for me, to use vernacular phrasing." Watching Corey's creased brow, Lucian felt some levity was in order to get things back on track. "Also, now we're being super honest, I have great stamina. Not just with sex but everything. Despite my small stature, I'm athletic, and I've participated in the New York City Marathon for years."

Corey's eyebrows shot up. "Really? Wow, that's impressive. Nice." His smile at the end confirmed Lucian had made the right call.

"What about you?" Lucian asked, acting coy. "Tell me something true."

Corey frowned, more baffled than miffed. "Well, I'm, uh… I'm a dog person."

Lucian rolled his eyes. "Goodness, what a profound revelation. Oh, and by the way, I'm a cat person myself. *Meow*." He made a claw of his hand as he meowed.

Corey chuckled. "Yeah, I kind of figured. What was with that big kitty anyway?"

"Long story. Maybe I'll tell it to you someday." Lucian liked to remain enigmatic.

"Fine. For now." Then Corey cocked his head, as if assessing the situation. "So, what's the next step on our path to healing me?"

Lucian gave a naughty grin, for he had specific designs for Corey. "Next up, a veritable feast for the eyes."

CHAPTER 9

"OKAY." COREY swallowed nervously but decided to trust in Lucian's judgment again. After Randolph visited Lucian, Corey knew he had to be on the right track. Not because his dad disagreed with Corey's plan, while being oblivious of the details, but because Randolph's reputation gave him no right or justification to judge his son.

Corey had to walk his own path. And he really wanted to get better, to be truly close to another human being and feel, feel, feel. God, how he wished to be able to do that.

Lucian glanced at him under his lashes, a cutely demure look. "I realize that with my actions I have violated our confidentiality agreement, so if you'd like to speak with your attorney first and perhaps amend the contract and its—"

"No. I'm good." Corey did not want his family's stodgy lawyer, Mr. Upton, to have a single glance at the papers. Besides, that man's sense of loyalty always extended to Randolph first, no matter what. "So, are we going back to the club?"

Lucian shook his head. "No. Not yet. Before we proceed tonight, however, I have been meaning to ask you about your reasons for seeing Doctor Kingsley. What has recently changed in your life? What precipitated your initial contact with her? Depression or stress, perhaps?"

Corey hesitated, more unsure how to reply than reluctant to answer. "I'm tired of feeling like an outsider. I'm at an age when the few people I call friends and acquaintances are getting paired up. You know, people getting married and popping out two-and-a-half kids in their house with the dog and the white picket fence. The American domestic dream. So, yeah, I guess I've been depressed. I'm not saying that's my particular dream. I suppose I just want… something more. I thought a shrink might give me some clarity and perspective. That's basically it."

"I see."

Corey narrowed his eyes. "How do *you* know Ms. Kingsley exactly?"

"Sorry. Doctor-patient confidentiality."

Wheels were turning fast in Corey's head as he imagined Lucian and Adelaide having sex on that plushy divan, and that untoward and unbidden vision caused him to blush intensely.

"Corey?" Lucian interrupted Corey's embarrassing speculations, evidently ready to begin the session. He pointed to one of the bookshelves. "Take that book, please. The dark red one in the back."

Corey followed Lucian's instructions and grabbed a huge, thick book with a dark red leather cover. It had no title or author's name. He gave it to Lucian, who with a chin lift indicated Corey should sit in one of the two leather chairs on the opposite side of the room from the desk. He did as he was directed.

"You often have books with no names?" Corey asked, curious.

Lucian chuckled, his green eyes twinkling. "A few. I'm a collector."

"Of books with no name?"

"Of erotica."

Lucian placed the book on the small cherrywood table between the two armchairs and lovingly caressed the surface with his delicate fingertips. Lucian had the most feminine hands Corey had ever seen on a man. An image of Lucian's fingers flying on a piano popped into Corey's head—and then the vision morphed into Corey's torso, where Lucian's fingers were familiarizing themselves with the soft nubs of Corey's nipples.

Expelling the image out of his mind, Corey shivered.

Lucian didn't seem to have noticed as he spoke quietly, "My grandfather Julian—God bless his soul—was a shameless rake in life and remained disreputable in death. My parents hated him while he was alive and were embarrassed by him after he was gone."

"That's Alexander's father?" Corey had done his research, learning about Lucian's past history and lineage: Alexander Allard, the politician, diplomat, and Lucian's father, and Chastity Allard, the scholar, philanthropist, and Lucian's mother. Corey had especially liked how Chastity's name was so similar to his own mother's name, which was Prudence.

"Yes. He lived in Italy, in an old mansion in the hills. I was close to him, more than anyone else, I think." Lucian smiled fondly, and Corey liked the look on him. It softened the sharp pixie-like features into a dreamy portrait of a caring man. "You see, Julian and I conversed a lot. He wasn't shy about admitting why the rest of my family shied away from him." Lucian seemed upset, displeased. "My family weren't repressed or anything, but they always felt sex served a biological and social purpose, not selfish acts of pleasure. Offspring and rising status in society. As politicians they typically had other interests besides sex."

"Is that why you focus so much on sex?" Corey teased a bit.

Lucian seemed to realize Corey's goal and chuckled, shrugging. "Perhaps so. Julian was a lecher, and I adored the stories of his sexual conquests. I was a teenage boy at the time, and everything he had done felt like a victory of sorts on a battlefield of sensuality, beauty, and love. I was a romantic back in the day."

"That's nice. Not modest, though."

Lucian scoffed playfully. "Modesty is another word for prudish. I was never prudish."

Corey laughed, relaxed. "Perish the thought!"

"When my sexual interest in men was piqued and I realized my main fascination centered on the male gender rather than the female, Julian was the first person I came out to. Formally. Later my parents told me they had suspected for years I was gay despite my many dalliances with the ladies." Lucian didn't appear fazed by this, his expression neutral. "Julian warned me that the biggest challenge came from myself, from my own judgment. I had to accept I was gay because it was my inner truth, in my soul. He said it would be my freedom. It took me years to figure out what he meant."

"Sounds familiar," Corey agreed quietly, not wanting to interrupt Lucian.

Lucian smiled again, his gaze glazed over and lost in some distant memory. Corey was mesmerized by the sight. "Indeed. I expected the world to pass judgment on me for flair, for being shameless, for being a homosexual. Sometimes people did. But it was me, myself, and I staring back at me in the mirror that was the hardest trial of all."

Corey nodded, though Lucian didn't see it. "Yeah, that sounds familiar too." It was a tough contest which was worse, admitting the truth to yourself or coming out with it to others, especially in a world that seemed to thrive on hate and prejudice. With all too painful clarity, Corey recalled his own struggles about this. It was hard to know the truth conclusively, one way or the other, when you'd never had sex. Fantasies weren't enough, and Corey didn't have many of those either.

"Yes." Lucian's gaze refocused on Corey, serious and profound, seeking something in deep. "In some ways being gay is a choice of sorts, isn't it? The pressures of discrimination, hate, and violence force us to choose sides. Gays have had to become political to protect their own basic human rights, which should be the same as everyone else's."

"I guess." Corey had to admit Lucian had a valid point. Still, for Corey being gay meant essentially that he had sex with and loved men. What should have been a private matter between two people in love, or in lust, had become public due to the hatred LGBT people faced every day.

Then again, he wasn't having sex with men *or* women, so for him it was a moot point.

Lucian seemed to sense Corey's shift in mood, and he patted his thigh gently. A shiver ran through Corey at the touch. "Anyway…. Julian asked me did I *think* I was gay or did I *know* I was gay. Considering I had kissed a boy in the fields of the closest village a mere day before, I had to reply I knew for certain. Julian understood. He never judged. I imagine he would have reacted the same had I told him I had kissed a girl instead."

"He sounds like an awesome guy."

"He was. I miss him greatly." Lucian frowned, but only briefly. "Strange, but I haven't thought about him for a while." His gaze landed back on Corey, grateful. "Thank you for giving me the chance to reminisce."

Corey's cheeks flushed with heat, and he bowed his head, allowing his falling hair to hide his blush. "You're welcome."

"In any case, Julian gave me this book. Bequeathed it to me, to be precise." Lucian's grin was conspiratorial and wicked. "My parents haven't seen it, or what's inside."

Now Corey was positively teeming with curiosity. "Julian wrote a book?"

"Not exactly." Lucian gave the book to Corey. "Open it, and find out."

Corey accepted the book with caution, not wanting to damage the family heirloom that was Lucian's legacy. The leather creaked, and the vellum rustled dryly. As he opened the tome, he saw it for what it was. *An album.* Erotic pictures dotted each and every page. Some were photographs or leaflets, others drawings or paintings. "Wow…." He admired the rich assortment of imagery, slowly flipping forward.

Not wanting to rush, though, he returned to the first page where an old, gritty black-and-white photograph of a beautiful brunette caught his eye. She was looking straight at the camera, her eyes big and black, framed by long dark lashes. She had on an elaborate jeweled headdress, echoing the age of sultans and deserts and harem girls. Only a thin veil, held together by pieces of jewelry, covered her body. But the silk was so thin one could see everything: her barely obscured brown nipples, her belly button, and the bush where her thighs met. Old-fashioned erotica, Corey surmised, enthralled by the vision.

Lucian touched the rim of the picture gently. "Do you remember Rudolf Valentino? He was a famous actor long ago in those grainy, black-and-white films? He played sultry heroes, like sultans in the desert, seducing women with a mere look."

"A bit before my time, I'm afraid," Corey replied with a smirk.

Lucian rolled his eyes and chuckled. "Fine. How about Marlene Dietrich? She sang in movies, her voice raspy, her eyes smoky, a seductress extraordinaire, a mystic charm present in every word and deed."

Corey shrugged, paying attention to the book. "I think I've seen a movie of hers. Can't remember which one, though." He glanced up at Lucian, pondering. "You miss the good old days? Do you long for those golden eras that never really existed?"

Lucian shook his head with zero doubt. "No. Time moves forward, not back."

"I thought I detected a hint of nostalgia is all."

"To long for times gone by is to live in the past. And I don't live in the past. I prefer to live in the here and now, in the concrete reality of the moment."

Corey watched Lucian's gaze travel from picture to picture, a soft smile curling his lips. It was a sensuous sight, though Corey wasn't sure how he recognized it as such. Was it an instinct he had assumed he didn't possess because of his lack of experience? It seemed a part of him did recognize certain signals and responded to them in some way. That was promising, he thought, excited about the prospect of feeling in response to another human being.

Lucian, however, continued with a more clinical tone, "Eyesight is inextricably linked to sexuality, for men especially since we rely on visual stimuli for sexual arousal, much more than women."

"Ah. I did *not* know that," Corey said. He grinned sarcastically.

Lucian laughed. "No need to be a bitch about it." Then he flicked his tongue at Corey.

Corey feigned a shocked expression, knowing he was failing at delivery. "What a potty mouth. Who knew?" Then he stared back at the album, focusing on the images. "Your grandfather had quite a hobby. It must've taken him years to gather all these."

"Decades and longer," Lucian confirmed. "Beyond generations. His uncle Pépin—my great-granduncle—started the tradition, I believe. I never knew him. He died long before I was born."

"And he was a rake too?"

Lucian winked. "According to family legends, Pépin would have given Casanova a run for his money. Predictably, he perished of untreated syphilis."

Corey was fascinated, lost in the story of true history and real people, so tangible and heartfelt because their descendant sat in his company. "So, Julian and Pépin were gay?"

Lucian waved a hand to dismiss the notion. "Oh no. Players, womanizers, ladies' men. As I'm sure you can see from the photos and art, all of it erotic, taboo, and illicit. Although... I did hear some rumors circulating, and when confronted about them, Julian was awfully secretive, hush-hush." Lucian tapped his nose and winked knowingly. Then he pointed at the picture of the harem brunette. "Oh, and this exotic lady was Fleur, my grandmother."

Corey's eyebrows shot up. "Your family tree sure has some intriguing characters."

"Yes. Too bad my parents are so stuck up. Pity."

Lucian shrugged, and Corey couldn't tell how much that fact mattered to Lucian. He could apparently keep a lot of secrets close to his chest.

Corey sought to divert the conversation back to lighter topics. "Did you ever add any pictures to the album?" he teased. "Are there any personal, real-life photos of you buried in here somewhere?"

Lucian smirked enigmatically. "Maybe. Maybe not." Then he straightened up, but that devilish look never really went away. "Back to business. Now, just because a man gets turned on by visual delights, that does not mean a man has no use for imagination. Take a look at that picture, for example."

Corey cast his gaze back down to the book.

The picture in the next spread was a colorful, realistically detailed pencil drawing of a half-dressed man embracing and disrobing a half-naked woman. Judging from their attire, the era was late nineteenth-century, or thereabouts. The couple was moving toward a big bed that dominated the frame, the cozy room illuminated by a single lamp on the bedside dresser. The intimacy of the scene came from the alluded nudity as well as the passionate kiss the couple was sharing.

But… under the bed lay another man, fully clothed except for his exposed, erect cock, which he was stroking.

And… to top that off, inside the broad cupboard by the side of the bed, peering out of a crack, a third shadowy man was spying on the couple, his hard penis jutting upward, barely visible in the dark.

"As you can see," Lucian said with amusement, "there can be many interpretations for this illustration. Are the couple husband and wife? Or perhaps a married man with his mistress, or the other way around? Is this a lovers' tryst, or are these two trying to rekindle the embers of their dying affair?" Lucian pointed at the man under the bed. "Who is he? The woman's other lover, or a total stranger and a pervert, or a lowly criminal even? He doesn't seem to mind that another man has taken his place. Does he only like to look? Is the couple aware of his presence and merely pretending he isn't there? Are they excited by the prospect of being watched?" With a wicked grin, Lucian glanced at Corey and then tapped the picture of the third man hiding in the closet. "What about this man? Look at his leer. Is he observing the woman so raptly, wishing to be the lucky man? Or… does he prefer tight muscles, scratchy stubble, and a hard cock, wanting to be the woman instead, to be taken and claimed by a man? Is he a vile rapist, biding his time?"

Corey envisioned each and every scenario Lucian proposed. In his mind's eye, he could witness every scene unfold, proceed, and come to completion.

This time when his cock throbbed and jumped in his pants, Corey knew he wasn't in bed just waking up with morning wood. This was a spontaneous, full-body, full-on waking moment of epic proportions. Unable to analyze the overwhelming sensations or their cause—the images, his imagination, or Lucian's seductive voice—Corey went with it.

His groin tingled, the base of his dick heated, his balls drew taut, and his cock grew harder with every labored inhale.

"One sight, one thousand and one stories." Lucian's whisper sounded reverent, as though he was aware of Corey's inner turmoil and deliberately remained unassuming and soft. He didn't look at Corey, not even once.

The atmosphere gripped Corey's soul, a hallowed weight that spoke of revelations and dark recesses within his lonely heart. "Show me more." His choked voice cracked. He heard it but didn't bother trying to hide it in a cough, not from Lucian.

For a while they sat together in silence, flipping through the album filled with long-ago and unchanging notions of erotica and sensuality. One spread depicted a series of pictures where a young man was getting undressed, only the frames of the artwork were keyholes. As the man slowly revealed his nakedness, he was being spied on, probably in his home, perhaps by a lonely servant girl or a neighbor boy with a crush. Lucian was right: A thousand and one possible stories hid in each picture.

Corey licked his dry lips and felt how sweaty and hot his hands were as they swept across the pages. This... heat... he felt was unlike any he'd experienced. New York could be hotter than hell in the summer, a scorching furnace of a maze with no way out. But this heat was internal, roaring up within him, blazing through his body like wildfire.

This wasn't desire to have sex, per se, but... closer than ever before. Palpable, visceral, sensual, almost tangible. Undeniably real.

A cavalcade of visions erupted in his mind as he perused the pictures, line for line. A young man from the Renaissance era presented to a seated higher-class suitor, his genitalia exposed and shaved; an older man, dressed all in black like a classic movie villain, shifting aside the blankets over a man—asleep or awake?—so he could look at his remarkably huge erection; a young woman in a lovely summer dress peeking through a hole in a wooden wall to spy on the two men fucking on the hay in the stables; a woman clad in a silk and lace negligee admiring her pussy in a hand mirror; two half-naked boys having a laugh together and comparing each other's buff backsides in a tall looking glass; a naughty-looking priest watching from behind a partition as a young man masturbates in a confessional, an expression of rapture giving his flushed cheeks a red glow; a man bound to a pillar and forced to watch his wife or mistress gaily having sex with another man in a bathtub; a young man surrounded by a horde of lecherous men, all of them erect, grabbing on to him, claiming him with eyes, hands, mouths, and cocks, and all the while his eyes are closed, as if he might hide from what is happening as long as he can't see....

"It was during the industrial revolution," Lucian said sluggishly, as if lost in thought, "when erotic paraphernalia began to surface all over, even on the covers of everyday items, such as cigarette cases or two-sided greeting cards. Commercial powers began to see the truth and value of selling sex. These days, of course, the world is highly sexualized, and not just through advertising. No longer is sexual artwork hidden away from the light of day, only to be seen in brothels and dark clubs. Carnal pleasures can be seen everywhere—on the walls of respectable galleries, in the wide array of available online porn, and even on the streets in the form of barely clad beautiful people, uncaring of how they might be seen by onlookers."

It was a relief for Corey that the historical lecture, so timely, gave him back some of the self-control that he'd been losing. Shivering and feverish, Corey swallowed hard, regained most of his composure, and then closed the album with a muffled thud, remembering to keep the book over his groin to cover the remains of his erection.

"Now what?"

Lucian smiled cryptically. "Boudoir."

"We're going back to the club?" Corey stood up, grabbing his jacket from the back of the chair. God, but he needed fresh air to cool off!

Lucian shook his head, a mischievous glow in his eyes. "No. *My* boudoir."

CHAPTER 10

WHATEVER COREY had expected, the sight of Lucian's inner sanctum—his private luxury bedroom—took him by surprise.

The walls were adorned with the expected sensual art, but the rest was far from what he had imagined. Italian Renaissance busts, Grecian urns, Japanese partitions with storks and flowers, art deco furniture, Oriental rugs, art nouveau paintings—it was a hodgepodge of various styles, eras, and cultures, with no discernible routine or pattern, only with a focus on aesthetic beauty. The bedroom was dominated by an old four-poster bed, built of mahogany, with a hardwood roof and damask curtains currently drawn out of the way.

At that point Corey simply stared, not really knowing where or what to look at first.

Lucian spoke out of the blue, "I'm a triple-E."

Corey stared back, dumbfounded. "Huh?"

"Eclectic, exotic, eccentric." Lucian grinned salaciously. "What? Did you think I was referring to my extra, extra large scrotum perhaps?"

Corey laughed. "I thought maybe it was a euphemism for your short attention span."

Lucian feigned outrage, his hand on his chest. "How dare you! I do *not* have ADD." He walked over to the bed and sat down. He petted the cover lovingly. "I've always seen homes as illustrations of family life, the emotional range from extreme to extreme, signs of lives lived in every artifact and object. I know this bed doesn't fit with all the rest of the decor, but I love it. I brought it from France, from my family's mansion."

Corey ambled closer, checking out the bed. The dark wood framework was excellent quality, the drapes thick and soft, and the scent was slightly musky but mostly clean. "A bedroom is a person's most personal space. You don't have to explain or justify your interior design choices to me, you, or anyone."

Chuckling, Lucian beamed, obviously pleased with the comment. "Thank you. That is so sweet of you." While Corey was busy blushing at the compliment, Lucian went on, "The places where I grew up—the sprawling estates I told you about?—they all had four-poster beds and heavy curtains and silk sheets. To me, they mystified sex, covering it behind veils of semiprivacy. But... I did still hear: the moans, the whimpers, the bedsprings, the slapping of skin.... And I could almost see sometimes, when a candle or a lamp was lit behind the curtains: shapes entwined, silhouettes of sensual bodies so close to one another and even to me, so close it... it physically hurt not to be a part of that world."

Carefully Corey sat on the bed next to Lucian. "You got to have all that, just not as a boy. How old were you?"

Lucian nudged him playfully with his shoulder. "Too young. Way too young. Perhaps not too young to know about it, but definitely too young to experience it." His gaze rose to meet Corey's, open and honest. "Does it hurt *you*? To see the whole world engaged in sex while you're still standing at the starting line?"

Rubbing his forehead—though to his surprise he was *not* having a migraine—Corey paused to think about it. "I... I don't know.... I mean, I must be because I see it as a problem, you know. The not having sex part." He looked away, down at his hands in his lap, feeling small and embarrassed. "Only... you had it all figured out at the right age, when you were still young. I'm too old for this."

Lucian snorted, but the spark in his eyes was filled with fury. "You are over thirty, not three hundred. You are most certainly not too old. I don't ever want to hear you say nonsense like that again, understand?"

At the command, like a teacher reproaching his student, Corey had to laugh and nod his acquiescence. "Sure. Okay. Fine." When Lucian offered him a grateful smile, Corey confessed, "You know, even though we parted on, um, less than cordial terms last time, I did do the homework you gave me. About listening to sexual signals around me."

Lucian appeared happy with the declaration. "That's wonderful. And...?"

Though Corey wasn't regretting his admission, he had trouble vocalizing all the things he had thought about and felt. Finally, after some soul-searching, he said, "I thought about us—um, you and I—listening to an opera together."

Quirking an eyebrow, Lucian studied Corey for a moment, until Corey fidgeted under the scrutiny, feeling quite naked under those all-seeing eyes. "I have a box at the Met. I'll take you some day. One day soon." He tapped his finger on his jaw, pensive. "*Don Giovanni* is a must. Yes, absolutely."

Corey barely heard him. He was lost, staring at Lucian's jaw, shaved and as smooth as silk. When he grinned in that mischievous way he did, there were dimples. Beautiful. Corey had tried beards and mustaches, but they made him look dirty and unkempt. Even stubble ill suited him, so he shaved twice a day. Lucian, however, didn't appear to need shaving even once a day. Corey wondered what Lucian's skin felt like, imagining it soft and pliant and sweet-scented....

"Corey? Are you all right?" Lucian stared at him, concerned.

Corey shook his head to clear the passion-red fog, giving a self-deprecating chuckle. "Sorry. Guess I spaced out there for a minute." The back of his neck heated, and he had to touch it to make sure his skin wasn't on fire. He hoped he wasn't babbling when he asked, "So, um, what do we do now? In your, uh... boudoir?"

Expecting a seductive glance and a lewd smirk, Corey was taken aback by the serious expression on Lucian's lovely visage. "There's an exercise I'd like to try with you." Corey was sure he was sporting *the* most panicky look ever because Lucian set out to reassure him, soothing his fears with words. "It does not involve me, unless you so choose." He pointed to the corner of the room where a tall, rectangular gilded mirror stood, awaiting viewers. "I would like you to see... you. I would like you to take off your clothes and go stand in front of the mirror. I want you to try to see yourself in a sensual light. To look at yourself as a sexual being." Lucian gave him a small, gentle smile. "I can leave the room if that's what you want."

At the crazy proposition, Corey wasn't sure what he wanted or thought at all. He felt ridiculous and stupid just considering removing his attire to stand naked in front of a mirror with no rational reason to do so. Just so he could, what, see himself? It was madness personified.

"Don't worry so much about how it seems," Lucian suggested softly, his hand landing on Corey's shoulder, a comforting warmth. "You have a habit of analyzing things, seeking rational explanations, hidden patterns, inner logic, but—"

Corey snorted. "You mean I *over*analyze the shit out of every little thing?"

Lucian chuckled. "Yes. This time, however, focus on how you feel."

Exhaling deeply until he felt utterly deflated, Corey stood and took the necessary two steps to reach the mirror. It was bigger than him all around, with that Empire era exaggerated look of luxury, including gilded carvings on the thick frames.

Lucian giggled behind him. "You're thinking about the mirror, aren't you?"

Corey blushed. "Maybe."

"Would you like me to step out of the room?" Lucian sounded sincere and somehow small too, as if he were trying to appear less noticeable. The thought of Lucian hiding from him didn't sit well with Corey at all.

But… wasn't that the billion-dollar question?

"No. I'd like you to stay." Corey was rather proud of his level tone. "I think you'll be able to see stuff I won't."

Lucian sauntered over to stand next to the mirror so Corey could see both him and his own reflection. He wasn't sure which scared him more. To be seen naked by another, well, that was unnerving. But to really look at yourself and try to see facets you'd never seen before? That was a whole new level of fright night.

Yet Lucian's expression was kind, inviting, and reassuring.

Mollified, Corey began to unbutton his dress shirt. The top buttons were already open. Now he worked on the rest but worried, questioning what Lucian could possibly see in him.

But as he spied out of the corner of his eye, Corey saw Lucian's intense gaze remain riveted on Corey's fingers as they popped one button at a time, revealing more and more skin. Was it Corey's imagination, or was Lucian flushed? His cheeks and neck seemed redder than before, and he was chewing on the inside of his lower lip, while his glazed-over gaze was fixed on Corey.

Generally speaking, Corey knew people could and did find him attractive.

But with Lucian that knowledge felt truer, more tangible, more real somehow, perhaps because he was right there, present in the bedroom, looking directly at Corey.

He wants me. I'm the object of his desire.

Corey could barely draw breath due to that epiphany.

"What are you feeling at this very moment?" Lucian asked, leaning his head against the mirror frame, a dreamy look on his face.

Corey spoke without thinking, as instructed. "Weird. Exposed. Nervous."

"Any positive feelings in there?" Lucian's smile was teasing but also a bit sad, which worried Corey. Was Lucian afraid this exercise was futile, hopeless, without a chance of success? Or was he sorry for Corey, whose first impressions were so negative? Corey looked away from his friend and at his own reflection. Couldn't he really see anything beautiful in his own visage?

Once again, he admitted the truth. "Honestly? I've never looked at myself like that, in that light. I mean, rationally I know I'm handsome, and that people may see me as hot and fuckable. But...." He fell silent, uncertain as to how to finish the sentence.

"I understand." Corey wondered if that could be true. People like Lucian had to be 100 percent aware how pleasing and enticing they were. "I want you to define the attributes of your appearance. What thoughts does your skin invoke? How do you feel about your muscles?"

"You mean, how I would rate myself?" Corey asked, confused.

"No. This is not a competition, not a comparison against standards of beauty that not everyone shares. I'm eager to hear your initial thoughts about your physical qualities." When Corey didn't respond, probably looked as uncomfortable as he felt, Lucian asked, "Would it make it easier or harder for you if I removed *my* clothes as well, simultaneously?"

Corey didn't have to doubt his answer. "No, it would *not* help!"

At the swift denial, Corey expected Lucian to get disappointed or even upset, but he simply offered an encouraging smile. "As you wish."

Nodding and taking a couple calming breaths, Corey finished opening his shirt, pulling the tails out of his pants, and letting the garment slide down his shoulders and arms into a bundle on the floor, a soft thump indicating the landing. Only then did he realize he had closed his eyes.

Come on, you pussy. You see yourself naked every fucking day of your life!

The mental reprimands helped, and Corey found the strength to confront himself head-on. Or face-to-face, as the case might be, as he opened his eyes and saw his reflection staring back at him. God, was that anxious face, turning pale, really his? It must have been because those dark eyes were his, desperate shadows and all.

With serious attempts to control his rapid heartbeat and heaving chest, Corey let his gaze slip lower to examine the revelation.

"If you can, describe out loud what you see and feel," Lucian urged softly. Funny how a man he had known less than two weeks could already seem so unobtrusive and soothing.

Corey hoped vocalizing what he thought would help pinpoint any problems he might have with his self-image. "I'm, uh… I'm tanned." As a wealthy bachelor with too much time on his hands, Corey naturally engaged in a lot of sports, indoors and out. Because of that and despite the temporary nervous paling, his skin held a rich golden luster, youthful and healthy. After a moment's deliberation, he concluded the look suited him.

"Looks good on you," Lucian confirmed with a grin.

"I'm muscular. I play a lot of sports and eat healthy whenever I can. Except when I eat meat, that is."

"Mmm, muscles are good. Not just for when aging, but for sex." Lucian giggled. "But you knew I was going to say that."

Corey blushed deeply, avoiding his companion's eyes in favor of the mirror. "So you think I'm sexy?" He would have slapped his forehead if he could. He couldn't believe the words that had escaped his rambling mouth. What in the hell had he been thinking? But he knew the answer. He hadn't been thinking at all. The image filling his mind wasn't his own reflection but Lucian's.

Frowning as if baffled beyond belief, Lucian replied slowly and cautiously, "Yes. You are very beautiful, Corey. A sight to behold."

"Why?" Cursing himself internally, Corey swore he'd sew his mouth shut if he kept blurting out stuff like this.

Lucian cocked his head, a lopsided smile gracing his lips. "Because your skin glistens like golden velvet? Because I want those thick biceps of yours to wrap around me? Because I dream of licking warm chocolate sauce off your nipples? Because I could probably grate cheese with those ripped abs? Because I wish to feel your weight on me as I lie in bed?" He let his gaze fall, hiding his thoughts. "All of the above?"

Breathless and hot in his skin, Corey choked out, "Yes…?"

"Or…." Lucian whispered, still not showing his eyes to Corey. "Or because I find you utterly fascinating: a good, kind, and smart man, who has riveted me with his mysterious being?" Before Corey could reply—though he doubted he'd be able to produce much that was intelligible—Lucian continued with a command. "Take off your pants. No sense in doing anything halfway. Not when you're on a roll."

Corey was certain he was about to have a heart attack. It felt awfully imminent, heated pressure in his chest making it hard for him to breathe and his head dizzy.

His brain took a second or two to register his hands working his belt buckle without him controlling them. Was that all it took to get him to bare himself? An order?

Corey pushed his pants down his thighs and then lower, bending forward to do so. As he straightened up, his pants dangled at his ankles, and all he had on were his black Calvin Klein boxer briefs.

Now that his brain had caught up, Corey felt like covering his privates, and he moved his hands to block his groin from sight. He felt vulnerable in his exposure, raw and on display, and he was sure he didn't like it.

"Look at yourself, Corey. Breathe deeply and evenly. Don't be afraid."

How was it that Lucian's voice always seemed to ground him? Corey swallowed his nervousness and then looked up, ignoring Lucian and observing only himself.

While he couldn't see his crotch, the rest of his body was on view. His thighs had hair but not much. His legs were long and lean, his muscles strong and defined. He wasn't bad looking.

"When you look at yourself, are any of your thoughts about sex?" Lucian asked.

Corey had only one answer, and *fuck*, wasn't that depressing? "No."

"Look at me. And then answer again."

On command, Corey turned his gaze to Lucian. And what he saw blew his mind.

Lucian was aroused. His eyes were wide and dark, his lips soft and glistening, his skin flushed and beaded with sweat, his chest heaving, his nipples hard, his penis erect in his pants. Lucian was… absolutely gorgeous, Corey thought, scared to breathe, as if that single act might break the spell.

Lucian licked his lips, his gaze dark and intense. "I want you, Corey. I want you for so many reasons. I want to do things to you. I want *you* to do things to *me*. I want us to lie together in my bed and make love until our orgasms blow us away, until neither of us can move an inch."

Corey couldn't hear more if there was more. His heart beat so hard and fast in his ears the drumming was deafening, echoing inside a skull empty of thoughts. All he could do was feel.

And his first instinct was to run, to cower and hide back in a life of familiarities he could control. He swiveled around and tried to run.

But he forgot his pants were bunched down around his ankles.

Like a tree cut down, he fell on the floor with a heavy thud, grunting with pain, all the while knowing he'd be bruised and sore tomorrow. "Shit. Fuck. Dammit." He stopped trying to get up, slumped in defeat, and buried his embarrassed face in his hands, wishing for the ground—or the floor, as the case might be—to open up and swallow him whole.

"Too soon for such words, I see. I apologize." Lucian knelt next to Corey who felt his knees brush against his arm. Then a gentle hand landed on his head, petting softly.

"Sorry," Corey murmured from his hideaway.

"No, *I* am sorry." Lucian sounded repentant too. As though he had committed an act of disgrace, one not to be forgiven. His contrite tone made Corey feel worse. "I push too much and too fast sometimes. I shouldn't have said all that I—"

"You didn't mean it?" Corey cut in, feeling now both ashamed *and* rejected.

"Oh, Corey." Lucian's sigh was melancholy. "I meant every word. You are beautiful and desirable and magical and…. You make my body hum, my heart flutter, my cock throb. I *do* want you. But… at your pace. Even if that means never. I hope, despite everything, you can still consider me a friend, someone you can trust."

Of that Corey had no doubts either. "I do trust you. Still."

"All right, then." Lucian gave Corey's shoulder a tender nudge. "How about you get off the floor, put your clothes back on, and I'll take you to dinner and a show?"

Was the man actually suggesting a date? Dumbfounded, Corey was too curious for his own good. "Sure, okay."

Though already way past midnight, the night ahead in the city that never slept promised to be a new experience, one for the books—or a disaster in the making. Corey wasn't sure which prospect unnerved him more.

CHAPTER 11

"YOU WISH to have a public or a private show?" Lucian asked, his usual quirk of the lip in place as he taunted Corey, who wasn't all that surprised to step back into the velvety gloom of Boudoir.

Both possibilities had merit—and held inherent dangers too. Corey was of two minds about the whole affair. On the one hand, a public viewing of… well, whatever Lucian had planned meant Corey could try to blend into the crowd and not be the center of attention. But on the other hand, he also couldn't predict how he would react to whatever was being shown to him—or if he would fail to react entirely. Neither made him particularly comfortable.

In the end, the embarrassment factor ruled out over other considerations. If he were unable to react in any meaningful way, or if he responded ridiculously passionately (although that was unlikely), better for it to happen in private.

"Private." He glanced at Lucian, suspicious. "What are you up to?"

Lucian shrugged, keeping a casual facade over his innermost thoughts. But that dirty grin made a quick appearance as he was walking off, leaving Corey fuming as he followed less than meekly. But in his heart, he knew he didn't wish to be anywhere else in the world.

Like before, the hallways felt stuffy and dry, with no sounds. Their escort once again was a handsome young man in immaculate attire, not much skin exposed. Corey might have called his uniform dignified if he hadn't known where they were. Like a ghost, the man walked on the thick carpet, a muffled whisper of movement, and Lucian mirrored him to a tee.

Unlike before, however, this time Corey got glimpses he wasn't sure he was meant or allowed to witness. A winding hallway diverged into the dimness, but Corey saw shadows, recognizing them as human by instinct alone. Clad in darkness, they stood behind windows, gazing into lighted rooms where sensuous scenes unfolded like unwrapping candies. These flashes left Corey confused and hot and sweating and weirded out. These had to be the public viewings Lucian had alluded to, so anyone passing by could stop and watch.

Bravely he soldiered on, trailing Lucian who never once glanced around him.

Finally their silent guide led them to a door, stepped aside to let them enter, and then closed the door after them, vanishing to places unknown. A copy of their previous visit, the room was dark but for a couple of long candles burning on a decorated and plated table. Lace doilies and luxury place settings, complete with silverware, fine china, and champagne flutes, weren't what Corey had expected. Steaming pots sat at the side tables, one to each side, and Corey couldn't wait to see what was on the menu.

"I thought our visit here tonight was a spontaneous thing," he commented, needling.

"Thank Amaya. She's the best assistant under the sun." Lucian winked at him.

"Exactly what does she do for you?" Corey was teeming with curiosity—and an odd spark of jealousy.

Lucian chuckled as he sat down. "Everything. Well, almost everything."

Corey sat in the other chair. "Have you slept with her?" Briefly, he wondered why he cared. Not only was it the past (it was, right?), but it was private and none of his business. He didn't own Lucian and had no say in his personal affairs.

"No." Lucian stared back at him with a soft smile and a kind gaze, as if he knew every envious thought in Corey's mind. "I mentored her before she came into my employ. She was as lost as you."

Corey frowned. "Frigid?"

"No. Repressed. She grew up in a fiercely traditional and conservative household in rural Japan. Before we met, she had not orgasmed in a decade, not since she was a teenager."

Blushing, Corey asked hesitantly, "Would she, um, like you telling me this…?"

Lucian shook his head. "Amaya is comfortable in her skin now. If her case can solve sexual problems others are having, she's fine with it. She's very accommodating in that sense. She often sees her past as a cautionary tale of denying who you are."

Corey pondered that for a moment. Then he had to ask to confirm what Lucian told him earlier about his sexual preferences. Appropriate or not. "You've slept with women in the past, though, right?"

Lucian let his surprisingly long lashes veil his eyes, and Corey felt alarm, the kind he couldn't explain but was sure he didn't like. "Yes. I've slept with both men and women."

Corey gulped, a lump in his throat. *What on earth's the matter with me?* Who Lucian had sex with shouldn't have mattered to him in any way, shape, or form. Yet... a hollow sorrow at the pit of his stomach pained him for reasons he couldn't define.

"And, uh... these days your preference is men, right?"

"I mentor mostly. And I have sex with men. I can be with women, as I'm somewhere between gay and bisexual on the Kinsey scale. Well, as I've told you before, I'm leaning toward the gay end of the spectrum." Lucian locked gazes with Corey, his expression inscrutable. "Does this bother you?"

Rolling his eyes ironically and waving his hand dismissively (though he felt anything but), Corey replied, "I'm familiar with basic psychology, okay? Transference and all that jazz. I don't care who you fuck." He sounded colder and crueler than ever before, and he immediately regretted his words and his accusatory tone. Man, when he fucked up, he fucked up good!

Lucian looked sad and hurt, but he concealed it quickly with a smile that didn't reach his eyes. "Have no fear. I will not let our professional relationship evolve into an unprofessional one. I will not take advantage of you or betray the trust you have in me."

Corey felt chastised and disappointed, though he had no right. "Great," he mumbled, avoiding Lucian's eyes as though they could kill him or turn him to stone.

"Of course, considering our professional relationship is basically about getting you all hot and bothered, with a *chance* of sex, that premise might change."

Shocked, Corey looked into Lucian's warm and smiling eyes that spoke of his ability to forgive every insult and slight. Seeing that had Corey struggling to breathe, grateful and ashamed at once.

Lucian snickered shamelessly. "I admit I'm one for making all kinds of rules, for myself and others, and then breaking them."

Corey could breathe easier, the reprieve giving his heart some much-needed levity. "Oh, you mean like rule number one? That only you get to ask questions? We've broken that rule a hundred times over."

Lucian laughed, tossing his head back to expose his pale neck. Corey's sudden urge to lick a line there made him super uneasy and terrified about what that meant.

"Yes, exactly like that! Well, it was such a dreary, boring rule anyway. Glad we abandoned it." Lucian's wink was amiable and conspiratorial, as though his rebellion was attributed more to Corey than himself.

Unable to do anything but laugh, Corey let his mirth show, and Lucian joined him. For a while they shared their amusement as the tension left their cozy little bubble. Corey was just happy Lucian didn't hold his rambling mouth as a negative. Nonetheless, he vowed to make this fiasco up to Lucian somehow, to show his appreciation and gratitude.

For now, though, he chose to move on with his first "date night" ever.

"So… what are we having tonight?" Corey leaned closer to the four round, metallic covers on the side tables that hid the dishes underneath and sniffed. *Yum.*

With a theatrical gesture, Lucian lifted the cover of the first dish. A sizzling hot steak emerged into view, a smoky scent reaching Corey's nostrils until he was salivating.

"Planked New York strip steak in a red wine and mushroom sauce with grilled vegetables on the side." Corey could taste the meat already, suddenly overwhelmed with voracious hunger. "Good?" Lucian asked with a sparkle in his eyes.

"Yeah. Delicious." Corey licked his lips, barely stopping himself from grabbing the platter and yanking the whole thing in front of him so he could devour it like an animal.

Lucian chuckled, took hold of the second dish cover, and raised it to reveal a dark pink fish in broth. "Lightly cooked Scottish salmon in a sweet and sour mushroom sauce with cilantro and cucumbers."

Corey smiled, practically tasting the sharp tang of the fish, a taste with which he was familiar and quite liked. "Ah, surf and turf. What a repertoire."

"Something for everyone."

"And the other two?" Corey pointed at the remaining two dish covers that still hid the savory foods underneath.

"Dessert, which shall for now remain a mystery, and—" Lucian lifted the third cover, exposing a dish that to Corey resembled a pile of fuming compost. Sure, there was also a fruit bowl, but it still looked a little weird. "—a vegetarian option. After all, you mentioned you like to live and eat healthy."

Corey shrugged, quietly preening over the compliment. "I lift weights and run track and stuff. I can eat whatever 'cause I usually burn it off at the gym later the same day."

"Your muscles sure show your tendency to enjoy the gymnasium." Lucian's gaze was appreciative to the point of making Corey blush and feel rather warm in his clothes. "I have a great metabolic system as well. Burns everything right off these old bones. I could eat éclairs all day, every day, and not gain a single ounce."

"Ah, so you've got a sweet tooth?"

"Actually, I prefer vegetarian diets. And I eat a lot of fruit. For obvious reasons." He winked as he spoke.

Corey was confused. "An apple a day keeps the doctor away?"

Lucian's eyebrows rose high. He seemed utterly surprised. "Really?"

Corey chuckled in disbelief. "You've never heard that old adage?"

Lucian bit his lip, his jaw quivering as though he were barely holding back a laugh. "I have heard it, yes. I was referring to the, um… other reason." Corey must have looked like a picture of perplexity because Lucian leaned closer to whisper, "The food we ingest has an effect on how we taste."

"You mean, like, my mouth…?" The notion that someone might not want to kiss him because of how he tasted made Corey actually consider all the crap he put in his mouth.

"Well, yes, that too. But I was mainly referring to…." Lucian quirked an eyebrow, his gaze dropping right down to Corey's crotch, homing in on it like a guided missile.

Corey's eyes widened. "Oh, you mean my…." He cleared his throat and tried again, hopefully without the less than masculine quiver and squeaky tone. "My spunk?"

Lucian nodded, pleased. "Yes." He popped a piece of sliced apple from the bowl into his mouth. "I like to eat a lot of fruit. It makes my semen taste sweet. Fruit is good for me and good for any lover who might—"

"Yeah, yeah, I get it," Corey cut in, his tone rising in alarm. He wasn't ready to talk about Lucian and blowjobs in the same sentence and risk the accompanying mental image, not yet anyway. "I'm not sure I wanna give up steak entirely, though."

Lucian chuckled seductively. "Most men love their meat." God, how he made a simple sentence sound *so* dirty. Corey flushed with heat. Lucian obviously decided to give him a reprieve as he leaned back, took on a polite expression, and raised his voice back to conversational levels. But his next words belied the casual mannerisms. "Of course, if you refuse to mind what you eat, then you're hardly in a position to complain if and when your lover decides to spit, *not* swallow."

The thought of any man either spitting or swallowing his cum made Corey dizzy with the veritable cornucopia of erotic imagery that overflowed his mind. He wasn't 100 percent sure, but he might have gurgled something unintelligible then, and he prayed he wasn't drooling like a village idiot.

Lucian cocked his head to the side and narrowed his eyes, obviously studying Corey intimately. Finally he said, his tone pensive, "Corey? Can you please tell me what you're feeling right now?"

Inwardly distraught, Corey refused by shaking his head violently. "No. I'd rather we, um, eat." He picked up his fork and knife, and only then remembered he hadn't yet chosen which meal he would partake of. Setting his utensils back down while his mind reeled, Corey yanked the steak platter closer and lifted several slices onto his empty porcelain plate. Then he shoved the tray back and began eating, hiding his embarrassed face in his food.

Thankfully, Lucian made no remarks. Corey heard him picking foods from various platters and beginning to eat as well.

"Champagne, wine, or water?" he asked all of a sudden, and Corey jolted.

"Huh? Oh, yeah, um…. Water's fine, thanks." He extended his glass closer to the jug of crystal clear water, ice cubes clinking against the sides, and Lucian poured him a glass. Out of the corner of his eye, he observed Lucian also drinking water. "You, uh, don't want wine?"

There was a smile in Lucian's voice. "I'm not much of a drinker. While I do enjoy the occasional glass of champagne at parties or white wine with dinner, tonight I wish to keep a clear head. I'm no use to you if I'm drunk. Irish courage has never been something I needed." He took a sip of his water. "You?"

"Me? Oh, uh, I may have a beer at night or a nice claret with a meal. That's about it."

"That's good to know, Corey. Do not read too much into me saying this, but excessive drinking can cause impotence."

That remark had Corey's head springing up like a jack-in-the-box. "I'm frigid, not an alcoholic!" How dare he imply Corey had a habit of getting too wasted to get it up?

Lucian nodded, his face irritatingly impassive. "Yes, I know. It was simply a statement of fact, not necessarily linked to your condition."

"*Necessarily!*" Corey was fuming by then, his dinner forgotten. "What the f—"

"I apologize if you interpreted what I said as a personal insult. Which it was not."

Corey counted to ten, fisting his hands on the table beside his plate. Why did Lucian sound so condescending all of a sudden? Or was Corey overimagining things? Knowing the answer made him sick to his stomach, and he grunted at the familiar tightening pain in his gut.

"Corey? Are you all right? Do you need to see a doctor?" Lucian's tone rose with every word until he seemed deeply concerned. He began to rise from his seat, concern etched into his pixie-like features. If he'd had pointy ears, he would have resembled those elves in the *Lord of the Rings* and *Hobbit* movies. A weird thing to think about at a time like this.

"No, don't get up. Just sit. I… I'm sorry. I overreacted. Sorry." Corey meant it too. As he had witnessed Lucian's response to his plight, it had confirmed he was being stupid. "I don't think you accused me of being a hopeless drunkard."

"No, I didn't. I wouldn't do or say anything to hurt you." Lucian sounded as sincere as his expression seemed. "All right, yes, I admit I do and say things to provoke a reaction out of you, to countermand your claim of frigidity, but to intentionally and for no functional purpose be mean just to—"

"My *claim* of frigidity?" Corey had to actually stop and laugh then, or he would have blown a gasket. Again.

"I phrased that wrong—" Lucian started to say, alarmed.

"No, no. I really need to stop reading too much into things." He gave a casual chuckle in the hopes of convincing his companion he saw the whole exchange as an attempt at levity. When Lucian showed no signs of seeing the humor in the situation, Corey continued in a soothing tone, "I swear, Lucian, I... I'm just rattled about this whole business, you know. I keep hearing things when you speak, reading between the lines, and I know they're wrong, that you wouldn't...." He ran out of steam, opening and closing his mouth like a koi out of its pond.

Seemingly placated, Lucian offered a shy smile. "I understand." He spoke softly and slowly, obviously choosing his words carefully. "I was only trying to ascertain possible reasons for your frigidity. Drinking is one such cause, albeit a temporary one. We had not discussed it before so I.... In any case, I never meant it as an accusation. After all, there's still so much we don't know about each other." He gave a nervous giggle at the end.

That told Corey Lucian felt he was in a precarious position. "Yeah. Perhaps we can do that tonight. Learn more about one another, I mean."

Lucian smirked, a mixture of bashfulness and temptation in the gesture. "Like a first date?"

The gentle teasing undid something in Corey, a tightness constricting his insides began to uncoil and loosen. The pressure in his belly and head eased, and he felt calmer again. Even at the prospect of his first date ever.

"Kind of like that, yeah."

And what a frightening and exhilarating prospect it was.

CHAPTER 12

"So, WHAT should we talk about?" Corey looked flushed and embarrassed, as though he wished he could slap his forehead for asking such a dumb question.

For Lucian, those reddened cheeks only endeared him more. "It depends. Do you wish to have a casual conversation or a deep and meaningful one, which could dredge things up?"

Corey frowned, and Lucian could practically see the gears turning in his busy head. "What's the difference?" Suddenly he shook his head, harrumphing in annoyance. "I mean I *know* the difference. I just mean, what's the right thing to do with us? I mean, you and I." Corey looked even more weirded out now, and Lucian suppressed a smile at how many times the word *mean* had sounded in those sentences.

"Let's cool things off for a moment, shall we?" Lucian suggested in his most casual and down-to-earth speech patterns, and instantly Corey sighed in relief, the stiffness in his shoulders vanishing. "Let us start with the basics. Like… what's your favorite book, and why?"

Corey smiled and relaxed. "Huh. What a loaded question. 'Cause there are books I value but I've read only once and will never read again. Then there are the ones I like to reread every once in a while, but I don't value for their literary merit but solely for the fun."

Lucian chuckled. "Spoken like yours truly. So, the book you rate the highest?"

"Easy. *The Catcher in the Rye*."

"Salinger. How classical of you." Lucian flicked his tongue at Corey, invoking a deep laugh from his new friend. "Why?"

Corey shrugged. "Holden, I think. His character is a mess, all over the place socially, emotionally, physically. But he's human. Irritatingly so. And he's honest. To a fault sometimes."

"You recognize yourself in him?"

Corey laughed while shaking his head. "God, no. Not even when I was a teenager. I was a different kind of mess. No, he's just a portrayal of the kind of young man a lot of people have been, when everything irks them, and they think everything's bullshit. Typical teenage stuff. He puts into words what some kids feel, even today." His eyes narrowed in a challenging way as he asked, "How about you? What's your favorite book? The one you value the most?"

Lucian had to pause to consider the options as a library of read books flipped through the index of his memory. "There were two that had a great impact on me in my teenage years. And no, I probably shouldn't have been reading either one."

"Oh?" Corey showed his curiosity even while chewing a forkful of food.

"*The Picture of Dorian Gray* by Oscar Wilde and *Justine* by the Marquis de Sade."

Corey laughed. "Depraved and disturbing psychologies and equally disturbing sexual imagery? Now why am I not surprised?"

Lucian smiled. Corey's laugh was a wonderful, bubbly sound of pure joy and amusement. He wished he could hear it again. "At the time I found the notion of eternal youth a fascinating one. Yet, even back then, I understood there was always a price to be paid for pleasures and pains. How every thrill comes with a cost, a price tag attached, and how they are rarely worth all the heartache that comes with them. And... sometimes the price was paid by someone else, with horrific results."

"Huh. Deep thinking for a teenager."

Lucian shook his head. "Sometimes I think no one understands the world better than a teenager. They live on the edge of ignorance and knowledge, precariously balanced over the abyss, ever ready to take the plunge into the unknown." He shrugged, recalling the weird way of thinking he was notorious for back in the day. "De Sade showed that virtue may be its own reward, which is good because not much else of value can be had from it. Philosophical pornography attracted me then. Later I learned de Sade was in fact wrong. Virtue doesn't necessarily lead to being taken advantage of by vice but in fact leads to boredom and a life left unlived, and I knew that path was not for me."

"So, you're not a libertine, then?" Corey teased, and Lucian liked that he felt comfortable doing so.

"I deplore rules set by others. But I like to have a couple in store for myself. I do not ascribe to a lifestyle where all moralities and ethics are abandoned for the sake of selfish pleasures. To me that approach shows the kind of intellectual lassitude and laziness that makes everything meaningless and diminishes new experiences to indifference. De Sade wrote about grotesque facets of humanity, which I believe are only one aspect of what humans are truly capable of."

Corey harrumphed, looking surprised. "You're fundamentally a person with a positive outlook on life. Huh. Who'da thunk it?"

"Hush, you," Lucian admonished with a wicked smirk. "I have a reputation of cynical notoriety to maintain." When Corey only laughed back, Lucian asked, "Are you going to tell me you never read any erotic classics when you were young?"

"Sure." Corey admitted with an air of insolence. "*Dracula* by Bram Stoker for all those sexual allusions. And Anaïs Nin, of course, for all those fantastical scenes she describes with such flourish. A lot of racy sex and... dub con, noncon, and such." Those terms were familiar to Lucian. Dubious consent and nonconsensual. Basically literary references to forced sex and rape in erotic or romance narratives. Corey's eyes flashed intently as he spoke.

Lucian caught on to it right away. Corey was keeping something a secret. Now they were getting somewhere. "How did those erotic scenes make you feel? They have a strong physical, sensual presence after all."

Corey gulped, his skin paling until a light sheen of sweat made his face glisten a bit. "I thought they were, um, the opposite of puritanical and patriarchal. A poetic way of writing about fetishes and unusual gender dynamics—"

"Corey." Lucian cut in with a single word, feeling in his gut how wrong that answer was. Not that it was incorrect in a literal sense but how unlike Corey the reply was. Lucian could have used those words, but from Corey's lips, they sounded... off. Avoidance. Evasion. Censorship.

Corey exhaled deeply, deflating before Lucian's eyes, and then in a hushed voice said, "I felt nothing. Not then, not now." His tone spoke of self-recrimination and shame and resignation and defeat, and Lucian hated hearing them. He *hated* hearing them.

Watching Corey gulp down a whole glass of water and then refill it silently, Lucian felt helpless in a way he never had before. In his heart he began to understand why that was, but he also knew he had to fight the instinct to reach out and let his emotions pour out of him. This took a delicate but professional hand, not a tender and loving heart. Not yet.

"Physically? Emotionally? Please, Corey, tell me. Don't shut me out." Lucian hoped he sounded like a proper confidant and not a hopeless romantic.

Corey closed his eyes, and his jaw quivered ever so slightly. Never had Lucian seen him so down, so beaten and broken by his situation. He had to dig his nails into his palms to prevent himself from grabbing Corey, yanking him into his embrace, and not letting go until they were both healed.

"I didn't get hard," Corey finally whispered, his lips pouting in a manner suggesting he was unhappy with himself. "I found those stories interesting, you know, intellectually. I did have fantasies, but they were purely mental exercises to see if I got the logistics of intercourse right. But an erection? No. Not a one."

Lucian nodded, though he felt anything but calm. Was he getting too close to this case and his client? That would be bad. "Do you have wet dreams?"

Surprised, Corey looked up, eyes wide—and noticeably bright with unshed tears. He had to swallow several times before he managed to speak. "I... I think so. I mean, I must have them since I wake up hard most mornings. At least I did in my twenties. Every other or third morning these days."

Lucian nodded, feeling more confident after hearing that. There seemed to be nothing physically wrong with Corey, and he had surely been tested for all the usual suspects. "Do you remember any of them? Vivid details or vague feelings?"

"Latter." Corey frowned, musing. "You believe I have no physical problems in, um, that area? That it's all in my head?"

Though somewhat uncertain of the answer, Lucian nodded emphatically. "Yes." It was a little white lie because Lucian, like Corey undoubtedly, *wanted* to believe it. "Speaking of which. Do you still wish to participate in what I have planned for this evening? A private viewing to show you what's out there?"

"Yes." Corey straightened up, blinked away the moisture from his eyes, and plainly regained his self-control. No hesitation, no doubt. Lucian was proud of his bravery. All of a sudden, Corey pinked slightly, looking sheepish. "Sorry we didn't get to have a nice casual and ordinary first date talk."

Lucian giggled. "You and I, honey, we're anything but ordinary. Come on. Let's finish our meal so we can savor a different form of entertainment."

With a small nod and a tentative smile, Corey picked up his fork and resumed dining, as did Lucian. The only sounds in the room were the clink of silverware on plates and the hum of the ceiling fan. The cozy solitude was one of the reasons why Lucian appreciated Boudoir and all it had to offer. The ambience seemed to relax them instead of filling them with tension and anticipation.

Once their plates were all but empty, Lucian asked, "So... I have several options for you to consider, from mild and innocent to wild and wicked. Your choice what you wish to see."

Corey patted his mouth with his napkin, probably buying time before answering. "Like what?"

"Nuh-uh." Lucian waved a finger between them in a scolding matter. "Don't you like surprises?"

Corey chuckled. His eyebrow quirked. "Not even a clue? You're cruel."

"Just naughty." Lucian winked. "Would you like to start with sweet and innocent? To get your feet wet before jumping off the deep end?" Licking his lips nervously and readjusting on the chair, Corey nodded his acquiescence quietly. "Good." Lucian pulled out his smartphone, tapped on the screen, and then put the little device back in his pocket, certain that his impish expression was enough to keep Corey on the edge of his seat.

But whether sanguine or intrigued, Corey said nothing, merely pushed his dinnerware back, and sat ready and waiting.

Finally, after a minute or two, Lucian's smartphone beeped. He grinned. "Showtime."

The curtains on their right parted. Judging from Corey's startled expression, he hadn't realized the drapes were on the other side. Corey stood up and ambled closer to peer into the room, and Lucian joined him.

The bathroom was done in cool colors—rich blues and whites and turquoises. An empty claw-foot bathtub stood in the middle of the room. Behind it was a small pedestal with a silvery marble statue of a nude young man. A bed was tucked against the wall on the right, while the door remained in shadows on the left.

Out of the corner of his eye, Lucian observed Corey taking in the sight.

Corey cocked his head from side to side, frowning in bafflement. "That's not... not a real statue, is it?"

Lucian followed his gaze, smiling. The long lashes fluttered ever so slightly, and the chest rose and fell with shallow breathing. Apart from that, the Grecian posture was perfect. "You're right. No, that is not a real statue. His name is Thierry."

Corey's body stiffened, as did his expression. "A lover?"

Lucian heard the unspoken jealousy but decided not to react. "No. I mentored him."

Corey nodded, his rigid shoulders relaxing. "What's his story? If you're allowed to tell me, that is. I don't wanna get you in trouble for spilling other people's secrets."

"Thierry wouldn't mind." Lucian knew the young man well and had no reservations or doubts about the lack of any veil of secrecy. "He's from up north. His former boyfriend was a class act. Well, on the surface, anyway. He demanded perfection from Thierry, in conduct, in appearance, in obedience."

A low growl emanated from Corey's throat. "Abusive?"

Lucian nodded, though Corey's gaze was aimed at the man pretending to be a statue. "Yes. For even the smallest infraction, he hurt Thierry badly. Sexually too."

Corey grimaced, angry for another. That was encouraging to see, Lucian thought with satisfaction. "Where's the fucker now?"

"Prison. Ten years for gross sexual assault and another ten for aggravated assault. But he had no priors, so he's likely to get out long before his twenty years are up."

"That's not justice." Corey shook his head vehemently, his tone fierce.

"Thierry was lucky the crimes against him took place in Maine when they had been living together in Canada before that. There the penalties for such crimes would have been much lower, with only a few years jail time."

"Lucky…." Corey all but spat the word, disagreeing with the law. Lucian had to agree with him. Many countries had ridiculously shoddy laws and disgracefully mild penalties when it came to sex crimes, especially those involving LGBT people. "So, why did he come to you?" Corey asked, calmer now.

"He was referred to me by a friend." Lucian stared at Thierry, remembering him lying in a hospital bed, the white sheets in stark contrast to the bloody gauze, swollen face, and black-and-blue bruises all over him. "Thierry was so young then, only seventeen. The judge had deemed him old enough to know whether or not to enter a relationship—"

"Oh my fucking God," Corey muttered next to him, fury in every sound and act.

"—so his abuser didn't get as long a sentence as he should have." Lucian had hated the verdict with all his being back then. Nowadays Thierry was better, and that was a comfort, even if at times it felt like too small a one. "To this day, at the age of twenty, Thierry does not speak about him, not even his name. But Thierry is part of a community now, and he has friends and family around him, so he isn't in any danger."

"That's good." Corey let out a long, weary sigh. "What community?"

Lucian smiled. "Mine."

Just as Corey gave Lucian a perplexed look, the door opened, and in walked a big, tall man dressed in jeans and a T-shirt, carrying a wooden bucket with bathing tools in it. He shut the door after him, came to stand by the bathtub, and placed his items on a stool. Then his gaze turned toward the statue, inspecting with his eyes before sauntering around the pedestal to do the same with his hands.

"Should we…?" Corey sounded concerned, his body fidgeting as if readying for battle on behalf of the statue boy.

"Intervene? No. That's Luther. He's Thierry's handler."

Corey shot a sharp look at Lucian. "His *what?*"

Lucian chuckled. "Well, his Daddy or his Dom would give the wrong idea. But Luther and Thierry are very much a devoted couple, I assure you."

While the two of them were talking, Luther had circled the human statue a few times, an increasing look of hunger on his face. Finally he stopped in front of Thierry, extended his hand in a gentlemanly fashion, and waited.

For a while nothing happened.

Then, as if by a miracle, the statue's chest heaved, and his eyes blinked, as if the stone had come to life and flesh. Lucian saw how Corey held his breath, rapt, and was happy that the man seemed to be sensitive to the emotional staging in the other room.

Thierry raised his hand slowly, shivering, until he placed it in his suitor's palm. Luther helped Thierry down off the pedestal and picked the man up in his arms, carrying him to the bathtub and placing him to stand there. The whole series of movements had been gentle, adoring, and loving to the fullest, Luther's gaze never leaving that of his charge.

Thierry watched silently as Luther turned the knobs and water drizzled into the tub. Luther moistened a sponge and with tender strokes began to wash Thierry clean. Trickles of silver ran down his pale skin, becoming rivulets and exposing new patches of white skin. The young man was fit, with defined muscles and tendons, all taut in stark relief to the softness of his skin. The blatant carnality was overshadowed by the air of romance.

And all the while, Luther spoke. Lucian saw his lips moving, but since the microphones to the room were turned off, he couldn't hear what the man was saying. Lucian had a feeling those softly whispered endearments and gentle demonstrations of affection weren't meant for an audience anyway. He was content with using his imagination.

"Is this show symbolic?" Corey asked suddenly, shaking Lucian out of his reverie.

"How do you mean?"

A flicker of a smile lifted the corner of Corey's lips, vanishing fast. "The stone statue, cold and rigid, becoming alive by the magic touch of a lover's hands?" He did sound cynical, yes, but a note of longing was buried there too. "Pygmalion and his desperate love for perfection that could only exist by the wonders of divine intervention? Should I wait for Cupid or Aphrodite to grant *my* wish next? Oh, if only I were a real boy...."

A certain bitterness rose in Corey's tone as he went on, and a chill rushed through Lucian. Desperation became familiar ground if allowed to fester long enough. But Lucian wasn't ready to admit defeat over Corey's heart, body, and soul yet.

"We're both educated men, and we interpret the world accordingly." Lucian shifted his gaze back to the sensual scene unfolding before their eyes. "But what you're seeing right now with Luther and Thierry, that is *their* fantasy, not one I chose for them to reenact. When Thierry came to me...." Lucian frowned, lost in the joyless memory. "He couldn't bear for anyone to touch him. Not like you who cannot feel. He was terrified to feel, crying himself to sleep and dreaming of what you unwittingly possess."

Corey shook visibly, fighting for breath, blinking hard. Obviously the idea of anyone wanting to be frigid shook him to the core. "He wanted to be... stone?"

"Hard as stone, cold as ice, unfeeling, uncaring. Safe."

Corey rubbed his temple, a grim expression marring his handsome face. Perhaps his headache had renewed. "But... his handler...."

"Yes. Luther has a gift. He listens. He can listen to silence and hear what is not being said, what is hidden beneath dead-calm surfaces. I asked him to listen to Thierry, and he did. For two years, without a single brush or caress. What you see now is the end result."

"The way Thierry looks at him...." Corey pressed his palm against the window and then laid his forehead on the cool glass. He seemed conflicted, gulping. "He adores Luther."

Lucian came to stand next to Corey, offering him answers and security, should he need them. "Yes. They are very much in love. They married last year."

Thierry smiled down upon Luther. The gesture was shy and sad and full of love. With his hand, he caressed Luther's stubbly cheek, following the curve of the cheek and line of the jaw, pausing at the neck where Luther's heartbeat might be felt. Luther turned his head, never breaking eye contact with Thierry, and kissed the bare wrist sweetly.

Corey looked away.

Lucian understood. In that one simple act, a whole love story could be seen. An intimate display, difficult to watch for someone who had never known such adoration.

Lucian looked away too. Though glass separated them, he felt too close for comfort to the pair's love that healed and held true through thick and thin. Lucian held back the sigh born from a longing heart, knowing it would do no good here.

In many ways Lucian was as lonely as Corey.

Sex had nothing to do with it.

CHAPTER 13

"SO, UM... what else have you got to show me?" Corey damn near choked on his words, pushing them past the stranglehold his emotions had on him.

Lucian gave him that enigmatic smile that could mean anything. "We don't have to go on if you wish to stop or take a break."

For reasons Corey couldn't fathom, the constricting knot in his stomach grew, the one that spoke of stress and anxiety and no, no, no. His head ached as well, the familiar heated pressure against his forehead and temples like fiery screws tightened around each and every nerve ending. Being with Lucian frequently calmed him, no matter what the novel experience. This time... no.

The problem was he couldn't rationally comprehend why the sudden coil of stress was emerging now. But... in his gut he felt the answer. Lucian cracked the lid of Pandora's box, granting Corey glimpses of a magical world where love, intimacy, and sex resided. But something darker was arising as well, temptations he knew not how to counter, emotions he had no name for, desires that frightened him.

Corey turned his back to Lucian, needing time to process. Still, he felt like a coward doing so, hiding from the sensual journey his companion was taking him on. Corey could trust him as a guide, couldn't he? Nothing bad would happen to him while he was with Lucian, right?

"Corey? Are you all right? Please, talk to me." Lucian sounded scared as he placed his hand on Corey's shoulder. Corey could feel it shaking.

Suddenly he stood calmly in the eye of the storm. Lucian's panic seemed to trigger an instinctive response in Corey, causing him to get a grip on himself so he could offer the same composure to another.

Elated at figuring out what aided him, Corey placed his palm over the back of Lucian's hand, squeezing for reassurance. "I'm fine. Headache is all." When he glanced over his shoulder and saw that Lucian was far from convinced, Corey went for the truth. "That scene with Thierry and

Luther. I guess it had a bigger impact on me than I thought at first. Emotional, you know."

His admission was the right one because Lucian's face softened, a sweet expression of sympathy rising to the foreground. "I admit I initially had a similar response. Seeing them together has always warmed my heart." Was Corey imagining the glimpse of melancholy on that beautiful face, hidden before he could confirm it? What possible reason could Lucian have to be sad? Surely a man like him, with wealth and importance, friends and lovers, had to be more than content with his life. Corey made a mental note to address the issue at a later date.

"Are *you* okay with us going forward?" Corey asked, hesitant.

Lucian smiled ruefully before he seemed to notice his faux pas, and his smile widened. "Yes, of course. I am comfortable in this venue. Your choice."

Corey shrugged but felt anything but casual. "I'm cool with seeing more." Slowly he was beginning to realize this descent into erotic depths might just be fraught with perils he had not perceived or anticipated. One of them being Lucian and the temptation he presented. Falling for him would be a very bad idea. A modern-day Casanova like Lucian would never return Corey's feelings, as he himself had said, keeping their relationship strictly professional.

Even if it involved sex to aid him.

But his attention was drawn to Lucian readying to leave, smoothing out any wrinkles that might have developed on his immaculate attire. His grin was as inviting as always. "Come then, young squire. Unto new adventures."

Corey choked a chuckle and followed Lucian out of the room.

The thick hallway carpets muffled their steps, and several doors were half-covered by curtains. Every scene around a new corner offered a sense of privacy and intimacy created by locked doors, veiled entrances, wax flowers and sensual paintings, low lighting and bottles of wine. Corey was all but smothered by the sensual atmosphere that hid and suppressed everything in suggestive appearances that a child could see through. He surmised that was the purpose of Boudoir.

They arrived at a door like any other, with no names, numbers, or symbols on it. Corey puzzled at how Lucian identified their goal so readily, so unerringly. Another mental note to add to an already long list, he decided as he ambled after his host.

The new room was a carbon copy of their former one, sans the table and the dinner.

Except… where in the previous room there had been a window to look through, in this one there were Japanese-style paper sliding doors. A young man dressed in tight leather pants and nothing else, including footwear, parted the doors and then backed out of the room, the lock on the door clicking shut as he went.

But Corey couldn't have cared less about any servant types, not when it seemed they were about to be catered to by a concert. On a low stage were two women, one standing, one sitting. The petite blonde standing was pretty and delicate, like a flower or a butterfly, and her long frilly dress was made of silks and satins, all see-through and pastel-colored. The other woman sat on a chair behind the blonde, with a cello resting next to her. Her raven black hair was cut short in roaring twenties style, and the dark, body-hugging dress on her skinny figure matched her sullen look. It seemed she didn't wish to be here, while the perky blonde waved at Lucian and Corey enthusiastically, practically bouncing on her feet.

Lucian turned to Corey. "French or English?" Corey had no idea what he meant, so he shrugged, indicating his response was "whatever." "French it is." The gleam in Lucian's green eyes was downright mischievous as he leaned over to whisper, "You speak French, Corey, or do you just wish to kiss that way?"

Corey blushed at the taunt but restrained any further acts of humiliation. "I'm up for anything." Two could play at this seductive game.

Lucian laughed low, debauchery in every tone.

The brunette spread her legs and placed the cello there, her fingers on the strings and the bow, her hands slender but sinewy, undoubtedly strong and steady. The blonde gazed at her, and the brunette began to play. From the first bars and the opening lines of the blonde singing, Corey soon recognized the aria, *"Mon coeur s'ouvre a ta voix,"* from the opera *Samson and Delilah.* He had heard it before, the echoing light lyrics in contrast with the dark tones of the instruments—though at the moment only the cello was playing—and the occasionally soft and deep voice. The aria was not one of his favorites, but the right mezzo-soprano could bring the lyrics alive and tears to his eyes.

Quiet in his seat, Corey listened to the woman singing in French,

"My heart opens to your voice like the flowers open to the kisses of the dawn.

So trembles my heart, ready to be consoled by your voice that is so dear to me!"

All of a sudden, the cellist played a sharp discord, causing Corey to cringe.

The aria stopped dead as the blonde swiveled on her heels and glared at her companion. "You inept clod! Your fingering merits a snap from my belt!" She twirled the ends of her heavy silken sash under her ample bosom, a clear threat in her voice.

The brunette blushed, grimacing in a warning of her own. "You didn't think so little of my fingering last night!"

The blonde gasped in shock, eyes wide and lips apart.

Corey expected a catfight to break out any second, but as he made to stand between the women and prevent fisticuffs, topped with long and sharp acrylic nails, Lucian placed a hand firmly on his arm and then shook his head. His expression was determined and serious, but Corey wondered if his friend had lost his mind.

On stage the blonde had stormed right up to the brunette, who pushed her cello aside and tried to stand. But the blonde shoved her back down on the rickety chair, which creaked under the sudden strain.

"I'll show you what I think of you," she murmured in a low reverberating tone.

Corey inhaled, ready to stop a fight, when the blonde promptly dropped on her knees, tore the black dress in half from the hem up, and exposed the brunette's... cock? As Corey ogled at the revelation, wide-eyed and slack-jawed, utterly dumbfounded, the blonde grabbed the hardening penis and then took the whole length down her throat. She gurgled while the brunet groaned, his head falling back as he patted the blonde's hair.

"She's a... a he...," Corey mumbled, glaring at Lucian, who should have warned him not to make a fool of himself by running to the rescue of a woman who didn't need rescuing. Even though, in all honesty, Corey hadn't done that because Lucian had prevented him.

Lucian smiled in his cryptic way. "Surprises are everywhere."

"Even under dresses, it seems," Corey replied dryly. "What's this supposed to show or teach me? What's this symbolic of, besides your, uh, surprise, surprise!"

"Why can't this be exactly what it is? A titillating sensual show for our pleasure, or for their enjoyment? Why does there have to be deeper meanings or more layers?"

About to start a world of arguments, Corey happened to glance at the stage to see the blonde climb into the brunet's lap to kiss him passionately—while the man was stroking the blond *guy's* exposed cock with vigor.

"They're both men? What the—" he exclaimed. Then he flushed with embarrassment as both musicians stopped kissing and faced him, a whole host of emotions from disappointment to anger displayed in their silent demeanor. "Sorry. I didn't mean it like that. I've got no problem with gays and transpersons or, you know, whatever. Please, um, go back to, uh… doing what you were doing…." Mortified, he ran out of steam and wished the floor would open up and bury him so deep no one would ever dig him out. Deflating, he muttered to Lucian, "Now can we go?"

"You don't wish to watch us finish what we started?" the blond guy asked, his voice still feminine and soft, a perfect singer's voice. And best of all, there was no animosity.

Corey looked up, surprised at the invitation, and frowning in disbelief. "You'd still…? Wouldn't you want some privacy after—"

The brunet harrumphed wryly. "We wouldn't have come to Boudoir if privacy was something precious to us." His gaze swept over Corey, impassive—or faking neutrality. "Watch or don't. We're cool either way." Then he went back to smooching the blond beauty until their rocking motions turned erratic and yearning moans filtered through the otherwise silent air.

Breathless, Corey couldn't avert his gaze no matter how hard he tried. Frozen in place, he observed as pieces of garments slipped away or got torn to shreds as the two men hurried to feel each other naked. When their torsos were fully bare, it was obvious they were men. Flat chests, ripped muscles, corded tendons, short hair, rough skin—all signs of masculinity hidden under the guise of femininity.

And the ardor these two felt for each other could be felt with every heated gasp, groping hand, feverish bite, demanding kiss, shredded clothing, and uncovered patches of skin. Watching porn online had nothing on the scene Corey was seeing. This was palpable, visceral, tangible, in-your-face real, and he had to see more. He needed to see this through to the end.

But even as the sexually exhibitionistic artists, all but naked, began to fuck each other with the shared motions of their bodies—no penetration was imminent, it seemed—Corey was painfully aware of the fact that his own cock was barely half-hard. His erection was a mere glimmer of the feral display of frotting taking place before him.

The trouble was Corey didn't get it. Why had his body failed him again? After all, when he had looked at the erotic album with Lucian, he had been so immensely hard, like a fucking rock.

Why not now when real live sex was taking place not ten feet from him? Corey was so frustrated he could have screamed. Inside... he did, disappointed beyond belief.

I hate myself. I hate you, you stupid dick. Get up, dammit! Pretty please...?

As expected, his pleas went unanswered, and what was left of his erection vanished after that pitiful pep talk.

It no longer mattered what transpired in front of him. Their passion stirred nothing in him, so it was wasted. Corey exhaled slowly, closed his eyes, and waited for the fat lady to sing and the show to end. Only the lady wasn't fat, or even a lady. He didn't care who sang the final note as long as someone did.

A warm hand landed on his arm. "Are you all right?" Lucian whispered, concern again tinting his tone. God, but Corey really liked that voice, kind of dulcet and melodic and sweet and smart and sexy....

And that was when blood rushed through him, blazing hot, singeing all in its path, surging to throb in his cock, which then began to show signs of renewed vitality. Or was it sexuality? He didn't give a flying fuck as long as his dick decided it was time to play in any way, shape, or form.

Opening his eyes, Corey faced Lucian, whose delicate features were scrunched up in worry lines. It actually felt as though he was seeing Lucian for the first time. Really seeing him. In the dim lighting of the audience area, Lucian's hair glowed deep red instead of the copper and gold it usually did. His pert little nose seemed to invite a tentative brush or a brief kiss. Lucian had quite high cheekbones, and the rest of his countenance had similarly sharpish edges, as though he had been sculpted daintily, and then some crispness added to his softness.

"Corey? What's wrong?" Lucian stared at him, eyes wide at first in anxiety, but then narrowing as he apparently suspected something was truly off.

Rushing to reply, Corey placated him by saying, "What else can you show me? Something in the hard-core department?" He was rather proud of how steady his voice sounded.

Lucian had his skeptical and reserved game face on, but Corey waited him out. Then, after a leisurely pause for thought, Lucian nodded lightly. "How about an orgy?"

Corey damn near swallowed his tongue.

CHAPTER 14

THE YOUNG dark-haired man being swarmed by three other men was nubile and pliant as they manhandled him into submission. One of them, a gorgeous tall black man built like a sex god, gripped the boy's hips hard enough to leave finger-shaped bruises and ramming his sheathed cock deep into his ass. Another one, a ripped athletic type with blond hair, was busy stuffing the young guy's mouth full of his dick, his hips rocking back and forth as he held the guy's head gently in place by his hair and jaw. The third man, a brawny bear with lots of hair and bulging muscles, was on his knees beneath the young man, sucking his cock while stroking his own in tandem.

Corey stared at the scene, mesmerized, which was like some kind of erotic monster, twisted and alluring. "Why's he wearing mask?" He pointed at the young man being used for sexual delight by three men. He wore a black silken theatrical mask, weirdly out of place and appropriate at once, plus a bit melodramatic.

Lucian replied matter-of-factly, "Some acts of debauchery and submission require a touch of anonymity, don't you agree?"

Shrugging, Corey had no opinion. How would he know what types of props orgies did or didn't require? He'd never attended one, as a participant or an onlooker. He'd only seen a couple on the Internet, and they had been choreographed in every detail. Realism didn't enter into it, only hard bodies.

The two of them were sitting in chairs in full view of the bedroom staging where sexy games were afoot. Watching, but not touching, seemed to be the theme of the evening, he thought. Well, he had requested something hard-core, and that was what he got. In plain sight, raw and exposed, less than fifteen feet away.

"You've, uh, watched live shows like this before?" Corey asked, just to create any kind of sounds in the room that weren't moans and groans, or skin slapping skin, or litanies of dirty sex talk, no matter how apropos.

Lucian nodded, his expression impassive once more. "Yes. Many times."

Corey turned to Lucian, studying his half-lidded eyes that had no spark, his stoic face that betrayed no emotions, the air of boredom that emanated from his stance. "It's gotten old for you, hasn't it?"

Lucian lowered his eyelids so that his lashes blocked his eyes. As usual, with a single gesture he hid so much of himself from Corey. "It has lost some of its prior charm, I admit."

"You don't wanna watch this, do you?"

Lucian faced him, smiling in a way that didn't reach his eyes. "This performance is not for me, but for your benefit. After all, this is all new to *you*. Ignore me and my jaded ways."

"You're not someone I can ignore." What he said was true, but Corey was surprised to see Lucian frown at the compliment before his feigned smile deigned to reappear.

"How sweet of you, darling." The melodic lilt that rose in Lucian's tone was definitely an act, just like the first moment they met, and Corey didn't like it one damn bit.

That only cemented his decision. "Look, I think I've seen enough for one night. I'm getting tired. I'm gonna go home and get some much needed shut-eye." He rose from his seat, not sparing a glance at the vigorous bed sports taking place nearby.

Lucian quickly joined him, readjusting his attire to match his perfect classy look. His gaze was uncertain. "Do you wish to stop our sensual journey entirely or—"

"No. Just for tonight." Corey reassured his host with his most charming smile, the one he had perfected over the course of hundreds of cocktail parties, swanky soirees, and fancy balls. Though, in all honesty, he had never really cared whether the gesture attracted someone or not. But alleviating Lucian's concerns seemed to be his top priority at the moment.

His words apparently put Lucian at ease because his worried features softened and a genuine smile emerged. "Of course. Very well. Let us adjourn for the night and come back later, refreshed and with new energy."

"Next weekend? Bright-eyed and bushy-tailed." Corey winked at Lucian, who seemed purely pleased to be the object of Corey's charms.

"Sounds wonderful." Lucian bowed his head slightly, a mischievous look replacing the apprehensive one. "I look forward to our next... date, my dear." Suddenly he frowned, exasperated and somewhat whiny. "Oh, bother. We forgot the dessert." With a sheepish grin, he added, "I'll ask for a doggy bag."

Corey laughed, and Lucian joined in, and side by side they strode out of the room.

For what it was worth, Corey considered the night a success. After all, he had gotten an erection outside the typical morning setting, which for him was a first and an absolute win.

But… could he repeat or recreate that stroke of luck? Corey had no idea.

Yet he was 100 percent sure that meeting Lucian had been the best thing that had ever happened to him.

BACK AT home in his expensive and luxurious high-rise apartment with a view of the Manhattan skyline, Corey made himself a drink. A Manhattan seemed like an appropriate drink as he stood in front of the floor-to-ceiling window, staring out into the night. No stars, just dark clouds above, casting a gloomy ambience over his already weird mood. As he sipped his drink, Corey did what he always did, which was categorize and analyze. He went over the events of the evening, one by one, scene after scene, but he felt like there was a gray dusk settling over his reason, forcing him to focus on his feelings instead. It was unnerving.

"I'm losing my mind," he whispered solemnly to his blurry reflection in the glass. He leaned forward and rested his forehead against the cool surface. It helped thwart his pounding headache, the heat of his skin subsiding as the cold glass eased the throbbing.

He wondered why he had a headache. This time it wasn't born of stress; he was sure of that. He'd felt the same relentless pain back at Boudoir, but that had been the result of his own odd headspace.

Maybe Lucian was right, and Corey was overthinking things, causing himself agony. Upon returning back home, Corey regretted missing an opportunity to study a naked man. Corey was certain Lucian would not have minded being an experimental sexual rat for him, at least for a night.

Speaking of Lucian…. Corey swallowed hard. Of all the things he had seen and heard tonight, Lucian was the brightest and the loudest spark in the dark of the classy dungeon. He was a man one could not dismiss.

Plus, he was a freaking frustrating puzzle of a man! Corey growled, annoyed at being unable to decipher the mystery that was Lucian Allard. As he had noticed the first time they met, Lucian had many facets and several masks that he alternated between, depending on the current situation. Corey pondered if he had seen even a glimpse of the true man.

His heart, though, knew he had. Corey had seen on three separate occasions the sad, melancholy expression that Lucian camouflaged with a charming smile—quickly but not fast enough. Again, Corey couldn't understand what on earth Lucian could have to feel woeful about. He seemed to have it all, and he didn't seem to need anyone or anything.

A person can be alone in a crowd. Corey remembered Prudence, his mother, saying that after one particularly exhausting meet-and-greet at a fundraiser where everyone doted on her—and wanted something from her, typically money for whatever project they had going. She had looked haggard and, yes, lonely. Randolph had been, as usual, a no-show.

Was Lucian lonely despite his filled-up social calendar?

Was his spirit dull, his mind bored, his body jaded—or his heart broken?

What in hell could Corey do about any of that? He was as lost as Lucian was, or more.

Maybe we can be alone together. Until we're not lonely anymore.

Angry at his heart's ridiculous capacity to romanticize everything, Corey tossed back his drink, shoved the glass on the tray with a sharp clink, and stomped toward the bathroom. What he needed was a good soak in the bathtub, to relax him and make him forget—

Forget that he had seen a statue come to life tonight by the powers of water and love?

Yeah, right. He rolled his eyes to no one in particular.

Fine, a simple shower had to suffice.

The blue marble bathroom was large, and the shower space could have accommodated six or eight people. The round showerhead offered a flow equivalent to a gushing waterfall, and the six jets on the wall made sure not a single nook or cranny remained unwashed. The floor was also sunken, with a seat on either side, so he could stand, sit, or lie down in a single space. He loved it; it was his favorite room in the apartment. The number one spot could not be occupied by his bedroom because no *magic* had ever happened there.

He stepped into the enclosure, turned the knob, and stood under the refreshing spray, letting it sluice over his stressed-out muscles and relax him. As the hot water beat down on him, a few minutes later he began to unwind, and he let out a long sigh of contentment.

Images of what had transpired that evening sprung to his mind. The gentle and sensual bathing the abused living statue got in the hands of his lover were fresh pictures before his closed eyes. He couldn't get rid of the scenario replaying in his head, like a lurid porno flick. Only… for him it wasn't tawdry or debasing or animalistic. The muscles rippling and quivering under a tender touch, hips undulating as pleasure within rose, the soft smiles aimed at one another, and the locked gazes full of love.

Love….

Funny how Corey could recognize it, though he had never felt it or sensed it aimed at him. Perhaps it was instinctual and universal and undeniable.

If so, why couldn't he reciprocate? Why could he not… *feel*… those better emotions, the ones that didn't make him feel like a loser, despondent and bereft of hope? Had it been nothing more than… *gasp*… a fluke?

Shaking his head under the spray, angry at himself, Corey went back further, to early evening when he had shared his time with Lucian alone at his study.

The erotica album. Yes, that might work….

When flipping through those pages, Corey had gotten hard. His cock had decided out of the blue that it liked erotic pictures. Frowning, he couldn't understand why that was. He had seen such imagery many times before, live and not, so why then and there?

Without conscious thought he gripped his limp dick and gave it a few tugs. Water was beating him hard, but the droplets did nothing for the stimulation of his sexual organ. *Fuck.* He sped up the strokes, searching for anything that might light his fire. But nothing happened. Frustrated, he stopped and let yet another defeat wash over him. How in the hell could he have a cock for thirty-three years and not get any action with his own special sex toy? *Dammit.*

He turned the knob, and the spray ceased. Dripping wet, he stood in the warm space, surrounded by steam clouds and slowly chilling air. He cast a hazy reflection on the shower's glass wall. He recalled studying himself in the mirror at Lucian's penthouse, seeing nothing worthy of getting hot and bothered about.

And yet Lucian's predatory eyes had devoured him with every leisurely glance.

All of a sudden, in the privacy of his bathroom, Corey heard Lucian's smooth, sultry voice in his head, whispering sweet nothings. "*I want you, Corey. I want you for so many reasons. I want to do things to you. I want you to do things to me. I want us to lie together in my bed and make love until our orgasms blow us away, until neither of us can move an inch.*"

The memory shook him to the core.

And, as if touched by a magic wand, his cock filled with hot blood, swelling and rising, hardening visibly with every breathless heartbeat. His head swam under a cloud of red-hot passion he had no control over. Corey closed his eyes and went with it.

In a seductive, hungry tone, Lucian murmured in his mind, "*You are very beautiful, Corey. A sight to behold. Why? Because your skin glistens like golden velvet? Because I want those thick biceps of yours to wrap around me? Because I dream of licking warm chocolate sauce off your nipples? Because I could probably grate cheese with those ripped abs? Because I wish to feel your weight on me as I lie in bed? All of the above.*"

Corey's heart thundered, like primal drums with the very force of the Earth. His fingers wrapped around his shaft and flew over an erection the likes of which he had never known, neither day nor night. With vigorous motions and an increasing pace, he took full advantage of the rare opportunity and beat his meat unlike ever before, partly fearing he would rub his sensitive skin to shreds.

But there was no way, nohow he was going to stop.

When Corey thought of someone else, of another man, even for a second, his hand stopped moving, as if forgetting in an instant how to masturbate, as if the skill were taken from him until the true object of his desire was put back on display in his mind's eye.

As far as Corey was concerned, only one man existed under the sun....

Flashes of Lucian popped into his mind, irresistible and beckoning, a masculine siren calling out to him. Those beautiful eyes—one green, one blue—that wicked smile, the promise of sensual and sexual fulfillment he represented. His delicate features and slender figure, like the stem of a flower or a reed or a young willow, bending but not breaking.

Chris Isaak sang softly and huskily in his ear about playing wicked games of love and sex that evoked dreams of that special someone. The memory of the melody and lyrics felt so real, like a touch on his skin, awakening and stirring something new within. How appropriate for his situation.

Was this what it took to start his engine? A man he barely knew? All his life Corey had watched people, men and women, and not felt a thing, worried what was wrong with him and his libido. But Lucian? He seemed the carefree, frolicking type, out to have sex for fun, not for any kind of meaningful relationship. In a word, he was unattainable, out of bounds for the likes of Corey, who had nothing to offer to a sensualist like Lucian.

But those doubts that kept plaguing him with their incessant voices had nothing on Lucian, whose image had apparently cemented itself in Corey's brain. His radiance outshone the shades that lurked on the edges of his awareness. Lucian behaved with a seductive swagger and appeared with an effortless glamour that was easy to see in his pristine attire and pure good looks, and at the moment, he had conquered Corey from within, granting him no quarter.

Leaning his back against the marble wall, Corey shivered, as if Lucian were there in the room, watching him masturbating. His head hit the wall as he stroked with a startling fury, panting madly. He groaned as the pleasure spiked through him, not rolling waves crashing over him but a relentless lightning strike that reached every cell and nerve in his body. With his cock in one hand, he cupped his achy, pendulous balls with the other, squeezing and tugging with a primitive instinct he was supremely glad of.

His hand was wet—and sticky? Corey glanced down and watched wide-eyed as the bead of precum turned into a gooey strand stretching from the slit to his fingers and attaching itself around his cock as he continued stroking. Mesmerized by the sight he had never bothered to look at in the mornings, too drowsy to open his eyes, Corey watched his uncut cock leak precum, more with every swipe over the crown.

At that moment he just had to. Corey rubbed his fingertips over the slit, wetted them with pearls of precum—and licked them clean. He trembled at the shocking sensation of it. The briny flavor exploded on his taste buds, a bittersweet taste he'd never before encountered. Savoring it, he let the droplets linger on his tongue, rolling them around to squeeze every possible tangy zest from his own juices.

This is how I taste. This is the flavor of my arousal, my excitement, my... sex.

Gasping loudly, he was well aware he was navigating uncharted waters.

His eyes rolled back. Every jolt of delight vibrated through him as he rocked back and forth, his sensitive dick cocooned in his own palm, flashes of something so intense and fluid and perfect he had no name for it. If this was what sex with himself felt like, what would it feel like with another person?

With Lucian? *Oh my God....*

In his mind's eye, like a scene replaying, Corey recalled Lucian's bedroom, or as he called it, his boudoir. That dark wood bed with its four posters and heavy drapes, the sexy odor of male musk that hung in the air. Corey was on fire, blazing like an inferno all over, and no one could touch him like Lucian.

Lucian's voice reached Corey across time from a mere few hours ago. *"The places where I grew up—the sprawling estates I told you about?—they all had four-poster beds and heavy curtains and silk sheets. To me, they mystified sex, covering it behind veils of semiprivacy. But... I did still hear: the moans, the whimpers, the bedsprings, the slapping of skin.... And I could almost see sometimes, when a candle or a lamp was lit behind the curtains: shapes entwined, silhouettes of sensual bodies so close to one another and even to me, so close it... it physically hurt not to be a part of that world."*

As if it were really happening, Corey envisioned Lucian's bed, the thick brocade curtains, the deep brown wood, the sturdy frame, the warm light beyond—and a silhouette projected on the fabric, akin to shadow theater.

Lucian.

That willowy body was bent, back arched, every line drawn taut, his nipples visible nubs, his head thrown back, and his graceful hand glided on his erect penis. And... his cock was huge! Totally disproportionate to the rest of his petite figure, like a real-life Priapus. But it was only a fantasy, Corey knew, as he watched Lucian masturbate behind the curtains of his bed, in private but really the object of an imaginary voyeur.

Lucian's body was surprisingly agile, his shape divinely angled to provide maximum pleasure to the one spectator. The shadow of Lucian stroked faster, his silhouetted hand only a blur, and his moans rose high, a shrill pitch of enjoyment reaching crescendo.

Corey watched, hypnotized, as Lucian's body quaked and shook. "*Corey....*"

Then shadows of long ropes flew high in the air as Lucian came, his hips thrusting wildly as his semen showered on the bed. Corey let out a gurgle so animalistic he had never known he was capable of releasing such a sound.

Holy fucking shit! My first sexual fantasy about a real person.

Corey's hips jerked as pleasure rocketed from his tightening, heated balls to his needy cock. No longer were his thoughts focused on the clinical details of his shaft, the length or the girth, the pink color or the silky surface. In fact, he had no rational thoughts whatsoever.

All that existed in the whole world was the cresting pleasure wave he was riding for the first time in his life, chasing the edge with a yearning that bordered on desperation.

"Lucian...." His whisper echoed from the marble floor, obscenely loud in the empty space, yet far more silent than the blood roaring in his ears.

With a single word and a single image flashing repeatedly behind his closed eyes, Corey shouted so high it was no more than frantic wailing. His balls constricted and drew up, his cock twitched and swelled, and then Corey erupted like a volcano.

His body convulsed, and his dick jerked, and hot liquid spilled over his fingers. His fist kept moving, milking every last drop of pleasure wrung from his tortured being. Spunk landed on his cock, his hand, his groin, the glass partition, the floor in creamy, white splashes.

With a groan that seemed to have no end, Corey let his shaky, weakened knees give out, and he crumpled to the floor, slumping in victory.

God, what a sweet benediction to give to a lowly human.

His chest and throat hurt as he slid to lie on the heated, wet floor. His breaths came so rough and fast he was only now catching the normal rhythm. And, *wow*, had he yelled. He must have because he felt the rasp in his throat, as when he'd been sick at the age of twelve with pneumonia and struggled to speak for two weeks after.

Only this time Corey wasn't sick. *Nuh-uh.* "I'm good. I'm great. No, better than great. I'm fucking amazing!"

He started to chuckle, a surprised and elated sound of pure wonder. He couldn't stop, so he lay in place and let it all out. The buoyancy bubbled in his heart and his wrung-dry cock, a levity that gave him wings.

Alone, naked, and wet, shaking on his bathroom floor, he soared to heavenly heights.

All of a sudden, like a lightning strike from a clear blue sky, Corey was crying. Really crying, blubbering his eyes out, a flood running down his cheeks, a terrible pain in his chest, a tight pressure behind his closed eyes.

Corey had no idea where the sudden sadness emerged from, but the feeling consumed him, like a typhoon, an unstoppable force breaking through levies as the tidal waves rose ever higher, drowning him in sorrow.

Though his headache had returned with a vengeance, his stomach unwound, and stress nails bore back, releasing him. Lying on the floor, he let it all out: every emotion he had held within, every feeling his condition kept buried. It all came flooding out of him through hot tears.

Lonely, bare to the bone, and dripping, he lay on his bathroom floor and broke apart.

CHAPTER 15

"DO YOU require anything, sir?" Amaya asked from the doorway. She was concerned, Lucian could tell.

"No, I'm good, thank you. Please, go on home. It's late." Simple platitudes fell easily from his lips, though he felt antsy and restless as he sat in the corner of his living room, with the floor-to-ceiling window pressed against his left side.

"I can stay if you need—"

"Amaya, I'm fine. Go home and get some rest. You've more than earned it." Lucian smiled reassuringly but also knew that Amaya had been with him long enough to be familiar with his quirks and moods—and was not buying into his bullshit.

Her brown, almond-shaped eyes flashed intently, but she nodded silently and vanished from the doorway. A few seconds later, the penthouse main door opened and closed, signaling her departure for the night.

Lucian sighed, feeling desolate and sad. He wasn't sure exactly why. After all, he and Corey had parted on good terms, plus with plans for next weekend. Yet, there was a growing fear in Lucian that he had pushed Corey too far. That orgy. Four men, all tangled in each other and in pleasure. Perhaps it had been too much for an innocent like Corey. Watching sex on a computer screen hardly matched seeing a live show of gorgeous hunks dedicated to making one another come as many times as humanly possible.

He let his head fall against the window with a low *thunk*, depressed and frenzied about what was to come. Was he getting too close to Corey's case? For that *had* to be all Corey was to him, and was ever going to be to him. A psychology case. A problem to solve. A newbie on his way to becoming an expert in the field of sexual endeavors.

But the more he tried to convince himself of the necessity of emotional distancing, the less successful he was. He had already treaded on that forbidden path, tippy-toes. His current state of affairs was proof positive.

I can't get any closer to him. I must not. He kept giving himself these simple orders, as if they alone held the power over his will, his determination, and his yielding.

"Then stop thinking about him, silly," Lucian scolded himself—to no effect.

His misbehaving cock wanted in on the action, feeling no recriminations or remorse but happily rising to fire-hot, rock-hard attention, willing and wishing to play.

The problem was that with Corey, it wasn't strictly play. It never had been. Lucian had known from the start that if Corey's situation necessitated it, they would have sex. After all, that was the whole point of Lucian's experiments with his companion's arousal. To find out what made Corey tick and how to set that bomb off in a spectacular orgasmic explosion.

The only emotions allowed onto the playing field were Corey's. How Corey felt about whatever had happened and was yet to come was key. Lucian's feelings? Well, they didn't enter into the equation.

The idea that Corey might be gay and sexually compatible with Lucian was a bonus for the task ahead, but it could not be the end goal in itself. And matters of the heart were a strict no-no when it came to psychological healing.

In essence Lucian was the doctor and Corey his patient. In addition to doctor-patient confidentiality, emotional transference was a double-edged sword. Like the sword of Damocles, it hung over their heads precariously. Unfortunately, Lucian knew if push came to shove, it was *his* head that would get chopped off, not Corey's. Or, more to the point, it would be his heart on the line, not Corey's.

Pulling his knees up to his chin, Lucian hugged himself, shivering from a coldness within.

It was then, when he felt sorry for himself and despondent over a loss he had yet to even experience, that Lucian received a phone call. The incessant ringing told him who it was, so with a resigned exhale, he answered. "Good evening, Father."

"Evening, Lucian." Alexander Allard had a deep, resonant voice that never altered in tone, as he was not a man to show emotions. An intellectual by education and a diplomat by trade, he was always in control. While as adults, their relationship was amicable, as a child Lucian had admired his father and loved his voice when he had read stories to him before bedtime. *The Arabian Nights* were memorable to Lucian even to this day.

Alexander's life traveling and living abroad was evident in his French accent. "How are you?"

Lucian had two choices: Tell the truth, speak of emotions, and listen to either silence or a lecture, depending on Alexander's situation; or tell a white lie, reply with one word, and move on with his life.

"There's a man I'm quite fond of, but he's all wrong for me. For a lot of reasons."

Alexander was quiet for a time, as if digesting the news. "Wrong how?"

Apparently he was in a mood to talk. "I suppose you could say he's a patient of mine."

"You mean that sexual mentoring program of yours?"

"Yes." Lucian had every reason to be proud of his achievements.

"Have you crossed any ethical lines?"

Lucian frowned, hesitant. "Actual physical lines, or the emotional kind?"

"If you have to ask, I'd wager a guess the latter rings true."

Lucian closed his eyes, ready for a moral bombardment from a professional of ethical guidelines. "As I said, I like him." Before Alexander could comment, Lucian continued, "Father, have you heard of Randolph Paige?"

While Alexander tone didn't rise in alarm, Lucian heard the underlying tint of concern. "Is he the one you—"

"No. He's a… a relation to the one I mean."

"Ah." Alexander said nothing for another moment. Lucian could almost hear the gears turning in his brain, which was never idle. "Is Randolph Paige important to this… case? Does his opinion or existence weigh on you or this other person you speak of?"

Lucian cringed, hoping it wouldn't be audible in his voice. "He has warned me off. He was quite adamant." That word, adamant, was one Lucian and his father used when speaking of a person who used low vernacular, vulgarities, or profanities, or one who had trouble or lack of will to control outbursts of emotions, especially rage.

"I see." Alexander took exception to people like that, to people who could not voice their negative opinions without curse words, as if their vocabularies consisted of only those. "And this person you've mentioned, the one who apparently has no name, does he know about this adamant posturing?"

"Yes. He wasn't happy about Paige's meddling in his affairs."

"Is this person Paige's... companion?" Another euphemism, Lucian knew, this time referring to anything from a mistress or a lover to an escort or a prostitute.

"I said relation, didn't I?" Lucian reminded, suppressing the scoff in his throat.

"These days any act seems to be sanctioned if it is pleasurable enough." There was no reproach in Alexander's voice, only detachment. He only commented on what he had learned but had no personal feelings about.

Lucian half snorted, half chuckled and decided to confide in one of the two people in the world who had never judged him. "And he does have a name. Corey Paige. Randolph's son."

"What is this Corey like? Is he... like Blake?" Again, even though Alexander's tone remained cool and aloof, his pause spoke volumes about his emotional investment.

Lucian's throat constricted, emotional bile rising to choke him with bad memories. "No, Father. Corey is nothing like Blake. Corey would never hurt me." Lucian wondered how he got the words past his lips, knowing they were a lie. Corey had gotten angry and shoved him. But he still remained certain Corey would never intentionally hurt him the way Blake had.

"Lu, you're nothing but a fancy, pretty, high-priced whore," Blake had accused Lucian snidely—right before delivering a savage beating, one Lucian never allowed himself to forget. The life lesson had been priceless. Lucian's slender build gave certain people the delusion that he was meek and vulnerable and waiting for a brute of a man to dominate him.

One error of judgment—Blake—had been all it took. No one would ever call Lucian a whore or Lu again.

"I admit I am overjoyed upon hearing that," Alexander said, wrenching Lucian back to the moment at hand. "Despite whatever assets or positive qualities this Corey Paige has, I was under the impression you had set strict codes of conduct for your mentoring sessions, unbreakable statutes you swore to yourself you would adhere to no matter what."

Lucian closed his eyes and hung his head, glum. "Yes. The rules…. I haven't forgotten them." Honesty, openness, and directness were rules number two, three, and four. But it was rule number one—absolutely no personal or emotional attachments—that held the greatest weight. And from that weight hung Lucian's guilt and regret. Professional objectivity and behavior had always been and would continue to be the cornerstone of his operation, or else the risks and repercussions would outweigh the benefits and rewards.

"But you are considering abandoning them for this man?"

Lucian's head grew silent as the grave. It seemed his mind was waiting for his heart to speak out. But he also knew if he gave that organ power over his decisions, he was done for. "I did. At first. Well, I did at one point. But… I am aware it can't possibly go anywhere." Images of Corey sprang to mind, unbidden, as if they belonged and had already made a home there. "He's an intriguing personality, Father. He seeks to understand the human condition. He is smart and strong and sexy and—"

"I think you have your answer right there, Lucian," his father's voice interjected with a kind of finality no one could ignore. Especially since he was right. "You must decide which is more important: aiding him with his predicament, whatever it is, or your attraction for him."

"My attraction…. I can't help him as long as it continues." Lucian said the words, and thus sealed his fate. He and Corey would never be anything beyond their professional relationship.

But… what if it is… love…? What if it is that, and I'll never feel it again?

Rationally, Lucian knew that was no real argument. After all, if and when Corey found his sexual mojo, he would undoubtedly want to take his newfound sexual energy and inspiration onto other playgrounds. Once that engine was kick-started, Corey would be in for a ride of a lifetime. And riding with only one person would be a waste of all that bursting prowess.

I have to let him go. I must let him go before I've even had him. There's no choice.

"Thank you for your counsel, Father. As usual, it has been invaluable."

Alexander's voice gentled. "You are dearest in the world to me, Lucian. You and your mother. I only wish the best for you. I wish you to be happy."

"Yes. But not under false pretenses." It wasn't a question, but a verbal, unanimous confirmation of Alexander's opinion. No matter how intimately Lucian was acquainted with Corey, the truth was that their common goal would not be served by engaging in a tryst.

"The time and place of falling in love is rarely of our own choosing," Alexander said wisely. "But what we can do is choose how to react. We are not animals. Our hearts do not have to gain control over our faculties. We master our own emotions, as it should be."

In this Lucian differed from his parents, who worshipped at the altar of logic, reason, and rationality. For them, knowledge, science, and scholasticism were top priorities. Lucian had chosen his own path to understand why his sexuality dominated him so from early adolescence. He had learned much and started his mentoring program for the benefit of others.

Though his parents did not always understand how Lucian thought and lived his life, they had invariably supported him, without fail. Their unwavering backing had made it possible for Lucian to find his own way in the world.

But to get to this age, adulthood, and experience and not know the devastating power of love laying waste to his resolve, fortitude, and self-control? Lucian was adrift. The only anchor to save him from the storm now was to ensure Corey would never find out how Lucian felt and how deep those emotional ties already ran.

Which is the better pretense, his heart demanded to know: to love and be silent or to refuse love and go down with the ship into the unknown abyss?

"Lucian?" Alexander's voice reached him from the tempest. "Whatever you ultimately decide, I will endorse you. I know you will make the right decision and do the right thing. I trust in your judgment."

Lucian swallowed past the lump in his throat, nodding even though his father could not see the gesture. "Th-thank you, Father. Please, give my love to Mother."

"I will, Son. I love you." Though Alexander's voice reflected the cool composure of his heart and soul, Lucian's upbringing had been filled with hugs and laughter and love. His parents might have been devout scholars, with a diplomatic skill to mask their feelings, but they had never hidden those from Lucian when he had been a child. Alexander and Chastity had ever shown the truth of their affection, with embraces and kisses and understanding a child's temperament. Lucian had been a happy, lucky child.

"I love you too, Father." Lucian hung up, and only then did he sniffle and let the tears run down his cheeks. "Do the right thing…," he repeated his father's words. "What is the right thing to do and by whom?"

As rare as it was for him to use vulgar vernacular, for Lucian falling in love sucked big hairy donkey balls.

CHAPTER 16

"WHAT'S IN store for our trip down sensory lane tonight?" Corey asked Lucian amusedly as they walked down the halls of Boudoir promptly at 8:00 p.m. on Friday.

"You're awfully keen to discover new sexual horizons tonight, I see." Lucian tried not to sound too dry so he ended up sounding wry.

Corey didn't seem to notice but basically beamed with an eagerness unlike any Lucian had seen from the man. "I suppose I am." He glanced at Lucian, fleeting as the wind, and a rosy hue pinked his cheeks. "Last time, uh, the whole... orgy scene might have been a bit too much too soon, if you get my drift."

Lucian understood. Wanting to be a part of something everyone else seemed to enjoy was vastly different from actually being confronted by it, dead on. "Have no fear. I have something else planned for this evening."

"Cool. Can't wait." And judging from the bounce in his step, Corey spoke the truth.

What Lucian observed of himself was that he was keeping a discreet distance from Corey, avoiding any and all chances of bodily contact. Not so much as a brush of clothing took place in the relatively narrow hallways. Lucian had vowed to keep things professional between them, and if sex became a necessity to get Corey to unfreeze, so to speak, Lucian would find a way to remain neutral at heart.

"Did you speak to your father?" Lucian asked instead as they walked onward.

Corey's shoulders stiffened at the mention. "No, I didn't. But I will."

Lucian nodded, though Corey walked slightly in front of him and couldn't see it. "I apologize if I ruined the mood for you."

Glancing over his shoulder, Corey flashed a bright smile. "You didn't."

God, that smile lit all kinds of fires in Lucian's heart and body, and with zero control over it, he smiled back, a new lightness in his feet now as well. "I'm glad." Then he just stared into Corey's gray eyes, like glimmers of steely skies, and remained transfixed by the gaze.

Corey narrowly missed stumbling into a wall as the hallway rounded a corner, and he let out a carefree chuckle as he blushed and rubbed the back of his neck. "Wow. I'm kind of a klutz today."

Lucian giggled along. "I'm sure you can be quite nimble when you wish to be." With an added wink, he made sure the atmosphere retained the levity and humor needed for games of the sensual variety.

"Maybe." Corey shrugged, a naughty grin playing on his lips. It seemed he could be cryptic too, Lucian noted with no small amount of enjoyment.

They reached their destination, this time unguided, and Lucian let Corey pass into a new dark room. Again, only chairs and a table occupied the small space. Corey didn't make any remarks about the minimalist decor but simply sat in one of the chairs and waited patiently for Lucian to join him, which Lucian did after closing the door.

"So, teach, what's the lesson for today?" Corey smirked.

"Can't you tell?" Lucian could play the teasing game as well as Corey, or better. But before Corey got to answer, Lucian went on, asking only now when they were in private. "I've been meaning to ask…. After all that you have seen and heard so far, have you managed to successfully become aroused? Have you witnessed anything you would like to try yourself? Have you fantasized about anything you have seen? Have you… touched yourself?"

At some point during Lucian's questions, Corey's gaze averted and darted all around the room, nonstop. He frowned and looked extremely uncomfortable, so much so that Lucian grew concerned, about to inquire what had troubled the man to such levels of anxiety.

All of a sudden Corey replied, his tone flat and his face scrunched up in concentration and dismay, but for what, Lucian had no idea. "I got an erection when I got home, after a shower."

Lucian inhaled sharply, absolutely thrilled about the news. This was record-breaking news. "Corey, that's amazing!" He was speechless, pleased beyond belief that positive results had come into effect so quickly in their series of sessions. He was about to offer more congratulations when he saw a cloud pass over Corey's face, a darker expression than that which spoke of victory and success. "Corey? What's wrong?" A chill ran up and down his spine, pooling in his gut to make his nerves knot. "Did it… not last long…?" *Did you not come?* He couldn't ask that, however, and give voice to failure.

Corey still refused to look at Lucian, who was damn near frantic with worry by then. "No. I mean, yes. No, I mean…." He paused, took a deep breath, and said, "I climaxed."

He had an orgasm! Lucian nearly leaped up and did a little end-zone victory dance. But Corey's closed-off face stopped him cold. "Wasn't it— um, how was it?" *Please, don't say you felt nothing.*

Corey screwed his eyes shut tight, as if warding against the world. "It was good. It was great. I've never come like that in my entire life."

Blinking to keep firm rein on his self-control, Lucian breathed in and out several times so he could think carefully what to say. "I am so terribly sorry, Corey, if you wanted to keep that to yourself. Sex can be a very private experience for some, and if I made you feel like you had to tell me a secret, then I am so very—"

Corey's gaze snapped up, his eyes widening in shock that displayed on his whole face. "You didn't force me to answer. I knew I was going to tell you. I just…."

As Corey's voice faded, with a couple of visible gulps following, Lucian tried to come up with a reason why Corey was so fidgety. But how to ask about that when words failed him?

"How did you come to terms with what, uh, turns you on?" Corey asked, his gaze once again removed from Lucian's inspection.

What on earth had Corey masturbated to if the mere recollection of that event made him this anxious? Lucian was beside himself with curiosity. "Well, I, uh… I suppose I realized the kinds of things that aroused me the same way most people do. With trial and error. But, Corey, it is important you know and understand that sexual fantasies should not be taken literally, nor should they be censored."

Corey let out a sarcastic chuckle without warmth. "So, if I fantasize about rape while I jack off, no one should worry?"

Lucian willed his breathing to calm in order to focus. "Yes. A lot of men and women can have forced seduction or noncon sexual fantasies. That does not turn the women into victims or the men into rapists. It is the same way with casual thoughts. No one should be judged based on what they think about in the heat of the moment. There is a difference between thinking and acting on it." What he didn't ask was whether Corey had fantasized about rape. Lucian did not have a clue as to how to ask *that* question, which was odd since he had dealt with taboo topics like that in the past with other people.

Corey seemed to mull over this, leaning his forearms on the table, his head hanging so low his face was hidden in the shadows. "Rape's not really my thing, in any sense of the word."

Inwardly, Lucian sighed in relief. "May I ask if you fantasized about men or women?"

Corey grimaced. "The former." What did that frown mean? Would he have wished to dream about women?

Lucian pressed on. "The body of a man or a whole man, with a face and everything?"

Corey picked on his nails, as if doing so was the most interesting thing in the world. "A specific man. Real, you know."

Lucian nodded, though Corey saw none of it. "It's all right in either case. Fantasies are always individual, every nuance and detail different. Fantasy men are safe because they offer no rejections or denials, only serve at your leisure, doing your bidding. Of course, they offer no true feelings, either, but no fantasy does. It is still acceptable to enjoy them, whatever they may be."

"Even if the object of your jerk-off session is a real person?" Corey scoffed loudly, as if Lucian's words weren't getting through. "Maybe you're right, maybe you're wrong. I don't know."

Lucian leaned back from the table to give his companion some space. "A lot of people masturbate to pictures of celebrities, movie stars, models, and the like. They are real people even though the vast majority of the populace never meet them in real life. Nonetheless, it is not ethically reprehensible to dream about them. Thoughts cannot be condemned."

Corey's face twisted in a snarl, which Lucian now interpreted as a defensive act. "And what if the person jacking off knows the real person?"

"It becomes a matter to deal with only if it begins to affect the life of the masturbator in a negative way. People fantasize about anyone. Their friends or their friends' spouses, their work colleagues or their next-door neighbors, people they see in the grocery store or at the post office, and so on."

"You're saying in the end it doesn't matter who the object of your fantasy is?" Corey's expression cleared as he digested Lucian's explanation.

"No, it doesn't." Lucian was certain of that. "Unless there's actual feelings involved. Then it becomes a bit more complicated." Corey had started to relax, but now he tensed up again. Why had Lucian added that wholly unnecessary piece of information? Silently cursing himself, he struggled to find the right words to appease the man once more.

But Corey got there first. "I was thinking about your album. The one with all the dirty pictures." His gaze flicked back to Lucian, locking with his in stark determination. "I got a stiffy when I was flipping through it back at your place."

Where the heck had Lucian been to not have noticed *that* development? "You did?"

"Yeah." Corey straightened up, like he had resolved whatever had plagued him until then. "I don't know why. 'Cause guys get turned on by what we see? Maybe." He shrugged casually, but Lucian doubted the sincerity of the gesture. Then he got a blissful expression, lost in the memory. "Back home, that climax was freaking phenomenal. I was sure I'd explode. Every nervous knot in my stomach and frayed nerve ending in my brain just... unwound and relaxed. I felt... free and sublime and perfect. I was flying...." His voice trailed off.

The look on his face was one Lucian had waited and prayed for, the ultimate goal of their sessions. And there it was, available for Lucian to behold to his heart's content. Yes, he was pleased. But was he happy? In his empathy, Lucian was overjoyed on Corey's behalf. The man had accomplished quite a feat in such a short amount of time. But... a weak part of him felt a twinge of jealousy, and it ruined the moment for him. And he hated himself for it.

But he masked that part of his baser self and let only the better angels of his nature show. "I am so very pleased for you, Corey. Very happy. You did it. You showed me and yourself you're not—"

"Not frigid?" Corey harrumphed, his face shutting down again. Why, Lucian had to ask. "So I got a boner when looking at dirty pictures. So fucking what?" He shook his head, furious for some reason. "So I got to have that one blindingly brilliant orgasm. Whoop-de-doo. Now what? What if I never get it again? Especially when thinking about—" This time his voice didn't trail off but purposely cut off. Corey obviously had a secret. But hadn't he just admitted his arousal had stemmed from the album? Why would that be worth keeping to himself?

"You don't have to censor your—" Lucian began to offer reassurances.

"I'm not!" Corey almost shouted and immediately closed his eyes and clearly fought to regain his self-control. When he spoke again, his tone was low and restrained. "I told you I was thinking about a specific person when I jacked off. The album was a whole other story." Lucian said nothing, opting to wait Corey out, holding his breath all the while. "That someone is in reality... unavailable."

Unable to do anything but stare, Lucian felt bereft, a profound loss he could sense like a lost limb in a place where his heart was. A hollow space in his chest ached. "T-that's the beauty of fantasies. They do not have to stand the test of real life." He coughed to stop his wayward tongue, but it was too late. "Unless, of course, this unattainable person is someone you would ultimately wish to have a relationship with. But that, uh, possibility doesn't have anything... um, not much to do with frigidity. Asexual people, for example, lack sexual attraction and the desire for sex, but even they can form relationships. Emotions are not inextricably linked with—"

"So, what you're saying," Corey cut in with a deliberately raised voice through Lucian and his apparent word vomit, "is that I could be with this person whether or not I'm able to climax or even get it up ever again? That for us to share feelings for each other, sex doesn't have to be a part of it at all?" The ice-cold, sharp edge of cynicism in his tone could have cut through solid stone.

"Do you want to talk about this person with—" Lucian hoped Corey would share the identity of this secret crush with him. It might help Corey's case in the long run, no matter what the fallout on Lucian's poor heart.

"No." Corey was adamant, as evidenced by his standoffish behavior. "I don't want to talk about it."

"With me? Because if you have other confidants, you could—" Lucian had to try being a mentor. Sometimes that meant relinquishing the right to privileged information. Another might succeed in his place.

"No. I don't want to talk about it with *anyone*. Not right now anyway. Maybe later." Corey twisted his neck left and right, his tendons and muscles crackling and snapping back in place with the stretching. "I *do* trust you, Lucian. I'm just not ready yet, okay?"

Lucian nodded, sympathetic with Corey's need for privacy. "Yes, yes, naturally, of course. Whenever you're ready. It's all right." He wondered if he might have overdone it a bit with the sentimentality. To master the situation again, he suggested, "How about we proceed ahead with tonight's program? To give us both the chance to decompress and process." He made his offer with an inviting smile.

Corey responded in kind. "Sure. Why not? It's why we're here."

Lucian hated to admit that whoever Corey's secret crush was he represented Lucian's rival for Corey's affections. Even if Lucian would not permit himself to pursue the man at the moment. So he had to accept the status quo and move on.

"I've got quite a treat for you, I assure you." He stood, went to the wall covered by a black curtain, and moved it aside to reveal a hidden door. "Follow me. If you dare."

Corey's expression was priceless.

CHAPTER 17

ANOTHER DARK hallway stretched out before them, like a tunnel to infinity. Corey had a sneaking suspicion all of Boudoir's maze-like interiors were like this, a honey trap to catch the lost and the unwary.

Meekly and quietly he followed in Lucian's wake. His gaze remained fixed on the tiny, tight, and bouncy butt before him. As usual, Lucian wore male chic luxury clothing that glowed in the dim lighting and caressed his figure akin to a second skin. Lucian's pants were as crisply white as his dress shirt. The only spots of color on him were his shoes and tie that matched the tint of his golden-red hair.

Whiffs of Lucian's fruity, sweet scent wafted into Corey's nostrils, and he inhaled deeply.

In his own tastefully ripped and worn, expensive jeans, Corey's cock jumped.

All of a sudden, Lucian stopped dead, and Corey ran right into him.

"What the—" At the last second he suppressed the curse word, the delicate air of the night ahead left undisturbed by a crass choice of vocabulary. "What's wrong?"

"Nothing. We're here." Lucian stepped aside a bit. Another dark door lay ahead. He waved for Corey to enter, his eyebrow quirked in a challenge.

Corey wasn't about to back down, so he scoffed haughtily, opened the door, and with confidence walked in. But he should have known by then with Lucian it was impossible to predict what he would encounter.

The large round room had a high ceiling with a skylight, but the only illumination was provided by spotlights pointed at tall pedestals, like museum exhibits. He couldn't see clearly what was on the pedestals, but they seemed to be porcelain bowls. A curious atmosphere of respectability cocooned the room, and without realizing it at first, Corey treaded more softly.

"What's all this?" he asked, baffled, his voice low in veneration.

"Your next session." Lucian closed the door behind them, walked over to Corey, and pressed a piece of black cloth in Corey's hand, which tingled at the brief contact. "Your equipment for the night, honey. Well, one of them." His wicked smirk was shadowed but audible.

Corey unfolded the bundle to find... a blindfold? "Why?"

Lucian was close enough to tap the tip of Corey's nose gently. "Tonight this shall be your guide."

Corey understood as he connected the dots in his mind. "Ah, I see. First session was about hearing, the second about sight, and now smell? Sensory experiences for the unfeeling man. Took me a while to figure out the pattern." Obediently he wrapped the blindfold over his eyes, tied it behind his head, and then extended his hand, which Lucian took right away. "You'll not leave me?"

"Never." Lucian's reply was deep and intense in the dark, with a crack so small Corey would not have detected it if his eyes hadn't been blinded. Corey tucked and stored the observation in his memory and then focused on Lucian's hand guiding him to where they needed to go. "Here. Your first sniff." His soft palm cradled the back of Corey's head, even tangling in his hair a bit, and carefully leaned him forward.

The sweet smell of strawberries wafted against his face. He smiled and licked his lips. "Yum."

Lucian chuckled. "Strawberries, like most fruits, can be considered an aphrodisiac. In a proper setting and use, they can enhance the pleasure of a sensual joining considerably." Then he escorted Corey onward. "What about this?"

With his companion's assistance, Corey dipped his head and inhaled. "Hmm, anise? Or maybe fennel? I can't tell."

"Good guesses." Lucian sounded pleased, and Corey warmed as he imagined Lucian's beaming face. His cock began to throb with renewed blood flow, pounding like crazy, demanding hands-on attention. "It's black licorice, a potent arousing odor, for men in particular."

Corey swallowed and shifted his hips to get his erection to flag. Willing his rebellious member to do his bidding wasn't all that easy, not when he was lead around a room full of sexy smells by one particularly erotic example of the male gender. He straightened up and breathed a few times to calm himself.

Since Lucian stood right next to him, his hand touching Corey's arm, the mission was a failure from the start.

But if Lucian noticed Corey's rising libido, he said nothing, simply moved on.

Corey bent forward and sniffed one bowl after another. Not being able to see what his olfactory sense was exposed to seemed to amplify the odors. "Vanilla. Lavender. Orange blossoms. Doughnut. Pumpkin pie. Jasmine. Peppermint. Oriental spices." Even if Corey had not been aware of the sexual and sensual aspect of these scents, he was able to recognize all of them, and showed he wasn't as sheltered and inexperienced as he had assumed.

While his body relaxed as an exercise that didn't seem to tax his senses or strain his stamina progressed, he loosened up further. And even if his libido hadn't made the connection between the pleasant odors and his sexual instincts yet, his dick decided it liked the proceedings a lot, throbbing keenly in his pants, swelling and stiffening with each new scent.

And all the time, Lucian kept speaking, his tone alluring and soothing, sneaking inside Corey like a lewd lullaby, a warm and cooling balm over his nerves. "All odors have a past. The history of patchouli, for example, is a fascinating one. For a long time, it was a popular scent among the highest rungs of society, but then it became associated with brothels and seedy places where illicit trysts and randy affairs were the norm, hidden in the shadows. The perfume clung to the skins of lovers, a deep, earthy scent, like sandalwood, and acted as a powerful reminder of sex."

The smell of patchouli was everything Lucian had said it would be, but Corey quickly learned he didn't like it. It couldn't remind him of sex since he had never done that, and the richness was somewhat suffocating.

"I don't like it much."

"I understand." Lucian probably did too, Corey believed. "Since the dawn of humanity, people have been trying, for one reason or another, to camouflage or mask the smells of the body. History is filled with periods where the divide between the rich and the poor, the powerful and the powerless, could be deduced from a person's state of hygiene. Not always, of course. Sometimes the privileged nobles cared as little for their cleanliness as the common rabble. Water and soap could have cured that, but they were considered useless, and therefore bodily odors were covered up under bottles of perfumes and colognes. They came from the animal kingdom first, like these."

Corey inhaled the smells from three different bowls and was certain he recognized at least a couple. "Musk. Ambergris. And... I don't know what this one is."

"Have you heard of a civet cat? This secretion, which is reminiscent of musk, comes from the gland of a male civet cat."

Corey's head was spinning and not just from the air thick with smells. "How do you know all this?" he asked, incredulous and impressed.

Lucian chuckled. "It is my business to know about everything and anything related to the sensual world." He moved Corey forward and resumed his lecture, which Corey found oddly comforting. He was in the hands of a professional in matters of sexuality. "Later, when modesty and prudishness and Puritanism grew prominent, popular scents shifted away from the powerful animal kingdom to light floral perfumes, like orange, ivy, rose, jasmine, and lilac. Women preferred them over the more primitive, warmer odors that exuded sex and raw sensuality. Of course, there was a strong social pressure being put on them by the patriarchal system to conform, to act coy and pure, to appear as idols of women instead of women of flesh and blood with carnal desires of their own."

"Men have had expectations put on them as well," Corey reminded sagely. As weird as it was to conduct a conversation while blindfolded, as time passed the experience began to feel as normal as any dialogue in any setting. Corey might have been standing and ambling, but he was also in repose.

"Yes, that is indeed true. Still is today." Lucian's knowledge of Corey's family life was evident even to Corey.

"I *will* talk to my dad. Soon. I swear." Corey insisted Lucian have faith in his ability to resolve this schism between him and his father. After all, there was so much Randolph didn't know about when it came to his son. The two of them definitely had a lot to talk about. The only doubts Corey had were how to do so without ruining their relationship beyond repair. Randolph had a propensity for stubbornness—much like his son.

Judging from Lucian's softer tone, he did. "All in good time. And he is not here now, is he? A moot point at the moment."

"Agreed." Corey ignored all other sentiments and refocused on the current test. It was then that he smelled an odor unlike any before. He reared back, shocked, and ripped the black cloth out of his eyes. "What in the hell is *that*?" He pointed at the bowl where a tiny pool of creamy liquid lay.

Lucian sniffed the contents of the bowl, a neutral expression on his face. "Fresh male semen, I believe. Well, relatively fresh. An hour old or thereabouts. Naturally, it is best hot and direct from the source. Hmm, I am thinking… strawberries and man cream." Startled, Corey stared at his smiling friend, unable to find adequate words to give voice to his confused state of mind. "The previous smells were to provide you with odors that could arouse the libido, awaken the senses, heighten sensitivities, induce relaxation, lower inhibitions, basically remind you of sex. But… nothing speaks of sex like the body odors of humans."

"I… I thought you were going to…." Corey gulped his anxieties down and took back his self-control. "I was under the impression you would try to rouse my scent memories, to see if I had any pleasurable experiences in the past."

Lucian cocked his head, an enigmatic but remarkably satisfied look softening his sharp features. "You have excellent instincts. That indeed was on the agenda for tonight."

"Oh." Corey didn't know what else to say. "Oh." He glanced at the circle of bowls still to go and had to ask, "Is the next one going to be a woman's… uh… what they… when they… um, come and…." He let out a breath in a loud huff, speech ceasing as fire spread across his cheeks and neck. Never had he felt quite this stupid and embarrassed.

"No." Lucian apparently took pity on him and thus relieved Corey's anxieties. "This is the only dish with a more, eh, personal touch. The rest are colognes and perfumes, soaps and body oils, soothing and calming, arousing and fever inducing, depending on your mood and take. What arouses a person is individual, you understand. Not everyone prefers the same scents or associates them with sex."

Corey nodded, shifting his weight from one foot to another. Coolness slowly returned, and he felt more like himself again. What was notable, however, was the deflated state of his penis. It was as if his cock knew that substance born of sex, alone or with another, had come from someone not Lucian, and because of that lost interest.

"So, uh, now what? Stop and go home?" Corey did *not* want to go back home without finding out more of what Lucian had planned for tonight—and the following sessions yet to come.

"I am willing to proceed. But it is your choice. If your discomfort level rises too high, then none of this will be beneficial to you. And that is, after all, the main objective here."

Lucian sounded rational and warm, and Corey wanted Lucian to want to continue to be with Corey. But he couldn't ask, not now, not like this. His motives would appear suspect, murky, and unclear, and that could drive Lucian away. That Corey could *not* risk.

So he shrugged, acting casual, and said only, "I'm still game."

"Very well. As you wish." Instead of proceeding to the next bowl, Lucian sauntered to the opposite side of the room from the door. There, behind another black curtain, was a secondary entrance. "Please, follow me."

Past the threshold opened a tiny vestibule with two doors on either side. Corey glanced at both, suppressing the itch to scratch his head in utter mystification. "Damn, but this place is like a fucking maze...."

Lucian grinned. "A Minotaur's maze, with a monstrous... penis at the other end?"

Corey rolled his eyes as he giggled. "Sure. Why not? I've seen crazier things." Then he waved a hand at the closed doors. "What's this? A puzzle?"

"A choice." Lucian stared directly, unwaveringly, at Corey, who began to get nervous. "Behind these doors is a line. A line of people. Their body odors await your choice." At that notion Corey could barely breathe, swallowing convulsively. "One of the lines is composed of only women and the other of only men." Now Corey understood Lucian's adamant gaze. "This, I suppose, dear Corey, is where you draw a line in the sand. Yes, we can try both rooms, if you like, but—"

"But I should choose only one, is that it?" Corey gritted his teeth, not knowing how to make the choice. He had scarce few fantasies, and those existed solely to push him toward climax in the mornings. His only other fantasy had starred Lucian. Did that mean he liked men and was in fact gay? Should that *possibility* rule his decision-making process?

"One or both. There are no rules or expectations written in stone. I may have said that this is a choice, but basically this only presents a choice if and when you wish to make one. It is not, however, an absolute requirement for us to proceed."

To Corey, Lucian appeared almost disinterested, his objectivity gone from neutrality to a nearly ice-cold disinterest. Warmth had completely crept out of his tone, and Corey wasn't fond of the change. Why did he act like that when surely compassion and empathy would better serve here?

Is he… jealous… of me…? That I might choose women over… him…?

The heady notion evaporated Corey's fears and doubts and solidified his resolution. "I choose men."

I want men. I want a man. I want… Lucian.

Decorum be damned!

CHAPTER 18

HIS HEART all but pounded its way out of his chest. Outwardly, though, Lucian kept up his cool facade. "V-very well." He hoped the tremor in his voice had gone unnoticed.

Without waiting for Corey to respond, Lucian turned to the door on the right, unlocked and opened it, and beckoned Corey inside. Once they had both crossed the threshold, Lucian flicked on the lights and illuminated the new room.

Another ring in a round room—only this time the circle composed not of pedestals but naked men. They all stood still, six feet apart, eyes front, like living, breathing statues of masculine beauty. Exactly according to Lucian's specifications.

So why was it that all he wanted right then was for the men to vanish into thin air so he had Corey all to himself?

Corey, however, seemed oblivious of Lucian's predicament as he observed the lineup leisurely. "So, what's the idea here? Watching?"

"Like candy, perfumes, drinks, or body powders, the task ahead consists of following your nose." Lucian kept his tone light, a wicked smile dangling on his lips, though he felt no mirth. "Do you remember when I mentioned taking you to an opera?"

"*Don Giovanni*? Yeah." He glanced at Lucian, winking. "I didn't get the chance to say I've seen the opera before, many years ago."

"I saw it when I was a teenager, with my school class." Lucian recalled the red velvet of their seats, the brightly lit chandeliers hanging high from the domed ceiling, the evening gowns and the tuxes, the luxurious perfumes and expensive colognes, the low murmurs, the subtle waves of excitement, the classy ambience—and the hints of pleasures he hadn't understood at the time. "It paved my way into this lifestyle and this line of work."

"They suit you," Corey commented, and without intending it, Lucian beamed.

"In any case, like *Don Giovanni,* in his bloodhound capacity, hunting women and declaring being able to smell a woman, so you are going to smell a man. Well, quite a few men, actually." With a carefree chuckle belying his true feelings, Lucian said, "Different body odors are attached to different men, for you to discern, like or not, and equate with sex. Work, exercise, sleep, sex, and so forth. The only condition is that you enjoy your exploration."

"Ah. Got it." As Corey inched forward, his gait was not even half as hesitant as Lucian had assumed—or secretly hoped—it would be.

To distract himself, Lucian said, "The many scents of a human body attach themselves to any kind of object, such as a piece of clothing tucked in a drawer or the handle of a perfume bottle or imprinted on fresh linen in a bed slept in only once or the inside of a glove or the most intimate garments worn against the skin. These sensual fumes can be intoxicating or repulsive, depending on the person using his nose."

Words ebbed and flowed typically as Lucian lectured on sensuality to his clients, but as he watched Corey step between two gorgeous hunks into the center of the ring of naked men, his tongue was glued to his palate, refusing to cooperate and move an inch. He was struck mute, only able to observe in silence as Corey studied the selection before him.

Without delay, Corey seemed to have made his choice when he approached a young blond man with a slender musculature, zero body hair, and a stylized tattoo of a red dragon on his hip. With an inscrutable expression, Corey scoured the man's skin with his eyes.

Lucian stamped down his fiery flash of jealousy. It wasn't Corey's fault Lucian found it all but impossible to remain objective and professional. No, this was Lucian's problem.

Finally, Corey leaned forward, without touching, and inhaled the scent of the blond man's hair. "I smell peppermint and citrus and… rosemary, I think. Clean, with a hint of moisture. He's had a shower recently so probably his shampoo or soap."

Elated, Lucian smiled to himself. Corey was speaking directly to *him*, describing the smells to him, incorporating Lucian into the experiment. He was not excluded after all. He spoke with a crack in his voice. "G-good. How does it make you feel?"

Corey shrugged, but when he glanced at Lucian, his grin was naughty. "Not horny, if that's what you mean. But it's a nice scent. For a shampoo. Earthy, masculine, with a bit of a tang."

"What else?" Lucian urged.

"What else do I feel or smell?" Corey sniffed at the man's neck, so Lucian gave him time to answer in his own pace. "He smells clean all over. I can't smell *him*."

Instantly, Corey moved away from the man and toward the next one in line. This man was robust and heavily built, with lots of body hair, a few scars scattered here and there, a strong five o'clock shadow on his square jaw, and broken fingernails. He was an acquaintance of Lucian's, a rough-stock Dom by the name of Colton, who worked construction.

Corey walked around the man a few times, sniffing as he went. "There's dirt and sand and maybe mortar. Sweat too. Not fresh. Pungent."

Lucian nodded. "Smells fire the imagination. Washed skin, all spick-and-span, is not always desirable, as it does not necessarily awaken the senses nor does it arouse. A person's truest smell is washed clean. Sometimes fresh sweat and earthy odors of toil and sex are the most alluring of all."

Corey frowned, possibly going over alternatives in his head. "His nails are broken; he has jagged scars and lines on his skin where a heavy weight pressed against him, like a... a tool belt and a harness maybe, plus he has flattened helmet hair. A manual laborer?"

Lucian was proud of Corey's deductions. "Construction work."

Corey stopped and stared at Lucian quizzically. "You know all these men?"

"I do, yes. I handpicked them for this occasion." Lucian could tell what Corey wanted to ask but hesitated voicing it out loud, making it real and irrevocable knowledge to hang in the air between them. "And to answer your *other* question, no, I haven't slept with all of them. A couple, but not all."

Corey's eyes narrowed dangerously, and Lucian immediately worried. But then Corey shrugged and looked away. "Okay." Then he moved on to the next man, as if nothing sensitive had been discussed.

Conflicted about how to deal with Corey's reactions and obvious deflections, Lucian focused on what was happening with Corey and the ring of men. He had a strong feeling the two of them would hash things out sooner or later, so he remained silent and patient. Their time would come one way or another.

The third man was beautiful in an effeminate way, graceful and delicate, the kind who might break if the wind blew too hard. The brunet's face had subtle makeup on, his ribs could be counted with a single glance, he had the tiniest nipples Lucian had ever seen in a twenty-year-old, and his hip bones stood out prominently. Noticeable was also the fact that his cock was at half-mast. Being looked at was a turn-on for a great many people, not just exhibitionists.

Corey stepped closed, scented the man, and immediately reared back with widened eyes. "This one has had sex recently. He smells of... of spunk." His tone dropped to husky at the last word, as if embarrassed to speak it out loud.

Lucian made his way to them and inhaled the slim young man's skin. Then he smiled. "No. He has chestnut body oil on his skin. The scent of chestnut flowers is extremely close to that of semen."

Frowning in disbelief, Corey closed the gap between them. "You sure?"

"The boy's skin glistens ever so slightly with it." Lucian backed off two steps to allow Corey to make the same observation, which he did since the frown cleared and he nodded in agreement. "Not many know about the similarity because chestnut flowers are not a commonly used substance in body oils."

Corey studied the young man in front of him, head cocked to the side. "It's funny, but I could have sworn...." He shook his head, let out a small chuckle, shrugged, and then moved on. "I guess you live and you learn, huh?"

"Yes, indeed." Lucian watched from within the ring now as Corey went on with his explorations. "Do you prefer to bathe or shower?"

Corey stopped to stare at Lucian, seemingly surprised by the odd question. "This may sound weird from a man of leisure, but I like to shower. Lack of time."

"In a hurry to go... where?"

"Out on business. What does it matter?" Corey replied defensively, serious now.

Lucian was unwilling to let the matter drop despite the audience they had. "I've been meaning to ask. What do you do for a living, Corey? Are you only a playboy, or does something else stir your interests? Have you no passions in life? For example, considering your father's career and success in communications, did you never wish to be a journalist or a writer?"

Corey shook his head, his expression and tone both brusque. "No. I like to read, not write. I'm not articulate or creative enough. I'll stick to signing checks and family legal documents, thank you very much." He was terse to the point of rude, but Lucian let that pass.

Conciliatory, Lucian offered, "It occurred to me you might have far too much time on your hands to contemplate your, uh, situation." It wasn't the most elaborate euphemism for frigidity, but needs must.

Corey paled, his discomfort obvious, and his jaw shifted as he gritted his teeth, as was his nervous habit. But for once he didn't seem to care about eavesdropping ears. "Like you, I don't need to work to earn a living. I have a trust fund. I'm not a big spender, so there will be funds there till the day I die, and longer."

"That is not an answer to my question, but an unnecessary speech about money. I was not talking about means or subsistence but of something beyond the material. Your situation may prevent you from getting fired up, uh, in certain conditions, but does nothing else blaze within you? You need a purpose in life. Find one, Corey. You do not want to become jaded like me."

Toward the end as Lucian spoke, Corey's rigid features eased and gentled, as did his voice. "Lucian, you're *not* jaded."

"Oh?" Lucian was amazed at the simple statement, spoken as if it were undeniable fact. "My experiences, my history, my state of mind…. For me, there is no place left unsullied, no time of day or night left untainted, no position left untried in sexual encounters."

Corey actually laughed then, and Lucian stopped dead, his brain empty of retorts and comebacks. "That's not proof that you're jaded. The only thing it proves is that like me, you're still searching."

"For what?" For some reason, Lucian was all of a sudden terrified to hear the answer.

Corey's half smile was rueful, and with sudden blinding certainty, Lucian understood the sentiment all too well. "For perfect companionship, for a soul mate, for a kindred spirit… for true love."

Out of breath, Lucian had no idea how to react. His body shared the confusion with his mind and heart, starting to quiver and heat up one moment, chill the next. In a devastating instant of sheer panic, he almost ran out of the room, out of Boudoir, desperate to get away from Corey, this man who seemed to see right into Lucian's lonely depths.

But then Corey was right there, in front of Lucian, gripping his shoulders, calming and scaring him at once. "I'm sorry, Lucian. That was uncalled for. I didn't mean to upset you. I spoke out of my ass. Forgive me."

Was denial the better part of valor, Lucian asked himself, the lie readily forming on his tongue, prepared to slip out into the world. It was so close he could taste the foul thing....

"No, no." Lucian offered a tentative smile to Corey, who frowned upon seeing it. "It is I who must apologize to you. I have grown so accustomed to the notion of being jaded and cynical and world-weary that the idea of... *not* being so shook me a bit. But I will be all right, I promise."

The hold Corey had on Lucian lessened slightly. "You sure?"

Lucian nodded, putting some emphasis into the gesture. "I am, yes." He dared to add a low, edgy chuckle. "As befitting the theme of the evening, like an armor, I wear an invisible cologne of a socially acceptable flavor to mask my, um, vulnerabilities. With it, I too hide my true self from the world."

Corey scoffed. "The world be damned! You expect honesty and directness from me. I expect the same from you." Then he quirked an eyebrow, a grin starting to form. "Even though we each tease the other, flirt and confuse and play games." Then he released his grip on Lucian. "What I want to know is why you asked me whether I shower or bathe. I suspect the ultimate reason was something other than a mere leading question to my passions."

Lucian played along, bringing lightness back. "Can't you tell? Use your imagination."

Corey grinned back. "Indulge me, good sir."

Lucian snorted. "That gentlemanly description hardly befits me." He exhaled a long, melodramatic breath. "But very well. Have you ever showered in a bathroom, locker room, or spa where someone has used it mere moments before you? Have you bathed in a tub still moist with droplets from the previous occupant? Have you sat on sauna benches where the body oils of another linger still?"

Corey seemed uncertain, his brow furrowing. "I, uh... I don't have a clue. Maybe. It's possible, I guess."

"I told you before that sometimes cleanliness washes away the unique, arousing scent of a person. The baser, earthier, rawer odors of the body. What do you imagine you will smell in a bathtub the occupant has departed from a heartbeat ago, when the water still remains before the tub is drained?"

Corey's eyes glazed as he became lost in thought, and he did not see Lucian for a time. "Hmm, soaps, shampoos, skin oils perhaps. Warmth of the water, possibly? There would be a slick, cloudy coating on the surface."

Lucian smiled. "Yes. Proof of bodily contact with water. Bathrooms have always been seen as intimate places where bodily functions and odors, the mere sight of a naked figure, could be hidden from view. Upon the arrival of indoor plumbing, hot water, and bidets, a whole culture of secrecy and sensuality was created around bathing. Every object from sponges and towels to bath oils and perfumes took on a poetic luster. This warm glow permeated past the veil of privacy to the bathroom and the bedroom that were no longer the dirty, ugly, and smelly necessities of old."

This time the dazed look Corey sported indicated intrigue, admiration, and amusement as he listened to Lucian, who kept wondering what the man was really thinking. "Mmm, the decadent, hot, moist clouds of bathhouses, luxurious and tempting...."

Though Corey grinned, Lucian didn't think his companion was making fun of him but getting in the mood and the spirit of things. "Dens of sin, yes. But the erotic vibe of nudity was used to advertise health and hygiene as well, a fresh sensuality of bare bodies glistening with water under the scorching sun. Attractive imagery, don't you agree?"

"Provocative too."

Lucian bowed his head in acknowledgment. "Cleanliness equals purity? These days, the expectation of proper hygiene in oneself and others is strong, in and out of bed. The reason why I asked about your habit of showering is because a freshly clean person has an artificial fragrance fixed on his skin. But like any exertion, arousal awakens the body's innate odors. Recognizing them is instinctual. Even for those who...." He let his voice trail off in the hopes Corey would catch on to his meaning without him having to say the *F* word, and he wasn't referring to the coarser of the two.

"Right." A flash of rigidity stiffened Corey's expression into a hardened mask but only for a moment. Then he seemed to return back to his relaxed self again. "Carnal scents of the flesh. Does it always... smell the same? Erogenous zones, I mean."

"No. Everyone is individual. There are many factors to the end result."

"Hygiene, for one," Corey interjected.

"Indeed. Body hairs also affect how pungent the odor is and how long it lingers." Corey seemed to mull this over, and his gaze went around the room over all the naked men. "Here you have the opportunity to see—well, smell for yourself."

Corey frowned, a displeased look encompassing his features. "Isn't it a bit too... damn intrusive for me to stuff my face in a stranger's crotch?"

"Did you know that no more than a hundred years ago, the stench of sweaty feet was rumored to be a fetish for homosexuals?"

Corey shook his head, and his frustration began to show. "No. I did not fucking know that. What's the point of that little historical tidbit?"

"Rumors are like appearances. They are both ultimately facades for truths that people usually do not know about or understand. What difference does it make to you what these men think of you should you sniff their privates? For all you know, you will never see them again."

Corey hedged. "It wouldn't be fair to experiment with people about *my* sexuality. My arousal is primarily about *me*, and so would any ensuing sex be. It would be about nothing more than me getting off in the company of another. There'd be no real connection." He paused to scowl at no one in particular. "Not that I admit to wanting *that*. The connection, I mean."

Lucian was dumbstruck. That was an argument he most certainly had never expected to hear from Corey. It had been presented angrily and defensively, in a manner Corey had spoken to Lucian when they had initially met. Lucian believed that self-guardedness had passed. Well, apparently not.

Then he uttered something he never would have said to anyone else under mentoring circumstances, and he regretted it immediately. "Whether making love with another human being or masturbating in solitude, we are all of us alone in the end."

Corey's eyes flashed intently, narrowing. "I hate to break it to you, man, but you're not exactly toeing the party line."

Lucian turned away, regrouping as fast as humanly possible. "You get negative all of a sudden, at times. I guess I had to show you that other people besides you can feel the same way." With newfound confidence, he straightened up and twirled back around. "But it does not mean either of us has to."

Corey stared back for a long time. Then he nodded ever so slightly. "You're right. I do get a bit… testy sometimes. Sorry." Then he glanced around the room. "Doesn't mean I don't feel weird sniffing strangers' genitals. Call me crazy, but that's just how I feel about it."

"Ah. I understand." And Lucian did too. The first time you touched, smelled, tasted a person, it was always different, frightening and enticing at once. At those moments it did indeed matter if that someone felt like a companion or a stranger. How had Lucian forgotten that sensation, that feeling? "Have you heard the terms 'temple of love' or 'the cave of Venus' or 'Cupid's arrow'?" Corey shrugged, puzzled a bit but obviously hungry to hear more. The intensity of his gaze was like catnip to Lucian, had he been a feline with a drug-like plant dangled in front of his face. "They are pretentious, yet innocent euphemisms for vagina and penis, the genitalia."

"So?" Corey grimaced. "They sound silly and old-fashioned now. I don't think there's a woman in the world today who would call her pussy the cave of Venus."

"Metaphorical and poetic licenses do not have to sound dated or gaudy. Why use a term like cunt, which is derogatory and filthy, when you could use a word that is beautiful and lyrical?"

Corey chuckled. "I get your point. Really I do. But I find it hard to believe any man would use decorative phrases for their dick. Why can't we call it plain old dick?"

"Would you call it a plain old dick in a romantic setting?"

Corey opened his mouth to speak but then stopped dead, jaw hanging open, conflicted. "Ah. Right. Well, in that kind of situation… no, I probably wouldn't. *But* that doesn't mean I would call it Cupid's lance either."

"Arrow."

"Whatever."

"The language we use during sex can be coarse, rough, boorish even. That is all right. What lovers whisper to each other during coitus is very much their business."

Corey stared, cringing in disbelief. "Coitus? Really?"

Lucian laughed. "Why not? Let us be accurate. After all, this scene we find ourselves in could hardly be considered romantic or delicate or sentimental. No. My point is that the language we use to describe new experiences can either attract or repulse us. Had you used a... a gentler word than crotch when describing the private place these men are offering for your sensual journey, perhaps your reaction would not have been so... quick to dismiss." He backed off a few steps and waved at the brunet boy whose skin held a flavor of chestnut body oil. "After all, you are not yet finished, as I recall."

His verbal challenge was met with silent determination as Corey squared his shoulders and prepared to continue the experiment.

But then, out of the blue, he cracked up, chortling like a hyena.

Perplexed, Lucian asked, "Are you all right? What's the matter?"

Right then, it seemed Lucian gained Corey's full and undivided attention because the man stopped laughing and moved toward Lucian, his gait slow and steady, sort of stalking, as if a predator circling his prey. Instinctively, Lucian began to retreat, his gaze fixed on Corey's eyes as they darkened with every step.

Lucian swallowed nervously as he passed the ring of men and his back hit the wall. "Corey?"

"Enough." Corey actually growled, and he crowded Lucian until he had Lucian pinned against the wall, Corey bracing his arms on both sides of Lucian's head, boxing him in. "No more of this."

"What?" Lucian wasn't sure if he was afraid or aroused. Chills trickled up and down his spine, but his groin ignited, like a match thrown into gasoline, setting him aflame.

"No more experimenting with strangers." Corey leaned forward until their noses were a breath apart. Lucian could feel the heat emanating from the other man's skin, his hot breath with a hint of coffee fanning over Lucian's face, and the weight of his words and actions, like a conqueror making his intentions known. "I want to smell *you*."

That was about when Lucian's brain short-circuited.

CHAPTER 19

THE DOOR of the private chamber closed with an ominous, conclusive bang, and the soft snick of the lock emphasized the finality of the scene about to take place. Lucian could not look at Corey, for he had too much trouble even breathing properly, and his heart pounded like a thousand drums. Lucian felt Corey moving behind his back, taking in their surroundings.

There was great variety in the secluded areas of Boudoir, depending on what kind of scene was sought. The BDSM dungeons, for example, had racks, chains, swings, and St. Andrew's crosses, while the more basic sex therapy session rooms had the standard doctor's desk and soft chairs and couches for the patients to choose their preference, a clinically traditional environment for those who only needed to talk.

But the room Lucian selected had none of those. The small space was intimate and warm and welcoming. Earth tones of red, gold, and brown dominated the space. Heavy rugs on the floor, upholstered chairs, dim lights with golden-hued shades, and a four-poster bed with dark, thick curtains.

Corey sauntered into Lucian's field of vision, but his gaze was aimed at the bed. "Well, what do you know? Get a load of that bed. Exact duplicate of the one you have at the penthouse. All the comforts of home." Corey's gaze shot at Lucian, who gasped quietly. "Speaking of which, when I suggested a more private setting, how come you didn't bring us back to your place? I mean, all this experimentation on my behalf must be setting you back thousands of dollars a pop. How on earth can you afford all this mentoring on a regular basis in a swanky place like Boudoir? Take me, for example. I'm not paying you anything. You sure haven't indicated I should." He chuckled. "Unless the bill comes after?"

His mind distorted with flashing images of what he wished to do with Corey. Lucian had trouble figuring out what to respond to first. "Why we came to this room instead of my place? Well, you didn't seem predisposed to wasting time by moving to a different location. Expediency, you understand. Why the bed reminds you of mine and why you aren't being billed for this experience? Well… that's because I own Boudoir."

While Corey had studied Lucian's body intently as he spoke, now he regarded Lucian with a new intensity. "You… what?"

Lucian had predicted this confrontation was coming, but he had hoped for a time and place not there. Alas, he was out of luck. "I have owned Boudoir for seven years now. My main motivation was to find a special venue, private, secluded, and secure, for my mentoring program. As the place grew and gained renown in the city and beyond, I hired managers to take care of it for me as I focused on my clients. Nowadays Boudoir caters to a grand variety of people seeking aid with sexual issues or simply privacy to explore sensual options."

Corey stared at him, lips a thin line, eyes narrowed, expression closed off. "Why didn't you tell me?" He sounded more hurt than furious. "And don't you dare say an opportunity to come clean never came up 'cause that'd be bullshit."

"In the beginning it didn't seem relevant. Then I forgot."

The flummoxed snort that emerged from Corey told a whole story. But then suddenly he started to laugh. "Yeah, okay. When we first came here, no, I wouldn't have cared whether you owned the place or not. In fact, I still don't."

Frowning, Lucian felt puzzled. "Then why—"

"I'm just disappointed you didn't explain to me why you value this joint so much. One or two words would've sufficed, you know. 'Hey, Corey? I love Boudoir. Oh, and by the way, I own it.' See how easy that was? Didn't take five seconds."

"You're right, of course. I should have said something." Lucian cast a glance at his toes, as if the answers to all the world's riddles were found down there. "Are you terribly upset with me?"

Corey's eyes flashed, like steel swords in the glint of the sun. "Go stand over there." He pointed at the foot of the four-poster bed where a soft dark red rug lay. "Now."

Lucian shivered. This new facet of Corey's, this assertiveness, was damn hot. Without saying a word, Lucian complied. The air in the room was warm and a bit stuffy, with no scents of any kind lingering. A clean space for this sort of sensory exercise.

Corey took a step closer, his demeanor one of prowling, his gaze dark and focused. "I'm in charge, Lucian. You will do exactly what I say and what I want you to do, no matter what. Nod if you understand."

It had been ages since a man had truly dominated Lucian. Most men knew the act, the role, and what to expect in terms of behavioral patterns, but they either went too far or not far enough, never quite understanding the meaning and purpose of domination.

Not that Lucian was a submissive. He was, in fact, a switch.

At the moment, though, the thrill of being commanded by Corey gave him hot flashes, so he merely nodded his acquiescence. He had to admit he was deeply curious to see what Corey would do.

"Don't move or speak unless I allow it." Corey inched closer again. Even though there was a distance between them, Lucian could feel his companion's presence and weight on his skin like a real touch. Finally Corey stood less than three feet away, their gazes locked. "I can tell what you're thinking, Lucian. You wonder what I'm up to and how is it I'm behaving like this. Right?"

"Yes." Lucian was dying to discover what Corey had learned from their lessons.

Corey grinned lopsidedly, daring. "You should know the answer to the first puzzle by now."

Lucian had no trouble recalling Corey's demand. "You want to smell me."

Corey grew serious, as if strained to the extreme. "Since I'm not going to touch you—that's a whole other lesson, yeah?—you're going to undress yourself. Slowly, though, at *my* pace. Not yours. I'm calling the shots."

Glad to hear there would be no touching or tasting involved, Lucian inclined his head a bit to show his compliance. Corey's sudden act of power was wreaking havoc with Lucian's body, his skin goose bumpy and his insides on fire. Lucian hadn't honestly expected this from Corey, not yet, perhaps not ever. This side of Corey's psyche took Lucian by surprise, but he was determined not to interfere—unless things went sideways.

Using only his fingertips to seductively caress the silky tie he wore, Lucian raised his hand to unknot it. With leisurely motions he let the fabric slip between his fingers like a cascade. He made an erotic show of it, exactly as his companion had requested.

Corey watched like a hawk, his jaw working as though he was gritting his teeth, and at his sides, he fisted his hands. Like a statue of a god of strife, he stared, not uttering a word or letting out a sound. He was transfixed.

Lucian dropped the tie on the bed behind him without looking back. Then he moved on to the top button of his dress shirt.

"Wait." Corey's voice was gravelly, as if he had great trouble controlling his emotions. Lucian stopped immediately, his hands hovering over the shirt buttons, and waited.

Corey dipped his head down and inhaled Lucian's neck.

Lucian was about to have a (heat) stroke right then and there. His heart pounded with the fierceness of a jackhammer, and he didn't seem to be able to draw proper breath. Corey was so close, Lucian had to close his eyes or lose his cool in a blink of an eye from the visual stimuli.

Was that a brush of Corey's warm, wet lips on his pulse point? Trembling, Lucian was two seconds away from creaming his pants.

"Mmm, I smell… oranges and lemons," Corey whispered, and Lucian heard the smile in his voice. "And lavender, jasmine, and vanilla. Beneath… patchouli and musk and… civet?" He pulled back, and Lucian opened his eyes to see Corey's reaction. He appeared pleasantly surprised that Lucian's scent resembled the test bowls from earlier, putting him in a position to be able to make the connection with recent experiences. "Your own concoction, maybe?"

Lucian smiled, beaming and blushing at the look of awe in Corey's gray eyes. Corey had a remarkable olfactory sense, one Lucian admired. "I wish I could take credit for the potent perfume, but, alas, I cannot. The cologne is Ungaro pour L'Homme II, my favorite. The initial scents are fruity, which I appreciate for many reasons, but the baser notes are a mix of flora and fauna. And yes, you are correct about civet."

"Well, now I'm a fan. The fragrance suits you." Corey's eyes glimmered with sensual appreciation, and Lucian gulped hard. "There's a curious raw power to it, hints of brutal masculinity and a spicy boldness that matches your unique beauty."

His poetic phrasing made Lucian feel ten feet tall, an object of desire for a man who had never paid attention to men in any sexual way. Lucian was indeed unique for he was Corey's first experience.

Rueful, he said, "Since the first sniff, I have adored the cologne. Unfortunately, it has been discontinued."

"Shame." Corey sounded as genuinely apologetic as Lucian felt. "The scent definitely adds to your mystique."

"I do still have a couple of bottles left for special occasions."

Corey grinned. "I'm honored you picked your time with me as such." Briefly he leaned forward again to smell Lucian. "You're not wearing a lot."

Lucian giggled. "You mean I haven't bathed in cologne like some men do?"

Corey snickered in return. "Oh, Lucian, I don't think there's anything other men do that you can't do better."

Flames licked Lucian's cheeks as he flushed at the compliment, loving every word and softly spoken nuance of Corey's voice. "Thank you."

"You know, it's funny, but all these... smells brought back a memory from my school days." Corey frowned, his eyes losing focus as his thoughts turned inward, searching for a recollection. "There was this guy in my class, a new pupil from one of those Rudolf Steiner schools, Waldorf or some such, I can't remember exactly. I remember he was very neat, clean, and precise in actions and appearance, like a model of a good boy. Anyway, he wore this expensive cologne, which was kind of strange since the rest of us barely used deodorant. In any case, that scent clung to his clothes and skin, a constant cloud around him, announcing his presence before he came in sight. That air of a grown man, of sophistication and maturity, it felt weird then. Now.... Damn, there were times when I, like the few school chums I had, used to smell like the back end of a goat stuffed in a jock strap for a week."

Lucian wrinkled his nose in amused disgust. "What an appealing image."

Corey laughed. "Yeah. We grew up to appreciate the *lack* of body odors. Still, I guess you proved your point. Our sensual sessions seem to awaken my dormant sense memories. For what it's worth, I'm just glad I have them. Without these experiments, I probably wouldn't even have recalled that guy. God, what was his name? It started with an... *R*...." Suddenly he shook his head. The memory evaporated as his focus was evidently right back in the game.

With an elegance of languid motion Lucian had not observed before, Corey ambled around Lucian, never touching but breathing him in. Swallowing, Lucian fought the urge to fidget under the scrutiny. He had showered before their "therapy date," plus he wore cologne, so he should smell sweet. But what would Corey think of his natural scent, eau de Lucian?

"Is this your natural hair color?" Corey asked all of a sudden, like a shadow looming behind Lucian's back. Lucian felt Corey's nose brush his hair, and goose bumps appeared all over his skin. His erection grew hotter and harder, pleading for attention.

Lucian tilted his head so that Corey could see his profile. "Yes. But… if you don't believe me, I can think of one way for you to find out."

Corey chuckled. "Only one?" he whispered into Lucian's hair in a sultry voice.

A teasing Corey was wonderful to be around, Lucian thought, smiling happily. "Not telling."

Corey shifted to stand at Lucian's side. "Continue undressing."

With a deep, shaky breath, Lucian resumed unbuttoning his dress shirt, all too aware of his companion's poignant gaze on his every move and each patch of skin revealed. Corey grew serious once more, seemingly taking in the sight of a man removing his clothes with earnest devotion, apparently unwilling to miss a single move Lucian made.

"I've been thinking," Corey said ominously out of the blue. "What exactly do you do?"

In obvious surprise, Lucian cocked his head to the side to see Corey better. "You mean besides the mentoring program, the sexual therapy, and owning Boudoir?" Corey nodded, so Lucian replied, "These days I am dedicated to aiding people through the three avenues I mentioned. They consume most all of my time."

Corey seemed to ponder the news carefully, a pensive look on his face. "I see."

Lucian felt an overpowering need to dig deeper into Corey's psyche so he asked, "You didn't answer my question about *your* passions. What inspires you? What motivates you? And I do not mean racquetball at the country club or your latest spa treatment with a serving of gossip or shopping for a new, faster sports car." Lucian used this tactic to retake charge of the situation, but he had a feeling he was about to fail fantastically.

Corey snorted and grinned. "I don't do any of those things."

"You know what I mean," Lucian retorted reproachfully.

Corey shrugged, but his smile remained. "Maybe I haven't found my shtick yet."

"What about architecture? You studied it for many years."

Corey circled to stand in front of Lucian, but he stared down at his feet, frowning. "I guess I don't feel any real inspiration for it. I don't want to make a career out of it."

"Why did you start studying it in the first place?"

"Partly to piss off Dad, partly because the subject required severity, eye for detail, and need for coherent structures, all of which I understand and appreciate. Architecture can be creative, but it's also rigid in that certain aspects must be done in certain ways to be functional." Lucian opened his mouth to comment, to offer an affirmative, but Corey waved him quiet. "No, no more of this, Lucian. Enough chatter. Take off your shirt."

It seemed their pause for learning through dialogue was at an end. Lucian acquiesced and finished popping the last buttons open.

He had wanted to see if this tempting situation would loosen Corey's tongue so he would let slip something personal that would enlighten Lucian as to why he was so sure he was frigid instead of simply being neurotic, repressed, or inexperienced, any of which could be dealt with through therapy. Alas, this new sensual situation had apparently only focused Corey more and given him single-minded purpose to see and smell Lucian naked.

Slowly Lucian parted the flaps of his shirt to reveal his sculpted chest. He had precious few chest hairs, and he tended to shave it all off. His muscles had definition but not much mass. He was well aware he was skinnier than looked becoming on a man. Unfortunately, Lucian was not the physical type that gained weight, so he would undoubtedly remain svelte for the rest of his days. Thankfully he was short enough to compensate for it, because being thin and tall would have made him feel awkward in high heels.

Nervous, Lucian wondered how Corey saw him as he let the shirt fall off his shoulders and pool on the floor. He did his best to tamp down his insecurities. After all, Corey had not seen many naked men in real life, so Lucian had a good chance of coming out on top, so to speak.

Didn't he…?

CHAPTER 20

COREY TOOK in the sight of Lucian's partial nudity, his gaze unwavering as it slid up and down Lucian's bare torso. Finally he murmured, "You're beautiful, Lucian."

Relieved, Lucian smiled and blushed. "Thank you, Corey. I'm glad you think so." He confessed to himself his nerves had almost gotten the better of him.

"I can't imagine anyone foolish enough to think differently." Corey's relentless gaze caressed Lucian's bare form like a touch, and Lucian anticipated Corey would soon be so enthralled in his visual exploration that he forgot his pledge not to touch and would do so willingly. "You have very little body hair, I see."

"Only a bit, I'm afraid. I shave off the rest." He resisted the urge to run his hands over his skin, as he often did when emphasizing his meaning. But he had a feeling Corey would not like him doing something Corey himself tried to abstain from.

Corey cocked his head as his eyes drifted downward. "Not the treasure trail, though, I'm glad to note."

Lucian glanced at his navel. Below it a sparse path of burnt orange hairs led down to his crotch. "I prefer my pubes trimmed and the rest shaved off." He looked at Corey and winked shamelessly.

Corey's eyes widened. "You shave your...."

"Balls and ass. Around my cock I only trim." Lucian preened at seeing Corey shaken so by the fresh erotic images that undoubtedly arose in his imagination. The more Corey wanted to feel aroused, and did, the better their chances that he would get an erection and be able to sustain it to climax. Especially in an experience with another person and not just a masturbatory act. "I like the cleanliness and sensuality of the practice. Are you... au naturel?"

Abashed, Corey shrugged, but his cheeks pinked. "I like it shorn."

Pleasantly surprised, Lucian said, "Intriguing. How does it make you feel? Trimming your pubic hair?"

Corey seemed half-bemused, half-sarcastic, and chuckled mildly. "Why should it make me feel anything? I don't like to have a smelly bush, or smelly anything, so I cut it. Simple as that. That's like asking me how I feel about cutting my toenails. Ridiculous." Before Lucian could offer a comment, Corey stopped him with a warning glare. "Now shush."

For a brief moment, Corey hovered his hands near Lucian's skin, so close Lucian could feel the warmth emanating from him. He held his breath, waiting to see what Corey would do. Corey continued gliding his hands through the air, a hairsbreadth away from Lucian's skin. Whatever he was testing, it was driving Lucian mad with want.

"Lift up your arms," Corey commanded, and Lucian complied.

Circling, Corey moved to follow Lucian's raised arms with his hands, never quite touching. Then, standing at Lucian's side, Corey leaned forward and inhaled Lucian's exposed armpit.

Heat flashed through Lucian's body. Never before had he had such a potent reaction to an act that did not touch him. His imagination, and the mere presence of Corey, did the trick. Lucian was extremely aware of Corey and everything he did—and didn't do. His skin prickled, his heart beat faster, his balls tingled, and his cock twitched. His physical responses were spinning out of control.

Corey chuckled deeply, rich and sweet like the darkest chocolate, and he murmured, "You even shave your armpits. I've never heard of a guy doing that. Even in order to be clean."

Lucian tried not to shiver but failed. "I prefer my armpits clean-shaven. I am aware it is not considered very masculine. But… I am not pretending or wishing to be a woman. Trans men, female impersonators, and gentlemen like me do shave where we need to. There is nothing wrong with that."

"I didn't say there was." Corey inhaled and whispered an *mmm*, as though his lungs had filled with something sweet and yummy. "Your own scent is stronger here."

"Bends, nooks, and crannies of the body, as well as the places where hair grows, retain a pungent natural, personal odor, it is true." Lucian found it hard to speak intelligibly when his mind raced with red-hot images, and his body was awash on a sea of sensations.

"We'll see. Nothing like empirical research, eh?" Corey grinned and winked. Then his gaze dropped to Lucian's groin where his erection strained the fabric of his expensive, tight pants. "Final frontier. Well, almost." He looked into Lucian's eyes, determined. "Pants down."

With a deep inhale, Lucian began to unbuckle his white leather belt. He had to get a tight rein over his wayward imagination or risk coming the moment he dropped his pants. But a single passing thought of Corey's soft, lovely, luscious lips on his cock... and an orgasm was pending already.

"Something up?" Corey asked, feigning innocence poorly. Apparently this position of power was growing on him, matching the pace of Lucian's rising libido perfectly.

Lucian wisely ignored the barb but rolled his eyes and slipped his belt out of its loops before letting it fall to the floor beside his shirt.

Corey's smile cracked, and now it was Lucian's turn to smirk. "No. You?" To give emphasis and weight to his words, he unzipped.

Corey visibly gulped, and his gaze was riveted on Lucian's actions. "C-continue."

With deliberate, slow movements, Lucian gripped the waistband of his pants and began to inch them down his hips, revealing more bare skin.

In all the years Lucian had mentored people with sexual problems, he had never felt this raw and vulnerable and yet this natural and fair. He was used to being seen naked for his clients, if the need arose. That didn't mean sex was in the picture.

Corey's merciless gaze didn't seem to miss a thing, peering into Lucian's very being, into his core where he had doubts and fears but where his goodness and beauty lay too. Some of his handsomeness and sex appeal was a mask behind which hid his truest self.

But it was all right for Corey to catch a glimpse.

That was Lucian's mantra as he slid his pants and underwear down to midthigh before straightening up and showing himself in his full glory to his companion.

An odd sound, reminiscent of a gurgle, escaped Corey's throat, and he stood in place, sweaty and red and apparently mesmerized by the sight. Then, like a robot given an electrical jolt, Corey stepped closer. He didn't seem to be breathing at all.

All of a sudden, a mere foot away from Lucian's body, he dropped to his knees. With widened eyes, he took in the vision of Lucian's erection, surrounded by neatly trimmed red-golden pubic hairs.

Corey inhaled in surprise, dropping his gaze too low to be aimed at Lucian's cock and balls. He frowned. "Your underwear.... I did not expect *that*."

Lucian blushed, glancing below. "I love the touch of silk and the feel of lace. I assure you, despite their appearance, my boxer briefs *are* for men." Lucian wore boxer briefs made of pale blue silk and natural white lace, designed for a man with a flavor for luxury.

Corey said nothing. Lucian watched him closely and saw exactly when his gaze rose from his bunched up underwear to his crotch. A sharp exhale mixed with a surprised chuckle. "You know, when we were dancing here the other week, when you were in my arms... I imagined what you would look like without a stitch on." Corey's gaze flicked upward briefly to lock with Lucian's. "I wondered if your skin would be pale as moonlight all over or sun-kissed brown where I couldn't see." He stared down at the milky white expanse and smiled. "I had a hunch...." His fingertips almost brushed over Lucian's hipbones, hovering over them like feathers.

"W-would you have preferred...." Lucian started to speak but was too breathless to go on, so his voice trailed away, vanishing into the ether.

"God, how delicate you are, with such frail bone structure." Corey didn't seem to have noticed Lucian's half question. He was lost in a subspace of sensuality, the one Lucian wanted him to sink into. Corey stared, taking in every detail and inch. "I bet I could count your ribs with my eyes and fingers. What if we... made love rough? Would you... bend or break?"

Lucian trembled. The thought ignited his lust, the one he could not sate with this man, not yet. Maybe never. "Bend."

"Good to know." So, apparently Corey wasn't entirely deaf. He leaned forward, his nose all but pressed against Lucian's erection, and inhaled. "Passion fruit. Just like before. The first time I smelled you, when we danced." He took on a dreamy look, eyes glazed over, far away. "Your skin was so soft then, and I bet it's silky smooth and warm now."

Lucian did his best to keep it together. "I thought there was to be no touching."

Corey smiled and nodded. "Yeah, I did say that." His open palm glided an inch away from Lucian's stomach. "I really want to, though." He all but pressed his face into Lucian's skin. "I had a feeling you'd be soft and smooth everywhere. I like your flat belly. I think it'll feel wonderful against me. Silky, you know. Ripped and bulging? Not so much. But you're sinewy too, and strong in a hidden sort of way, I think. Stringy and taut. You'd have to be if ballet was your hobby." Briefly he glanced up at Lucian. "I'd love to see you dance. For me alone. With no one else around. Just you. Naked."

Lucian swallowed hard, anxious about being able to form words or sounds of any kind past his dry throat. "I… I th-think I could do… that… for you."

Corey flashed a sudden, impish grin. "Oh, I know you can—and you will."

Lucian again played along. "Why? Just because you want it? I do not always obey if and when someone wishes it."

"You want to. For me." Corey's insistence was hot and domineering, and Lucian kept asking himself why he should deny either of them what they wanted. But Corey had already moved on, his gaze utterly focused on Lucian's groin. "When we danced, I figured you could have a pretty pink dick, small and unassuming, or… one of those monstrous cocks, a meaty battering ram that would send any ass into a twitching fit. Would you be circumcised or au naturel? I couldn't decide which of the ideas I preferred."

Having lived with himself and his physicality his whole life, Lucian was intimate with his… well, intimate parts. He was well aware his dangly bits were well above average. No, he didn't have a gargantuan scrotum or a colossal penis. But they weren't on the Lilliputian size scale either.

Corey seemed pleased with what he discovered. His fingers hovered above Lucian's red-golden hairs, as if itching to touch. Lucian was hard, and his cut, pink-hued dick jutted upward like the proud prow of a ship, ready and willing to wage war—or plunge into asses, like treasure troves. His hairless sac was a shade darker, at the moment drawn tight, hot and heavy, also ample and full, prepared for lovemaking.

Corey inhaled deeply, and Lucian could have sworn he felt the man's nose tickle his pubic bone, shifting the fine hairs about. "Mmm, musky. And sweet too. Guess you were right. The fruity diet, I mean. I wonder if you taste as delicious…."

Lucian's cock reached the point of imminent explosion, either on top or at the seams, whichever came first, but he tried to maintain control. "Delectable treat, that's me."

Corey pulled back a bit, frowning now, serious. "What does cum normally smell like?"

"Bleach."

Corey's eyebrows shot up. "Really?"

"A lot of people would describe the odor as resembling bleach, chlorine, or even chalk, and so would I. Genes, diet, and health are all factors, affecting the overall scent and taste."

Corey seemed baffled still, but at least he nodded. "I remember you saying that. Meat is bad. Fruit is good."

"Pineapples are the best for both odor and taste, as are fresh melons, celery, cinnamon, and plain old water. But it takes a steady diet of them, not just a cursory bite prior to sex."

"No easy remedies or quick fixes, then."

"Does that surprise you?" Lucian teased.

"No." Corey chuckled, but then his smile vanished. "I'm not sure I want anything that tastes like bleach in my mouth, though. Or even on my skin." He grimaced. "No, scratch that. I'm sure I don't want it."

Lucian recalled Corey's overthinking when it came to physicality, his hang-ups and anxieties about things such as nose hairs or unclean teeth, and so on. "When you masturbate, have you ever tasted your own cum?"

To Lucian's surprise, Corey's face reddened in an instant, and he rubbed the back of his neck with a look of complete discomfort on his handsome features. "Once."

Lucian was bubbling with questions, but he reined in the curiosity threatening to consume him. "Once?" Since any other form of question could have been seen by Corey as intruding, Lucian thought some repetition would help and encourage further exposures.

"Yeah. After... you know, when I told you I'd gotten off after a shower."

"Oh, yes, of course." Lucian had to bite on his lower lip to stop himself from asking more intimate queries—and from smiling at his companion's success in the sexual field.

Corey's eyes glazed over a bit as he lost himself in the memory. "Can't remember the smell as much as the taste, which was salty and bitter but also sweeter than I had imagined."

"You mean precum or cum?" Corey's gaze was baffled, so Lucian continued, "Was this tasting before you climaxed or after?"

"Before."

Lucian smiled, understanding. "Precome can taste sweeter than cum. It is usually mellower and more sugary. The two liquids are different in many ways, such as consistency and amount. Precum is thinner than cum, which is more, um, substantive, and stickier and stringier. Some men do not produce much precum at all, and it is also translucent while cum is creamier and thicker in texture and more ample in volume."

Corey chuckled. "Wow. You're like a… a spunk specialist."

Lucian felt his cheeks flush with heat, a mix of pride and mild embarrassment. "Thank you. Years of sampling from the finest specimens." He winked, hoping to convey the levity of his practices without seeming like, well, a slut. Meaning every word, he quickly added, "I would wager yours would blow my taste buds out of this world."

Corey's eyes flashed like steel swords in sunlight, hard and piercing. "I don't taste as sweet as you, I'm sure." He wasn't smiling anymore but seemed angry for some reason, only a tough exterior showing.

"Every man has a unique taste. Their mouth, skin, sweat, penis, semen. For every taste there is someone who will love it."

Corey frowned, but his features softened a bit. "You really believe that?"

Lucian smiled. "I do not need to believe it because I know it to be true."

"Have you ever met a man whose taste… repulsed you?"

Lucian grimaced, unable to prevent the tell. "Several. The worst, however, was a rich, powerful businessman, Richard, who had terrible habits, and they all affected his taste and smell. He was a chain-smoker, a meat-eater, a caffeine-addict, and he had an unfortunate propensity for disguising his lack of shower time with loads of expensive cologne."

Corey shared Lucian's cringe. "That doesn't sound good."

Lucian snorted. "Sound, smell, or taste. Not good at all." But he remembered the man very well, and sympathy flooded him. "But not all of it was his fault. He came from a family where a tyrannical father figure demanded his sons be real men, strong and successful. And real men ate meat, smoked like chimneys, drank their coffee black—none of that fruity tea for men—and would be known for their pungent, masculine scent. Instilling horrible values in children is hardly a rarity in any part of the world."

Lucian looked away, recalling vividly the shame and embarrassment Richard had felt about not being able to find a life partner. Richard had come to accept his homosexuality late in life, in his forties, and he had suffered from clinical depression when he compared himself to other gay men. The loneliness, sorrow, and pain had consumed him and brought him to the brink of suicide. Lucian had a difficult time convincing Richard it wasn't too late for him to change and become the man he wished to be.

"You helped him?" Corey asked carefully, peering up at Lucian.

"An ongoing process." Lucian wasn't trying to be evasive, only honest.

Corey nodded, solemn. "I'm sure you can help him overcome his issues."

Lucian beamed at the compliment, warmth spreading from his heart throughout his body. "Thank you." When Corey smiled in response, Lucian brought them back on topic by saying, "When we met, you told me of the things you worry about when thinking about sex, like nose hairs, bad breath, and so on. Corey, I want you to take a good look at me. Observe my physical qualities, and ask yourself if they invoke similar reactions in you, like the ones you mentioned. Look at me. Is my skin greasy or smelly? Do my nose hairs protrude unattractively? Do I have something between my teeth? Is my face asymmetrical or ugly in your opinion? Are my eyes beady? Tell me, Corey. What about me turns you off? Describe to me how you feel."

For a nerve-wracking moment, Corey did nothing but stare up at Lucian, who began to squirm under the relentless scrutiny. Finally he said blankly, "That's just it, Lu. All my life I've had those kinds of thoughts about everyone I see and meet. Everyone but you." Lucian gulped, shocked, and his eyes widened as breath caught in his throat. "When I look at you... I feel... good."

Lucian blinked hard, attempting to rationalize how Corey could seem so levelheaded, determined, and certain about what he was saying. Lucian had expected the man would require time and space to come to *that* conclusion. According to Corey, Lucian was an anomaly, a sexual fantasy come to life.

And Corey had called him by a nickname! With *that* particular nickname, the one he had sworn no one but Blake would ever use, a memory of despicable hate and violence. And yet... he didn't have the heart to tell Corey to never use it again. Probably because Lucian knew it had come from Corey's heart. And that made all the difference.

Lucian found it hard to keep it together when everything was moving so fast. He was off balance, and had no idea how to regain equilibrium within himself and between the two of them.

But before Lucian managed to master himself, Corey said, "I can hear your big brain spinning from down here." He smirked, adding humor to a situation gone serious. "Don't panic or get your panties in a twist. Your very pretty panties...."

Lucian harrumphed. "They are boxer briefs, you fiend. For men!"

Corey shrugged with a grin, obviously intended to provoke. "If you say so."

"I do say so!"

Corey chuckled low, seductively. "Anyway...." He licked his lips with a hungry look on his face, his gaze directed at Lucian's cock. "How long can you keep that up? Your hard-on?"

Lucian swallowed. "I can sustain an erection for quite a while, in truth. Edging is one of the many methods I employ." He had to close his eyes to keep control when the sensation of Corey's hot breath fanned on his most sensitive skin. "However... I believe I have to climax soon. I am on the edge."

Corey looked up, part empathetic, part devilish. "You gonna jerk off for me?" Was it Lucian's imagination that the man's voice had dropped to husky and wicked? "Or would you like me to...." His voice trailed off, leaving the blowjob unspoken. A hint of apprehension colored Corey's expression. "With your diet you must taste... sweet as sugar."

Lucian shivered at the notion of Corey's lips wrapped around his cockhead, sucking hard. He dispelled the image with great difficulty. "No. Not tonight."

Corey must have noted the crack in Lucian's voice because while his eyes narrowed at being rejected, he quickly schooled his features to display only passion. "You don't want me to...?"

Lucian sputtered. "You know that is not true!" With a couple of calming breaths, he took his tone down a notch. "What I mean is—"

"So, as nice as this scenting intimacy is, touch and taste are for our next session?" For Corey's benefit Lucian nodded emphatically. "Why not right here, right now?" Corey insisted.

Lucian searched for a way to say what was on his mind, which was troublesome since his mind was muddled with lust. "I... I have preparations to make. Or did you think all that you have experienced here at Boudoir magically appeared by me simply waving a hand and wishing for them?"

"Preparations...." Corey repeated, and his skepticism and sarcasm could not have been more evident.

"Yes." Lucian sighed in relief. Perhaps Corey understood. "There is still so much for you to see and—"

"No, Lucian. No." Without warning Corey stood up and stared Lucian down, his gray eyes intense and unyielding. "I don't want to experience anything more with men who aren't you. So you're going to get dressed again, and then we're going somewhere more private and intimate and continue our touch and taste lessons there. With *you* as my sole test object."

Being an object of desire was no novelty for Lucian. But being that for a man like Corey Paige who, despite his inexperience, knew what he wanted, was for Lucian a turn-on of epic proportions. Corey had clearly formed an emotional bond with Lucian, and now he was exercising that realization. Corey had power over Lucian as Lucian was supposed to aid Corey to confront his sexual demons.

I must help him. No, I must run away as fast as I can. No, I cannot leave him now. No, I must run and hide, or he will....

Lucian had no words and no thoughts, only frantic, sporadic emotions flickering in his hazy mind. All he could do was stare back, dumbstruck at this act of dominance and power play that demonstrated a determination he had never encountered in a virgin before.

I am in so much trouble.

CHAPTER 21

GOD, LUCIAN was a master at charm and evasion. Corey gritted his teeth as he paced the length of his living room back home in his apartment.

Somehow, even after Corey made his ultimate demand of private intimacy with just the two of them in a room somewhere, Lucian had managed to convince Corey that after their scent session, they needed a break before plunging headlong into the next phase of their mentor-novice relationship. How Lucian had won Corey over to his point of view was still a mystery.

But Corey's frustration wasn't born of Lucian's reticence alone. In accordance with his mentor's advice, Corey had tried his best to masturbate to fantasies of other men and even women, to some extent. Well, that had failed spectacularly! As soon as he got his fist around his half-hard dick and brought images of women and other men to mind, his erection disappeared the way of the dodo.

At the moment Corey was hopping mad because after the last session a week ago, he now got a boner at the oddest hours. His cock sprung up in line at Starbucks for coffee, at a restaurant waiting for his dinner, and at his favorite bakery to satisfy his incessant sweet tooth with some cream puffs. In point of fact, he got a raging hard-on at the most inopportune times imaginable.

The worst thing was that at every one of those moments his mind had been overcome with flashes of his sessions with Lucian. And Corey was super *extra* mad because he wasn't hard thanks to Lucian's teachings but because of the man himself. That sure didn't bode well for Corey's chances of getting an erection whenever he wanted to and with *whomever* he wished.

No. It had to be Lucian or no one. Always Lucian.

Corey shook his head, furious at every complication he had ever faced when it came to his sexuality. "How the hell does he make me want him so fucking much…?"

Thankfully his anger dissipated slightly when a firm knock on his door distracted him.

Corey hurried to the door and yanked it open, hoping to see Lucian so he could vent all his pent-up rage—and then to grab the guy, slam him against the wall, and ravage his mouth for an hour before pinning him to the floor, stuffing him full of cock, and pounding into him till Lucian begged to come…. And that was just for starters.

Unfortunately for him, the visitor was his father.

Since Corey promised Lucian he would speak with his father, Corey grudgingly let his fury subside. "Dad. Come in." He stepped aside, and Randolph walked past him silently, as usual taking a look around him, though he had seen Corey's place many times. Corey had no idea what the man expected to find, but he didn't care either. "What brings you here, Dad?"

Corey's laconic tone made Randolph frown. "Do I need a reason to visit my son?"

Corey resisted the urge to roll his eyes, but he did cross his arms over his chest. "You usually do, yeah. You never just *pop by*." He used air quotes for the last two words.

Randolph coughed and straightened up, apparently gathering his thoughts. He clutched his business suit jacket in his arms like a soft shield, which was strange since Corey didn't think his father had ever needed a defense against anything.

"Very well. I'm here to ask about your continued, um, relationship with Lucian Allard."

Corey bristled, his jaw tightening in anger. "What about it?"

"You must be aware of his notorious reputation in regards to—"

"Yeah, fully aware. That's why I hang out with him."

Randolph's face reddened slightly. "Do you care so little for your self-image that you would socialize with—"

"With who, Dad?" Corey was on the edge of blowout, fury fueling him. "Someone of questionable lifestyle? Or should I be more low-brow and call him riffraff or trash?"

Randolph growled and in a frenzied act tossed his jacket onto the couch. "Why do you insist on throwing away every advantage in life your mother and I have tried to provide for you? Surely there are better people you can—"

"Better! What would you know about that? What would you know about anything, least of all me?" Corey was so angry about his father's meddling he was shaking like a leaf, his fists trembling at his sides. "Do you have any idea what my life is like?"

"Then tell me, and I—" Randolph tried to cut in, his voice low and commanding.

But Corey was deaf to his father's authority. "Did you know that thanks to Lucian I had my first ever true orgasm that wasn't an unsatisfying, automatic, mechanical ridding of morning wood? My first sexual experience with another human being at the age of thirty-three? No, you didn't because you're too busy passing judgment on things that have nothing to do with you. This is *my* fucking life! How dare you pass judgment on me? Or on Lucian, who is a complete stranger to you? Do you have the slightest notion of what life has been like for me, not feeling a damn thing for anyone? Not wanting, not feeling, not needing? For twenty years, Dad! Try to get it through your thick skull that all I want is what you and Mom take for granted with each other. Closeness, intimacy, relationships, a future together with someone special, a loved one. And you frown upon and disapprove of me for seeking help from a professional? How dare you be so hypocritical? You think I was blind, deaf, and dumb as a kid? You think I didn't notice you and Mom playing your stupid little games with men *and* women at your parties? You really believe after all this time I don't have a clue about your Park Avenue mistress, or Mom's lovers in Milan and Monte Carlo? God, Dad, you must think I'm a complete fucking idiot!" His tirade ended with him breathless and shaking, unable to stop because fury flowed through his veins like liquid fire, burning him up. "This is my life, my choices, my need for help. And if you can't grant me that freedom, then fuck you!"

Corey ended his rant as he tried to regain control over his emotions and his physical responses. He longed to sink into cool, calming waters, but he also yearned to rip something, or someone, into shreds, beat and hit and pulverize until his apartment would be in utter shambles. He doubted he had ever felt this enraged.

Randolph only stared, jaw hanging open, seemingly dumbstruck. Finally, after a long while, he began blinking, and his throat worked convulsively. Then he let out a ragged breath, and his shoulders slumped.

When he spoke his voice was hoarse and shaky. "Corey, I… I had no idea you…." He rubbed his forehead where sweat was beading, and a muffled curse escaped him. "Fuck, I need a drink." He all but ran to the open liquor cabinet, grabbed a glass with a clink, and poured it full of whiskey, neat, and then tossed it back with one swallow and a grimace. Then he filled the glass again but didn't drink this time. He held the glass and stared at the wall, his eyes glazed as though he looked right through it.

Corey began to worry he had gone too far, said too much, crossed a line. But he clenched his teeth, refusing to give in to the impulse to speak first. The ball was in his father's court.

When Randolph took another sip, his hand trembled. With an exhale, he spoke quietly, "I, uh... I had a feeling you'd seen things you shouldn't have when you were a boy. Things your mother and I weren't all that, um... discreet about." He swiped the back of his hand over his upper lip, exuding nervousness. "But you have to understand all that... not only is it in the past, but...." He groaned painfully, hanging his head. "God, how I regret those times. When I was your age, Corey, I made so many bad decisions and acted so foolishly, as though consequences happened to other people, not to me, not to your mother." He lifted his head to stare at Corey, an achy, pleading look in his eyes, which were glistening with moisture. "I wanted to spare you those humiliating experiences. I desperately needed you to avoid making the same mistakes I did." He shook his head, angry at himself. "I was young and rich and popular, and I thought those days would last forever. I was so stupid. Orgies, booze, drugs, run-ins with the law.... I never wanted you exposed to that kind of life, so I... I may have been awfully hard on you."

It was Corey's turn to stare, dumbfounded. His father had never shown weakness in front of him before. And falling apart emotionally certainly classified. Corey stared at the surreal tableau, feeling insane himself.

"But, Dad... my relationship with Lucian is nothing like that. He's mentoring me. He has a program to help people with sexual problems. My therapist recommended him to me. I didn't just go to some damn night club and hook up with him."

That clearly wasn't the explanation Randolph had been waiting for because his eyes widened impossibly large, and an odd gurgling sound emanated from him. "Your therapist...? A program...? But I thought...."

Corey snorted. "I know what you thought. That Lucian's some kind of sexual deviant taking advantage of me. Well, he's not. In fact, if anything, I'm using him. He is willing to do anything to help me solve this problem I have. He's selfless and good and understanding, and I need him, Dad. You have no right to tell me what to do or how to conduct my affairs. And even if this thing between me and Lucian became something else, something more, it still wouldn't—"

"Wait. Are you saying you're... gay...?" Randolph might have cut in, but it was the quiet subdued tone that had Corey falling silent.

Corey sighed. "Fuck, I don't know! All I know is he makes me feel, Dad. For the past twenty years, I've waited to feel something, anything, for anyone, male or female. But it's all been for nothing. No one feels real to me, substantial, or then too much so, drowning me in their physical... stuff. Lucian.... He helps me, Dad. I need this."

Randolph nodded a few times frantically before setting his untouched whiskey glass down. "Corey, Son.... All right, fine, yes, of course. I... I may not understand exactly what it is you do with Allard, but... you're right. I don't know the truth of your relationship, so I shouldn't butt in." His look grew steadier as his voice grew stronger. "I do want you to know, however, that if you are gay... that's fine. If you're straight, that's fine too." He let out a mirthless chuckle. "God knows I've done things in my time. I can't condemn you for... well, any of it. I just want you to be careful, Son, okay? That's all. Careful."

Corey managed a ghost of a smile. "I am, Dad. Besides, Lucian and I, we're *not* having sex. Yeah, he is teaching me about sex. But him and me? We haven't done anything."

Randolph's eyes flashed, much like Corey's did at times. "Yet?"

Corey shrugged. "I don't know. Maybe. Maybe not. He's a... a tough nut to crack, hard to get a handle on, difficult to decipher." Repetitive as he was, answers weren't falling down from the sky as he beckoned them.

"But you, um... like him?" Randolph sounded hesitant but curious too. For that Corey had no answer to offer, for either of them. Randolph seemed to sense this because he nodded. "All in good time, eh?" He appeared pensive for a moment, mulling things over. "How about a game of racquetball with your old man tomorrow at the club?" Randolph suggested, obviously having shifted into his placating mode.

Corey burst into hapless giggles, clearly confusing his father further. "Sorry. It's not you, I swear. It's just something Lucian said about racquetball."

Randolph appeared taken aback by the remark. "You talk about sports?"

Corey smirked. "No, not really."

Surprisingly Randolph reddened a bit upon hearing that, and he rubbed the back of his neck nervously. "It seems you two have become quite close in a short amount of time."

"Dad...," Corey warned, his tone low. While this new bonding moment with his father was nice, Corey wasn't about to suffer another interference when he didn't need it.

Randolph bowed his head a bit in a show of acquiescence. He sighed deeply, turned on his heels, ambled to the couch, and sat down heavily.

After he tossed back the rest of his drink and put the glass down on the coffee table, he swiped his hands over his face, murmuring something. "You have to understand, Son, that this is all new to me. New news. I never thought you'd be gay, let alone, um, inhibited."

Sauntering over to the opposite couch and sitting down more gingerly, Corey did not want to get mad at his father anymore. "The clinical term is frigid," he said stiffly.

Randolph shot a sharp look at Corey, shocked. For once, he was speechless, opening and closing his mouth like a fish on dry land. Corey had never seen him like that, completely lost.

"Lucian doesn't think I am frigid, though," Corey added to give his father some peace of mind.

As Corey expected, Randolph's look changed from stunned to hopeful. Corey had a feeling his dad's opinion about Lucian had just done a one-eighty. "Really? And that is the, uh... problem you two are working on?" Corey nodded, offering no more details, mostly because he was unsure of them himself. Randolph frowned. "What about your... personal feelings for him? Seems to me that's a can of worms about to explode in your face. Pardon the mixed metaphors."

Dismayed as he was, Corey could not deny his father's words were wise. Any teacher-student, mentor-client, or healer-patient relationship, where hierarchies and authority figures came into play, demanded objectivity, neutrality, and detachment. Corey was well aware he was treading on thin ice. But... his body craved Lucian something fierce. How could he forbid his sex-starved self this man who ignited him like a spark in a dormant volcano?

"I do like him," Corey admitted grudgingly. "I think he likes me. I mean, he's attracted to me. Of that I'm sure."

"Do these feelings hamper your professional relationship with him?" Randolph spoke warily. "Watch your step, Son. If you take the wrong path, you won't get the help you seek, just more complications."

"You're a master of stating the obvious, Dad." Corey rolled his eyes and snorted. "I'm not a kid. I may be pure as the driven snow sexually, but I'm not an idiot."

Randolph swallowed hard, his skin pale, a tick in his jaw. "You mean, you're a…."

"A virgin? Yup. How's that for a curve ball?"

As ill as Randolph appeared, he managed to nod understandingly. "There're many kinds of inexperience. When I met your mother, I knew nothing about true love. I took it for lust. Damn, did she show me how wrong I was." A wistful expression softened Randolph's stark features, and Corey was mesmerized by a sight relatively new to him. "Prudence was unlike any woman I had ever met, self-reliant and independent, whip-smart and vocal with her opinions, beautiful and graceful. Marrying her was the best decision I've ever made in my entire life."

Corey was baffled to hear that, considering what he knew about their separate lives. "But you fu—sleep with other people." Though he realized he should react with discomfort to the topic of his parents' sex life, Corey counted himself lucky Lucian had shown him there was no topic to feel squeamish about.

Randolph shook his head, as if infuriated but not quite there. "It's complicated."

"You love her still, don't you?" Corey was briefly puzzled at the crack in his voice that sounded an awful lot like a child on the verge of tears. What the cause was for this emotional and even childish reaction, he refused to ponder further.

"Oh, yes." Randolph looked and sounded adamant, absolutely confident and mellow somehow, warmer and softer. "Your mother is the love of my life. I will never leave her." He took on a more serious tone. "But Pru and I are both consenting adults, and we figured out a long time ago that we are not monogamous by nature or personality. Instead of divorcing, which neither of us wanted then or now, we made an agreement to see other people. Spice of life. We tell each other everything, full disclosure and total honesty. She doesn't love her two lovers, and I feel no such thing for my mistress in the city either. Our other affairs have no effect on my marriage with your mother."

"You have an open relationship. I get it." To Corey that idea tasted bitter, and the fact that his parents were engaged in such an entanglement only made it more undesirable. But why would he think so negatively? Corey had never been in love, never longed for the touch of one person alone, never had to choose between love and lust, never had to consider his faithfulness or fidelity in practice.

Randolph shrugged, but the dark glint in his eyes, as gray as Corey's, told a different story. "Unconventional attachments seem to be all the rage these days. But you must understand I would have given your mother anything—the sun, the moon, and all the stars in the sky. When she suggested that we—"

"That was Mom's idea?" Corey couldn't believe what he was hearing. He had always assumed Randolph had been the one to insist on affairs outside the marriage bed. This news forced him to look at his family under a new, harsher light, and frayed edges began to show in the previously perfect family portrait.

Randolph smiled affectionately. "It was Pru's suggestion, yes, but we both agreed. She values her freedom while also valuing her love for me. I have no doubt, not a single doubt in my mind, that if push came to shove she would choose me. As is, I cannot and will not limit or control her freedom in any way. If I yanked the rope and tied her to me, I'd be the one ending up hanged."

"You afraid you'll lose her if you push the issue?" Corey had to press, had to know how tenuous his parents' marriage was. Which was odd, because he wasn't a child anymore. He was a grown man, responsible for his own choices and basically his own life. It shouldn't matter to him if Randolph and Prudence decided to conclude their relationship of thirty-seven years and file for divorce. But... for some reason it mattered a whole hell of a lot.

"We were teenagers when we got married. Well, she was. Nineteen, you know." The reminiscence gave Randolph a warm, mature, and even tender look that Corey really liked. "I was barely twenty myself. But I had been around the block a few times, I can tell you. So had she. Pru knew who she was, what she wanted, and how to get it. Us falling in love didn't change that part of her personality."

Nodding, Corey recalled his childhood days when his parents had always seemed so loving around one another, playful and kind, and these memories filled him with a radiant glow. Then Corey grew up and saw another side of their love, and it had confused, frightened, and even angered him for a long time. Now, to hear Randolph and Prudence still loved and cared for each other was music to Corey's childlike ears.

"I came from a middle-class family. Lower middle class, to be exact," Randolph said, seemingly oblivious to Corey and his musings. "Pru, however, she was rich, beautiful, popular, and from luxury all the way. But... she rebelled, attending protests for the environment or abortion rights instead of cocktail parties and fundraisers." Randolph chuckled ironically. "In that, you remind me of her. The rebel *with* a cause."

Hearing the compliment felt awesome, and Corey smiled, happier than he had been in a long time. He had wondered at times if he resembled either of his parents. To get a sense of his heritage in this manner was heartwarming.

Corey was also well aware he was privileged to be able to live the way he did, having gotten a first class education from start to finish, living in a huge apartment in a skyscraper, and being able to afford anything his heart desired. He was indeed fortunate in many ways despite his sexual difficulties.

"My mom and dad worked all their lives. They couldn't afford to retire until I made my first million with the company." Randolph frowned as he spoke, his expression shutting down.

Randolph had established an East Coast newspaper, *The New York Standard*, and now it was on par with the *New York Times* and *Financial Times*. That was how he had worked his way out of the middle class and into the upper crust, financially and socially, becoming a self-made success. His educational background as a journalist and a financier helped him lay groundwork for his future endeavor, which was to build a newspaper and communications empire that now spread from coast to coast, and even farther online.

But Randolph's father, Robert, worked first as an apprentice to a clockmaker and then as an accountant most of his professional life, while his mother, Bonnie, had been a court clerk before she became a homemaker. Financially they had struggled at times but managed to keep their heads above water. Randolph's self-made success had been, according to them, their greatest achievement, and Randolph's marriage to an heiress, Prudence, had been a stroke of luck. The alliance had granted the Paige family access to the highest rungs of society. Prudence's family, the Winthrops, had never let Randolph forget the debt they considered he owed them. The Winthrops were related (distantly) to the Astors and the Vanderbilts, who were New York aristocracy. Thankfully the Paiges didn't have many dealings with those sides of the family tree.

Corey knew their family history, and it just made him more thankful for everything he had in life. To know that going back a mere two generations, his kin had been a step above working class was a humbling experience. It kept Corey grounded at times when vast amounts of money and other resources were easily at his reach, and his morals and values were at the mercy of temptation.

The wise words of Gabriel Garcia Márquez echoed in his ears: "No, not rich. I am a poor man with money, which is not the same thing." Corey was glad his roots came from hardship, struggle to survive, and fighting for basic subsistence. This legacy had taught him the true value of money as a means to an end, not the end itself.

"Are you thinking about retiring, Dad? You're still young."

Randolph chuckled. "Young? Perhaps young at heart. I am fifty-seven after all, so not a spring chicken. Sometimes I think about it, I admit it, not having the job as a reason to get up in the morning. But then I shake off those ridiculous thoughts and get going. That's the Paige way." He gazed at Corey knowingly. "Just like you chose to find someone to help you with your problem instead of sitting on your ass, waiting for everything to get worse."

Corey laughed, briefly considering how long it had been since he had shared a laugh with his father. Not since childhood, surely. "Nope, Paiges aren't quitters."

"Ask me about retirement in, oh, say ten years from now." Randolph had a gleam in his eyes that Corey recalled seeing when he was a teenager. At some point at around thirteen years of age, Corey lost touch with his father. Not in the physical proximity sense. But in the relating and understanding and empathy department. It was as if they spoke two different languages on the rare occasions they talked. This right here, this was nice, Corey thought.

But he still had other concerns to tackle. "Do you think Mom will feel the same way? About me maybe being gay? About me and Lucian?"

Randolph scoffed with a grin. "When has your mother ever been judgmental about anything? She'll be fine. In fact, she might insist on meeting Allard herself—and then start planning for a June wedding."

"Jesus Christ, Dad!" Corey exclaimed. "Are you insane? It's not like that between him and me." But did he wish it to be? Was the only reason Lucian occupied Corey's every waking and dreaming thought that Corey was so hot for the guy? Corey had to shake his head to discard the madness plaguing him, the kinds of wants and needs he had never, ever considered before. His sole focus had been to feel, to get close, to fall in lust. But marriage, or any kind of union, had not once entered his mind—until now.

Randolph chuckled. "Pru will undoubtedly take one look at the situation and deem you to have chosen the right course of action. Finding help. Liking someone. And getting laid."

"Dad!" Corey tried not to shudder but couldn't prevent it. Despite all they'd shared in the past hour, he still felt uncomfortable with the topic of his sex life—or lack thereof.

"Am I grossing you out, Son? So sorry." But Randolph sure didn't *seem* sorry. In fact, his expression was whimsical. And whimsical Randolph was *not*.

"You think maybe we should've cleared the air a long time ago, Dad?" Corey didn't want to sound bitter, but he did, and he hated it. The past was the past. Those days would never repeat for do-overs, so what was the point of carrying around anger, fear, doubt, or regret?

Solemnly, Randolph nodded, his gaze dropping to the drink on the coffee table. "I am an old man, set in my ways. I made mistakes in my youth, and the shadows of those regrets cast upon you. They shouldn't have. I'm sorry."

Corey swallowed hard, his throat constricting with a lump of emotional baggage. "Me too. But, Dad? For the record, you're not that old."

"Thanks. It's funny, but I've never been the jump-to-conclusions type," Randolph said pensively. "I guess only you got the brunt of that personality quirk. I am your father, after all, and I thought I saw something to get concerned about, so I acted... poorly."

"That's one way of putting it," Corey remarked dryly. Before Randolph could speak, Corey got there first. "But, you know, this isn't all your fault. Communication is a two-way street. I could've opened up a dialogue with you myself at any point in time."

"Why didn't you?" Randolph didn't sound accusing but sad. Perhaps he had regrets about his son too.

He shrugged. "I don't know. Guess back when I was a kid, learning about how you and Mom conducted your, um, affairs, I took it personally. Or maybe I was just a typical teenager who overreacted emotionally to every goddamn thing on the planet. I don't know." He stared down at the floor too, like his father, and an odd hollow pressure squeezed his chest. "I was thirteen or fourteen when I kinda felt like you didn't want me around anymore. All you did was work. I barely ever saw you. I guess I kinda lost touch, you know, even though we lived in the same house."

Randolph sighed, a weary echo of the way Corey felt within. "I know I worked too much. Pru told me so many times, chastising me. She told me I was missing it, your childhood and the chances to bond. I always told myself there was plenty of time." He closed his eyes, and for a moment he looked twenty years older, a frail and rueful old man. "By the time I realized how badly I had messed up, you were a grown man, living on your own, doing your own thing. I didn't know how to repair that fracture between us, to bridge that chasm. I was disconnected. So... I did what I thought was the very least I could do, which was to save you from poor decisions, like the ones I had made as a kid, and to protect you from bad influences."

Corey snorted, rolling his eyes. "Like Lucian."

"Yes." Randolph managed a small smile without much humor in it, a pale imitation of the happy gesture. "I should've talked to you first before going over to his place and accusing him of—"

Corey understood why his father had clipped his own words, and righteous indignation stirred inside him once more. "Of being a deviant and a pervert and other disgusting things? Yeah, that was a huge error in judgment on your part. You had better apologize."

Randolph's face reddened in blotches of embarrassment, and he nodded. "Yes. I know that now. I will, Son. I promise."

"Good. 'Cause Lucian has only my best interest at heart." Of that Corey had no doubts, regardless of any attractions simmering between them.

"I hope you know I also did what I did with the best of intentions, as misguided as they were." Randolph wasn't pleading but only stating his stance and hoping Corey understood and forgave.

"Not to mention rude and petty and—"

"Yes, yes. All that." Remarkably, Randolph appeared amused at the reproach, and Corey felt the rift between them closing, if not entirely, then at least quite a bit. "Name the time and place, and I'll apologize to Allard. Now… your mother is coming back from Paris next week. I was hoping we could arrange a family dinner at home. What do you say?"

They did usually come together as a family for formal holiday dinners, such as Easter, Thanksgiving, Christmas, and such. But for no official reason at all? Corey couldn't remember them doing that since… well, not in a long time. This should be interesting.

"Sure, yeah. Why not?" The agreement was easily made. Corey allowed himself to have high hopes for their next familial gathering even though their track record didn't exactly shine with success.

Randolph stood, smoothing the wrinkles out of his pants and straightening his tie. "I hope you settle your, um, relationship with Allard by then. 'Cause if I know your mother, and I do, she'll have a ton of questions. And you'd better have answers, or she'll track the poor guy down and ask *him*."

Corey grimaced, not at the prospect of his parents meeting Lucian, but the three of them meeting before Corey himself knew where he stood with Lucian and what their relationship was like exactly. For now, their arrangement lacked definition because the sexual tension between them was unexpectedly strong and now muddied the waters. Were they mentor and client or good friends with benefits or future lovers in the making?

Corey rose too. "I'll see what I can do. Don't rush me."

Randolph laughed, obviously having caught on to Corey's lack of seriousness. "All in good time." For a second Corey was certain his father was going to hug him. But Randolph only squeezed his shoulder gently and then dropped his hand at his side, a shaky smile lifting one corner of his mouth. "You're a good boy, Corey. I really have nothing to worry about with you. I should try to remember that. For both our sakes."

To say Corey was teary-eyed might have been an exaggeration, but there was a blurry wet veil in his eyes until he blinked it away as they said their good-byes at the door.

Once Randolph was gone, Corey sat down heavily on the couch, exhaled deeply, and let an emptiness fill his mind. He would think about all that had transpired later. For he was sure this would require a lot of inner reflection. Seeing his father in a new light was peculiar and demanded some adjustment. For so many years, Corey had come to accept he just wasn't that close to his father. Now he had to change his thinking, his views, his once firm understanding of his family. He would have to sleep on this. Maybe several nights. He would have to adapt to a new point of view or let the distance between him and his father grow even greater.

He vowed to try and do all the above.

Well... after he spoke with Lucian.

CHAPTER 22

"HEY, LU. Is this a bad time?" Corey's voice sounded sultry smooth on the other end of the line, and Lucian shivered. Thankfully the man was actually across town, so Lucian was safe.

Corey's ability to use nicknames and familiarities with such ease did not help matters.

"No, Mr. Paige. Of course not." Two could play at that game, Lucian thought, with no small amount of amusement.

Corey merely laughed. "Fuck, how formal of you."

"How may I be of assistance?"

"Well, I was thinking…. Before our next session—you know, with the touching and the tasting—I thought we might go out on a date."

Lucian was flummoxed. "A date…?"

"Yeah. I mean, I've never been on one. And isn't that the relationship protocol? Wining and dining, plus a movie or something, before you let me get to first base?" Corey's tone teased in a lighthearted way, and Lucian couldn't help but smile.

"Oh, how I love baseball analogies when it comes to sex." He giggled, unable to stop the bubbling, effervescent sound of pure joy from escaping his chest.

"I got lots more in store just for you," Corey whispered seductively. Lucian blushed. If that was Corey's first attempt at vocal flirting, he had it down in spades. "So, Lu. How about it? A night out on the town with little old me? Not Boudoir, though."

"No. Someplace else." Lucian had to cover the cell phone or risk Corey hearing him sighing like a smitten, swooning teenage girl. "I am wide open to suggestions."

"Geez, Lu. That didn't sound like sexual innuendo at all!" Corey's sarcasm was laced with good humor, and they shared a laugh. "I'll text you with the time and place. If you accept them, all you need to do is show up."

With a silent sigh, Lucian felt light as a feather and couldn't wait for their date. But he felt like needling a bit too, so he asked, "So, Corey... what are you wearing?"

Corey sputtered. "*What?*" Then he cackled almost hysterically. "Hell no! This is *not* that kind of call, okay?"

"Aww, why ever not?" Lucian grinned wickedly even though Corey was unable to see it. "After all, this could be another first for you. And me? Well, I am always ready, willing, and able to expose you to new layers of the sensual world—and yourself within it."

Corey breathed heavily into the phone, be it excitement or nervousness, Lucian didn't know for certain but banked on the former. "A-another t-time, okay...?"

"Can't wait," Lucian whispered seductively, his tone husky.

Corey must have gulped hard because Lucian could have sworn he heard it, and he tucked the revealing tell into his heart. "G-good night, Lu" was all Corey finally said, his voice warm and intimate in a way Lucian loved, plus a bit shaky, as if emotional.

Lucian ended their call on a positive note.

And just like that, Lucian had agreed to his first date with Corey, outside the setting of the mentoring program. To say he had butterflies in his stomach was a vast understatement, and he had to wonder if he was ever going to survive waiting for their date night to arrive.

WHATEVER LUCIAN had expected, having dinner in the comfort and quiet of Corey's own apartment had not been it. Personally, he would not have chosen such an intimate site for a date when they were supposed to be keeping a professional distance. Then again, they were on a date, which sort of countered the whole detachment aspect.

"This place okay with you?" Corey gestured Lucian to enter from the hallway. Lucian heard the hesitance in his voice, the worry the place would be unsuitable for Lucian.

"It is perfect," Lucian assured his host with a smile, stepping into the apartment.

Corey closed the door and beckoned Lucian in farther. "Sorry about the mess."

Lucian quirked an eyebrow as he inspected his surroundings. *What mess?* The whole residence was spotless and immaculate, not a dust bunny nor speck of dirt in sight. "How long have you lived here?"

"Since I finished college, so… I don't know, eleven, twelve years?" Corey vanished in the direction of the kitchen, leaving Lucian to familiarize himself with the flat.

The color palette ruling the spacious living room that spanned the height of two floors was dominated by deep, masculine blacks, browns, and dark blues. Two black leather couches sat opposite each other on either side of a dark wooden and glass coffee table. The gray, deliberately texturally unrefined walls were exposed, save for a couple of watercolor landscapes of skies, seas, and mountains, while the floors were smooth parquet. The floor-to-ceiling windows undoubtedly lit up the room in the day, and now, in the evening, revealed an impressive view of dark sky fronted by the Manhattan skyline, filled with tall, dark buildings glimmering with dots of lights. A whitewashed electric fireplace stood tall and imposing between the living room and the kitchen, and on both sides grew braided ficus and bamboo palm trees, adding a flash of green to the otherwise dark, ultramodern interior with strict geometrical lines and lack of clutter.

Lucian quite liked the minimalist, masculine decor, and that the living room and the kitchen were connected by an open floor plan, with the fireplace as the only partition. "Who designed the decor, if I may ask?"

Corey laughed in the kitchen, out of Lucian's line of sight. "Why do you automatically assume it wasn't me?"

Lucian liked playful, confident Corey a lot. "Was it?"

"Now I'm not telling." Smiling, Corey walked past the fireplace toward Lucian. "Care for a drink? I've got pretty much everything. I keep my liquor cabinet well stocked."

Lucian chuckled, appreciating the subtle flirting that went with a first date. "What? No wine room? Many apartments like these have both chilled and room temperature wine rooms."

Corey shook his head. "I don't go *that* far."

"I'll have a champagne cocktail, if you can make one." Lucian offered the challenge with a carefree attitude, hoping Corey would not be offended by the request. He decided to add a teasing twist as an alternative. "Or a glass of white wine. 2008 Domaine Leflaive Batard Montrachet Grand Cru, perhaps?"

Corey laughed. "At six thousand dollars a bottle, it's a bit out of my price range for a simple bottle of white, I'm afraid. Plus I'm not a fan of Chardonnay." He glanced at the open liquor cabinet with a discerning eye and a crooked grin. "How about 2008 Littorai Thieriot?"

"I hear it is excellent," Lucian complimented his host's choice, which was in fact better in taste and aroma than the other more expensive option anyway. Yet, he pretended he'd never had it before, for Corey's sake. "Thank you, I'd love a glass."

Corey turned around to pour the desired liquid into a wine glass. "I'll make champagne cocktails for your next visit."

Lucian beamed, realizing he really liked the idea of a return visit to Corey's sanctum sanctorum. "My palate thanks you in advance." He graciously took the offered glass.

As he did so, he had an opportunity to discreetly check out his host while Corey poured himself a glass of spring water. For tonight, Corey had dressed the same way as during his first visit with Lucian, a handsome casual. Blue jeans that looked like they were painted on, a slim-fit Henley shirt of similar shade with the long sleeves rolled up to the elbows, and nothing more. No socks, no shoes, no tie. As inexperienced as he was, Corey epitomized a laid-back dater, and Lucian was smitten, which probably wasn't all that wise.

"So...." Corey swayed back and forth on his heels, trying to look nonchalant. "What does a person do on a date exactly?"

Lucian smiled and nodded toward the couch. "Why don't we start by making ourselves comfortable?" Setting the example, he sat down on the plush leather cushion, leaned back, relaxed, and crossed his legs. "Like this."

Corey chuckled and joined him, surprisingly on the same couch, though keeping his distance. "Okay, that's done. What's next? Making out on the couch? I hear that's all the rage, among teenagers at least."

Lucian giggled. "How about a little conversation? After all, small talk is a vital social skill in dating and several other social situations."

"Waiting for that normalcy to kick in?" Corey joked but bowed in acceptance. Then his gaze swept over Lucian, intrigue sparking in his eyes. "You're certainly wearing... white today."

Lucian looked down at himself. He wore white, form-fitting chinos, a crisp white dress shirt, a tight white vest, and a matching natural white silk tie, plus white leather brogue shoes. For him, this was casual wear.

"Do you approve?" he asked coyly. White was his favorite color, at least when it came to fashion.

Corey chuckled, his cheeks pinking a bit. "I like." Then his gaze locked with Lucian's. "What else should we talk about on our date, other than sharing our appreciation for each other's attire?" Though he appeared pleasantly blasé, Lucian doubted the man felt as at ease as he seemed. After all, this was Corey's first date. Well, his first real date, outside the confines of Boudoir.

"There is no strict protocol when it comes to date topics," Lucian replied, grinning as he teased gently. "The usual, however, includes work, hobbies, family, friends, fun and games, that sort of thing. Not exes, though, as that particular subject is reserved for a later date, if ever."

"I really don't see what possible use there could be for you to know trivialities about me, like whether I'm a fan of the Yankees or the Mets. Oh, and it's the Yankees, by the way." After a wink Corey digested the rest of the news with a pensive look. "Anyway, we've covered a lot of those, haven't we? For me, at least. You know a lot more about me than I do about you."

"Is there something you would like to know? Please, ask away."

Corey frowned, hesitant. "Are you okay with this? Us being on a date? I mean, you are my sex mentor too. Is this, um... appropriate?"

Lucian had asked himself the same question. His brow furrowed as he contemplated the right reply. "It's complicated. But I suppose a lot of it depends on what you perceive to be the goal of tonight's... activities."

Corey chuckled, shaking his head in amusement. "God, I fucking love the way you talk. All formal and shit."

Lucian blushed. "Was that a compliment? If so, then thank you."

"The goal for tonight? I don't know." Corey shrugged. "Feeling normal, being alone with you, liking your company, learning how to do this whole dating thing."

"I think we can do that." Corey smiled in that oddly grateful way he did sometimes, and the gesture had Lucian preening but made him doubtful too. "In the spirit of dating, I've been wondering what it is that you do to get your mind off your sexual problems. Most people, when trying to dispel worries and concerns, they focus on their work or hobbies, sometimes to a grueling extent."

Corey rolled his eyes and blew out a breath. "Wow. You sure take the casual out of casual dating. Just dive right in the deep end." Lucian tried to cut in, but Corey waved him silent. "I didn't mean it badly. I like how you don't beat around the bush. Your directness is a positive thing, I swear."

Lucian's cheeks flushed with heat, and he ducked his head, murmuring a thank you.

"Anyway," Corey went on, probably for Lucian's benefit. "I have been working out at the gym a lot lately. Lifting weights, running the treadmill, doing push-ups—they blank out my mind pretty effectively."

"You like going to the gym?"

"Yeah. Plus, I've got my own gym in the back of the apartment." Suddenly he grinned wickedly. "Why? Are you gonna tell me how gay it is to like pumping iron so much?"

Lucian burst into hapless giggles. "Goodness, no! But I appreciate the inference. Not to mention how amazing you look as a result of your daily regimen."

Corey let out a self-conscious chuckle, blushing. "Thanks. I like the way you look too. Especially in all white."

"Must be my feminine bridal tendencies rising to the surface." They both laughed. "So, Corey. What do you do for fun?"

"I read. It's both relaxing and thought provoking. I like to watch action flicks, thrillers, that sort of thing. Plus, I work out, as you know." He got a faraway look in his eyes. "When I was younger, late teens and early twenties, to distract myself from my sexual problems, I did a lot of crazy shit. I was something of an adrenaline junkie. I sought the thrill, you see. The edge. If people couldn't make me feel, then perhaps exciting situations could. So to provoke reactions I tried rock climbing, deep-sea diving, skydiving, bungee jumping, snowboarding, racecar driving, motocross, whitewater kayaking, all that and more. There was a tiny, *really* tiny wish somewhere in the back of my mind that I might become an adventure guide or something like that."

Staring back in surprise, Lucian wasn't sure how to adjust to what he was hearing. To know how cavalier and careless Corey had been with his life and safety in order to feel something, anything, that both humbled and frightened Lucian. That kind of reckless attitude lent itself to dangers, but it was also kind of admirable, the unabashed willingness to take risks to find that elusive connection with the world and its inhabitants.

Corey stared back, eyes narrowing. "You okay, Lu? Did I say too much?"

"No. No." Lucian shook his head, finding his voice again. "I am in awe of the life you have lived. It is at once admirable and scary. All those risks you took…."

"Are they really so different from the risks I'm taking with you?" Corey refuted, dead serious. "It's just as—or even more—thrilling to be here or at Boudoir with you, learning about sex in this experimental way. Yeah, okay. Maybe my life isn't in jeopardy quite the same way, but still. Learning curves come in all shapes and sizes."

"And? What was the result of all those… life-threatening activities?"

"You mean did they make me feel? Yeah, they did. I felt everything. You can't know fear until you jump out of a moving plane and watch the earth come closer as you freefall, with only a piece of fabric between you and a gruesome death as you hit the ground. You don't understand excitement until you sit in a racing car driving 200 mph in the middle of a desert, the view all but unchanging, G-forces compressing you like a heavy weight, your peripheral vision blurring as your speed increases." Corey frowned but chuckled too, as if surprised by his own words. "I've done a lot, seen and felt plenty. But with people? Not so much."

Lucian nodded. Corey had revealed much of his inner workings by describing how he tried to make himself feel in the past. Was he still so rash? Lucian doubted it. The man had obviously mellowed and found other avenues of exploration.

"Well, next to you I seem quite drab and predictable." Lucian smiled shortly. "I attend the opera, theater, and ballet on my rare vacation days. A bit cliché, I admit, but I find high culture sophisticated, cerebrally and artistically challenging, and simply beautiful."

Corey shook his head. "Nothing wrong with your recreational pursuits." Then a shrug followed his words. "Besides, I may have engaged in some risky behavior, but I did counter it with other, less dangerous hobbies, like reading and stuff. One in particular led to me go to college to study architecture."

Lucian was intrigued, and he leaned forward. "Oh?"

"You know how teenagers have cliques in schools?" Corey asked, and Lucian nodded, all too aware of the tendency of youths to congregate among like minds and exclude others. "Well, I attended the finest schools, right from the start. I was new money, so kids from old money circles rejected me. I made friends with book geeks and science nerds. Well, I befriended them, but it was always casual, you know. I guess I never really connected emotionally, not even with friends."

As Corey spoke, he frowned, apparently only now remembering certain aspects of his past, little details that had heralded his solitary, celibate way of life in the future.

Lucian wanted to reassure him that past wasn't always prologue, so he said, "Social connections are complicated. As a child and as a teenager, I was an oddball. We moved around a lot because of my parents' academic and diplomatic careers. I never really had friends. No, I did have *one* friend. Unfortunately, he was imaginary." Lucian chuckled, even though the story was true, and Corey smiled again, in that sad, understanding way he did at times. "In any case, I am an adult now, and I have a remarkably large social network of friends, companions, and associates. I am not alone anymore."

"I get what you're trying to say." Corey seemed calmer again, more relaxed, so Lucian considered his speech successful. "Thanks."

Lucian blushed, happy. "You're welcome."

"Anyway," Corey went on. "My so-called friends at school tried to recruit me in their RPGs."

Lucian grinned. "I really can't picture you role-playing at a game table, throwing dice and waving a plastic sword about, wearing an 'I heart Mr. Spock' T-shirt."

Corey chortled so hard he actually bent in half at the waist for a moment. "Jesus. What an image you have of gaming geeks!" As his mirth subsided incrementally, he explained, "Like I said, they tried. I watched a couple of gaming sessions. The thing is, what interested me most of all were the detailed maps and floor plans of dungeons and castles and towns. They just blew me away with their intricate beauty. I was hooked. So, whenever I wasn't jumping out of planes and diving with sharks as a teenager, I lay on the floor of my room, drawing maps and building layouts. It was the best time of my life, I think, looking back upon it now."

The wistful tone and deep sigh from Corey made Lucian's heart flutter with warm emotions. That gorgeous, dreamy look on Corey's face had an undeniable effect on Lucian, who tried to maintain his distance. Only now he was beginning to realize he more than liked Corey. And that unnerved Lucian greatly.

Still, he acknowledged Corey's reminiscence with a smile. "That sounds wonderful, Corey. We do not always realize where our motivations and inspirations come from. I would hazard a guess a happy childhood is conducive to a positive outcome."

Corey laughed huskily, his gaze directed 100 percent at Lucian. "I guess so. God, it's been ages since I've last thought about those days. I had completely forgotten. Thanks for reminding me."

Lucian preened but attempted to hide his reaction behind his hair as it flopped over his eyes a bit. "You did it all, not I. Thank yourself."

Corey shook his head, apparently unwilling to concede defeat. "Stop arguing with me, Lu. Just accept the gratitude."

"Fine." Lucian smiled back and suddenly found it hard to breathe or look away. Corey was fascinating and mesmerizing, and Lucian no longer knew how long he could resist the temptation the man represented. He decided to ignore the fact that they were on a date and progress their professional relationship instead. "I've been wondering…. You told me people have shown an interest in you romantically and sexually, even if you felt nothing in return. How did you determine if a person was interested in you? What kind of signals did you detect?"

Lucian expected Corey to become disappointed or even angry with the change in topic, as it hinted an end to their date. But Corey actually grinned wickedly, as if the question was some kind of flirting method. His eyes sparkled, and Lucian realized his own folly.

"Well, women tend to giggle more. It's kind of annoying. They bat their eyelashes, pout their lips, push out their breasts, flip their hair. I suppose they accentuate their feminine… wiles."

Lucian suppressed a giggle fit of his own, disguising it poorly as a cough. "Ah. And men?"

Corey let his gaze drift leisurely over Lucian, who began to feel hot in his skin, like the room temperature had gone up a few degrees toward the tropical. "Men... well, they rub the back of their neck often. I thought at first it was a self-conscious act, but I learned soon that by raising their arms, their muscles bulge and their shoulders appear wider. In general, there's a lot of straightening up and trying to appear taller, bigger, more imposing. Guys put their hands on their hips or their belts, not quite handling their junk but close, so I guess that suggests where their ideas are headed. Their voices lower too, drop to a husky tone, and they smile and laugh more than usual. Some guys blush, but not everyone." Corey frowned, seemingly musing. "I guess these signals are identifiable but not necessarily so commonplace as to include every single person in the world."

Lucian cocked his head, examining his companion. "Did you notice you said men and they instead of we?"

Corey rolled his eyes. "You asked me how I perceived sexual signals from women and men. That's just how I phrased it. And really, you're one to comment on how I speak!" But right then, as the words left his lips, he frowned, playfulness gone, and added, "I didn't mean it like that. I like the way you speak. I wasn't trying to offend you, Lu."

"Yes, I know." Lucian did too. Corey was not a mean or cruel individual. Even when he had shoved Lucian around, that had been an emotional breaking point, not indicative of his true nature. "Don't worry about it." He turned sideways on the couch, brought his left leg up, tucked it in under himself, and leaned a bit closer toward Corey. "So, what kind of signals can you read about me? Would you say I am attracted to you?"

With a salacious grin, Corey shifted on the couch to mirror Lucian's posture, a relaxed and confident move that incited a rapid response in Lucian. His dick swelled as hot blood filled the shaft in a rush, and his nuts tightened to almost unbearable discomfort. Lucian felt dizzy.

"I already know you're hot for my rocking bod," Corey declared, chuckling and flirting with surprising ease. "I can see it. You're leaning toward me, intrigued, seeking casual touches and whiffs of my scent. You're smiling, unable to prevent it. Kind of like me. When you were naked in front of me at Boudoir, you were nervous and fidgety, aroused and horny."

"W-were *you*?" Lucian interjected, needing to know, not only for the sake of their sensual experimentation but for himself too. As ludicrous as it was to expect anything real to come from this relationship.

"I was shaking like a fucking leaf in a tornado," Corey admitted bluntly, smiling. "But you were right there in front of me, and I didn't want to back down or hide just because it was all so new. Because, you know, it was thrilling and damn amazing, and you were breathtakingly beautiful. I couldn't take my eyes off you." He winked. "I almost succumbed to touching you."

Lucian giggled. "I remember that." He locked gazes with Corey. "I almost did too."

Corey's eyes narrowed, and Lucian's breath hitched. Corey seemed to see directly into Lucian's soul, and it unnerved him a bit. Corey seemed to have no compunctions at the moment about showing his fascination and knowledge.

"Yeah, I know. You couldn't take your eyes off me. Back then or now. Prolonged eye contact is a pretty strong signal, isn't it?" He didn't wait for Lucian to speak, but went on. "When you look at me, your pupils dilate, the tips of your ears redden, you wet your lips more, most likely in the hopes of catching my attention. I assure you, I'm riveted, so you have my undivided attention."

Trying to breathe became a true hardship as Lucian became increasingly aroused by his companion, who might be inexperienced but was neither blind nor stupid. All the sexual signs he witnessed around him were accurate. So why not act on the promise those signals suggested and throw caution to the wind? Many people could and did have sex by being a passive participant. It happened. Corey might initially take that role and learn through trial and error what, if anything, excited him.

Unfortunately, Lucian did not get the chance to ask because Corey's cell phone beeped loudly, startling them both out of the erotic cocoon they had begun to build around them. Lucian's burgeoning erection dwindled at the interruption. But the warmth of being with Corey never left his heart or his spirits.

Corey fished the infernal device out of his pocket and offered Lucian a cute, bashful, lopsided grin. "*Sorry*," he mouthed as he flipped the phone lid open. "Hello?" A minor pause, and a happy smile lit up Corey's face. "Mom, hey. Dad told me you were coming back to town next—" His smile faded, and a frown creased his forehead. "Mom, wait, slow down. I can't understand—" Lucian watched as abject horror rose on Corey's face, his skin paling and his breathing speeding up. The next words confirmed to Lucian that something was horribly wrong. "W-which h-hospital?" Corey swallowed hard, his grief-stricken eyes blinking with unshed tears. "Yeah, yeah, I'm leaving now. I'll be there as soon as I can. Bye." With a flip of his wrist, he snapped the cell phone shut as he sat there, frozen.

"Corey, what's happened?" Lucian tried to keep calm, to offer serenity to his friend in a time of trouble.

Corey let out a half sob, half exhale. "My dad's had a heart attack."

CHAPTER 23

IF LUCIAN had not been holding his hand, Corey would have crumbled to pieces. His eyes itched with tears, as did his cheeks, where a flood had already fallen and dried off. The waiting sucked, plain and simple, especially since they didn't know anything beyond Randolph being admitted.

Lucian squeezed Corey's hand gently, their fingers interlaced. The small gesture was enough to ground Corey, to act as an anchor in a turbulent sea of emotions that threatened to drown him.

"Thanks for coming here with me," Corey whispered, his voice too hoarse and craggy to speak properly. He was well aware he sounded horrible, muffled, and almost unintelligible.

Lucian inched a bit closer, pressing their sides together more firmly. "Of course. There is nowhere else in the world I would rather be."

Corey took a shaky breath, and more tears welled and spilled out of his eyes, no matter how hard he tried to blink them away. A terrible hollow pressure filled his chest, compressing him with a sorrow so encompassing it felt like emptiness. This was the worst he had ever felt. A part of him wished to go back to a time when his emotional connections with people were less potent.

"When is your mother arriving?" Lucian asked tenderly.

Corey struggled to find even a thread of rational thought in his messed-up head. "As soon as she can. Shouldn't be too long."

They had already waited two hours at the hospital with no fresh news. When his mother had called, she had been in midflight above the Atlantic on her way home to New York. She was Randolph's in-case-of-emergency contact, and that was why she had been informed of his heart attack and not Corey. Last time they texted, Prudence was three hours from landing.

"It will be all right," Lucian whispered directly into Corey's ear, his warm breath fanning over Corey's skin, the air brushing his hair. "Not all heart attacks have fatal consequences. And your father is in the care of some of the best doctors in the world." Lucian sounded so sure, so strong in his belief.

Corey wanted to believe him. But it was hard. A deep despair gripped his insides and would not let go. Yet he offered a tiny nod, hoping that would convince Lucian that Corey did not need further reassurances.

But Lucian suddenly tugged his hand. "Come with me, Corey. Please."

Like a child, Corey let himself be led away from the dreary waiting area into the vast maze of both vacant and busy corridors that made up the hospital's private wing. Lucian did not stop until they reached a set of double doors. With a quick, soft glance at Corey, Lucian entered, pulling Corey along.

The chapel was empty. Colorful stained glass windows were lit from behind, offering the barest illumination into the minimalist space. Lucian dragged Corey to the second pew from the front, and with heavy feet, Corey followed. They sat, side by side, and for a long while neither spoke. The noises of the hospital faded. Only their breathing could be heard, and Corey's wheezed as though he smoked three packs a day.

"Is the quiet better or worse?" Lucian inquired, his voice concerned.

Corey leaned in to Lucian for support, and as if knowing exactly what Corey needed, Lucian wrapped his slender arm around Corey's shoulders. "Better. 'Cause you're here." There was no thought of appearing weak. Corey didn't care about such things anymore, not now when Lucian offered whatever Corey asked for without asking for anything in return.

Lucian threaded his fingers through Corey's hair, massaging his scalp and neck with a caress so tender it brought tears to Corey's eyes. Yet his heart felt a little bit lighter, as if some of his worries dissolved under Lucian's sweet presence. The bond he had formed with Lucian seemed to outweigh even personal tragedy.

"Do you know the story of Damon and Pythias?" Lucian asked quietly, with no echo of his voice in the chapel. Corey nodded, remembering the tale from his school days. "Pythias was facing death at the hands of a tyrant king, accused of conspiring against the wretched ruler. When Pythias pleaded with the tyrant king to return home and bid farewell to his loved ones, his truest friend and comrade, Damon, offered to take his place—even in death should Pythias not return. The tyrant king agreed. Finally the day of execution came... and went, without Pythias. As

Damon had vowed to take his place, the tyrant king was about to order Damon's death. That was the moment Pythias returned, having been detained by pirates. So deeply impressed with the friendship, loyalty, trust, and devotion of the two young men was the tyrant king that he set them both free." Lucian leaned his head closer to Corey until they touched, and Corey knew then how solace felt. "You and I may not have been childhood friends like Damon and Pythias, but I am your friend, Corey, and I will be here for you for as long as you wish. Forever if that is your desire." His tone softened to a near-whisper. "Corey, my sweet *eromenos*...."

Corey swallowed hard, a spark of fire igniting in his heart and groin. He had to close his eyes to keep the memory of those precious words tucked in his soul. Eromenos, beloved. It was as close to a confession of love as could be spoken without saying the actual word.

Without noticing it at first, Corey was smiling so much he only felt it when his cheeks all but hurt. "Lu.... And here I assumed I would be *erastes*, the older... lover." He sighed, a new joy spreading through him. Somehow it didn't seem so hard to use the word *lover* as he had surmised. "Despite your age, which I'm sure is not as ageless and eternal as you like to pretend, you are more experienced. But... are you the dominant one? Could it be... me instead?"

At the ageless remark, Lucian let out a muffled giggle. But he waited until Corey finished before he said, "Experience does not equal the sexual roles we undertake while having—while making love." The change of phrasing did not go unnoticed by Corey, who realized the two of them were entering a new phase in their relationship, one more intimate than before.

And they had growing emotions to either blame or thank for that development.

Corey also liked the implication that Lucian was open to alternatives. Perhaps he was a switch. The options that presented in regards to sex—no, to *lovemaking*—certainly promised exciting times ahead.

Because at that moment, Corey knew without a shadow of doubt that lovemaking was ahead of them in the near future.

But was this the right time to ponder such matters?

Corey turned to face Lucian, who looked up, his eyes glowing in the dim light of the room, with an unasked question in those different-colored depths. A silent consensus formed between them, born from glances and held breaths.

"Please...."

Corey neither cared nor noticed which one of them whispered or moved first.

Lucian's lips brushed against Corey's, a soft and fleeting touch, a hint of warm flesh in contact with his own. Lucian's eyelids fluttered closed, and he let out a shaky, desperate sigh. Corey could scarcely draw breath himself, an overwhelming need expanding within him, like a supernova about to explode. His mouth actually hurt from absence of touch, from want and need.

This time it was Corey who moved first, pressing his lips more firmly over Lucian's.

My first kiss. Oh my God....

Corey slipped his hand over Lucian's neck to the back of his head, his fingers combing through the red-gold locks and entangling in them to tug the man closer. Lucian gasped, and his lips parted, trembling.

Tilting his head, Corey slanted his mouth over Lucian's, sharing a hot breath with the man, pressing his tongue and body forward and closer on pure impulse. Corey felt Lucian's quivering hands grip his waist, his shirt, as he angled his body toward him more. Yet, despite the newborn urgency, the kiss retained its innocence.

A hot, wet tongue licked across Corey's lower lip, and he shivered uncontrollably. His heart pounded so hard he felt like his chest might burst. The simple, moist glide over his lips had Corey panting, and then Lucian's tongue slipped inside.

Corey shook all over. Some of his instincts cried out to get away from the intruder in his mouth. The disturbing *ick* factor threatened to expand and drown out all these new and pleasurable sensations. Fleeting repellent thoughts of bad breath, food lodged in teeth, and bacteria in saliva passed through Corey's consciousness.

But a considerably larger part of his psyche, and most all of his body, demanded more. The kiss was sweet and enjoyable, and none of his worries came to pass. This was something he had never experienced before, never even really dreamed of. He had feared it, a piece of another person inside him.

But this was no stranger, no anonymous nightmare to fear, hate, or detest.

This was Lucian. A man who with a single holding of hands had saved Corey tonight from despair akin to emotional death.

Lucian's tongue withdrew, and he pulled back entirely, but only ever so slightly, leaving a puff of air against Corey's face.

Corey couldn't wait. With a quick intake of oxygen, he dove right back into the kiss. He opened his mouth out of pure reflex and let his tongue out to delve deep and explore. He was tentative at first but quickly grew greedier, and a moan spilled out. Lucian's unique, sweet fruity flavor exploded over his taste buds, so goddamn good his head swam. This was nothing like the detestable things Corey had been so concerned about for so damn long.

I'm in heaven.

But he wasn't. Not until the tip of Lucian's tongue brushed against his. A frantic groan escaped his gut into his lover-to-be's mouth, and then all restraint, every ounce of self-control evaporated. Corey gripped Lucian's face, the skin soft with a hint of coarseness from stubble, and drew him close roughly, sucking his tongue into his mouth. Lucian clawed at Corey's back, pulling him nearer. Their tongues entangled, and they shared breaths, flavors, saliva, and more. Every new sensation built on the one preceding it, sending them both headlong into a fiery-red haze of passionate frenzy.

"Ahem."

A low, embarrassed cough yanked them apart, panting and blushing, need coursing through their veins like a living being. Corey turned his head to see an old man at the threshold of the chapel, his cheeks red, but a small, understanding smile flicking on his lips. The clank of a metal cane hitting the floor accompanied the old man; he limped to a pew in the back and sat down with a painful sigh. He crossed his hands, closed his eyes, and bowed his head in prayer.

Cheeks flaming with embarrassment at forgetting both his dad's dire situation and decorum in a public place, Corey turned back to Lucian, who was apparently on the same page. His chest was heaving too, and his eyes were dark with lust.

Corey cleared his throat, whispering, "Um, maybe we should, uh...." He couldn't quite find strength for his cracking voice.

Lucian nodded repeatedly. "Y-yes, I th-think we should go." He sprung up like a jack-in-the-box, passed Corey, and headed toward the door. Awkward and silent, Corey trailed after him quickly.

It wasn't until they reached the worn sea green couches of the waiting area again that they both suddenly started talking at once—and stopped at the same time too.

"I'm sorry," Lucian said, his smile flaky and uncertain. "You go first."

Corey watched his delicate features and thought he saw... remorse? The mere notion that Lucian wished they had not kissed made Corey's stomach knot painfully, and nausea rose to his throat, causing him to bend forward in pain.

The words spilled out of his mouth, a desperate edge to them. "You regret the kiss?"

Lucian's eyes widened. "No!" He sighed. "Only the timing. We are in a hospital, after all. In a chapel, no less. It was not the best—"

"Apart from that?" Corey insisted, the pitch of his voice rising as his alarm grew.

Lucian placed his hand on Corey's thigh and squeezed gently. He spoke in a soft tone, sweet and kind as he always was. "I do not regret kissing you, Corey. It was...." His cheeks pinked, his tongue darted out to moisten his lips, and his eyes darkened. "Wonderful. Perfect." His fingers swept over Corey's lower lip and traced the Cupid's bow of his upper lip, the touch arousing and itching at once. "I knew it would be all that and more."

Corey exhaled in relief. He was glad there was no reason to feel sorry about what had transpired between them. Whether the kiss was born of consolation or desire did not matter in the end.

"Okay. Good." He dipped his head and rested his forehead against Lucian's, relishing the smooth warmth of Lucian's skin. "I'm grateful you're here. Even if we hadn't kissed."

Lucian smiled, blinking hard as his eyes glimmered with moisture. "The time and place may not have been ideal, but I am glad that happened." He wove his fingers amid Corey's. "I will stand at your side through this. As long as you need me."

Corey knew Lucian meant more than the kiss and his father's situation. The bond they shared was growing stronger. He wondered how long it would take for it to be indestructible. And would that mean they would be inseparable? Would they be... together?

IN THE stark fluorescent light, Lucian looked pale, with dark circles around his eyes. He appeared tired, and Corey felt much the same. He had woken early to prepare for their date, agitated and in dire need of working with his hands to distract himself from flights of fancy—or fantasy, to be exact. The adrenaline and the endorphins had begun to wane and vanish. Soon the full brunt of this ordeal would hit him like a truck on a collision course.

Corey just needed to stay awake and rational for a while longer. Until they heard back from the doctor who was currently performing Randolph's bypass surgery. For the news of the outcome, whatever that might be, he required Lucian at his side, holding him together.

As if sensing Corey's reflections, Lucian wrapped his arms around Corey's neck and hugged him tight. With a sigh Corey embraced Lucian back, tighter than a coil, and longed to pull him into his lap and bury his face in the crook of the man's neck, to drown in his scent and warmth, to forget the big, bad world and what might happen to his father....

"Corey?"

A woman's shocked voice startled him, and he pulled back from the hug only to find his mother standing there, staring at him and Lucian wide-eyed. Corey disengaged from Lucian, got up on his feet, and went to her.

"Hi, Mom." He didn't waste time or breath explaining Lucian just yet. "Dad's still in surgery as far as I know. The doctors and the nurses haven't told us anything. Hospital policy. No news, sorry."

Prudence nodded, her jaw quivering slightly and her hazel eyes wet. Though she was fifty-six years old, she looked to be in her thirties, as she'd had work done. That made her striking, but it was a false kind of beauty, stretched and unnatural. Corey had never liked her having plastic surgery, but it was a constant in the social circles of the rich and famous.

Her long brown hair was gathered on top of her head in an elaborate hairdo, but threads were loose here and there. For her this was a disheveled state, proof of her anxiety. She wore high heels and a dark brown, sleeveless sheath dress that fitted her sleek form admirably. But there were wrinkles in it, and her makeup had not been touched-up in hours. In essence, Prudence was not in a good frame of mind.

"Mom, let's sit down," Corey suggested, taking her arm and escorting her to the couch. He noticed Lucian had moved to the next couch, giving them space. That bothered Corey for some reason. Perhaps because Lucian was a friend and as such practically family. No, Lucian *was* already family as far as Corey was concerned.

Prudence seemed to be aware of Lucian's presence because although her body was turned away from Lucian, her head whipped in his direction, a frown marring her high forehead. She clearly had questions, so Corey decided to beat her to them.

"Mom, this is my friend, Lucian Allard. Lu, this is my mother, Prudence Paige."

Lucian offered a cute, if somewhat polite, smile, leaned toward her, and extended his hand. "Nice to meet you, Mrs. Paige, even under these circumstances."

Prudence shook Lucian's hand, but Corey could see her heart wasn't in it. The gesture was cold and standoffish, and he felt bad for Lucian. Yet, Lucian's smile never faltered, and Corey had to give him credit for keeping up an amicable facade.

Corey knew why his mother was behaving in this cool manner. For her, family matters were strictly private affairs. For a stranger to be present at a time like this was tantamount to an offensive intrusion.

"Mom, Lu was with me when you called about Dad. I was too shell-shocked to get here by myself. I couldn't really function. Lu helped me." *He has every right to be here.* But Corey left that part unsaid, praying his mother would not be rude or dismissive of Lucian. At least one thing was for certain, and that was that Prudence would never cause a scene. Avoidance of scandal was important to her reputation as well as her values.

All of a sudden, she nodded and slumped, turning back to Corey. "Yes, I understand. Your father informed me of your... new relationship with Mr. Allard." She sounded weary, and she clutched her handbag firmly, with a white-knuckled grip. "Corey, there is something I need to tell you." Corey was instantly on alert, holding his breath for whatever bad news was to come. "Your father would not want me to speak of this with you, as he was adamant you not know, but…. He's not here to refute me, and it's my decision." She straightened her back and locked gazes with Corey. "This isn't the first time your father has had a heart attack."

"What the fuck?" Corey damn near shouted, jumping up on his feet and waving his hands about. Blind rage attacked his self-control and caused it to buckle under the strain. "What the hell are you talking about?" The news was *this* close to being the straw that broke the camel's back. Red spots danced in his field of vision, and he concluded he was in serious risk of passing out for the first time in his life.

Prudence stood up as well, her back ramrod straight and her expression grave and taut. "He had another heart attack last year."

Hot flashes of rage warred with the cold shivers that ran up and down Corey's spine. He recalled his father staying at their house in the Hamptons after an apparent twisted wrist during a racquetball game. "His wrist…."

Prudence nodded, her lips thin, either angry or disapproving. She did not appreciate Corey putting them under a spotlight like this. But Corey didn't care about her feelings. He was too angry at being kept out of the loop.

"Yes, that was a ruse. If it came out that Randolph had had a heart attack, the stock prices would have plummeted and—"

"Oh my fucking God." Corey couldn't believe what he was hearing. "You're using the stock market as an excuse for not telling *me*? I'm his son, not his VP! You think I give a flying fuck about the company—"

"You may not care, but your father does." Prudence's voice was chilly as it cut through the interference of Corey speaking. "He gave me specific instructions not to worry you. Besides, he is fine."

"Fine?" Corey scoffed, gesturing toward the doors to the ICU. "He's in surgery!" He was well aware he was shouting, his face undoubtedly red, his whole body shaking.

But only when Lucian slipped his hand into Corey's, the touch gentle and familiar and caring, did Corey realize he should calm down. Nothing would be served by fighting in the hospital waiting room.

He exhaled long and dropped his gaze to the white linoleum floor, letting the sight cool him off. Arguments with his parents were a new development in their relationship, and they drained his energy.

Besides, Corey understood that Randolph Paige was a proud and private man, and this was exactly the kind of thing he would do.

He looked up at his mother, the anger receding and affection taking its place. "Mom, I'm sorry. I get it. Dad's... reserved and protective. He's always been that way. And I know how much the company means to him." Though he felt betrayed, he pushed those feelings aside as counterproductive.

All of a sudden, Prudence let out a shaky breath, crossed the gap between them, and embraced Corey, dislodging Corey's hold of Lucian. "I argued with your father about telling you. But you know how stubborn and adamant he can be. Damned old coot."

Corey chuckled, the sound watery and hoarse. Prudence cursing, however mildly, had to be a sign of an impending apocalypse. "Yeah. But he's our miserable old coot." Her arms tightened around him as she shook with half sobs, half laughter. Holding her like this was a rarity for Corey, especially in a public venue. But he was determined not to be the one to let go first.

Soon she stepped back, but her hands cupped his face, stroking his jawline gently. "He should have told you himself, and sooner too." Tears formed in her eyes, and a few errant droplets trickled down her cheek. She quickly wiped them away. "When he gets out of surgery and wakes up, I'll be sure to let him know how we both feel about it." While Corey liked the sound of that, he didn't get the chance to comment, when Prudence turned to face Lucian. "I'm sorry, Mr. Allard, for being so dismissive."

Lucian smiled back kindly and shook his head. "No need to apologize. I understand. These are difficult circumstances."

"Excuse me?" A man's rough, weary voice startled all three of them, and they turned toward a doctor wearing light green surgical scrubs. He had a trimmed beard and dark circles around his eyes. "Mrs. Paige?" His gaze was aimed at Prudence, who nodded without saying a word, her chin lifting in a show of bravery. "Your husband's surgery went well."

It was as if a massive balloon deflated when Corey, Lucian, and Prudence all exhaled at the exact same moment. Their relief filled the room, and the doctor smiled a bit, an understanding and sympathetic gesture.

"As you're aware," the doctor continued laconically, "Mr. Paige's acute myocardial infarction was more than likely precipitated by, not only the previous MI, but also his chronic stress and high blood pressure. They both make him susceptible to coronary artery disease, which narrows the arteries that provide adequate oxygen-rich blood flow to the heart."

"There was a clot in his arteries?" Corey asked for clarification. The relief he had felt was already dwindling, and fear resumed its earlier place in his heart.

"Yes." The doctor's game face was dead serious. "Mr. Paige's arteries were already narrowed by his hypertension when a clot formed, blocking the blood flow. His heart muscle doesn't appear to have sustained irreparable damage, so with a few lifestyle changes, he can go on to live a long, productive life."

"What kind of changes?" Prudence asked, frowning.

"Regular exercise, a healthy vegetarian diet, absolutely no alcohol or smoking, and of course decreasing stress, job-related *and* everything else." The doctor gazed at Prudence sharply. "I understand your husband has suffered from palpitations for a few years now?"

That was news to Corey, but Prudence nodded slightly, with a grim expression. Corey wanted to scream and shout, hit or break something, to act out and blow off some steam. But he did none of those things and stayed in place, silent. At least the waiting for the other shoe to drop was over. What more could go wrong?

"In general," the doctor went on, oblivious to Corey's agitated state. "Mr. Paige is in good health. Maintaining a healthy weight and eliminating alcohol and smoking will undoubtedly help in his recovery. However, from what I understand from his patient records, there is the continuous state of job stress he endures?"

Prudence nodded again, her face and body deadpan and immobile, like a statue.

"He will need to avoid stress because that, perhaps most of all, has contributed to his hypertension, which in turn led to his heart attack," the doctor declared neutrally.

"You mean he has to quit his job?" Corey spoke the words, but they didn't really sink in. Randolph Paige *was* the job, a newspaper and communications technology magnate. Beyond that, Corey had no idea who his father was—or could be. If faced with the choice between his life and his job, Randolph might be inclined to ignore the risk to his health and safety. In short, the man loved his job.

The doctor shrugged. "If that is the only means by which to reduce his stress levels and subsequently his high blood pressure, then yes, I would strongly advise he do so posthaste."

For a while, the waiting room was filled by an awkward, heavy silence.

Finally, Prudence asked, "When may we see him?"

"He's out of surgery and in recovery. It'll be a couple of hours before his anesthesia wears off and we move him to his room. I would suggest getting some rest while we wait for the latest test results." With that, the doctor said a quick, neutral good-bye and walked away, disappearing into the bowels of the hospital.

Prudence was the first to take a seat on the couch, and Corey and Lucian followed her example. But no one spoke.

Still, Corey sought the unwavering support Lucian offered and found his hand, interlaced their fingers, and held on for dear life. His eyes burned with hot tears, and his chest hurt to the point he wondered if he was going to have a heart attack too.

But Lucian pressed against him, squeezing his hand gently, and was a steady rock for Corey to lean against. Never had he felt this grateful for a true friend like Lucian. As if knowing what turbulence existed within Corey, Lucian petted Corey's hair, neck, and shoulders, his touch comforting and soothing. Corey closed his eyes and went with it, instinctively following the motions of his friend's fingers, all but purring.

"Corey?" Prudence spoke softly, and Corey didn't bother to open his eyes.

"Yeah?"

"Will you stay here and wait to hear from your father? I have to make a few calls."

That did rouse Corey from his momentary serenity. "Calls?" His blood chilled. "You don't expect me to—" His pitch rose as he waited for the request that might kill him.

"To take over the company while Randolph recuperates?" Prudence shook her head, determined. "No. For one, you're not a businessman like your father. You have never worked for the company and know very little, if anything, about its operations. No. Your father is chairman and CEO, and that will not change. Not until he so decides."

Corey bristled. "He could die before he agrees to step down."

Prudence's hazel eyes flashed with fierce sparks. "No, he won't. That is an option I will not allow him." She could indeed be a force to be reckoned with, Corey concluded, happy she was holding the reins. Randolph might have fought back with Corey but with Prudence? Not a chance. "I will call Arthur Lowe and Jane Whitehall for an emergency meeting. We'll figure out how to deal with this matter swiftly and with the least amount of fuss."

Corey knew both those mentioned. Arthur Lowe was the company's chief operations officer, while Jane Whitehall was the chief legal officer. Lowe handled the day-to-day operations of several of the newspapers, and Whitehall acted as general counsel in all legal matters pertaining to the company. They would know what to do. Bad press was a publicity nightmare in situations like these, threatening to send stock prices into a downward spiral. Corey could only hope that after his father's previous MI, Randolph would have created a contingency plan for just this kind of problem.

Corey nodded. "Sure. I'll stay here. Not like I have anywhere pressing to go."

"Thank you." Prudence's smile might have been less than stellar in its radiance, but it was genuine and grateful. She rose and came over to hug Corey, who stood up to embrace her back. Her final glance was aimed at Lucian. "I'm glad you're here for my son, Mr. Allard." She looked like she had more to say, but she snapped her mouth shut, bowed her head a bit, and left. Nothing in her steps showed how vulnerable she must have felt.

Corey sat back down with a heavy sigh, burying his face in his hands. "Well. Looks like it's just you and me now, Lu."

CHAPTER 24

"STOP FIDGETING, Dad, or you'll give yourself a damn hernia."

Randolph Paige growled impatiently, reminding Corey of a petulant child who didn't get his way. The man actually pouted. "It's been three days since the surgery. As nice as this private room is, I want to go home."

Corey groaned. "Yeah, that's right, Dad. It's only been three fucking days. If you don't relax and recuperate in the hospital now, you may never get out of here. So stop acting like a child and rest, goddamn it!"

Randolph looked like an impending storm cloud about to thunder and roar. But a calm female voice rang out instead. "He's right, Randy. So quit it." Corey suppressed a smirk when his mother spoke succinctly, her voice quietly intimidating in its pure coolness. No one called him that but her.

Randolph had the good grace to redden and appear sheepish. He grumbled something under his breath but leaned back in the hospital bed and got comfortable again.

"Thanks for the assist, Mom." Corey smiled, sat back down in his chair by the hospital bed, and let out a deep breath.

"You're welcome, darling," she replied in her most honeyed voice, clearly designed to rub it in to her poor husband. Her sickeningly sweet smile was proof positive.

Randolph grimaced. "If the two of you are going to be lounging here for long, at least get me some entertainment. A movie, a book, the last fiscal year quarterly report. Anything!"

"Aren't we enough amusement, dear?" Prudence asked, deadpan.

Unable to help it, Corey burst into guffaws, holding his belly. Prudence smirked, and Randolph shook his head as if mad, but the corners of his lips were twitching, and his eyes crinkled in a relaxed way.

The door cracked open, and a head full of red-gold curls peeked in. "Hello?"

Corey jumped up from his seat, startled at seeing Lucian. "Lu? What are you…?" His voice trailed off as his heart began to hammer. After their interrupted date and consoling in the hospital, Lucian had been a no-show—at Corey's insistence. Randolph was a proud man, and for anyone who wasn't a family friend to hang around while he was stuck in a hospital bed would only lead to grumbling and perhaps more.

"I invited him, darling," Prudence said casually. She tapped on her tablet, lost in her… whatever it was she was doing. "He seems like such a nice man."

It wasn't like Corey could refute that, not in his smitten state. "Oh, I, uh…." Struggling to find a suitable excuse for his stammering, Corey sputtered, "I thought we had an appointment that I'd forgotten or something. Sorry. Um, please, come in." His face flamed with embarrassment, but he waved the once again white-clad beauty into the room.

Lucian flashed a perfect smile that did funny things to Corey's stomach. It sure didn't help him cool off his blush. "Don't mind if I do." Gingerly, he slipped in and closed the door behind him. "Mrs. Paige, you look as lovely and ravishing as ever. I swear, you must have discovered the spring of eternal youth." Prudence smiled without raising her gaze from the tablet and nodded in acknowledgment of the compliment. "Mr. Paige, may I say you look much improved. With people like you, hospitals might go out of business."

It was shameless but so like Lucian, Corey mused, smiling.

Randolph muttered under his breath but didn't appear too offended by Lucian's arrival. "Thanks."

"I come bearing gifts." Lucian brought up a brown paper bag, and something sloshed inside. He strolled over to Randolph's bed and offered his belongings. "Can you smell that delicious flavor? Ah, the likes of nectar from the gods, surely."

Corey moved to stand next to Lucian. He told himself he did it to be watchful over his father, but feeling Lucian's body heat and scenting his fruity cologne were the real reasons, if he dared to admit the truth.

"What is it?"

"Tea."

Randolph frowned and grimaced, pushing the bag slightly away from him. "Thank you, but I'm a coffee drinker."

"And he's not allowed coffee at the moment," Corey reminded them all, adamant. That only had Randolph cursing more, his actual words thankfully mostly muffled.

But as usual Lucian remained undeterred, and he giggled. "Take a sip, Mr. Paige. If you do not care for it, which is impossible, I promise I will find your doctors and use my masculine wiles to get you out of here by tomorrow at the latest."

"Lu!" Corey couldn't believe Lucian would endanger Randolph's health for damn tea.

But Lucian only gave him a smug smirk and a confident wink before turning back to Randolph. "What say you, good sir? Up for a challenge? A win-win situation, as I see it."

Alarmed, Corey watched as Randolph's eyes narrowed. He was not one to back down from a challenge, and when he reached for the bag, the deal was done. Corey fumed, about to drag Lucian out of the room and demand he never return.

Randolph unwrapped the bag and revealed what looked like a plastic coffee cup from Starbucks. Corey tried to grab it, but Lucian stopped him with a hand on his arm.

With a careful inhale, Randolph looked suddenly surprised and then suspicious. But Lucian only smiled, seemingly without guile. Randolph took a sip, put the cup down, smacked his lips as he rolled the liquid around in his mouth before swallowing. Then his eyebrows shot up, and Corey was speechless. Not much shocked his father.

"This is tea?" Randolph asked, bemused. Then he took another, longer swig. This time he was clearly savoring it, and some of the tension in his shoulders and back seemed to drain away. "Amazing. It tastes like coffee."

Corey was about to yank the cup away and check for himself when Lucian laughed. "It is tea, I assure you. One of my own concoctions. Unlike you, Mr. Paige, I am not a fan of coffee, but I appreciate the value it has in our busy, rushed society. So I conducted a few tests. And voilà! A tea that retains the sweet odors of tea but one that has a distinctly detectable coffee flavor. Plus, there is a tiny amount of actual caffeine in it. Not as rich as real coffee, of course, but a hint. Nothing to hamper your current physical recovery, naturally."

The charming ease that Lucian seemed to radiate had Randolph smiling and Corey all but pulling the hairs out of his head. Lucian had a magic touch, that much was apparent. "This is really quite good. Have you thought about patenting it?"

Lucian giggled, his cheeks pinking. "Goodness, no. I would not have a clue as to how or why to inflict such a heinous punishment on a world so terribly addicted to coffee. The western world might never recover from the sudden loss of drugged efficiency."

To everyone's surprise Randolph laughed. "Well, a good businessman understands the market—or lack thereof. If you ever change your mind, though, give me a call, Mr. Allard, and I'll put you in touch with the right people to get this product onto the shelves."

Lucian bit his bottom lip cutely, and Corey had a sudden urge to do the same and nip that luscious pout, drag it between his teeth and pull gently, and then soothe the sting with a swipe from his tongue.

Blood roared in his ears as his heart pounded a mile a minute. What was happening to him? Was this all it had taken in the end to awaken his desires? Any person he allowed to get close enough to stir shit up? Or... had his body and heart merely waited for someone like Lucian, a man who related to him and understood what Corey was going through?

Or someone *exactly* like Lucian...?

Corey could scarcely draw breath after that thought.

Prudence spoke in a cool voice, but Corey heard the underlying curiosity she usually kept to herself. "Mr. Allard, I've been fascinated by this sexual mentoring program of yours. Can you tell me a bit more about it? If we are not keeping you, that is."

Lucian waved a casual hand about. "I do have duties and a busy schedule, but I would be happy to answer any questions you have. After all, Corey is my client." His smile was dazzling. "And I am in no hurry. I have concluded my affairs for today."

Corey bit his lip hard to suppress showing verbally his sudden burst of jealousy, fire-hot and overwhelming. His knees buckled, and he would have fallen if he hadn't been holding on to the metal railings of his father's hospital bed.

"A-at Boudoir?" His voice cracked at the implication Lucian had been loving someone else today. That unbidden mental image didn't sit well with him at all, as irrational as the whole emotion was. Lucian didn't belong to Corey.

Lucian shook his head. "No, I have not been at Boudoir today. I was actually doing my rounds at Heather House."

Corey frowned, baffled.

But it was Prudence who asked first. "What is Heather House?"

"As you might be aware by now," Lucian said politely but with clear affection in his tone, "I have a mentoring program for people with sexual problems. At Boudoir as well as at my apartment, I, along with other professional mentors, work mostly with adults. Heather House is part of New York's outreach program for LGBT children."

Corey's jaw dropped as shock washed over him. "You never told me about working in an outreach program."

"You never asked, and the topic has not come up yet." Lucian continued, addressing Randolph and Prudence. "Outreach exists to bring matters of equality to the foreground, be it about age, race, religion, politics, gender, or sexual orientation. Society needs reminding that there is still a long road ahead when it comes to equal civil rights for all sexual orientations. Typically the outreach program works in the confines of community centers for LGBT affairs, or other suitable locations. LGBT kids often end up on the street after their families throw them out, and they are exposed to prostitution, drugs, alcohol, and sexually transmitted diseases. Some cities have no shelters for these homeless LGBT kids, while some church shelters focus on proselytizing and preaching, and even reprogramming." He shuddered, and Corey did too.

"I assume that's where Heather House comes in?" Prudence clarified, her voice, eyes, and posture all speaking to her deep interest.

Lucian smiled. "Yes. I established Heather House about a year after I took charge of Boudoir, so it must be at least... oh, nine years ago by now. Boudoir was initially founded by my grandfather, Julian Allard. Nonetheless, Boudoir is not a suitable place for anyone under twenty-one because some of the programs deal with hard-core issues. Heather House, on the other hand, deals mainly with sex studies and sex problems among teenagers but also offers aid with housing and schooling."

"What kind of issues?" Prudence asked, her head cocked as she focused utterly on the conversation. That boded well for Lucian since Prudence had a habit of sponsoring and funding programs she believed in. Not that Lucian probably knew anything about that.

"Any kind of matters pertaining to sex," Lucian explained. "Encouraging these youths to be themselves despite the dangers society poses to them is a tough pill to swallow. STDs are one of our main points of focus, but the primary lessons deal with sex education. Basically, we teach about anything from the proper use of prophylactics to sexual positions."

Still processing Lucian's statement about having mentored for nearly a decade, Corey gasped, and his eyes damn near bugged out of his sockets as he listened to Lucian describing his work. "Sexual positions? Are you serious? Like Kama Sutra 101?"

Lucian chuckled. "It is more complicated than that simple interpretation. Street kids, for example, know a lot about blowjobs. But being able to identify a sexual sadist at the start of his career in exploitation by his use of hard-core sexual positions, S&M paraphernalia, and demeaning, manipulative psychological tricks and violence? Some kids have an instinct about these things but not all. Sexual positions people prefer can reveal much about their basic psychology."

It was Corey's turn to chuckle. "Psychology again, eh?"

Lucian joined in, his eyes sparkling. Corey wanted to spend days gazing into them.

"Your organization is nonprofit?" Prudence asked, snapping Corey out of his idolatry.

"Yes. I am founder and major contributor, but there are others too. I was fortunate to start in cooperation with other NYC outreach programs." Lucian sounded immensely proud of all he had achieved, and Corey was proud of him too. Lucian was far from a wealthy dilettante with no purpose or interest beyond sex.

"You reach these youths through outreach programs and arrange their stay at Heather House?" Prudence inquired, tapping her tablet again but her gaze flicking to Lucian every other second.

"The housing is temporary for most because, in addition to a shelter for the homeless, one of the main services we provide is medical care for young rape victims and teenage sex workers. About half of the inhabitants of HH consist of them as they are in the direst need of a place to go after hospitals send them back out on the street because they have no insurance."

Corey had never seen that hard, icy glint in Lucian's eyes or heard that brutal edge to his otherwise smooth, sultry voice. Lucian took this personally and was emotionally involved. That spoke volumes about his dedication to his profession—and had Corey falling for Lucian without a chance of preventing it.

I'm falling… falling, falling, falling… I'm falling in love….

Corey's stomach plummeted into an unknown darkness. Dazed, his head spun, and he grappled the metal railing of the bed with both hands, white-knuckled.

Falling down, falling apart, falling behind... falling in love... falling into love, falling into darkness, into depths... falling in love, in love, in love....

"Son? Are you all right?" Randolph's big, warm, dry hand landed on Corey's arm, the weight familiar, comforting and grounding.

He offered a weak smile. "Yeah, yeah. I guess I kind of spaced out there for a minute. I'm fine."

Randolph squeezed gently. "I understand. This is hard for us all."

Thankfully, Randolph was referring to something else. Corey sighed in relief, and then nodded. "Yeah. I'm glad you're gonna be okay." He placed his own hand on top of his dad's and let the touch soothe his aches and fears of losing his father before his time.

"Me too." Randolph smiled encouragingly. "How about you go with your mother and Allard?"

Puzzled, Corey frowned. "Go where?"

Randolph chuckled. "You haven't heard a word, have you? Pru asked Allard to show her Heather House. Might do you good to visit the place with them." His sudden wicked, knowing smirk hinted to Corey that his old man might not have been as blind as he had assumed. Pushing Corey and Lucian together seemed to be Randolph's aim du jour. If Corey had known all it would take to get in Randolph's good graces was coffee-flavored tea, he would have chosen a career in the chemical industry.

Corey rolled his eyes and snorted, but he decided to go with them. Time was well spent with Lucian, he mused. If he was lucky, Corey might even get the chance to hold the man's hand....

"BOTH THE city and the state of New York are among our major funders, along with our corporate sponsors," Lucian explained to Prudence as they walked through the main entrance into Heather House, with Corey following on their heels.

Corey was duly impressed. The four-story brownstone building was huge, with wood-paneled walls, parquet floors, dark velvet curtains, and an air of refinement. Corey had not expected that in a LGBT shelter, not one situated in the heart of Manhattan.

But he had, on their way over, prepared for teenagers lounging about in tattered clothes, worn shoes, and with tired, bored, and blank expressions. Well, as much as humanly possible—without knowing anything about how they lived every day.

Kids were coming and going, while young men and women stood in the front hall with nametags, leaflets, and welcoming smiles. Lucian introduced them as the house peer counselors who came from hard circumstances but had overcome them with the help of Heather House and the outreach programs.

Trailing aimlessly behind Lucian and Prudence, Corey sneaked peeks into the various rooms they passed. The first floor consisted of lounges, classrooms, a large open kitchen, and one massive dining hall. Corey managed a glimpse of a backyard with trees, bushes, and even a picnic area. Lucian had gone all out in establishing a safe haven for troubled kids without homes or family. Every minute had Corey appreciating and idolizing Lucian more.

Upon passing what appeared to be a music room, Corey halted midstep as he heard an eerie melody, played on a flute. The piece was slow and playful but with a melancholy sound that gave Corey shivers, recognizing it as Debussy's "Syrinx."

Following the beautiful harmonies almost in a trance, Corey stopped at a room where a lone boy of perhaps fifteen played, his eyes closed. His brown hair cascaded over his face and hid his appearance. He wore nothing but dirty tennis shoes, baggy faded jeans, and a T-shirt with a picture so faded no colors, images, or text could be detected.

Corey leaned against the doorjamb, listening raptly. The melody wasn't long, but it was one of the few flute pieces he liked. The timbre reminded him of lush woods, flowery meadows, the springtime—plus a few running satyrs thrown into the mix.

Suddenly the music stopped as if hitting a wall, and the boy lifted the flute from his lips and peered at Corey through his mess of hair. "Are you spying on me or something, weirdo? Leave me alone." His voice was low, but it cracked to high-pitched a few times, indicating he was in puberty.

Corey tried to defend himself. "I was just admiring your playing. Debussy, isn't it?"

"What of it?" The boy looked and sounded wary, getting more suspicious with each passing second.

"Nothing." Corey smiled, hoping to look casual and harmless. "What's your name?"

"What's it to you, dickhead?" The boy got up and placed his flute in a small case, also worn and filthy.

"Guess I was just curious, trying to get to know you," Corey said.

The boy scoffed. "Yeah, right. Fuck off, pimp. I ain't interested."

"Pimp?" That shook Corey to the core. Exactly what about him screamed pimp?

The boy glanced at him over his shoulder, brazen. "Yeah. Those clothes you've got on. What did they cost you? Four, five hundred bucks?" He turned to his task at hand, snapping the latches on his flute case closed. "Entitled rich jerks don't hang around here unless they want something. I'm no one's bitch."

A sinking feeling made Corey feel worse. Not the least of which was the knowledge his luxurious casual attire had actually set him back *six* hundred dollars. His cheeks burned with shame at the way this boy saw him, as an entitled and privileged moron who went around talking to young boys and stirring up shit, like a pimp or a pedophile.

"Sorry. Didn't mean to bother you." Corey made to leave but almost bumped his nose against Lucian's forehead since the man was standing just outside the doorway with Prudence.

Lucian didn't look at Corey once but instead focused on the boy. "Hey, Dylan."

The boy—Dylan, apparently—whipped around, and smiled. "Hey, Allie."

Allie? Corey did his best not to grimace or growl, but it was a damn close call. How close was Lucian to these youths anyway? And by what right did that... kid... call Lucian with any kind of endearment or nickname?

"Aren't you supposed to be in math class?" Lucian asked, still smiling.

Blushing, Dylan ducked his head, hiding behind his thick hair, and muttered, "Yeah. I forgot. Sorry."

Lucian stepped aside. "Get your stuff, and get to class. Come on now." There was no harsh recrimination in his voice. It was as beckoning and sweet as ever, and Corey wanted to go to sleep listening to that divine cadence.

Dylan grabbed his flute case and a backpack and rushed past Lucian and Corey. But not before shooting a glare at Corey, as though Corey stood in his way or something.

Once the boy was out of earshot, Corey rubbed the back of his neck and murmured, "Geez, what did I say?"

Lucian quirked an eyebrow, grinning. "What did you expect? That with a few choice, wise words from you, he'd have everything figured out, every problem solved, and he could go on to live a long and productive life as a proud gay man? I expect newcomers to fail in their first attempt at reaching these youths." His gaze was reproachful and amused at once, and Corey reddened more. "But I am overjoyed you made the effort to speak to him."

"It wasn't a chore," Corey muttered, wringing his hands and worrying his lower lip. "He was just so… hostile."

Lucian frowned, more bewildered than furious. "These teenagers have lost everything. Families, homes, money, safety. If they gave up their trust to the first nice person too, what would they retain themselves? There are a lot of emotions storming within them. They're adolescents. *And* they are homeless, friendless, and purposeless, with virtually no resources to speak of. Would that not make anyone hostile?"

Corey had to admit it would. He didn't know how to feel, embarrassed or confused. "Is he going to be okay?"

Lucian smiled. "You could try to find that out for yourself. Come back and speak with him again. Do not be a one-off, and you might be able to get him to open up."

"A one-off?"

"A transient person, a flyby, someone just passing through. Someone who doesn't stick around." Lucian smiled sadly, the look reaching his eyes, a rueful glimmer shining in their depths. "These youths have come to expect that no one cares about them. That everyone leaves. That is why it is so hard for them to trust anyone, even the people here trying to help. They believe a lack of trust makes them stronger, more self-reliant, independent. How else can they view their situation when those they loved and had faith in abandoned them?"

"They've all been thrown out of their homes?" Corey asked, depressed for Dylan and others like him. He had never been in their shoes, and that made it hard for him to understand.

"No, not all." Lucian looked around at the hallway where boys and girls wandered like lost souls in limbo. "Some are runaways or orphans or poor or simply confused and overwhelmed. In these halls there are a thousand and one stories, and they can all break your heart."

"Like Thierry…." Corey recalled the sad young man who had been so abused he had wanted to be like Corey, a block of stone and ice, never to feel anything again, desperate to be set apart from a cruel, bruising world.

Lucian's gaze was sympathetic as he nodded lightly. "I have the advantage of having been here far longer than you who just showed up on their radar. I am a permanent fixture by now."

Then Lucian lifted his chin to indicate Corey and Prudence should follow after him. They did, but Corey's mind wandered to other places, darker and more desolate. His gaze trailed after these youths as he tried to guess what their situations were.

But what really boggled his mind was the knowledge that he was thirty-three, wealthy and independent, with a huge apartment, vast resources—and he had never had to face the kind of truth these kids had when he had been their age. Only now was he reconciling with the fact that he was more than likely gay. To go through this hectic self-discovery during adolescence when hormones did a number on you and your freedom was dictated by people who might or might not understand you? He shuddered just thinking about it.

Corey was lost, still trying to find out who he was, his current life empty of purpose and meaning. He had everything else in his life worked out, but he *was* privileged, entitled, and spoiled. No wonder Dylan had not related to him.

Was Corey really a one-off?

More confused than ever, Corey followed Lucian and Prudence through the endless hallways of Heather House, which was apparently named after heathers, resilient little plants. That analogy suited these fleeting travelers who were lost inside and out but could endure anything. If only….

But what could Corey do? Other than loosening his purse strings, what good could he do for this place? He wanted to help, though. And surprisingly, he wanted it for himself more than for Lucian. But damned if he understood why.

CHAPTER 25

DO YOU want to touch or be touched?

Corey shivered thinking about the words Lucian had huskily whispered to him on the phone as they'd made plans for their next session. The next sense, it seemed, was touch. At the time, Corey'd had no answer for his companion as he was busy coming apart at the seams, gasping and gulping.

It was Friday, and Lucian was due to arrive any minute at Corey's apartment for their appointment, and Corey was a wreck. This was it, he knew. This session would measure if he could ever feel something from an intimate caress, a rough grope, or anything in between.

Though he wore his snuggest jeans and his favorite T-shirt, with a bold text saying I Aim to Misbehave, a quote from one of his favorite sci-fi TV shows, Corey didn't feel at all comfortable. He was sweating bullets, and every two minutes he checked his armpits in the mirror to see if there were wet rings on his shirt. His forehead was damp, though he wiped his face every five minutes. He was so anxious he'd spent the last twenty minutes pacing the length of his apartment, a fidgety bundle of raw nerves.

The doorbell rang, startling him so badly he jumped about a foot in the air.

Corey rushed to the door, eager to see Lucian after so many days, and yanked the door open with too much force. "Hey, Lu—" He stopped dead, his smile slipping and his back stiffening as he stared at Lucian— and a big, buff man carrying what looked like a portable cot.

Lucian smirked knowingly. "Do not worry, Corey. He will not be staying with us." He gestured for the third man to enter, and on automatic, Corey stepped aside to let them in. "In what room do you feel the most at ease?" Lucian asked.

Corey followed the huge man's movements. "Huh?" He had to shake his head to clear it, irritated at having a stranger traipsing through his home. Then, all of a sudden, he realized the man was not a stranger. To Lucian, he replied coolly, "Any room. They're all mine. No difference."

"All right." Lucian addressed the third man. "Set it up there, by the fireplace." He said to Corey, "Could we start a fire?"

"Yeah, sure." Frowning and gritting his teeth, Corey felt like adding a what-the-fuck-ever to this odd turn of events, but instead constrained himself to merely glaring and crossing his hands over his chest.

With swift efficiency, the third man opened and assembled the cot—which turned out to be a luxury portable massage table, wide and long and sturdy—a mere foot above the ground, situated right in front of the fireplace. Corey breathed in and out to calm himself, in part heating up, in part chilled to his spine at the implications of the device.

To touch or be touched? Corey shivered as he began to accept this was really and truly happening. He was going to touch another human being, with intent, with the aim to please—and to be pleasured. The notion was frightening, nerve-wracking even, since touch was the only sense he had no firsthand experience with, no memories he could draw on for strength or confidence other than his parents from childhood. But he wanted this so badly he could taste it.

Once the man finished preparing the massage table, he stood, nodded to both Corey and Lucian, and silently left the apartment. No weird glances, no knowing smirks, no verbal banter or casual innuendo. A professional at work, clearly.

"I recognize him. From Boudoir. He was there during our last session." Corey was glad the man had gone. It had been unnerving to stare at him and know exactly what he looked like naked. How on earth did people manage to interact intelligibly with people they had seen naked and had sex with? He simply could not wrap his brain around the lewd teaser trailer, so he shoved the disconcerting thoughts out of his mind.

Lucian nodded with a pleased smile. "Yes. The construction worker. Colton. He is a Dom. Plus, he is used to carrying heavy equipment, so I asked him for help. Paid for his time and services, of course."

"Of course." Corey recalled Lucian mentioning his prior affairs there. "Have you and he… bumped hips, so to speak?" He grimaced at his own words, while Lucian giggled. "Yeah, stupid euphemism. You and he fuck?" The crassness he used almost made him cringe again, but he was dying to know.

Lucian hedged. "It was not what you might call conventional sex. He orgasmed, as did I, but we did not exactly touch each other." The answer puzzled Corey, but thankfully Lucian explained. "It was a scene. He was the Dom, and I was the submissive. Like I said, there is a great deal of pleasure to be had even though no cocks penetrate any asses."

Corey considered the reply, trying to assimilate the information. As weird as it was for him to grasp, his baser instincts cried out in relief that Lucian had not fucked or been fucked by this rough-and-tumble Colton, who was apparently quite experienced in the BDSM world.

"Okay." He turned to the readied cot and gestured at it. "So, what's this about?"

"That is to acclimatize you to being touched. If you so desire. Incidentally, you have not yet told me of your decision. Touch or be touched?" Lucian removed his jacket, peach-colored this time, just like his slacks and tie, and tossed the garment on the back of the couch.

Blushing, Corey busied himself with the gas fireplace, and soon a lively fire roared, illuminating the space with dancing lights and shadows. "W-which do you recommend we start with?" He remained kneeling in front of the fire, staring at it but not seeing it, as his body was attuned and hyperaware of Lucian behind him. Goose bumps rose all over his skin as he knelt, waiting for a reply just to hear the man's sweet voice.

Lucian's footsteps inched closer until Corey knew the guy was standing right behind him, all but touching Corey's back with his knees. "If you do the touching, you will be in control. If I do it, I will have a certain amount of control, but I will be at your command. One word from you, and this stops."

Corey had zero reason to doubt Lucian would do exactly as he promised, proceeding or halting if Corey asked. The idea of a massage from those nimble, delicate fingers intrigued him to no end. Hot shivers ran up and down his skin, so close to a real touch that the hairs on his body stood up, craving the caress.

"I wouldn't mind trying this massage bed. After all, you went to such trouble getting it here." He glanced over his shoulder and grinned impishly.

Lucian laughed. "Ah, yes. Thankfully, like the gods of India, I have multiple pairs of hands to carry out any required tasks." Then he winked shamelessly. "If I only had those in real life... oh, the things I could do to you, my gorgeous Corey."

Corey flushed, his skin heating so intensely that he wished briefly he were nude. Then he blazed all over even more at the mental image of standing buck naked in front of Lucian.

"Goodness, how I wish I knew what went through your mind just now," Lucian said with a seductive purr as he ambled closer to Corey, who climbed to his feet. Once Lucian was near enough to touch, he locked gazes with Corey. "What I'm about to say I've wanted to say for many weeks, ever since we met to be exact. Corey? Take off your clothes."

Corey gulped. "Um, a-all of them…?" It was a silly question considering all he wore were jeans, T-shirt, and underwear. It would take all of five seconds to get naked.

Lucian tittered. "Let's start with the shirt and see where that revelation leads us, yes?"

Fighting embarrassment, Corey turned around, pulled his T-shirt over his head, and tossed it onto the couch. He swiveled back to face Lucian and his catlike green and blue eyes. He hadn't been sure which would unnerve him more: Lucian giving him that all-consuming, hungry stare or… not.

His chest heaved as he gasped for breath, and his heart hammered, making him dizzy. Lucian did stare at him, his beautiful gaze taking in every inch of Corey's bare torso. Corey wanted that look to last. He *wanted* to be seen.

His thoughts took a darker path then—even as his cock stirred in his pants, pushing restlessly against the zipper.

Corey had wished for someone to notice him. His real self, his true being, his inner man. Life was easy but hollow without someone to share it. But… would his life really be easy and happy with a person to love and to be loved by? Even if that someone was… Lucian?

At this point, staring into the mirror late at night with eyes like pitch black stars, he didn't want to go to bed lonely at heart and empty inside, crying himself to sleep, dreaming of a forever kind of bond, a mating he had never experienced, yet magically, instinctively, knew to wish for.

Loneliness constricted his gut, and his cock began to deflate. He was indecisive, torn. He had always believed knowledge was good but understanding was better. Now he was leaning in the whole ignorance was bliss direction, which was ludicrous.

He had to ask. He had to know. No matter if the road led to perdition or to bliss. "What's it like to fall in love? How was it for you? You know, for the first time?" Without noticing it at first, Corey held his breath, anxious to hear Lucian's response, silently hoping for bright colors, fluffy bunnies, joyful dancing, and perfect synchrony between two hearts.

Lucian's expression shuttered. "Would you mind terribly if we got started with the massage? I would feel more comfortable if...."

"If I couldn't look at you?" Corey felt his stomach plummet to icy depths of doubt and insecurity, but he fought to keep that from showing on his face. "Sure, fine."

He paused, his hands on the top button of his jeans, wondering if he should remove them. A part of him felt disenchanted and disappointed at Lucian's apparent cold shoulder. But he also knew that sometimes it was indeed easier to talk about sensitive, private things out of eyesight, the way the two of them had in the pitch-black room at Boudoir.

So he resumed unzipping his pants. This time Corey's half nudity wasn't coincidental because of a shower or bedtime. No, this was deliberate, planned, intentional. A sensual intimacy, perhaps more with himself than his current companion. After all, it was Corey's sexual experiences that were the goal here.

But were they the key to solving this riddle that Lucian posed? Probably not.

As he shoved his jeans down his legs and began yanking them off, Corey said, "You don't have to tell me anything if you don't want to. You know that, right? I'm not trying to pressure you or anything. I mean, just because I'm getting exposed here." He added a smirk at the end, trying to coax a positive response from his companion.

Thankfully, Lucian smiled, a tentative, soft gesture that lit his face right up. "Yes, I know. Forgive me." Then his gaze swept over Corey's body, bare except for his underwear, and a bold hunger sparked in Lucian's eyes. "Oh, Corey. You are truly a sight to behold."

Corey blushed, recalling Lucian's previous words when he stood naked in front of a mirror, those declarations burned into his memory like etchings on a stone. "You still want to lick stuff off my skin?" He had meant it as a tease, but Lucian's darkened stare was enough to get him to gulp as his rattled nerves prickled his skin.

Lucian grinned. "Perhaps I will use flavored massage oils, then."

Corey ducked his head to hide the massive grin widening on his face, and he shucked his jeans the rest of the way down, one of his pant legs still clinging to his ankle. "So, um, how do you want me?" Then, as his cheeks fired up with sudden embarrassment at the unintentional double entendre, he quickly stammered, "I mean, on the massage board?"

Lucian giggled. "Why don't we start facedown so I can work on your back?"

With swift clumsiness, Corey settled onto his stomach on the surprisingly comfortable massage table, tucked his arms by his sides, and rested his face on the doughnut-shaped face cushion. He felt awkward in just his boxer briefs, waiting to be touched, passive and immobile. He guessed that accounted for his ungainly movements, attempting to finish settling down on the massage bed as promptly as humanly possible.

He heard rustling, fabric sliding against skin, and flushed with heat at knowing his friend was removing his attire as well, getting ready to put his hands on Corey's bare skin. His cock again began to swell and harden in his tight undies, and he had to wiggle to accommodate the compression against the unyielding material and the table.

Corey heard Lucian saunter closer by the padding of his footsteps. A warm, light weight landed on Corey—*ohmygod, he's as close to naked as me*—as Lucian straddled the backs of Corey's thighs. The cool silk of Lucian's underwear felt amazing over Corey's inner thighs. Lucian shifted a couple of times to find the best position, and those seconds were blissful agony to Corey, who was shivering with building anticipation.

Lucian's delicate hands came to rest at the base of Corey's spine. There was no real pressure or hard groping, just a full-palm touch, fingers spread wide. "Are you all right?"

Corey swallowed, unable to find his voice, and nodded.

Those at once calming and unnerving hands abandoned him, and then Corey heard a bottle cap popping open. Liquid—most likely body oil—splashed, and then Lucian's slick, hot hands slid from the small of Corey's back up to his shoulders with just enough force for him to feel his muscles being kneaded like soft putty.

Corey groaned, relaxing into the touch, unwinding all over.

Lucian made a cute, muffled little giggle that had Corey smiling. "If I am too hard on you, please tell me, all right?" Corey suppressed a startled chortle at the suggestive words and how they could be misinterpreted. As was customary, Lucian seemed in tune with Corey's ponderings, and he too chuckled. "Oops. Poor choice of words. I am bad."

But Lucian twisted a bit, and the firm length of Lucian's cock pressed against Corey's buttocks, sliding into the crack as if belonging there, regardless of the two layers of clothes between them. Corey closed his eyes and wondered how on earth he could still draw breath. He was on fire, from head to toe, and his hips bucked.

Wow, that's new.

"Mmm, yes," Lucian murmured, his hips rocking back and forth ever so gently, barely moving at all. But the press of his hard shaft still nudged at Corey's private place, the one he had not believed would ever get much action. "Once more, darling, tell me if anything I do makes you... uneasy. That is the last thing I want."

Corey licked his dry lips, parched for something to drink. Anything. Even... Lucian's juices. And that... urge... shocked him to the core. "Just... stay there," he muttered, out of breath, needing Lucian to remain exactly where he was.

With the weight of them both on it, Corey expected the massage table to go all wobbly, particularly considering they were shifting on it constantly. But it never wavered, and Corey was able to decompress and cool off. Well, relatively speaking, since there was a totally hot body on top of him, manhandling him to sensual rapture.

Scents of lavender and chamomile wafted up to Corey's nose from the body oil, and he inhaled deeply, luxuriating in the soothing essential oils. "Nice smells."

Corey could hear Lucian's smile in his voice. "Thank you. I picked a relaxing scent instead of one more... arousing."

"Why? Isn't getting all hot and bothered supposed to be the idea tonight?"

"Are you in a hurry?" Lucian worked on Corey's muscles with surprisingly strong and adept fingers. His thumbs, especially, were sublime at finding all the pressure points where Corey was most tense. Corey moaned, loving every second of the almost excruciatingly firm touch that somehow melted his muscles and tendons and left behind a mass of jelly. "Or may I touch more of you as I please?"

"Yeah, yeah. Anything." Corey grunted in delight. "Just don't fucking stop."

Lucian laughed while rubbing Corey's neck and shoulders, back and sides, all the way down to the small of his back. Those nimble fingers traced every bump in Corey's spine, squeezed and stretched open every muscle with his flattened palms, and applied exquisite pressure to every inch of Corey's loosening body.

"You're a hell of a lot stronger than you look, Lu," Corey purred, relishing the caress of the man who was slowly but steadily acclimatizing him to the touch of another human being.

"Would it surprise you to know I went to an exclusive boarding school?"

Corey snorted. "Not really."

"Well, I did, where I excelled in gymnastics along with ballet. Doing that, I learned a great deal about the human body and how simple skin-to-skin contact can make you feel better."

"You mean, like, touch therapy, or something?"

"Yes. This session, this massage, is intended to make you feel restful and relaxed, to show you a touch can be nonsensual and still give you pleasure and enjoyment."

Corey mumbled out his pleasure, smiling, his eyes closed. "Mmm, check."

"But… because it is *I* doing the touching—" Lucian leaned down to whisper in Corey's ear, a slow seductive sound. "—I am also trying to get a rise out of you, to demonstrate how easy the shift from casual contact to a sensual caress is."

Immediately Corey's eyes popped open. Lucian's willowy body held a hairsbreadth apart from Corey's skin, which went goose bumpy in a heartbeat. He held his breath, waiting for that first brush of skin, that tentative, soft, light touch on his back that would send his senses into a spiral of satisfaction.

But it never came.

Lucian straightened up, and Corey didn't know whether to sigh in relief or scream his outrage at being denied again. But when Lucian resumed his powerful, perfect ministrations, Corey let it go. They would get another chance to explore, as they were in very close quarters indeed.

Lucian kneaded and extended Corey's knotted, stiff muscles, and tension oozed out of Corey like sweat through pores in a steam room. With each stroke and glide, Corey uncoiled, his anxiety waning and his stress vanishing, and his body became pliable, flexible, and soft. His whole mind turned hazy, softening around the edges as if the sharp pains in his head and the dull aches in his stomach no longer mattered. Never in his entire life, as far back as he could remember, had he felt so chill, so blissed out, so unwound.

That was when things got weird. He felt the tremors first, the uncontrollable shaking of his whole body, and had no willpower available to contain the reaction. Then came the moisture on his face.

Before he knew it, Corey was crying. Subtle sobs at first, then escalating into deep gulps and intense blubbering. Hot tears trickled down his cheeks, flowing out of his itchy, half-lidded eyes, and he watched them fall on the floor, splattering like raindrops.

Corey had never realized, not with the total awareness of this moment, how much he *ached* to be touched. His raw, palpable loneliness permeated his whole body, from skin to soul. Perhaps the constant solitude had fried his brain, making him mad, delusional, and wanting impossible things. But in his heart, he had more than an inkling it was this isolation that left him hollow and hurting, touch deprived and in desperate need for contact.

"Fuck. I'm sorry." Corey was glad his face was hidden by the cushion, but he wasn't stupid enough to believe or hope that Lucian hadn't noticed. His large frame shook from weeping.

Lucian's hands never stopped, their pace slowing, gentling. "It's all right. It happens. Nothing to be ashamed of or embarrassed about. I promise." His tone was as tender as his touch, and Corey was grateful for his understanding.

For a long time, though Corey had no comprehension of its passage, Lucian continued to rub and massage him, up from his bulging arms to his broad shoulders and hairy scalp, and then down his long, lean back to his buttocks, dipping beneath the waistband of his underwear to move over the soft skin and firm mounds. Though his sobs subsided in due course, the trembling didn't end as quickly as Corey would have wished.

"Corey?" Lucian's voice was small and shy, as if he didn't want to disturb Corey in his weakened state. "Do you want me to stop, or would you roll over to lie on your back?"

Corey couldn't move, not so much as budge.

"I will get you some water. It is important to hydrate after a massage." Lucian started to slide off, but Corey couldn't have that, so he pleaded.

"Please, don't go. Not yet."

Halting, Lucian shifted gracefully to regain his former position, sitting on the backs of Corey's thighs. His warm, oily hands lay on Corey's skin, their touch now familiar and soothing. Corey needed that grounding presence right then.

"It really is all right," Lucian whispered. "Many people, men and women of all ages, have strong emotional reactions to massages. When skin is touched and the body worked on, we learn how inextricably linked the physical and emotional are."

Corey let out a wet snort. "Strong reactions? Crying their eyes out?"

"Yes. That, and more. I assure you it is the truth."

That calmed Corey, the knowledge he wasn't alone in his emotional breakdown, that others could experience the same sudden epiphany, the empty loneliness, and then find release, letting that feeling go in a huge outburst.

With that certainty in mind, he confessed, "I cried after that first awesome orgasm too. The one in the shower, you know. Is that... normal?" God, how he needed Lucian to say he was not a total basket case.

He more felt than saw Lucian nod. "It can be, for both men and women. Especially for you because it was your first time climaxing with specific intent and not simply ridding yourself of a morning erection. It was your first foray into the sensual realm, the one hiding within you, so it was natural and even to be expected it would stir many different emotions and reactions from you."

It took Corey a moment to digest this, the truth of a blinding, shattering instance when he had let out everything he'd held back, each drop of despair within him. "I... I couldn't stop. I just... had to. It was all... too much."

"I understand." Lucian sounded sympathetic, and he caressed Corey's back for a time, long, languid pettings that told Corey he would be okay. "You are dealing with a great deal of stress right now. Not just from our sensual sojourns, but with your father too. How is he?"

Corey snorted. "A cantankerous old bastard is what. He's out of the hospital, but he's on 24/7 supervision by a live-in nurse, and he's being such a pain in the—"

"I hope this nurse maiden is able to take care of a... a PITA."

Corey chuckled a bit, lighter in his heart, however briefly. "You and your euphemisms and abbreviations. But... the nurse is quite a strong *guy*, so I daresay he can handle my dad." After a minor amused snort, Corey grew serious again. "I don't want Dad to die."

Lucian comforted Corey with his presence. "Tough old coots die last or not at all."

"I just started to connect with him. And it's so stupid, you know. All it really took was one single conversation to lay our cards on the table. Why he and I never tried that direct approach before.... Fuck if I know." Corey sighed, feeling tired and lethargic. "Stress does seem to be my constant companion. And this, you know, what we're doing... it's taking a lot out of me."

Lucian rubbed Corey's shoulders gently. "Many, if not the majority, of people awaken to these physical and sensual realizations during adolescence, when their whole beings are already in turmoil, so what is one more novel experience added to that turbulence. A lightning strike seems less potent when it happens during a storm than out of a clear blue sky."

"And I'm dealing with this shit as an adult," Corey remarked, glum.

All of a sudden Lucian pinched Corey's back. Hard enough for Corey to yelp. Lucian growled. "If you're about to say that makes you a loser or a failure or a freak, I will spank the living daylights out of you." Lucian sounded like he meant business, and immediately Corey felt better, lighter, and stronger. He could handle this, and the consequences too.

"I would never say that. Not in your company." Lucian pinched him again, but Corey chuckled. "And I won't say it to me, myself, and I again either. I promise. Cross my heart and hope to die. So would you please stop? I thought corporal punishment was passé."

Lucian leaned forward, draping himself over Corey's back. Corey's breath hitched when Lucian whispered in his ear, "Oh, I don't know. I have a hunch you wouldn't mind a little slap with your tickle." To accentuate his innuendo, Lucian slipped both hands under Corey's boxer briefs, clutching and gripping his buttocks hard enough to sting *and* leave marks.

The image of finger-shaped bruises on his ass cheeks *and* Lucian's timely touches had Corey's deflated cock standing at attention in the blink of an eye. And when that fantasy received an added slap from Lucian's hand, Corey was certain he was going spectacularly insane.

Chapter 26

"Do you wish to turn over and continue?" Lucian asked, waiting for Corey to accept Lucian's tempting presence.

It occurred to Lucian as he sat patiently on top of Corey that once their mentor/client relationship was over, Lucian would be free to see Corey in any capacity. No more rules to prohibit their emotional and physical relationship. *Right?* Or would it still be unethical to have an affair with a former client? Repression and regression were the obvious risks involved, he concluded, torn in two, caught between want and duty. He would have to think on it—later.

"W-what else you got planned?" Corey sounded hesitant, unsure, obviously in need of a break, a cooling off period.

"I told you I required time to make preparations." Lucian rested his forearms on the thick, relaxed muscles of Corey's back. "Of course, now that our sessions are one-on-one tutorials instead of more complex displays and experiments at Boudoir, I've had to readjust my designs."

Calmer and curious, Corey asked, "Are you gonna tell me in advance or just spring up one surprise after another? Can't wait."

Lucian blew a breath over Corey's neck, rustling his hair about. Corey's skin bristled, and he inhaled sharply, exciting Lucian. "Are you going to turn over?"

For a while Corey did not reply. Then out of the blue, he began to shift and roll to lie on his back. Lucian moved up on his knees to accommodate his movements, but then, as soon as Corey resettled, he sat right back down, his balls pressing against Corey's.

Lucian gleefully observed Corey's obvious aroused state. His cheeks and neck were flushed, his pupils dilated, his breathing shallow, his hands gripped the crevice of Lucian's thighs and hips, and his cock was fire hot and rock hard in his black boxer briefs, tenting and stretching the fabric into a delicious bulge that Lucian craved to mouth and wet.

A thin sheen of sweat made Corey's taut muscles glisten, and without thinking, Lucian glided his palms over Corey's forearms and biceps, past his clavicles and jugular notch, and down his firm, round pectorals, stiff pink nipples, cute little belly button, and those flat, tight, and ridged abs. By the time his fingers scraped over the salt-and-pepper treasure trail of hair leading to Corey's cock, Lucian was mad with desire, while Corey squirmed, apparently ticklish.

Lucian giggled. "Like or dislike?" His fingertips danced over Corey's rippling belly.

Corey grunted, a smile fleeting on his lips. "H-haven't decided yet." Then his gaze shot up to lock with Lucian's. "You gonna answer me about falling in love? What was it like for you? How did it feel?"

Lucian stopped what he was doing. His first instinct was to recoil and deflect. But this was Corey, and he could not tell a lie. "It is... difficult to describe. It is so very personal, intimate, and different for everyone." It was even odder and more discomforting to speak about his first love when sitting on top of a mostly naked *other* man.

Corey petted Lucian's thighs, catching his eyes and smiling softly. "You don't have to tell me if you don't want to."

Lucian frowned, conflicted about what to confess and what to hold back. "Does the idea of me being with other men bother you?"

Corey grinned then, with no sign of jealousy. "I wouldn't have asked if I didn't want to know. Genuinely. Honestly. I swear." His hands were a warm weight on Lucian's skin, and he liked having Corey touching him.

So he made his decision. "Remember when I told you about the boy I met in Italy at my grandfather Julian's mansion?"

"The boy you kissed in the fields? Yeah."

"His name was Paulo. He was my first kiss. But he was *not* my first love. That came much later in life." Lucian had to look back to a past buried, peer inside his hidden memories, and it wasn't an entirely pleasant experience. "I was sweet sixteen when I met Max. A late bloomer. He went to the same private school as I did. He was new, so naturally he was fascinating and attractive to me."

Corey smiled. "And you fell head over heels for him, huh?"

Lucian smiled back but felt lacking in true joy. "Max was larger than life, addicted to living life to the fullest. I could never keep up with him. I fell... behind."

Corey's smile faded as understanding dawned on him. "The love was one-sided? Oh, Lu, I'm so sorry to dredge up the past."

"No, no." Lucian waved a hand about, dismissive. "I have cowered from the memory of him long enough. And no, it was not entirely one-sided. He had me whenever he felt inclined to do so. I let him have me because I was in love with him. I learned a lot about love in my two and a half months with him."

Corey grimaced. "No offense to your taste of men, but I don't think I like the guy. If he didn't want you, then fuck him. Loser." He grunted, obviously certain in his conviction about Max's character.

That defensive streak warmed Lucian's heart. "Thank you, Corey. That means a great deal to me." He recalled the last time he and Max had talked, and it had not been sweet and loving. "For a time, in the beginning, falling in love was… amazing. Empowered, I felt alive, full of energy and light all the time, as though I could take on the world. I walked on air, dazed and with a grin on my face all the time. But… there was a flip side to it. The deepening of my emotions was indeed like falling without a safety net into a terrible, vast emptiness, a darkness I could not see into."

"Were you scared?" Corey sounded frightfully concerned, his grip on Lucian's thighs tightening.

Lucian nodded. "Afraid, happy, sad, hopeful, blissful. Everything at once. Emotions took me over, encompassing me, filling me."

"I'm sorry it didn't end well."

Lucian tried to shrug but was aware the gesture was anything but carefree. "In a way love is always one-sided. No one but you can truly feel it. The object of your love may or may not be in love as well, but their feelings are never exactly equal to yours. Love can be shared, yes, but it is never perfectly on par between both, or all, partners."

Corey frowned, seemingly puzzled. "You mean, in reality only one ever feels the love? Or that there are stages and phases to loving, and when one is deeply in love, the other might be just falling in, or out of, love?"

Lucian was pleased Corey tried to understand Lucian's meaning. He felt bad because he could hear his own loneliness bleed into his words, adding an edge of despair he did not wish for Corey to adopt.

"The latter." *And sometimes the former, but you don't need to know that.*

Corey nodded, apparently placated by the definite reply—even though Lucian was not a believer in his own teachings. Not anymore. "H-have you been with many men?"

Swallowing hard and wishing he were someplace else, Lucian licked his dry lips and tried to find a suitable answer. "Yes." Corey's eyelids fluttered almost closed, hiding his expression as the rest of his face went blank. "I asked you if you were bothered—"

"That's not why I asked." Corey shook his head. "I was wondering… you probably weren't in love with all of them?"

"No. Not even half. I have learned to… to guard my heart from ache."

"It… it hurts… badly…?"

Lucian felt a twinge in his chest, sharp and cruel. "When your heart is broken?" He let out a breath, a sudden burst of air, as if exhaling anxieties along with oxygen. "Physical pain can be sharp or dull. But a broken heart? The ache is at once hollow and full, with a kind of deep sorrow that penetrates your entire being, until you feel empty and drained, heavy and completely at a loss. It is as if you are at the bottom of a hole, dark and dismal, and you cannot climb out. Like a piece of your soul is missing, and you're never going to get it back."

Corey swallowed hard, and Lucian could see he had a hard time assimilating this new information. "N-nothing makes it better? Ever…?"

Lucian gave a reassuring smile, praying it would be interpreted correctly. "Time heals all wounds. Even broken hearts. Sometimes… it helps to keep the faith that even though things did not work out, you are still worthy and capable of love."

"Falling in love *again* cures all ills, is that it? In the hopes next time everything will turn out perfect?" Corey did not sound convinced.

"If you fall off a horse, you get right back in the saddle, as the adage goes." Lucian gave Corey a small nudge, his palms just below Corey's pecs. "I am not saying it will never get any easier. But it is not the end of the world, even if it feels like it for a while."

Corey bit his lower lip, obviously still worried. "Have you ever been in love that didn't end in heartbreak, so that it all worked out?"

"Yes." A few names sprung to Lucian's mind.

"Then how come you aren't together with that person, or any of them?"

"Mostly because when you fall in love, it feels as if you are… for the lack of a better word, high. Intoxicated with love, with the other person. All rough edges are smoothed. But… no one is as perfect as they appear through romanticized, rose-tinted glasses. When you are in love, a part of you is blind to reality. When that haze wears off… true colors appear.

Character flaws and annoying habits, it all becomes visible. Most relationships strain under reality's harsh grip, and as a result some end. For some, though, love deepens, becoming one with reality, no holds barred. With the ones I cared for... I was lucky. We parted amicably."

For a long time, Corey seemed preoccupied, weighing Lucian's words. "I see."

Lucian felt it was time to inquire further. "Corey, let us be realistic and straight here. These sessions we are having.... Have you pictured yourself after our sessions end? Beyond sexual experimentation? Having an actual relationship? Do you see that in your future? What kind of relationship would we be talking about? Casual or exclusive? Gay or straight? Monogamous or polyamorous? Marriage or bachelorhood?"

Lucian might have continued bombarding Corey with questions, but Corey placed his hand firmly over Lucian's still bubbling mouth. "Lu, stop. No, I haven't thought that far ahead. I can't. Not until I know if I can ever cross *this* bridge."

Ashamed at being so callous to Corey's predicament, Lucian felt rebuked. "Yes, of course. I understand. I.... Please forgive me for being so insensitive."

Surprisingly, Corey smiled softly, shook his head, and caressed Lucian's thighs. "You challenge me, it's true. But insensitive? That's the last thing you are. Not with someone vulnerable who you are trying to help. In fact, not with anyone." In the blink of an eye, the mood shifted when Corey rubbed up and down Lucian's thighs, an amazed, all but reverent look on his face. "Your skin is so fucking soft. Even your thighs. Hairless and smooth, like silk."

The air thickened and crackled between them. Lucian was suddenly out of breath and in desperate need of fresh oxygen. His skin was on fire, and his groin joined in on the fun. His dick elongated and grew as desire coursed through his veins, pumping blood into his needy member. The simmering ambience was gone in a flash, and it was replaced by a rapid boiling.

"I-I'm glad you like my...." Lucian's voice cracked, and he couldn't finish.

Not when Corey slipped his hands past Lucian's hips to cup his buttocks.

But Corey's gaze was aimed directly at Lucian, a piercing, studying look. "Is this too forward?"

Lucian was trying very hard not to pass out with sudden overstimulation, so it took him a moment to answer. "W-we are s-supposed to progress at your pace."

Corey nodded, licking his lips slowly as his gaze wandered down Lucian's body, as if taking in the scenery at his leisure. "What kind of preparations were you gonna make at Boudoir? You know, if we'd gone there instead of here." His eyes mesmerized Lucian as they locked with his. "What kind of touch experiments did you have in mind? Tell me."

That was Corey's confident tone again, working overtime, with a casual power that Lucian had in a short time come to admire, adore, and savor. "I was going to introduce you to different kinds of touches in a sensual environment. You are already familiar with the erotic caress of water, as your experiment in the shower demonstrated, yes?"

Corey grinned. "Yeah. Can't argue with that assessment. What else?"

"How about the touch of food?" Lucian smiled teasingly as Corey appeared baffled. "I would have arranged for you to serve as a platter, with a variety of fine cuisine and five-star dishes placed on your naked body, while I and perhaps other men would have eaten off you. Slices of fruit devoured off your chest, honey sipped from your lips, sweet beverages drunk from your navel. How does that sound?"

Clearly it sounded exciting because Corey's face and neck reddened, and he started to pant. But he managed to say nothing, just gawked, eyes wide.

"What about fabrics?" Lucian flirted with every gesture, unyielding in his attempt to provide Corey new material for his fantasies. "The airy caress of silk, the erotic luxury of lace, the warm musk of leather, the ticklish heat of fur. All that and sex too. What say you now?"

Corey's lips moved, but no sound emerged. His eyes were huge as saucers, his pupils blown as his arousal grew.

"I had planned on giving you a tour of sex toys as well. To offer you the opportunity to touch and familiarize yourself with sensual paraphernalia that may one day be very intimate with your inner physique." Lucian let his gaze take a leisurely course over Corey's body. "I personally think you would you look divine wearing a cock ring. And perhaps a cock cage as well. No, I think we'll have two different sessions for those. And, of course, let us not forget whips, canes, chains, and everything else under the sun. How red your skin would be after a kiss from the flogger...."

For a moment there was nothing but silence, heavy as both men held their breath. Then Corey exhaled in a burst of air, chuckling. "Wow. Just... wow." Corey grinned suddenly, all of his eagerness on display. "We're gonna do all that, Lu, I promise." Then his smile faded, and a wistful look replaced his joy. "But not tonight. No more talking. I just wanna... feel." Like steel in sunlight, his determination shone. "You had your turn. Now... I wanna touch you."

Lucian swallowed hard, as if there were a cinderblock lodged in his throat, but he managed to nod as well. All the time they had spent together, every sensual test they had undergone side by side, they all came down to this. To this moment, this time and place.

"Please, touch me." Lucian heard his own voice quiver, but he didn't bother to censor the reaction, loving the sight of Corey's eyes darkening at the tremor in his tone.

"How do you, um, like to be touched?" Corey gripped Lucian's ass cheeks tighter, as if worried his about-to-be lover would abscond any second.

Lucian giggled softly, playfully. "In a matter of heartbeats, you are about to become my lover, so... I am sure you can figure it all out for yourself. After all, Corey, lovemaking should be unhurried and leisurely, a voyage of sensual exploration. I am confident you can do the journey justice." Lucian straightened up, his heart hammering. "Do what you will. I promise I will be quite vocal if we encounter a hard limit."

Corey's brow furrowed. "Hard limit?"

"Oh, forgive me. It is a term used in BDSM sex. It refers to prohibited issues, aspects of a scene that would take the play onto undesirable, too uncomfortable, or even hazardous ground. Basically, it refers to things that are off limits. If these boundaries are crossed, the scene should end. Always. Safe words should prevent scenes from going wrong in this fashion."

Lucian watched with curiosity as Corey's eyes took on a dangerous glint. "I see." His body immobile, Corey seemed to become a statue, digesting the news. "And what are your hard limits?"

"I have a great deal of experience with sex. I have done a lot. Most of my limits are soft, which means they can be negotiated—as in, enacted but requiring a careful approach. For example, I have fair skin, and I bruise easily. To avoid any domestic abuse allegations and rumors flying about, I tend to shy away from the cane, even though it too can be handled with care so no bruising occurs."

Corey seemed to bristle. "So, there's nothing you wouldn't do?"

"I do not engage in scat or blood play. Those are hard limits."

For a while Lucian worried their tryst would be over before it began. But then Corey shrugged. "Likewise. No poop, no vital fluids. Also, no zombie fantasies or animals. Just plain old human sex." He winked at the end, and the mood was back to upbeat and enthusiastic.

"Ah, that old black magic." Lucian rested his elbows on Corey's smooth, muscular chest, dipping his head to hover above Corey's lips. "Now what?"

Corey stared at Lucian's lips hungrily and licked his own luscious lips Lucian desired to devour for hours. "Well, obviously I can't kiss you." Lucian backed off a few inches, puzzled and a bit disappointed. There must have been a question on his face because Corey smiled in that smug manner he sometimes did when his self-confidence got a boost. "According to you, this session is about touch, not taste. I can't kiss you without tasting you."

Annoyed at the reminder, Lucian growled, though it sounded like a purr. "We could agree tonight is a no-limits, no-holds-barred session, with no senses out of bounds. But only if you wish it."

"No. Tell me what *you* want." Corey's eyes narrowed, and there was a stark wariness in his voice and posture. He seemed to be waiting for something.

It only took Lucian a second to figure out the mystery, the need for acknowledgment and assurance of mutually shared desires. So he took a leap of faith. "I want *you*, Corey. All of you. And I want you to have me in return. In every sense."

CHAPTER 27

COREY GURGLED something unintelligible as the truth hit him.

I'm going to have sex. I'm going to have sex with a man. Sex with Lucian. With Lu.

My Lu. Mine.

The first thing he noticed was Lucian's warm breath fanning over his face like hot air from the tropics as the curve of his tempting mouth curled up. Next was the dark yet luminescent glow of Lucian's huge eyes in the firelight, one midnight blue, one deep forest green. Lucian's taut body trembling against Corey's, his quivering muscles flexing, the skin of his cheeks, neck, and chest growing pink from arousal.

But then, blanketing all other observations, came the nerve-wracking sensation of their crotches pressed tightly together. Lucian's dick jumped against Corey's equally rigid member.

Corey gulped. The small weight of another man's balls in contact with his, plus a hot, hard length of cock next to his, they were totally new experiences. He had to…. Corey shifted his hips from side to side, feeling Lucian's sac and dick move.

His hips bucked, involuntarily, and a gasp escaped his mouth.

"Mmm, yesss…." Lucian murmured softly, and his eyes fluttered closed. Corey, on the other hand, could not have closed his eyes if his life depended on it. Lucian was utterly beautiful, caught up in rapture. Corey fantasized about Lucian's orgasm face, knowing the term but never having seen it firsthand, not even his own.

Should I kiss him now? Is he waiting for me to initiate…? What do I do?

Questions plagued Corey's mind, preying on his vulnerabilities and weaknesses. But this time he wasn't about to let those fears stop him.

It's just one damn kiss, dumbass.

Roughly, but immediately gentling his grip, Corey cupped Lucian's face, dragged him down, and kissed him. Their lips stayed closed, a mere press of flesh against flesh, smooth and dry, with a hint of more as they both held their breath. The kiss was tentative and even shy, as if neither wanted to take it further first.

Corey slipped his right hand around to rub Lucian's nape—and the silky strands of his red-gold locks slid through his fingers, almost like water. His cock stirred as if his hands were connected to his dick in some tangible way. Corey stroked Lucian's soft hair, threading his fingers through the thick mane, worshipping the sensation.

Panting into the kiss, he murmured, "God, I love your hair. It's like silk."

Since Corey's eyes were closed, he didn't see but felt Lucian smile. "Thank youuu...." His voice trailed off, muffled as Corey's tongue prevented Lucian from being coherent.

Corey's fingertips were so sensitized his hands trembled. He yanked on Lucian's luscious locks a little more sharply than he had intended. The curls wrapped around his digits.

"*Ouch!*" Lucian pulled back from the kiss, and Corey was mortified. But Lucian just giggled with a look of pleased, surprised contentment on his face. "Tugging on hair during sexual ardor? I approve." Then, without further ado, he dove back into the kiss, as though the interruption had never happened.

Corey gave up trying to figure out Lucian's intricacies. He was a personality all right, and deciphering him seemed pointless. The initial, barest hint of pressure on Corey's lips during the first kiss had changed altogether. Lucian was clearly hungry for Corey, kissing Corey like he meant it, like it was all he wanted and needed to do. And, *damn*, how hot was that?

Their tongues pushed against each other, slippery slides and deep entanglements that drove Corey out of his mind with lust unlike any he had ever felt before. His shower fantasies about Lucian paled in comparison to the real thing. Lucian hummed into the kiss, and the sound tickled and reverberated inside Corey so profoundly he felt it all the way down to his curling toes.

Lucian clutched at Corey's big biceps, as if hanging on for dear life, and his hips were moving, downright humping the man beneath him. Corey flushed with heat when he felt the silky fabric Lucian wore growing hotter and wetter and a rigid column of flesh pressing against his stomach, rubbing.

Lucian's cock.

Corey didn't know what to do: To hold on to Lucian more firmly or to take charge, flip them over until Corey was on top, and then simply fuck—

Fuck! He had no idea how to do that, how to get to the fucking. No, the lovemaking. Not that the precise term mattered. Well, his ignorance wasn't entirely encompassing. He did understand the mechanics of gay sex. But in practice, with a perfect, nubile, writhing man in his arms? Not a clue.

So, since he didn't know what else to do, Corey threw himself headlong into the kiss. He gripped Lucian's jaw with one hand and the back of his neck with the other, controlling the feel of the kiss, the depth, the angle. Corey breathed heavily through his nose, unwilling to be separated from Lucian even for a second. Lucian's fruity scent filled his nostrils, and the flavor of melons sated his taste buds.

But it was Lucian who was evidently in charge. He fused their lips together, sealing the kiss into one unbroken touch. Lucian mashed their tongues against each other, long and hungry consumptions that became endless. Corey had never in his life been kissed by another man; no one but Lucian had ever touched him like this. But now as he was engaged in the act, it was the most natural and sublime experience he had ever undertaken, and he didn't want it to end.

I am so freaking gay I should tattoo it on my forehead in neon.

It was Lucian who tore his mouth away, to gasp and gulp hard, his skin flushed and his eyes almost black. "Ohmygod, Corey...." His voice dropped in tone down to husky, as if he had lost the ability to use normal inflections.

"More." That was the only thought in Corey's mind and body. He needed more, or he feared his heart might stop beating.

"As you wish." Lucian's voice cracked and quaked, and Corey loved it, knowing he was the cause of Lucian's slow but steady unraveling.

Then they were kissing again, long play of tongues, heavenly slippery friction, taste to rival that of ambrosia and nectar from the gods. The reality of Lucian thrusting his tongue virtually down Corey's throat like there was no tomorrow made Corey happier than he ever remembered being. Not a single one of his past fears, not even the ick factor, made an appearance.

Lucian moved in a rising, rocking tempo as he ground against Corey, who was certain his mind blew a fuse. His eyes rolled to the back of his head, and he groaned loudly, though the sound was muffled by Lucian's mouth. As far as Corey was concerned, if this was what he had to look forward to with sex, the kissing could continue into eternity.

Lucian was passionate and self-confident in his kissing but also gentle and soft, and the touch of his mouth was... perfect. For Corey, it was all perfect. Lucian's unique taste teased his senses, demanding more uninterrupted sensuality and intimacy. Corey's cock screamed to be let out to play, a first for him.

Then a firm hand cupped Corey's erection.

Corey moaned desperately, like a wanton sex slave, and the two men pulled apart, but only by a couple of inches. "Holy shit...."

"Oh, yes, indeed," Lucian murmured back, rubbing his hand along Corey's shaft over and over, the grip hardly punishing, but strong and relentless nonetheless. Above Corey, Lucian wet lips that seemed redder now, more luscious, glistening, swollen. *I did that to him. Gave him kiss lips. I'll give him dick lips next.* As if reading Corey's smutty mind, Lucian whispered hoarsely, "I may be a devoted vegetarian, but right now I want to eat your meat."

Corey was struck silent by the crass and even corny comment. But his body had no qualms about how to respond as his arms wound around Lucian's lower back to pin him close, unyielding. And all the while, the insistent grinding continued, their hard cocks side by side, separated only by two layers of clothing.

"Fuck yeah. Anything you want, Lu. Have at me."

Corey wasn't naïve. He was well aware this was a cardinal sin for newbies and virgins. The dangerous lure of the "oh please, don't stop, whatever you want is fine" phase where inhibitions were lowered by ravenous need and where threats loomed ahead in acts of pure recklessness. The beckoning temptation to surrender was overwhelming, and because it was Lucian Corey was with, that attraction increased a thousandfold.

"I won't hurt you. I promise. We won't have to do anything you're uncomfortable with. You say slow down or you need a minute or for me to stop, and we will." Lucian spoke reassurances that, to his surprise, Corey no longer felt he needed. He did believe Lucian was sincere, but Cory didn't require vows of safety protocols to be with the man he desired. Not anymore.

"I know, Lu." Corey locked gazes with Lucian, unhesitant but still asking the question. "Can I… undress you…?"

Lucian moaned softly. "Yesss, anything, sweetheart."

To prevent himself from becoming the prey of doubt, Corey slipped his hands down to cup Lucian's buttocks and then squeezed them gently, not wanting to hurt his lover. The soft yet firm mounds of flesh flexed a bit under Corey's touch, trembling. The velvety smooth skin was cool at first, but then the curves heated, though Corey couldn't be certain if that warmth emanated from his palms or poured out of Lucian, or both.

As Lucian devoured Corey in another heated kiss, Corey quickly pushed the offending underwear out of his way to gain access to every inch of Lucian's exposed skin. Corey was shaking so badly he worried he might come prematurely. His cock leaked precum profusely, dampening the front of his boxer briefs and his lower belly.

Is all that precum mine, or are some of the droplets… his…?

Corey sure wanted to believe so, working one of his hands back to weave through Lucian's hair, the silky locks calling out to him. He tugged a little, eliciting a soft purr from Lucian. In fact, Lucian kept making sweet, delectable little noises when Corey simultaneously wound his fingers around Lucian's curls and squeezed Lucian's ass.

"Oh, Corey, the sweet things you do to me," Lucian whispered breathlessly, his mouth forceful and gentle on Corey's lips.

Corey couldn't stop staring at Lucian, taking in every minute detail of the gorgeous guy sitting on top of him. Well, more like lying at the moment. "God, Lu. When you kiss, I feel it everywhere, from head to toes," Corey murmured, unable to keep his feelings inside. "I feel it right here." He touched his chest, gently beating the place over his heart.

Lucian smiled into the kiss, and Corey felt the man's teeth with his kiss-sensitized lips. "As do I." Lucian closed his eyes, as if he were having a pleasant waking dream. But quickly he followed with his barely parted lips, brushing them over Corey's, side to side, gliding their flesh together, no pressure, no urgency, only the briefest erotic contact. Corey whimpered, and his lips tingled all over. "You have such delicious lips. I could attach myself to them for days."

The heat within Corey reached volcanic levels. "Yeah. Me too. You, I mean."

Lucian snickered and then retreated, a puckish grin on his face. "I leave it up to you to decide whether it is fortuitous that my lips are headed down for an altogether different target." He winked wickedly and then began to slither down Corey's body, like a snake recoiling.

This time Corey didn't need to use his imagination. As Lucian progressed, he kissed, licked, and sucked all over. Corey's neck received some lavish full-tongue action, his clavicles were softly sucked, and the curves of his muscles were traced with the tip of a tongue and tickling fingers. Corey's nipples gained special attention as Lucian used his lips to tentatively brush over the hardening, fleshy nubs, his hot breath giving Corey goose bumps. Lucian licked all around the areolas, getting the pointy tips wet and achingly solid before he opened his mouth and sucked on the right one while fiddling and tugging on the left, adding a little twist, half-painful but entirely sensual.

"Holy fucking shit!" Corey's hips jerked upward, his cock banging against Lucian's chest.

Lucian's teasing laugh vibrated on Corey's skin. Then he bit at the tender nipple, gently but hard enough to sting. The resulting electric jolt of mixed pain and pleasure raced through Corey, and he cried out.

God, how badly Corey wanted Lucian to stop his procrastinating and advance to their mutual goal. Lucian looked up, his breath whispering on Corey's chest. "Like?"

Corey was dimly aware he might have muttered or freaking gurgled, but his hands at least seemed to know what to do as they gripped Lucian's hair and pushed him down. "Please…."

Lucian's mirth never subsided, even as he allowed himself to be unceremoniously shoved toward Corey's groin. The soft puffs of heated, wet breaths tickled Corey's body until he believed he would come apart from all this stimulation.

"Y-you know, our s-session…." Corey swallowed hard, his thoughts a jumble, hard to get a handle on. "Touching, tasting. How were you g-g-gonna keep them separate, anyway?"

Lucian considered this, pausing briefly. "You know what? I honestly had not figured that out yet. Thankfully, by now the question is moot. Inseparable sensations of sweet lovemaking, mmm…."

Then Lucian placed an openmouthed kiss below Corey's navel with a lewd suckling sound. Corey's stomach muscles contracted. He shivered all over. Laving a wet, scorching path, Lucian smooched downward, gracefully shimmying Corey's boxer briefs down and then off, until he came to the base of Corey's cock, surrounded by closely-trimmed dark pubic hair. Lucian sidled lower until his cheek brushed one side of Corey's shaft.

Masturbating really didn't adequately prepare Corey for the way all the nerve endings in his cock suddenly lit up like a star being born. Corey moaned, his voice cracking, and he had to let go of Lucian's hair and grip the sides of the portable table or risk yanking out tufts in his wild, passionate abandon.

"Mmm, how good you smell," Lucian murmured while rubbing his face all over Corey's cock. Corey was pretty sure his brain was melting into goo. "Masculine, strong, in heat."

Corey had no idea if those were scents at all or just Lucian's way of putting things. He didn't care either, not as long as Lucian kept doing what he was doing.

"You know," Lucian muttered as he explored, "When I was a teenager, I used to spend an inordinate amount of time masturbating. Sometimes half a dozen times a day, or more. Almost anything would set the infernal thing off." He glanced up at Corey wickedly. "Good thing I did not know you back then, or I would have rubbed my poor cock to shreds in a week."

Corey shuddered at the images bursting into his head.

Then Lucian slid his palms from Corey's sides, causing him to jump a little, down past his hips to his thighs, caressing and squeezing, flooding Corey's brain with new sensations. Lucian pushed Corey's thighs apart, hooked his arms under them, dragged his body down—and then he swallowed Corey's cockhead, his lips fastening around the crown like an unbreakable seal.

Screaming, Corey felt his eyes roll to the back of his head, and his hips bucked up fast and violently. The fear of suffocating Lucian with his dick had Corey trying to control the reaction, but Lucian's hand around his thighs and hips were far more effective.

Lucian released the tip with a soft pop, licking his lips. "It's all right. You can push."

"D-don't w-wanna hurt you…." Shaking, Corey was weak in the knees, in his thighs, weak in the heart, everywhere.

Lucian giggled playfully. "While your size *is* impressive, I have a… deep throat." The imp waggled his eyebrows, and Corey blushed but grinned back because, *damn*, he was just happy. And then they were both chuckling, a bubbling levity filling Corey until he was sure he radiated joy.

"I-is t-this what we're gonna do tonight…?" Corey asked, wondering if Lucian would stop his sensual ministrations after giving Corey his first blowjob ever.

"Not by a long shot." Lucian winked and then resumed by unhooking one arm from under Corey's thigh and clutching the base of Corey's dick, holding the thick, aroused piece of meat upright. For a long, unnerving moment, Lucian studied Corey's cock. "I love how you are not circumcised. You feel so warm and fluid, like velvet."

Experimentally, Corey assumed, Lucian moved the foreskin back and forth over the tip, covering and exposing the head, again and again, the motion slicked by precum. All Corey knew was how fucking good it felt to get jacked off. Especially with someone *else* doing it. How come it had never felt his good with his own hand?

"It's not, um, ugly or anything?" Corey recalled how Lucian was cut, his cock pretty, silky, and pink, with a rosy-hued tip that somehow managed to look much bigger than his own.

Lucian glared at him and then rolled his eyes. "You will never say anything that stupid to me again, do I make myself clear?"

Corey had little choice but to nod in compliance. Inside, he was pleased Lucian liked what he saw. Of course, if he had to, for Lucian, Corey might even… get circumcised. They did that to adult men too, didn't they?

When Lucian let go, Corey's foreskin drew down, taut and stretched to reveal the peak of his cock, where in the slit a glistening, translucent pearl held motionless but growing.

Lucian smiled as he gazed adoringly at Corey's cock. "I also love knowing I can taste you fully because you have not been with anyone else. I can suck your cock to the root, you can come down my throat, and we will both be safe."

The thought of ejaculating into Lucian's mouth made Corey's mouth dryer than a fucking desert.

"I do not mind the taste of latex, but skin and come are better." Lucian gave Corey a naughty smirk, and then he descended on Corey's dick like a ravenous beast, closing his mouth over Corey's cock tightly and sucking on the head gently. His tongue swirled around Corey's crown, leisurely tracing the shape.

Corey might have shouted then, but blood roared in his ears, deafening him.

Then Lucian pulled back. Through half-lidded eyes, Corey saw Lucian red in the face, panting. Arousal was a state they shared. Lucian flattened his tongue and swept it over Corey's slit, catching the fluid gathering there.

Like flicking a switch, Corey was so turned on it actually *fucking* hurt.

Shuddering, he begged, "Oh God, Lu. Please...."

Lucian looked up, a mischievous glint in his eyes. "But I still have so much to teach you." He dipped his head and flicked the tip of his tongue below the crown. A bolt of fire shot through Corey in an instant, and he actually doubled over, as though he were doing crunches. "That, darling," Lucian whispered reverently, "is called the frenulum. Or as I like to call it, the outer sweet spot. Like a flower bud in sunlight, it awakens to full bloom at the mere touch of a tongue."

"Oh fuck...." Corey could do naught but stare, leaning up on his elbows, watching raptly to see what his lover would do next. How the hell had he missed this magical seat of pure pleasure in all the times he had taken care of his early morning needs?

Lucian flicked his tongue at the same spot again, and Corey's brain fried. How such a tiny touch could yield so much pleasure was beyond him. "The frenulum is a just a band of elastic tissues but there are a lot of nerve endings there, and the sensation when being caressed...." Once more, Lucian swirled his tongue over the area and then pressed on it harder with a flattened tongue. Corey whimpered as jolts of pleasure coursed through his veins, and more early seed pumped out of his slit. "It's so very, very erotic, don't you agree?"

Corey hovered on the precipice of oblivion. "Jesus Christ, Lu. Gimme a break. I'm dying here." That had to be the most words he had been capable of since Lucian started this new form of slow, torturous seduction. But he doubted he had much more to give.

"Hush, sweetheart. I will take care of all your needs." Lucian clearly enjoyed this revelry as much as Corey, or perhaps more since he was in control. But when Corey saw how blown Lucian's pupils were, he reconsidered just how much in charge of himself Lucian really was.

By then Lucian was giving Corey's cockhead so much lavish attention it bordered on excruciating delight. He moved his lips up and down the length of Corey's shaft, smothering it in heat and moisture.

Every time he reached the top, Lucian sucked on the head, a bit harder with each new pass, until Corey was a writhing mass of impatient need. The slick heat was his undoing, and he felt the tremors of orgasm begin.

That was when Lucian backed off.

"Oh man, that's just cruel," Corey whined at the cold-shoulder treatment.

Lucian quirked an eyebrow in a rebuking manner. "I have a question for you before we proceed. I am aware it is safe for you to come in my mouth. My query is about your willingness. Do you wish me to drink of you now? Or do you wish to wait while we explore further landscapes of sex tonight?"

Corey gulped. He had not considered that coming would end tonight's activities. Then again, his blood hadn't actually provided for the functions of his brain lately, busy with an altogether lower organ. "If I.... I mean, if you.... That is, if we... do this, meaning me, um, coming... does that mean the night's over?"

Throwing his head back, Lucian burst into a loud, deep-belly laughter. "Absolutely not! Now that I have you under my thumb and tongue, I am not releasing you until I am good and ready. And that, my dear, might be awhile. So... get comfortable and relax. Because you will spill down my throat soon. And that will only be the appetizer."

Stunned, Corey had zero objections.

CHAPTER 28

OH, HOW cute that fawn-like look was on Corey, Lucian decided, smiling at the deer in the headlights expression. "I take it that plan works for you, my dear?" he teased.

Corey murmured, reddening, "Y-you're all talk…." It was needling back, and Lucian loved it.

He responded with a wink and a smirk and ducked his head to take Corey's hot, hard cock in his mouth, all the way down to the root. The cockhead touched the back of Lucian's throat, then slid past it. One swallow forced Corey's dick snugly against Lucian's palate.

Corey groaned, his hips stuttering. "Holy fuck!"

Lucian's mind was blank, as his only desire at the moment was to give pleasure to his lover. His fingers found, as if by their own volition, the firm, fleshy globes of Corey's ass, squeezed, and kept the man close. Corey's beautiful erection fit Lucian's mouth perfectly, so he milked the shaft lovingly.

The sugary essence of Corey's precum coated Lucian's tongue, and greedily he drank every droplet. He used his other hand to clasp Corey's balls, to jiggle and roll them in his palm, not once letting up, even tugging a bit. Corey thrashed around, unable to lie still, and in his wantonness he began to babble incoherently, with a distinguishable dirty word buried here and there.

Lucian's mouth watered as thrills of anticipation ran through him. He was overjoyed he didn't have to contend with latex, the way it intruded in the act, making his throat typically constrict or the taste of spermicide causing nausea. Tasting Corey was a bonus to the session he wasn't about to miss.

Corey moaned, and his thighs shook, and his muscles flexed as he fell into the throes of passion. Lucian took Corey's length deep, over and over, sucking until his cheeks hollowed. With every flick and glide of Lucian's tongue against each sensitive spot, Corey moved more erratically, his hips jerking, and the noises he made turned louder and more high-pitched as time passed.

Corey smelled clean, the hint of soap still clinging to his skin, though a sheen of sweat began to coat his body, making it slick and hot. A musky odor, masculine, sweet, and pungent, filled Lucian's nostrils as he inhaled. Though he typically preferred to breathe through his mouth during oral sex, when there was a cock lodged deep in his throat, sucking in air via the nose or the mouth became impossible. This time he had to sense every last bit of Corey, even if a sensory overload threatened him, so he deep-throated Corey's delicious dick.

"Ohmygod, Lu," Corey cried out, his voice hoarse and breaking. "Please."

Feeling his own cock heavy and smoldering, the wet tip kissing his belly, Lucian realized by proceeding at this leisurely pace he was tormenting them both. "Soon," he vowed.

Knowing in his heart he wanted more of Corey, Lucian guided Corey into a rhythm by bobbing his head, devouring Corey's cock. He made sure his tongue glided over the slit and under the ridge of the crown, licked along the length of the shaft, and followed the throbbing veins. His suction remained strong as his desire grew, and Lucian cupped his own erection, wrapped his hand around his dick, and began to tug.

"W-what are you doing?" Corey asked, breathless but demanding. Lucian looked up and saw Corey watching him again intently as he braced himself up on his elbows. "Are you... touching yourself?" Lucian was unwilling to let go of the scrumptious piece of meat in his mouth, so he only nodded. Corey grimaced and shook his head. "Don't, Lu. Please. I wanna... suck you off too. R-return the p-pleasure." His voice cracked and faded because Lucian would not stop.

But Lucian also knew he should if they were both to enjoy the experience. With a wet plop, he let Corey slip from between his tingling lips. His breathing was labored and harsh as he fought for words. "Get... down... from the... table...."

Naked as the day he was born, and just as awkward, Lucian scrambled off Corey and slid down in the small space between the fireplace and the massage table. His cock bobbed up and down, hard and heavy, his balls aching.

Corey followed suit and tried to slide down the portable table. Unfortunately, he got snagged on something, and he landed on the floor with a soft thud, in a heap of limbs. "Damn, how smooth was that?" he cursed at himself, shaking his head. But he straightened up and shoved the table farther away. His gaze found Lucian again. "Now what?"

Lucian grinned, hungry for more. "You are aware of the position sixty-nine?"

Judging from Corey's blush and darkening eyes, he knew. Quickly Corey repositioned himself, his face aimed at Lucian's groin, and Lucian stared once more at Corey's delectable cock. Then Lucian gulped Corey's penis all the way to the hilt again, swallowing and sucking.

Corey groaned. "W-what will it—*you*—taste like? These, um, areas…?"

Lucian heard the hesitation and immediately released Corey. He cleared his throat to give better voice to his knowledge. "If one has showered or bathed recently, then cock, balls, and anus all taste and smell like clean skin. Exactly like anywhere else on the body. A word of advice, though. Until you grow accustomed to the pungent odors that *might* be there, I suggest you breathe through your mouth in all oral sex situations." As he spoke, Lucian was mildly surprised he was able to string together enough words to make sense.

Corey frowned, puzzled. "How can I, um, blow you *and* breathe at the same time? I only have one mouth."

Lucian giggled. "Go slow at first. Familiarize yourself with your new… terrain."

Snorting and rolling his eyes, Corey nodded. "Okay. Here goes."

The first lick over Lucian's glans was tentative, so soft and airy it was barely there. Lucian only felt it because the cock was a sensitive organ. He could not avert his gaze as Corey tried again, swiping his tongue across the slit where pearlescent precum formed. Corey seemed to digest the flavor carefully, closing his eyes.

Lucian was on pins and needles. "If you would prefer a condom, I have a variety with me. Even flavored ones." Yes, he would miss the more intense sensations of going bareback, but he was not about to do anything to jeopardize Corey.

But Corey shook his head, adamant. "No. You said we're safe. And I wanna taste you. Not a condom. What's that gonna teach me, other than a safe sex lecture I've already had or how to control my gag reflex with latex?"

Lucian laughed. "Understood. Proceed at will."

"Thanks, Lu, but I was already gonna." Corey grinned shamelessly.

Then he took the head of Lucian's cock in his mouth and sucked on it gently, as if he were purposely avoiding applying too much pressure, seemingly worried he might hurt or injure Lucian. It was really quite endearing.

But sooner than Lucian expected, Corey appeared to take the situation in hand, and with vigor and courage first doubled his efforts, and then tripled them. With every determined dip down, Corey swallowed more of Lucian's not inconsiderable length, getting the whole shaft wet, hot, and tingling.

Lucian whimpered around Corey's cock in his mouth when he felt his cockhead brush Corey's throat.

A gurgling sound followed, and Corey pulled back, panting roughly, looking quite befuddled and upset. "How the hell...?"

Lucian did not need a secret decoder ring to decipher Corey's meaning. "This is only your first time. Do not force it. There will be other times." His voice was rugged from all the sweet cocksucking, yet he managed.

Corey frowned as if pissed off. "But I want to do it now!"

Lucian smiled and reassured his lover by caressing his inner thigh, causing him to shiver. "No need to rush, Corey. We have all the time in the world. Just... follow your instincts. Do as you please."

With his gaze locked with Corey's, Lucian parted his lips and dragged Corey's ball sac into his mouth, suckling on the twin orbs as though they were the most delicious meal he'd ever savored. And in a sense, they were. Virginal and untouched was apparently his new flavor of choice. Rolling the tender sac in his mouth, he gave it every lavish attention he could come up with.

Then he was distracted by Corey swallowing his cockhead again and flicking the tip of his tongue first into Lucian's slit and then at the frenulum. God, the man was a fast learner. Lucian had trouble concentrating on his own task, but he tried. As soon as he found a rhythm he liked, he realized Corey was mimicking every move, every suck and lick he assayed. It was truly as if they had one mind, and their bodies were on the receiving end of that perfect synchronicity.

Lucian parted Corey's thighs farther, making room between them, and hooked his arm to grab one of Corey's trembling glutes. Corey followed suit, and it was Lucian's turn to moan as his ass cheeks were fondled, caressed, and squeezed. He craved Corey imprinting him with bruises as marks of ownership, no matter how temporary.

Trembling with need, Lucian held Corey's cock once more with his mouth and took him deep down his throat. Corey shook and gurgled, this time not because a cock was lodged in his throat but because he was clearly enjoying every second of getting blown. Corey tried again to go as deep as Lucian, but he backed off quickly, coughing.

"I can't get the whole thing to fit in my damn mouth!" he cursed, sounding miserable.

Lucian pulled off, panting. "Get my cock wet all over. Then use your mouth and your hand in tandem. Match the rhythms. Then you will see how glorious that can be."

Corey did as he was told, licking Lucian's shaft to moisten it with his saliva. A hot, wet tightness surrounded Lucian's dick, and all over his body, his muscles trembled, and his skin vibrated. Corey was making noises, humming as he sucked, and the sound was no longer audible as much as it was… a feeling, a sensation, a touch.

His head fuzzy, Lucian chuckled as a thought occurred to him, and he said, "In the spirit of the exercise of t-t-touch…. How did primitive man have sex? Trapped in the dark, perhaps with a dozen other hunters sleeping in the same cave? How did they recognize their partners in love, the ones they desired? Same as us. Through scent. Through touch. Through t-t-t-taste…."

That was as far as Lucian got when his orgasm crashed over his body and mind, shutting down all nonessential functions, like his running mouth. He cried out when the sensation unraveled his very being, sending him hurtling through universes of pleasure until he no longer had any sense of his self.

Corey coughed loudly, bringing Lucian back from the abyss, and then gulped hard enough to be heard through even the racing whoosh going on inside Lucian's ears. Twisting his head to witness the scene unfold, Lucian saw how overwhelmed Corey was at the sheer volume of come Lucian produced. Corey gulped and gasped, spewing spunk here and there over their bodies, the rug, even the wall. Yet, it was evident to Lucian that Corey tried as best he could to keep Lucian's cockhead in his mouth, fighting against the surges, keeping his mouth open and swallowing continuously, that lovely Adam's apple bobbing up and down.

"Ohmygod, ohmygod. Oh. My. God...." Lucian screamed, catapulted to some new and unknown subspace beyond a common universe-expanding-through-pleasure orgasm—which was pretty awesome too—by the sight of Corey furiously blowing him, using his hand at the base to pump Lucian dry. Lucian's balls felt like they were shooting sparks, like a tightened coil with metal fatigue about to blow apart. Miniature explosions cascaded over his whole consciousness until he was lost in sensation.

For a long time, Lucian could hear nothing. His heart pounded, his blood thundered, his breathing whirled.

Then, a small voice reached him. "Was that good? Was it okay?"

With heavy eyes, Lucian managed to get his head up enough to see Corey swiping the corners of his mouth, where sticky droplets of Lucian's load still clung, like white globs of curdled cream. Corey put his wet fingers in his mouth, obviously savoring the flavor.

"Words... fail me... in describing... how divine... that was." Lucian could provide no more, his mind dizzy and his body limp, languid, and sated—for the moment.

Corey smiled, the gesture so open and honest, innocent and astonished, that it left Lucian quiet in awe. "You were right. Your taste.... Salty, a hint of bitter, mostly sweet. So fucking sweet. I could eat this all day. Yours is a taste of... of life, Lu, of vitality and beauty and sex and love and everything." Corey was clearly caught in the haze of rapture. Lucian was disappointed in the knowledge it would not last. But he was also overjoyed the ick factor Corey had described when they met, the concern about exchanging bodily fluids, had not come up.

That was when Lucian observed that Corey was in fact caught in the haze of *Lucian's* rapture, not his own, since he had not come and was still rock hard. "My turn, if you please." His voice was hoarse and rough, undoubtedly from shouting his head off. Thankfully, the low tone had the desired effect on Corey, who snapped out of his previous exaltation and had the epiphany he had not yet climaxed.

"P-please" was all Corey said, a mere whisper, as if Lucian might vanish at any moment.

Lucian wrapped his hand around the base of Corey's cock, which stood out like a rigid flagpole, saluting with translucent beads of precum. The penis felt soft and hard against his palm, yielding flesh but also so turgid it could not be bent. With the fingertips of his other hand, Lucian tickled his way up and down the shaft, tracing throbbing veins and feeling the heft of the piece of meat, relishing what that would mean once the two of them got into the thick of things.

Then Lucian licked, planting wet openmouthed kisses all over, and he fisted Corey's cock and tugged, his hand moving smoother. But he kept the cockhead for his mouth. He rubbed the tip against his lips, and Corey whimpered. The silky, hot, and wet head held a musky aroma of sex, and Lucian inhaled it deeply.

He wondered if these sensations were similar to what Corey must have experienced a moment ago and felt a little thrill at the possibility. "You are so beautiful, Corey. I could stare at you all night and day."

Corey chuckled breathlessly. "No one's ever said that to me. Not about my face or my cock."

"Fools. More for me." Lucian leaned forward and kissed the tip, devoting himself to the task like a true aficionado. Lucian ran his flattened tongue across the head, swallowing the tangy and yet sweet fluid that emerged like a leaky faucet.

"D-does it t-taste okay…?" Corey asked, concern tinting his voice.

"Delicious, I assure you." To show the veracity of his words, Lucian suckled on the cockhead, milking new drops of precum as they appeared. Corey sucked in a sharp breath, shaking and groaning. "Now, the question of teeth."

Corey looked up at Lucian, startled and a little frantic with fear. "Huh?"

"Your eloquence never ceases to amaze me," Lucian teased, smiling. "Some men like a bit of teeth against the shaft, a hint of pain with their pleasure. Others do not care for it at all."

Nervously Corey nodded his understanding. "W-well, I guess I won't know until you try. Right…?"

"Do not fear. I will be gentle." Then Lucian smirked. "Well, up to a point."

Without further ado he took Corey's cock down his throat, and on the rise up, he let his teeth ever so slightly graze the sensitive foreskin. As he reached the crown, he had a bit of the foreskin caught between his teeth, and he tugged very gently. Corey groaned, his hips bucked, and he gripped Lucian's shoulders hard enough to hurt.

Lucian pulled away. "You did not like it?"

"Gimme a sec," Corey panted. Slowly his death grip on Lucian eased, and his muscles relaxed. He looked down at Lucian, his gaze glazed and dreamy. "It was…. It wasn't bad. But, um… maybe not this time."

Lucian smiled, nodding. "We can revisit this theme whenever you like."

So Lucian tucked his lips around his teeth for a smoother ride and proceeded to devour Corey's cock to the root. He wrapped his hand firmly around the base and bobbed up and down, his saliva and Corey's precum making the column of flesh slippery enough for a fast pace. With a slick fist, hard suction, and a swirling tongue, Lucian went in for the kill, lashing out an onslaught no man could resist.

Corey moaned, thrashed about, his sinewy body taut and writhing. Corey's cock was so big and hard in Lucian's mouth it threatened to suffocate him. But Lucian didn't stop. He increased his pace, sucking tighter and pumping his fist harder.

Then Lucian sneaked his other hand to Corey's balls, massaging them more roughly than before, quickly moving past them to the silky stretch of skin beyond and then to the twitching hole. Corey's pelvis lunged forward the moment Lucian's fingers caressed his opening, and his head came up, a stunned look in his wide eyes.

"I will do nothing against your will," Lucian vowed in a whisper, his abused throat making his voice hoarse.

Their gazes locked, Lucian tapped on Corey's asshole with his fingertips and then went round and round on the sensitive skin. Not once did he enter. But it seemed the mere hint of penetration did the trick.

Corey's back arched off the floor as he cried out, as if in pain, when the frantic thrusts of his pelvis peaked. For a blink of an eye, Corey remained motionless at the crest of the wave, strung taut and silent in between moans.

Then Lucian's mouth was filled with Corey's bittersweet essence. Long, deep pulses of come pushed out of Corey's cock, and Lucian swallowed convulsively. Not a single drop escaped. The thick, creamy fluid tasted divine, and this time it was Lucian who moaned loudly around his lover's dick, drinking the briny man juice like nectar.

As Corey's climax ebbed, Lucian eased as well, licking the shaft clean until only the cockhead remained in his mouth, which he also lapped. Finally, with an intimate openmouthed kiss, he released Corey's penis, which slapped against his belly wetly.

Out of breath, Lucian lay down on the floor, gasping. It took a while for him to come down, considering he had gotten hard again from blowing Corey and had not yet climaxed for the second time. He had a feeling this sensual height was the result of giving Corey so much pleasure.

I gave Corey his first blowjob. Hopefully he liked it.

Then a shocked voice aroused him back to awareness when Corey murmured in awe, "Holy shit, I'm still hard. Look."

With some effort Lucian used his elbows to rise up enough to witness Corey's cock lying on his stomach, still rigid and turgid. "Well, would you look at that."

Corey stared at him, half-proud, half-anxious. "What do I do with it?"

For some reason that struck Lucian as the funniest thing he had ever heard, and then he rolled around on the floor, laughing his ass off, holding his belly because it hurt to laugh so much.

Corey sounded more confused than mad. "What's so funny?"

Lucian's mirth subsided as quickly as it had started. With swift movements he got up, rolled on top of Corey, and asked, "Do you trust me?"

Blinking and frowning, Corey took a moment. Then he nodded, though a bit unsurely. "Yeah. Why?"

"If I promise you that you will not hurt me… will you let me ride your cock?"

WAITING FOR Corey to reply, Lucian remained patient. So soon after coming, Corey wouldn't be hard enough for anal sex, so Lucian gave his lover as much time as he needed to bounce back. After all, for Lucian, this was not merely a question of a second orgasm. No, he sought this greater unity with Corey for a lot of reasons, maybe even some he wasn't consciously aware of. He did not want to steal this first-time experience from his lover out of selfishness, though, so soon the doubts flowed.

But following a period of silent introspection, Corey halted the rising tide of hesitation. "God, Lu…. I've thought about my cock inside you so many times. I want it. I want this. I want… you. Do it."

Straddling Corey's thighs and facing him, Lucian nodded, determined. He reached for the bag Colton had brought in with the massage table, fumbled inside it, and came up with lube and a condom wrapper.

Looking straight at Corey, Lucian held up the condom and said, "Always be safe. Always. No matter what your partner says about being clean as a whistle. No matter how hot and bothered you are to just get to the fucking. No. Matter. What."

Corey chuckled breathlessly and rolled his eyes, which suggested he had most likely heard safe sex lectures before. Nonetheless, he nodded his compliance and understanding.

"Oral sex can be an exception. But even then…. Oh, I should have…." Lucian tore the wrapper open with his teeth and slid the condom over Corey's still slick and now fully hard erection. Grunting, Corey doubled over, grabbed his nuts, and yanked on them, his eyes closed in concentration. Pouring a rich dollop of the lubricant over his palms and rubbing them together to heat the liquid, Lucian spread the substance all over Corey's shaft, perhaps taking a bit too great care in making sure it covered every inch.

"Are you all right?" Lucian asked, somewhat worried. "It is not too late to stop."

Corey shook his head fiercely and opened his eyes. They blazed like two suns. "Do *not* fucking stop."

Nodding, Lucian didn't waste time. He squirted some of the shiny, sweet-scented gel on his fingers, and reached behind to prepare his channel for Corey's cock, slipping in with ease of experience.

Corey watched, rapt, eyes unblinking, his jaw hanging open. Then he blurted in haste, "What are you doing? Can I do that?"

Lucian halted, hesitating. "A lot of men do not like to do this for other men, fingering I mean. Besides, I require very little prep."

"How will I know if I don't like doing it to you if I don't try? Let me, please."

Swallowing hard, Lucian tried to regain self-control before he blew prematurely. It had been a while since a man had taken the time to get acquainted with this part of his anatomy, unless it involved eating his ass preceding a cock's crude, graceless insertion. Which was fine some of the time.

"All right."

Corey sat up, clearly eager to proceed. "Tell me what to do."

So Lucian showed him, coating Corey's fingers amply with lube. "Use a good deal of lube. Too much is always preferable to not enough."

Corey studied the gel briefly, his head cocked as he observed how the slightly sticky substance behaved on his fingers. "It's cold at first. Then it gets warmer."

Lucian smiled. "Your body heat induces the reaction. You do not use lube when you masturbate? A lot of men and women do. When wet, whether thanks to lubrication or by one's own juices, the sexual contact is enhanced."

Corey shrugged, his gaze still aimed at his hands. "I only jerk off in the morning, and it's pretty much done on autopilot. Doesn't take long to finish. So no, I don't use lube."

"I see. Now…. If I were doing this for the first time, I would ask you to go slow. Start with slow circles around my opening until the muscle eased, like yours did during my massage. Then you would ease one finger in, to the first knuckle to begin with. Then deeper. Then you would add a second finger, and then a third. Some would go further, to all fingers, even a whole hand."

Corey gasped, staring at Lucian like he was crazy. "The whole… hand…?"

"The rectum is flexible enough for that, but it can take a long while. Some find fisting extremely pleasurable, by themselves or with a partner."

The expression Corey wore suggested he was by no means ready to tackle that novelty any time soon. "I'm, uh, gonna pass on that, if you don't mind."

Lucian chuckled, understanding the daunting image the man undoubtedly had of the act. "As you wish." Then he sobered up to continue with a level tone. "My instructions would be applicable for virgins, such as yourself, or for those who bottom rarely. I, however, require little preparation."

Corey's eyes flashed intently. "You, uh, bottom a lot?"

"I prefer it, yes, to other sexual roles." Lucian waited to see if Corey's jealousy got the better of him, but the emotion seemed to pass as suddenly as it had appeared, like a fickle cloud over the sun. So Lucian felt confident enough to go on. "Please, put your fingers inside me."

Corey frowned. "How many?"

"Two. Do not fret. You will not hurt me. If you do, I will tell you. I promise."

At first Corey hesitated. His touch was a mere brush, tentative and concerned about how much pressure to apply. His slick fingers twirled leisurely around Lucian's hole, trembling as he went on despite his obvious case of nerves. Finally, much to Lucian's delight, Corey slipped two fingers inside Lucian's fluttering channel.

"H-how does it feel?" Corey asked, his shaky voice strained and nervous. "Am I doing it right?"

Lucian sighed as Corey filled him, his fingers moving around a bit, circling, gaining ground as they glided in deeper. "Oh yes, so very good. Please, continue."

Lucian's reply seemed to make Corey more confident and bolder, as he began to push in and pull out, mimicking the rhythm of the previous blowjob and the coupling that lay ahead.

Then, like a bolt of lightning from a clear blue sky, a hot thrill of ecstasy shot through Lucian when Corey accidentally brushed past his sweet spot. "Oh God, yes!" he cried out, tossing his head back, his body arcing, his hips bucking.

Corey froze. "What?"

Lucian panted, trying to focus on speech, which was difficult. "My prostate. My inner sweet spot. You hit it. Oh God above…."

"I'm sorry. I won't do it again," Corey hastened to say, alarmed.

Lucian giggled because he felt so amazingly great. "Yes, you are most definitely going to do it again. It feels heavenly. Again, if you please." He knew he would not last long if Corey kept touching his inner sweet spot, but goodness gracious, how absolutely excruciatingly blissful it felt. The caress was less than a cock sliding past it, more like a button being pushed.

Corey seemed to ponder Lucian's reassurances for an interminable time before he inched his fingers deeper inside Lucian's quivering rectum.

He appeared to be searching for something, since he moved tentatively. When he touched Lucian's prostate and sent Lucian into a fit of moans and writhing, Corey nodded, as if satisfied he had found what he had been exploring after.

"It's so tiny," Corey muttered, not looking at Lucian as he was mainly focused on the movements of his hand, unseen. "Such a soft, small lump. I almost missed it." He actually chuckled then, amused by his own thought patterns. "I mean, I know anatomy. I sort of knew where it would be. And still I forgot. The front wall. The size of a walnut, kind of." Then he laughed harder, a joke at the moment only he was privy to. "You know, my first thought was of a soft rubber ball." He erupted into a storm of chortles, and Lucian joined in. Humor and fun had a place in sex, and he was happy Corey had discovered that aspect.

But Lucian had no intelligible reply to offer, no sophisticated input, no wise words for advice. He was teetering on the edge, and he needed to get his ass stuffed *now*. "Corey, please."

Shocked by the begging, Corey became aware of Lucian's plight, and he nodded. "Yeah, yeah. Okay. So, uh, now what do I do?"

"Replace your fingers with your cock." It was the best Lucian could come up with, at least without taking matters into his own hand, and that remained a distinct possibility. His groin was enflamed, and his hips would not sit still.

For someone who could not see his dick and was doing this for the first time, Corey adeptly pulled out his fingers, reached behind Lucian's buttocks, and aimed his slick cock at Lucian's quivering hole. The moment Corey's cockhead brushed against Lucian's opening, they both inhaled sharply.

"Holy fucking shit," Corey mumbled, his eyes wide and dazed.

"When I bear down," Lucian murmured, breathless with want. "You push up. Do you understand? It will help."

Corey nodded, though judging from his somewhat stunned expression, he was in need of a moment of adjustment. Corey held his cock firmly at the base, a rigid shaft that poked against his lover's opening.

Then, as if of one mind, they both pushed at once, one in, the other out. The wide head of Corey's penis popped in past the ring of muscle, and both men shuddered and whimpered. Lucian was so far gone in lust he had to brace himself on Corey's shoulders, and slowly but surely he impaled himself on Corey's dick. With each inch gained, Corey shook more, his hands coming to grip Lucian's buttocks hard enough to bruise. Corey seemed unaware of what he was doing, lost in the haze of pleasure.

"Oh my God, that's so… hot and tight," Corey said through gritted teeth, as if holding on by a thread. But not once did he say he wanted to stop. Lucian saw Corey was feeling his way around, sensing every minute change and shift, and those things obliterated all doubts and fears. At least, they had for Lucian during his first time.

Still, out of a sense of responsibility, Lucian inquired, amid pants, "Are you all right? Do you wish to stop?" He shifted on top of Corey, trying to find a good position to adjust to Corey's rather sizable penis.

Corey moaned, shaking. "God, that feels good. You feel so fucking sweet around me. Like a vise made of velvet or something. Shit, so damn amazing." The ecstatic expression on his face went a long way in alleviating Lucian's concerns about pushing anal sex into their repertoire for tonight. "You gonna move, or what? Fuck, I need to…." Corey frowned, as though he wasn't sure what he wanted, only that he needed something.

Lucian descended on Corey's rock-hard cock, determined to reach his goal, and then his spread ass landed on Corey's hips. Lucian felt the base of Corey's cock and balls hit his perineum, Corey's pubes tickling the sensitive skin of his crack. He shifted again, ensuring his slender weight would not hinder Corey's actions.

"You are all the way inside me," Lucian said, shoving Corey's torso back down on the floor so he could brace himself against Corey's considerable pecs, squeezing the firm, well-rounded muscles simply because he could. "How do you feel?"

Corey grinned, eyes sparkling. "Like the king of the fucking world."

Lucian giggled breathlessly, loving Corey's self-confidence, boldness, and sense of humor. "Adonis himself, you are."

Corey made a face, pouting theatrically. "You mean I am the most beautiful man ever to grace the world but also the spawn of an incestuous lust between father and daughter?"

"I see you know your mythos." Lucian leaned forward, as if to dip down to kiss Corey. Instead, his new angle almost let Corey's cock slip from inside him. But Lucian stopped while the cockhead was still inside, and then he plopped down hard, grunting as he did so.

Corey's eyes rolled to the back of his head, and he groaned, his legs splaying open. "Holy. Fucking. Shit."

Lucian snickered. "That seems to be the most frequent phrase of yours."

"You're such a—" Corey started but got interrupted when Lucian developed a rhythm of merciless motions, up and down, slowly and steady at first, but with the pace quickly increasing.

Corey seemed out of his mind with passion. His back arched as he gripped Lucian's hips fiercely, pulling Lucian down on his cock before Lucian even got to the top of his ride. To get some breathing room, Lucian added a twist by clenching his ass muscles whenever only the tip of Corey's dick was inside, a tight squeeze that left Corey spasming and crying out.

They no longer bantered or traded quips. Lucian did not need respites anymore, and he did not try to gather his thoughts or analyze sensations for either of them. He gave in to the pleasure of the coupling, threw himself headlong into the wild ride, and together they rocked, grinded, and swayed, bouncing up and down like there was no tomorrow.

Then Corey planted his feet on the floor and started to thrust up hard, fast, and deep, bringing Lucian to the precipice of what he could bear. The aggressive rhythm of their fucking drove Lucian insane, and he whimpered, gripping Corey's muscles, in desperate need of an anchor in the midst of a mind-blowing experience.

Corey growled, and Lucian purred. Their mating turned rough, erratic, out of control, chaotic, wild to the extreme. Soon they were thrashing together, and Lucian dropped down to kiss the breath out of Corey.

Corey wound his arms tight around Lucian's back—and then he suddenly tipped his lover over, rolling them both until Corey was on top.

"Oh, yes, sweet God," Lucian whispered, his voice muffled due to Corey's tongue invading his mouth, plunging in and out with the same speed and lack of finesse as his cock.

Corey backed off, hooked his arms under Lucian's knees, and brought them up over his shoulders, like a sexual pro. The strokes of his dick were precise as he pounded against Lucian's prostate with each deliberate, fierce jab. Lucian moaned, half sobbing, and he scratched his nails across the broad, muscular expanse of Corey's back, undoubtedly leaving marks.

Lucian's cock jumped atop his heaving belly, hard and heavy and dribbling precum until he knew an explosion was imminent. Corey fisted Lucian's dick, causing Lucian to babble incoherently, part dirty pillow talk, part utter gibberish.

Corey plowed into Lucian like he had something to prove. Lucian figured he probably did too, as though it was Corey's responsibility to make sure his sex partner had a good time. Corey was conscientious like that, it seemed. That forceful fucking, in addition to the pumping of Lucian's cock, apparently pushed Corey toward climax as well.

Corey's thrusts became shorter, faster, more focused, and jerky as his body took over, moving of its own volition, without rational commands. Then Corey began to groan and shudder violently, and his muscles quaked. Lucian's sweet spot felt like it grew from the size of a walnut to a coconut under the continuous onslaught from Corey's cock.

Soon they rocketed into orbit and soared to the heights of orgasm. Corey cried out, his voice cracking, and he pumped and froze, repeating the cycle over and over. Even through the latex barrier, Lucian felt liquid heat fill Corey's condom. Lucian's ass spasmed, milking his lover's cock, demanding every last drop he had to give.

Simultaneously, Corey squeezed his fist around Lucian's dick so tightly on the upstroke that there was no chance to stop the orgasm that overloaded Lucian's senses and system, like a tidal wave dragging him down with the undercurrent. All he could hope for was not drowning as new splashes of hot, sticky come spilled out of his slit. The moment seemed to drag on for an eternity.

They crashed back down to earth as one too. Their orgasms subsided slowly, ebbing and receding. Lucian's groin and chest were dotted with white, creamy splatter. It smeared when Corey lost support of his arms and tumbled on top of Lucian, who *oomphed* but bore the weight of the man he had just made love with. Wild, mad, pure, pleasurable lovemaking.

"Corey? I do not mind snuggling or cuddling by any means, but you are making it very hard for me to breathe." Lucian nonetheless still kept petting Corey's back, firm round buttocks, and neck, where sweat made his hair curl a bit.

With a displeased grunt, Corey managed to roll off Lucian until he landed next to him on the floor with a thud. As their breathing slowed and silence reigned in the apartment again, the hiss of fire from the fireplace became audible. As the only light source in the living room, the flames cast lively shadows all around them and on their skin.

"Corey? Are you all right?" Nervous, Lucian turned his head on the soft rug in front of the fireplace to observe Corey's reactions. What he saw made his heart stop—and then beat again.

Corey was staring at the ceiling, his eyes wide, barely blinking. His chest heaved, his skin glistened with sweat and spunk, and his lips were parted in short gasps.

Finally, his voice filled with awe, he said, "That was freaking awesome. Now I get why people want to do that all the time. Have sex, you know. I just did it, and all I can think about is doing it again. Soon."

Lucian giggled. "Anytime, anywhere. Whenever you are ready." He sighed, happy and relieved, and let himself rest a bit, closing his eyes to savor the moment. They had accomplished a monumental task. Corey was *not* frigid, and neither was he a virgin anymore.

All of a sudden, Corey declared, "I wanna feel what you feel when I'm inside you."

Lucian's eyes flew open in shock, and he turned to face a determined Corey.

Alarmed, Lucian hedged, attempting to find the right words to convey his message of patience. "Corey, you need to consider carefully what you're saying. Too much is changing for you too fast. That is the reason why I chose the slow progression of our sessions, so you would not get overwhelmed and end up making poor, life-altering decisions in the heat of the moment."

Corey sighed, his voice patient but slowly becoming more agitated. "Please, Lucian. I am a grown man. I know who I am and what I want. I am not confused or scared or rutting in heat. I have waited all my life to feel this way. I'm as mentally, emotionally, and physically prepared and ready as a human being could ever be. You've just got to trust me on this." Instead of anger, his tone dropped to pleading, and it hurt Lucian within. "Do you trust me, Lu?"

"I do, Corey. I would trust you with my life." Lucian cupped Corey's face, holding close the man he cared for more than he should. "Listen to me now, please. What you ask, we will do. I promise. But not tonight. There are, um...."

As Lucian's voice trailed off into uncertainty, Corey snickered, his gaze softening. "You need to make preparations, am I right?" Lucian let out a relieved breath, sagging, and nodded. "Okay. I'll wait." Then his tone grew deadly serious and his gaze stern and adamant. "But I won't wait forever."

Lucian smiled tenderly. "Be it a heartbeat or eternity, I will give it to you."

While Corey's surprise was evident in his widening eyes, it was Lucian who felt the brunt of the shockwave. What on earth had he just promised this man?

And why was Lucian so utterly reluctant to take it back?

CHAPTER 29

THE NEXT three months were the best of Corey's life. It was as if he had been frozen from birth, but now he had melted and awakened into a new existence, one full of sensuality.

Corey had Lucian to thank for his resurrection. Not to mention Lucian living up to his promise of showing and doing everything he vowed. All those sensual and sexual delights he had planned and described, well, they had reenacted over half of them, some of them more than once, plus several Lucian had not mentioned at all.

THEIR FIRST morning together—after their first night of lovemaking— had been heavenly.

Waking up with an erection was the norm, even for Corey, though he rarely enjoyed the process of getting rid of it. Now he had a warm lover next to him as he awoke in bed, and taking full advantage of the situation might have been called selfish, or even rude, except for the fact that he devoted himself to giving Lucian as much pleasure as he himself received.

The slender weight of Lucian's svelte body on top of his had Corey writhing against his lover as he fought to stave off the inevitable climax. It was a quiet Saturday morning, and he longed for leisurely lovemaking.

Lucian kissed him nimbly. He tasted a bit stale, a flavor of sleep, but it wasn't bad, and certainly not unpleasant enough for Corey to stop. In fact, he responded with an equally hard, demanding kiss. He thrust his tongue inside wet warmth, licking and tasting, while simultaneously grinding against his beautiful partner's figure. Their hot cocks slid side by side, catching and dragging, delivering warm, wet kisses all over their skin.

They were submerged in a private cocoon of sex, where the scents of their previous engagements lingered, a light gloss covering their skins where semen had landed and gotten smeared. The skintight pressure and friction of sweating bodies was a novelty for Corey, or at least it had been since yesterday. Now he found he couldn't get enough, and he wrapped his arms around Lucian, gripping so tightly he briefly worried for Lucian's ability to draw breath.

Lucian seemed to be satisfied with breathing the air from Corey's lungs as their kiss kept them sealed together. Touch and taste became inextricable.

Finally, as if by one mind, they drew apart, panting heavily.

"Fuck, Lu. I love kissing you." Corey's mind was filled with a red haze of passion, and he was apparently experiencing a short circuit in his brain-to-mouth control.

Lucian giggled, so damn cutely, and Corey had to caress his red-gold strands, letting them slip through his fingers, like a cascade. "This is called frottage, in case you are wondering. Also known as rubbing."

Corey chuckled, shaking his head in disbelief. "Still the teacher, eh, Lu? I don't give a flying fuck what it's called as long as we keep doing it." And he went back to kissing the pants off Lucian—had the man been wearing pants at the time, which he wasn't.

Corey flipped them around so he was on top of Lucian. He tried to hold his weight off by bracing his arms straight at Lucian's sides, but Lucian threw a leg over Corey's backside and used a hand on the small of Corey's back to drag him down until their bodies were in full contact again, from lips to hips.

Small smooching noises were drowned out by deep, guttural groans as they rubbed against each other, their rhythm faltering, their pace quickening, becoming frantic and jolty. Corey rested his forehead against Lucian's, and they watched one another intently as they raced toward the finish line, their bodies fitting together perfectly, their actions synced.

They clung to each other, seeking that blinding edge as one as their hips bumped and humped and their cocks pressed together, sliding on top of one another, their smoldering shafts not once breaking contact. They pushed their pelvises together, and their eyes, lips, and hands explored every nuance of pleasure they could find.

"Oh God, Corey, I'm coming...." Lucian cried out, spilling the sweet, sharp sound into Corey's mouth.

Then Lucian tensed all over, going rigid, and his cock pumped jets of volcanic jizz, soaking them both at the midsection. Corey followed mere moments behind, loving the feel of his lover coming and overjoyed he hadn't missed that in the sheer enormity of his own climax. Lights flashed behind his closed eyelids as the pressure exploded in his balls, and he spurted fiery liquid everywhere, thick ropes of creamy come.

As they slowly came down from dizzying heights of orgasm, Corey luxuriated in the firm knowledge that they were only beginning their torrid affair. For the day, and beyond.

Following some hands-on friskiness in the shower that same morning, Lucian showed Corey that sensuality existed everywhere if one only bothered to look. Anything could be sensual when it came to touch. Such as… shaving.

With a fluffy white towel wrapped around his hips, Corey stood in front of the sink, with Lucian behind him, cooing in his ear. "Everything worth doing should be done properly. Let me, please."

Corey learned that Lucian found pleasure in even the most mundane, everyday acts, never letting cynicism take over and squelch his high spirits. "I'll take your word for it."

Lucian purred. "Have you ever been to one of those old-fashioned barbershops where they utilize razors and smooth shaving soap? You should. They are divine. Here." Lucian used a shaving brush to create a frothy lather, which he applied to Corey's face, and a soothing scent surrounded them. "This soap is made of real tallow. It is far superior to oils. How does it feel?"

"Surprisingly good," Corey had to admit. Like liquid silk on his skin.

"As predicted," Lucian quipped, rounded Corey, and slid backward to sit on the counter next to the sink. He tilted Corey's head back to finish applying the lather wherever there was stubble. "Now, do not move."

Goose bumps formed all over Corey's skin as chills ran up and down his spine. Part fear but mostly anticipation, the feeling made him nervous, but he remained absolutely still, willing to hand over the reins to his lover. The first slow, cautious swipe of the razor followed the grain as fluidly as a finger might, and Corey was once again surprised at how wonderful the sensation was.

"That feels so great," he murmured.

Lucian smiled and looked up at Corey, about to say something. But then he suddenly blinked hard, as if caught off guard by something he saw in the depths of Corey's eyes. Air crackled as though there were an electric charge between them, and they both breathed heavily. A new kind of heat simmered between them, filling the space with heady promises of the future.

Lucian gasped before lowering his gaze and breaking the mood. Corey swallowed, disappointed at Lucian's retreat. But he had a feeling he knew why Lucian had done so, and it only strengthened his own resolve.

He will be mine. Because he... needs me.

Love....

When Lucian raised his hand again, it shook only for a second or two, then stabilized. The cool, professional mask rose to replace the youthful exuberance from a moment ago. Corey let it go, knowing he would have his moment of sharing truths with Lucian. The proper time and place would come along.

So he obligingly cocked his head back and let Lucian resume the shaving. The gentle sweeps covered first his cheeks, then his jaw, and finally his chin. With every pass of the razor, Corey felt better, understanding how this common practice could become a sensual experience. He smiled at learning how sometimes the only thing needed was a new perspective on old experiences.

Lucian saw him smile and returned the gesture, the sparkle returning to his eyes. "I am happy you have found this to be a pleasant novelty."

"I'll have to remember this," Corey agreed with a grin, and then they were back to the burning sexual chemistry between them. Lucian toweled Corey's face, though there was not a single remnant of soap on him, and then they were kissing like mad.

THAT MORNING had only been the first of many sensual encounters that followed in the next few months.

On one fine day, Corey had gotten to enjoy Lucian's company in a bathtub, all in the name of sensuality training. Lucian had mentioned the eroticism of bathing. Before, Corey would have considered this an exercise in futility and improper hygiene, but the moment he felt Lucian's back tucked and pressed against his front, Corey had no longer cared about those things.

Only Lucian mattered.

Though they had lain together for a while in the huge oval tub, with the jets sending out soft bubbles here and there in its lowest setting, the lapping water was still warm and fragrant, and the bubbles had not burst or dispersed. Corey used a soaped-up sponge to wash whatever parts of his lover he could reach, a lazy progress as he cared more about touching than cleaning. Lucian made swirls in the soapy water with his delicate hands and long fingers, a dreamy practice, his head lolled back against Corey's shoulder.

"This feels wonderful," Corey murmured in Lucian's ear, planting a tender kiss on his earlobe.

Lucian squirmed until he seemed to have burrowed deeper into Corey's embrace, and he sighed happily. "Yes, it is. I wish—" But he stopped abruptly, and Lucian's muscles tensed, startling Corey. The relaxed mood was a thing of the past.

"Lu?" Corey had to speak fast because he suspected otherwise the beautiful, magical creature in his arms would fly away, never to be seen again. Lucian was retreating, emotionally if not physically—yet. "You told me you've been in love. A few ended well, others were unrequited. Was there ever a… a bad love?"

While Corey worried he might have pried too deep or not been very clear, Lucian remained silent. Then he spoke in a hushed tone, "Yes. His name was Blake." A bemused chuckle broke free. "You could say our love was born from the hands of other men."

This perplexed Corey, but it was so like Lucian, mysterious and beguiling. "How so?"

"I was at a night club. I was dancing. Three men were around me, pressed against me, grinding on me." Corey gritted his teeth and snarled silently but didn't interrupt, so Lucian went on. "They began to take liberties with my body. Actions I had not sanctioned. In unison, they began to undress me, as if their intention was to violate me in public. It was madness. I felt trapped."

Corey gulped hard, realizing his hand was motionless, soap oozing out of the sponge, and he began to swipe it across the plains and curves of Lucian's body, offering the comfort and touch of a friend.

"That was when Blake arrived on the scene. He was chivalrous. He rescued me and whisked me off to the bar, where he bought me a drink to calm me down." Lucian frowned, his gaze glazed, lost in the memory. "I think I must have fallen in love with him right then and there. I was much more cavalier and careless with my heart in those days. Later, as we began a relationship, we often joked about how it all began with the hands of other men. That was my first lesson about touch that I could feel everywhere." His brow furrowed more, and a harsh expression arose to replace the contemplative one. "As time went by, he was… cruel to me."

This time it was Corey who stiffened as rage spiked within him in an instant, blazing like wildfire. "Say again?" he ground out.

Lucian shook his head and pulled Corey's arms around himself. "It was not like that. He was physically violent only once. The day I left him. Before that, Blake was… demeaning. He thought very little of me despite his initial gentlemanly conduct. My sexual mentoring program? He said it was an excuse for me to act like an unfaithful slut."

It was extremely difficult for Corey to remain calm. The instinct and desire to kill had never been so strong a motivation inside him, threatening to spill out and do damage. "It's not true, Lucian. None of it. You help people. You've helped me more than you'll ever know."

Lucian tilted his head so he could show his smile to Corey and kiss him on the lips. "I know. Only a few of my clients and I are ever intimate, as in actual intercourse. I am not ashamed of the program I created. I was at the time, though. I loved Blake. But his love was possessive and degrading. He lived to humiliate others. And he had other… partners."

Corey exhaled sharply as a painful realization hit him square in the chest. "That's what you meant. When you spoke of the teachings at Heather House. The sexual positions? The sexual sadist starting his exploitations? That all came from Blake, didn't it?"

Lucian let out a small, fleeting sob. "Yes, in a manner of speaking. Blake was deeply into the hard-core BDSM scene. A sexual sadist in the making. Well, he was a lot of things besides that too. But the sadism aspect grew to become his most defining characteristic. I am embarrassed and infuriated it took me so long to see the signs."

"Sexual sadists can be very manipulative." Corey hugged Lucian tighter. "It wasn't your fault. You're not to blame for his… assholiness."

Lucian giggled. "That's *not* a word."

Corey smiled and nuzzled Lucian's neck. "I'll petition the authorities to add it to all the dictionaries, with Blake's picture alongside it so everyone will know what the term means and who inspired it."

That suggestion had Lucian laughing so hard he slipped lower in the water and damn near drowned. Sputtering and blinking water out of his eyes, he muttered, "I would pay good money to see you do just that. Insolent brat."

Ignoring the teasing, Corey maneuvered Lucian's willowy body in the tub until he was positioned straddling Corey's hips, their cocks slipping and floating next to each other. "Can we do it now, here in the tub?" he asked.

Lucian's eyes darkened, and his smile faltered. Then he shook his head. "Unclean water is a hazard. The anus is highly susceptible to bacterial infections. Let's go to bed."

As they climbed out, Corey chuckled in disbelief. "Only you can be fully aroused and say stuff like *highly susceptible* and *bacterial infections*. You're really something. You have no idea how much I admire and desire you."

That statement had Lucian stopping to stare at Corey, mouth agape and eyes wide. For a while they did nothing but look at each other.

They never got past the bathroom sink. With Lucian on top of said sink, Corey sunk his cock deep inside Lucian's beautiful backside and fucked his lover to oblivion.

Twice, for good measure.

THE NEXT weekend Lucian demonstrated yet again how full of surprises he could be. They returned to Boudoir, and he promptly guided Corey to the BDSM area of the building, where Corey ventured for the first time.

This time they entered the room instead of watching it through a window. A big, burly man was attached naked to a black leather swing, his wrists and ankles bound on the sides, so he was splayed open and vulnerable, like a Thanksgiving turkey waiting to get stuffed. Corey had a hard time reconciling the image of a huge, hairy, muscle-bound man willing to be tied up, but judging from the expectant, darkened eyes and the blissful smile, he was.

Another man came into the room, the strong, silent type with a brooding expression, a bald head, and enough stubble to light fires. Wearing nothing but boots and black leather pants, he walked straight over to other man, unzipped his pants, pulled out a massive, hard cock, unsheathed, and shoved it in the man's lubed-up rectum in one stroke.

The bound man in the swing howled, his head thrown back, and Corey could barely breathe, his mouth dry and his hands sweaty.

When the top began a swift, unrelenting pace of deep thrusts—adding a harsh slap on the bottom's... bottom, on occasion—Lucian tiptoed to Corey's back, insinuating himself closer, and whispered in his ear, "Does the sight turn you on or off?"

Corey swallowed hard, trying to find his voice. He had no answer, for his cock was not hard. But then, in the blink of an eye, a fantastical image arose to replace the reality before him. In it, the two men fucking were replaced by him and Lucian. And his cock grew fully erect in a flash.

"On."

Lucian shifted to whisper into the other ear, "Which one do you see yourself as?"

Familiar faces, his and Lucian's, exchanged places several times but finally set in for a resolved image. "Bottom." He could scarcely believe he had uttered the word, but he knew in his heart he desired that role, that illusion of forced submission, even for a mere moment. He briefly considered the insanity of wanting to... bottom... for the first time in such a slavish manner.

Then he pushed the doubt out of his mind.

Lucian murmured, his excitement clear in his tone, "Who is the top?"

Corey turned his head to look straight into Lucian's eyes. "You know who." He was serious, and he did not want to play games. He wanted Lucian. Badly.

Lucian blinked, as if he was aware of the truth but was having a hard time believing it. Finally he licked his lips, nodded ever so slightly, and asked, "Shall we do that tonight, then?"

"Yes."

Half an hour later, they were back at Lucian's apartment, in his bedroom. No BDSM paraphernalia were required for Corey to know what experience he sought. No swings, no bonds, no whips, no canes. Just Lucian.

Corey flopped down on the bed on his back, naked. Lucian remained standing, slowly undressing, his hungry gaze aimed directly at Corey.

"Leave the tie on," Corey asked, bold and predatory. He wanted so many things he had no name for, but the sensuality of getting fucked by a guy wearing a tie? That was new and hot and exciting, a kink he had not known he possessed until that very moment, when the opportunity presented itself.

"As you wish." With only his white silk tie loose around his neck, Lucian climbed on the bed, crawling like a majestic beast. Like a big cat.

Which reminded Corey of.... "Say, where's that big kitty of yours?"

Lucian smiled enigmatically. "Not here anymore."

Corey whooped in glee, banging his hands against the wooden headboard. "Fuck, I knew it! I knew he was just for show. A little theatrical prop to scare off the new guy. Or... does the poor dear have sex problems too?" He made an exaggerated sad pouty face that had Lucian giggling like mad. "Did he frighten Oscar and Cas away? Did he make unwanted advances on the precious pussies?"

Lucian laughed some more, coming to lie on top of Corey, shaking with mirth. "Stop it, you fiend! Amaya is taking care of the little ones. And Lancelot is being tended to elsewhere."

Corey snorted, unable to prevent himself. "Lancelot? Really?"

"Great lovers in history and legend, literature and the arts. Why not?" Lucian moved to his hands and knees, hovering above Corey, who suddenly was no longer laughing. Lucian's mesmerizing gaze demanded swift surrender, and Corey happily obliged by parting his lips for Lucian's questing tongue to enter.

As Corey dove right into the kiss, allowing the world around him to fade to the back of his mind, he was suddenly brought back to reality when he felt his right wrist being bound by a firm leather shackle, attaching him to one of the bedposts.

"Wha—" He was too blissed out to really pay attention, and by the time his brain was functioning adequately again, his other hand was restrained as well.

Lucian grinned above him, straightening up. "This bound look becomes you. I shall bear that in mind for our future assignations." He frowned and blinked for a second, as though he were confused, but then he shook his head and chuckled awkwardly, like nothing had happened.

Still, Corey had seen and was not about to forget. Lucian might have been in denial, but Corey was determined not to let that fly forever.

Lucian was gone from the bed so fast it was as if he did a vanishing act, like magicians of yore. Yet he soon returned—with a sort of whip in his hand. Corey studied it, frowning. A short, braided, white leather handle with a wrist loop ended in a bunch of suede tails with tapered tips. To Corey, it resembled cat-o'-nine-tails, which confused him, since to the best of his knowledge, Lucian had no intentions of torturing him.

Flexing the object, Lucian asked, "Does this item frighten you?"

Corey shrugged, acting casual. "I don't know what it is exactly."

"It is called a flogger." Lucian stepped to the foot of the bed where Corey lay spread eagle, waiting. "The kiss of the flogger is sweet and sensual, with a touch of pain as well. May I use it on you? You can refuse. It will not interfere with what we are about to do. What I will eventually do to you. And do note that if this feels uncomfortable on your front, the flogger *will* feel amazing on your back and buttocks. Oh, yes, they will jiggle all red for minutes on end."

Corey swallowed hard. His brain fired on all cylinders, trying to find an escape. But his body remained relaxed, anticipating the event. It did not care about possible worries; it had no doubts about what it wanted.

So Corey chose to listen to his body. "Go ahead."

Lucian ambled to the side of the bed, in sight of Corey's body profile. "Close your eyes and focus on the sensations," he instructed, and Corey nodded and complied. He heard leather creaking, presumably from the handle of the object.

The first slap sounded and felt soft and supple, with barely any sting, as it landed on Corey's side lazily. The sensation had his skin tingling and turning goose bumpy. He had expected it to hurt way more.

"Are you all right?" Lucian asked, and to Corey he sounded breathless, expectant.

Corey nodded, fidgeting a bit in place, and tested the solidity of his bonds, which didn't budge when he yanked on them. "Fine. It wasn't… what I expected. Continue."

The following slaps from the suede flogger were soft, gentle, and slow. Nothing about them screamed sadomasochism or pain. The blows landed all over Corey's body, except on his face, cock, or balls. His thighs got a jolt, as did his stomach. When the tails scraped over his nipples, a sudden shock of pleasure had him gasping.

Lucian stopped immediately. "Corey?" He sounded concerned.

"I'm fine." Corey took a couple of deep, fortifying breaths. "Just my, um, nipples…. A bit sensitive, you know."

Lucian's low chuckle had Corey's toes curling. "I will be sure to… kiss away any pain my ministrations might cause, I assure you."

Corey shivered at the promise and envisioned Lucian's tongue lapping at his nipples. Right away, his cock swelled to full mast.

Before he knew what was happening, the bed dipped, and once Lucian unbuckled the wrist bonds, Corey's hands were free again. Corey opened his eyes just as Lucian straddled his pelvis, inching down to sit on his thighs. The look Lucian sported was dark and hungry, and Corey wanted him so much it hurt.

Lucian leaned forward, opened his mouth, and took one of Corey's nipples between his teeth, gently pulling on the tender nub. Chills ran up and down Corey's body. The shockwave was electric, awakening every bit of him that might have still been dormant or hesitant. Ablaze with want, Corey wiggled under Lucian's touches. Lucian licked around the areola and sucked on the teat while his nails raked over Corey's muscular sides, chest, and stomach.

"Oh, I can't take this anymore," Lucian cried out, sounding desperate and feral. "Turn over, please." But his *please* sounded an awful lot like an order, at least to Corey. Lucian moved off, muttering to himself. "I was going to use a feather on you. Tickle your cock. But I am…." His voice cracked, and he almost sobbed. Corey understood that Lucian was losing control, and he was asking for Corey's help.

As swiftly as he could without bumping any knees or elbows on sensitive body parts, Corey flipped over to lie on his belly, adjusting his hips until his rampant erection snuggled against his ripped abdomen, providing friction. Corey could relate to the haste, the rush, the overwhelming need since he had experienced them all with Lucian.

"Tell me what to do," Corey asked, keeping his tone level in counterpoint to Lucian's quivering, achy voice. One of them had to maintain a semblance of a cool head and inward serenity, even if it was a mere illusion.

Lucian seemed to be struggling as he said, "Lift up. I will put a pillow under your hips to raise your butt to the right height and angle."

Corey had no idea what that meant exactly, but he was more than willing to find out. His face pressed against a pillow, he beamed and grinned at the knowledge he was throwing his sex teacher off his game. It was Corey who was having this effect on Lucian. Not any other man. Corey. Making Lucian wild with desire.

Lifting his pelvis off the mattress, Corey felt a hurried hand shove a pillow beneath him, the move pushing his cock out of whack and forcing Corey to adjust yet again. Before he managed to get everything comfortably situated, Lucian grabbed Corey's hips, yanked him savagely backward toward him, and parted Corey's ass cheeks. Then a hot, wet... *something...* entered Corey's ass.

Holy. Shit. That's his... tongue. Lu's tongue is inside me!

Lucian continued to pry Corey's ass open with his delicate, firm hands and a slippery, darting tongue that speared into Corey like a water serpent, wiggling and squirming within. Corey moaned, clawed at the sheets like a maniac, and partly twisted to get away, partly thrust back against the slick invader. Corey's skin was on fire—from the inside. He got chills and hot waves at once. His muscles quivered, as if unsure whether to relax or tense up, so they did both, at three or four second intervals.

"Mmm, I knew you would taste divine," Lucian murmured into the lewd kiss, and the reverberations of his hoarse voice made Corey shudder.

"D-does it taste like, um...?" Corey couldn't finish. He had showered before the main event, and Lucian told him anus was like any patch of clean skin when, well, clean.

"No. Perfect." That was all Lucian replied.

Then he dove right back in. He jabbed his tongue inside, then pulled back out and with a flattened tongue, swiped over Corey's fluttering hole and began making lazy circles, slowly increasing the pace and pressure, until Corey was writhing and panting, and a second later mumbling incoherently and begging to be allowed to come. His cock lay heavy, hard, and hot against the pillow, which though soft and sensuous was too yielding to grind against, and he was leaking profusely too, getting stickier with each passing second.

Suddenly a cool finger entered Corey's ass, with such slick ease that Corey didn't even register it at first. He braced himself up on his elbows and twisted his head to look over his shoulder at Lucian.

"Does this hurt? Be sure to tell me. I need you to be honest." Lucian spoke clearly, but it was obvious from his harsh breathing, flushed skin, and dilated pupils that he was close to coming.

Corey nodded, staring, and then focusing on the sensations of a finger in his ass. It wasn't all that bad really. He had expected this, too, to hurt more. "Can't you tell if I'm in pain? You must have done this plenty."

"I have. I can tell if you are in physical discomfort. Your body will lock instead of spasming, your muscles will go taut instead of becoming pliant. That kind of thing. But pain is more subjective. I will need your feedback, your words, your honesty, your directness."

Just as Lucian stopped speaking, Corey felt the burn for the first time. It was different from the urge to push out that had started the moment Lucian stuck a finger inside him. No, this odd burning sensation was just plain weird. Not wrong, exactly, but... weird.

"Wait." Corey needed to breathe, and for some reason, having a finger inside his ass felt like having all the air pushed out from his lungs.

Lucian paused immediately. "Shall I pull out? We absolutely do not need to do this now or ever if you have any doubts. Please, Corey. Talk to me. Be honest."

The deep caring in Lucian's timid tone was all Corey needed to calm down. Corey was convinced Lucian would do nothing to harm him. "I'm okay." But he wasn't sure if he wanted to continue. "It just feels...." He didn't know what word would suffice to cover all the new and odd sensations he was experiencing.

"Weird. Yes, that sounds familiar." Lucian smiled softly. "The first time is always the strangest because you do not know what to expect. Some will tell you it hurts, as though you are being ripped apart, a hot tearing sensation. That can be true if the intrusion is done wrong, such as too fast or without enough lubrication. Is that how it feels?" Lucian still kept his finger in place, but he wasn't moving in or out. He simply held his digit in place, keeping Corey's spasming hole a bit open.

"I don't know how to describe it," Corey said, feeling dumb. His erection deflated too. At least Lucian couldn't see it. "Not painful exactly."

"Ah. The burn." Lucian seemed to relate. "That is normal. There will be a slight burn every time, but next time you will know to expect it." Corey wasn't sure if he felt better or worse at the thought of next time. Lucian, however, didn't seem to have the same compunctions. "Remember when you and I did this the other way around? With you inside me? I told you to push in while I pushed out."

"Yeah, I remember that." Corey frowned, catching on. "I need to... push out?" *Like I'm taking a dump?* But he wisely left that unsaid because nothing brought a sensual mood down like a discussion of feces. Unless one was into scat play. Which neither of them was.

"Yes. Bear down. Do not force it. I will not go in deep, I promise." Lucian did not move an inch until Corey had nodded his acquiescence. "Take a hold of your cock and masturbate. The pleasures will mix soon enough. I will be gentle."

Of that Corey had no doubts. "I know."

Lucian added more lube, and Corey felt very wet inside. Lucian's finger slid in easier this time, past the first knuckle, a simple in and out motion, kind of like seesawing. Corey still wasn't finding it particularly pleasurable. It wasn't painful either, but if there was a phenomenal bottoming experience to be had, he wasn't getting it.

Maybe I'm a top only.

Then all of a sudden, Lucian twisted the finger inside his channel—and hit a spot that sent lightning showers of pure, world-shattering pleasure coursing through his entire being.

"Holy Mother of God, what the fuck was *that?*" Corey groaned, his hips jerking as his body desperately sought to reexperience that blissful sensation.

Lucian chuckled low, a seductive purr that had Corey's toes curling. "That, darling, is your sweet spot. Your prostate. How did it feel? Good or bad?"

"Freaking awesome. Do it again," Corey urged, humping the pillow, his reawakened cock hard and dripping again. His whole groin felt warm, a steady radiation of heat that unfurled and spread to all corners of his body.

Lucian twirled his finger inside Corey's ass, coating the walls of his channel with ample doses of lube. And the circular motion was delightful, clearly designed to arouse every part of him and ignite his nerve endings to a blazing inferno.

Before Corey knew it, one finger had become two, and then three, with more and more lube added each round. Corey panted, feeling like he couldn't get enough air in his chest. His heart thundered, and his cock screamed for release.

"Lu, please, come on," he pleaded, grinding his hips up and down, searching for that sharp piercing pleasure that struck him each time Lucian brushed past or stabbed at his prostate. He was certain he would come without ever touching his dick. Lucian had advised him to masturbate, but Corey knew if so much as a breeze fanned over his cock, this would all be over in seconds flat.

"Normally," Lucian said quietly, strained, as if holding on by a thread too, "I would suggest using a sex toy, such as a dildo, to open you better and prepare you for my—"

"With other virgins?" Corey interjected, his patience waning fast. "No, Lu. *You*. I need you. Right the fuck now. I don't want a piece of plastic or silicone inside me. It has to be you. No more delays, no more excuses. Just do it. Please."

Lucian extracted his fingers carefully and wiped them on a towel. Then he slipped on a condom, coated his erection with lube, and on his knees scrambled closer, spreading Corey's thighs wider with his own.

He placed a warm hand over the small of Corey's back, making soothing circles as he asked, "Are you ready?"

Corey laughed, breathless. "I've been waiting for this for twenty years. I'm as ready as I'll ever be."

"Push out as I push in. And do not forget to breathe, no matter how full you feel, or out of breath you are." That was the last of Lucian's instructions.

Lucian's cockhead brushed briefly over Corey's twitching hole. Gripping Corey's hips gently, Lucian glided his cock back and forth in Corey's crack, the tiny contacts like whispered promises that sent Corey's hole into a fluttering frenzy.

Finally, after the teasing torment, Lucian pressed harder. Corey panted and pushed gently to relax his anus. After the rimming and fingering, Corey's sphincter had apparently come to the conclusion nothing would stand in the way of more pleasure because Corey felt himself open up to the touch of his lover's dick.

Then, as Corey probably imagined the wet pop that rung in his ears, Lucian's cock was inside. Well, the tip anyway. Corey's channel constricted around the intruder, while he tried to bear down on the new, stronger burn. For a moment it had indeed felt like he was being torn apart, a searing kind of pain. But it had been a mere flash, nothing more, gone now.

"The head is in," Lucian whispered hoarsely. "The biggest part. For me, anyway. It should be easier from now on."

That was a relief to hear, Corey thought, continuing to focus on pushing out and calming his breathing. Both were challenging, to say the least. *There's a huge cock inside me. Jesus fucking Christ, did Lu just grow a couple of inches in length and girth, or what?* Corey buried his face in his pillow, hugging it close, holding on to the new sensation like a ship holding on to an anchor on a stormy sea.

Inch by trembling inch, Lucian insinuated his considerable shaft deeper into Corey. He was so full that the urge to push out grew stronger with each millimeter Lucian gained. How on earth did gay guys do this on a regular basis? Corey sure hoped it would get easier.

Oddly, the mere notion of trying anal sex again in the future calmed Corey's nerves. The thought offered him the comfort that he would survive this experience and even learn to enjoy it. In fact, he was beginning to get the hang of it as his muscles relaxed, and the soft pressure of Lucian's hands on the small of his back continued to grant him his lover's composure.

After what felt like an eternity, Lucian was fully seated inside Corey. Both men sighed and groaned in relief and delight.

"H-how does it feel? Are you all right?" Lucian sounded hesitant and concerned, even fearful.

Corey twisted his arm back to caress and squeeze Lucian's thigh, the muscle taut. "I'm fine. It was a lot at first. But it's better now. I swear." Corey willed himself to unwind, to let go of all the tightness that clung to him, to find the peace of belonging to this situation that he had longed for, awaited, and dreamed of. After a couple of deep breaths, Corey loosened up and felt like molten jelly, practically oozing on the sheets.

Then, without explanation or warning, Lucian pulled almost all the way out, and then in a sudden whoosh, plunged back in, as deep as he could go.

"*Oh, fuck yeah!*" was Corey's response as he shouted at the top of his lungs, the feel of getting truly and utterly fucked a new and riveting one. The sensation was so real and potent, Corey all but started to weep, managing just barely to keep control.

Which was for the best because that was when Lucian really let it rip. After his first few gentle, short strokes, he escalated his tempo into forceful, deep thrusts, in and out, like pistons firing. The pause had done good, and Corey was open, wet with lube, and definitely willing, but was he ready for the pounding he was receiving? *Hell yeah!*

"Lu, do you have any idea how long I've waited for this?" Corey murmured, so lost in lust he had no real control over what he was saying. Yet the words rang true. His back bowed as he tried to push back, to get more of Lucian inside, as impossible as that was. Their rhythms began to match, get in sync.

"Thank you for giving me this gift of you," Lucian whispered, his tone ragged and drawn out, out of breath.

He dropped down, braced by his arms, and then came to lie on Corey, his chest to Corey's back. Lucian wound his arms around Corey's chest and neck, and started to fuck Corey as powerfully as he could. Or so Corey assumed, at least. Corey only knew he loved the tiny weight of the man above him, their bodies fitting together perfectly, as Lucian mounted Corey's ass, dragging his legs over Corey's until he was in effect straddling Corey's butt, keeping Corey's legs tight together.

This new position afforded Lucian great command over Corey's pliant, trapped body. He'd had his cock inside Lucian, but it hadn't been like this. Corey had assumed that anal sex, as in bottoming, was one thing, and he could acclimatize to it; but he had expected to be wary, nervous, and even unresponsive to being restrained in this manner by a lover's body, kept in place to get fucked.

But… Corey discovered there was nowhere in the world he would rather be. Yes, the idea of mounting Lucian in the same way and plunging his cock into Lucian was a hot one. It made his blood boil; there was no denying that. But… perhaps, once in a while, they could do this too. Corey's ass sure didn't seem to mind.

"Oh, Corey," Lucian muttered, his sizzling hot breath fanning over Corey's cheek and ear. "There are a million things I want to do with you. Feathers, silk, and lace draped over your skin like water. Leather whips, leaving red lines all over your firm, bouncy butt, my marks of ownership. Chains, collars, and cock rings, all at once, tying you up, trussed up for me and my pleasure. Anal beads, butt plugs, and jumbo dildos, opening you up for anything I put inside your beautiful ass, be it my cock, my fingers, or my tongue. You loved my tongue in you, didn't you?"

Corey turned his head on the pillow before either the plump object itself or the picture of it in his head smothered him. "Yeah, Lu. We'll do all that. I swear."

Lucian groaned, his pace quickening as he thrust in deep, fast, and hard, unrelenting, on instinct, feral and wild. Corey's cock and balls throbbed with need for more, like he required air to breathe. He ground against the pillow as Lucian rocked into him, both their motions intensifying as their pleasure expanded, and their orgasms raced, hurtling toward them at unimaginable speeds from some greater universe of delight.

Whether his channel was really tight, Corey didn't know, but he sure felt Lucian's dick rubbing every millimeter of his insides. Was this what it felt like to be horny, to be so randy all you could do was think about sex? Was this the depth and breadth of his sexual self, the assertiveness he used to dominate Lucian and the willing yielding he now experienced submitting to Lucian?

This is who I am. This is me having sex. This is me with Lucian. God, please, let Lu want me as I am, imperfect but perfect for him. Nothing more, nothing less. Please, Lu....

Spellbound by the sensations rocketing through him, Corey floated in a haze of desire, fiery red and pulsating. His body was ablaze, his skin too tight, his ass stretched full and to the limit of what he could bear. Or... could he take more? A jumbo dildo? Two cocks? A fist...?

Corey's head swam with sensual images, some created out of porn and erotica he had seen or heard, others born from his feverish imagination, from the depths of his yearning for more sex. He felt stripped of his defenses, raw and exposed to the world. Yet he was safe in the arms of his lover. He could and was allowed to let go of his trepidations and hang-ups.

"Corey?" Lucian had a hard time speaking, Corey could tell. "Can you turn around so we can do this face-to-face, please?"

Corey wanted to see emotions on Lucian's face, so he nodded. "Yeah."

Lucian didn't pull his cock out entirely, however, and yet somehow, in an odd tangle of flailing limbs, they managed to flip over so that Corey lay on his back with Lucian on top of him. Then Lucian thrust again, and Corey moaned.

But when Lucian gripped Corey's dick and started to jerk him off with deliberate force, Corey pretty much wailed. Lucian took possession of Corey's lips, drowning Corey's moans. Every glide of Lucian's tongue and dick in and out of Corey's orifices felt heavenly. Lucian sped up the tugs of his hand, the pounding of his cock, and the delving of his tongue, and Corey lost all sense of himself.

Corey locked his legs around Lucian's slender hips, seeking an anchor, and wound his arms around Lucian's neck. The shift in angle of thrusts had Lucian's cock swipe hard over Corey's prostate. Lucian growled and nailed Corey's gland again. Corey's eyes flew open at the sound from Lucian, so primal and domineering it shoved his libido into overdrive.

Nothing could prevent his orgasm. Years of pent-up passion broke free as he learned yet another truth about himself. *I fucking love bottoming!* Like an erupting volcano, Corey climaxed, his dick spewing come by the bucketloads. His body arched as his cock pulsed, encased in Lucian's fist, liquid fire burning in his veins, sinking him into a sea of lava. Pleasure unlike anything he had ever known exploded his senses, like a star being born.

Moaning, Lucian slammed into Corey once, twice, thrice before he jerked his hips, violent shudders wracking his svelte figure. Corey's abused ass muscles clamped around Lucian's cock, tight and unrelenting, until he fought to relax, and his hold of Lucian released. Hot spurts of semen filled Lucian's condom, that much Corey could feel, and he was disappointed there had to be barriers between them.

Right then, Corey vowed one day they would discard the latex and feel each other au naturel. *One day, Lu, I swear.*

Collapsing on Corey but trying hard not to, Lucian eased out, and Corey hissed at the withdrawing movement in his sensitized channel. He moaned at the loss, bereft, and knew without a doubt that he would bottom again. Well, maybe not today or even tomorrow, judging from the odd spasms his channel went through, feeling soft and roughed up. But soon, though.

Lucian slid off Corey but not out of his arms as he got rid of the condom. "I shall clean us up. We made a bit of a mess." He blushed cutely as he smiled, and to Corey nothing and no one had ever looked as lovely.

Corey tugged Lucian back before he could climb out of bed. "Nuh-uh. Later. You promised me a full experience. And I wanna cuddle." He made an exaggerated show of yanking Lucian close and embraced him so hard no man could have breathed in that bear hug.

Lucian giggled, wriggling and squirming. "We just had anal sex, so we should be anal about cleanliness."

The joke was ridiculous, but Corey laughed anyway. "You neat freak. Later." He swept his tongue over Lucian's pouty lower lip, snagged it between his teeth, and nipped tenderly. "Much, much later." Not a single worry about kissing Lucian after his tongue had been inside Corey's body emerged to plague Corey's mind. He was at ease in every sense of the word.

With hearty chuckles, slow caresses, and the occasional tickle, they snuggled the rest of the night, kissing and holding each other close in blissful afterglow.

To Corey, his first time bottoming had been a glorious success. Convincing Lucian that love had become a factor in the equation of their relationship would undoubtedly require more groundwork. Corey let slumber whisk him away to dreamland.

AFTER HIS first time bottoming, Corey assumed there was nothing new to learn besides new positions. But he was soon proven wrong. Two of the most memorable sexual scenes for Corey happened on the same day. The first was their initial real public date, spent at a five-star restaurant, even though it was lunch, not dinner.

The restaurant was packed, but since it was high-class, every private booth retained an air of intimacy. The background chatter and ambient music were both low, and the lights were dim. It was a perfect setting for their first public outing.

As was his custom, Lucian wore white, and Corey wanted to rip the clothes off him at the very instant he saw them. But he remained a consummate gentleman, even wearing artfully raggedy jeans and a gray polo sweater that matched the color of his eyes, none of which made him look as tasteful as Lucian. And *oh God*, how tasty the man could be!

"Our food has yet to arrive, but you are already devouring, I see," Lucian teased primly and grinned, his gaze aimed at the menu though they had already ordered.

"Careful, Lu," Corey said huskily. "I used to be bashful and proper, but now I know how to rev your engine, even in public, and I'm not above using any and all means at my disposal to make you... squirm."

The not-so-idle threat seemed to work because Lucian gulped, and his cheeks flamed. He said nothing, which had Corey grinning. Since their visit to Boudoir's dungeon and the subsequent bedroom calisthenics, Corey had a feeling his lover appreciated and yearned for the assertiveness Corey had mastered in the privacy of Lucian's boudoir. He had no idea where the empowerment came from. The source seemed to be buried so deep within Corey that he might never be able to dig and uncover it consciously, let alone analyze it fully.

Lucian could be subtly and overtly seductive and charming. Corey was more direct, it seemed, with an instinctual command presence. At least when it came to Lucian, who got all shaky and doe-eyed when Corey took charge. Was that Lucian's fantasy? To hand over the sexual reins to someone temporarily and be swept away by... love?

"I am still in the dark about the proper protocol of this... dating business," Corey said, trying to find a good opening line for their small talk. Lucian burst into a fit of giggles. Corey frowned. "What? Did that sound too robotic?"

Lucian laughed, an open and vivacious sound that sent thrills through Corey and made him feel even better than before. "How about... androi-dic?"

Corey chuckled. "That's *not* a word."

"Oh? And your, what was it, assholiness is? Seems rather unfair and discriminatory, the way you deny my dictionary additions and accept only yours."

Corey chimed in with a snigger of his own, feeling light and joyous. "Don't you think it's a bit, um... dirty?"

"Lewd words have their uses," Lucian reminded with an obscene wink and a grin.

"Maybe in the bedroom. But at a five-star restaurant?" Corey tutted theatrically.

The melodious sound of Lucian's laughter echoed in the room and reverberated inside Corey's chest, sending jolts into his heart that had nothing to do with voices and everything to do with... love.

Lucian's smile was dazzling, as always. "Gastronomy is inextricably linked to sensual desires. Oral pleasures can be derived from food and drink with ease as our palates refine and our taste buds experience novel flavors. Love potions and aphrodisiac appetizers, designed to awaken our senses, whet our appetites, grow our hunger. The kitchen offers a cornucopia of tantalizing fantasies. The master of the house in the dark with the scullery maid. The cook in the pantry with his waiter. Experiments with tastes. Such as cooking dinner with ingenuity—and without an apron. Or perhaps baking with a touch of sugar and spice and sex, hmm?" Lucian almost sparkled that night, a light burning within him that made Corey stop and stare and take notice. "What kind of memories do you have of taste? Prudence in the kitchen with flour and cake molds? Randolph in the study with brandy and fine wines?"

Corey chuckled, shaking his head. "Neither of my parents was ever really active in the kitchen. We did have a cook, though. Allegra was her name. She was Italian-American, robust and boisterous. And the dishes she could make, well, they would have any man or woman drooling with just a whiff carried through the air. Her lasagna was... *ah*, to die for." He smacked his lips, as his taste buds sure hadn't forgotten that dish. "I can taste the Italian sweet sausage now, and the ricotta and mozzarella cheeses, the herbs, the garlic...." He shook his head, hungrier than he had been before the reminiscing. "Damn, I should've ordered lasagna."

Their booth was tucked in a secluded corner, opening to a windowed view out over the Manhattan skyscrapers bathing in sunlight, since the restaurant was located on the seventy-seventh floor. Thick curtains hid them from the rest of the restaurant. Because of their prime location, dirty ideas fired up Corey's imagination in rapid succession, until finally....

"Unzip your pants, and take your cock out."

Lucian started, his eyes widening in shock. But he never once looked around to see if anyone heard or saw. Blushing, he licked his lips and then slid his hands underneath the edge of the table and the immaculate white tablecloth where Corey could not see. Corey watched, riveted by the motions of Lucian's petite hands, as much as he could detect. Judging from the up and down movement of his arms, Lucian had his dick out, and he was tugging it.

Corey swallowed, his hunger growing.

That was when the waiter returned. Lucian shifted forward so the table hid his exposed penis, and with a congenial smile, he let the server place his meal—red-wine-braised lentils with vegetable sausage—before him. With an equally strained, polite smile, Corey waited until his meal—honey-balsamic-glazed grilled chicken with asparagus stalks—was set.

The second the man had bowed, wished them bon appétit, and vanished, Corey wiggled his way under the table, and crawled the meter or two that separated him from Lucian. He gripped Lucian's hips, nudging his lower half entirely under the camouflage of the table, and proceeded to take the whole length of Lucian's cock in his mouth.

Oh God, how I love sucking this man's cock.

Above the table came a quiet, muffled moan that was quickly suppressed.

Corey grinned around the mouthful, a delicious appetizer, and began to swish saliva in his mouth, getting the hard, hot shaft so wet trickles ran down the thick column of flesh. Then, as he had Lucian where he wanted, all moist and easy and on the verge of collapse, Corey started sucking in earnest. He slurped; he drank; he nibbled; he tongued every inch he could reach.

Lucian's hand came to rest on Corey's head, trembling, and then he clutched at Corey's short hair, trying to get purchase but failing. His hips shimmied as his orgasm approached with the power of a steam engine. That prompted Corey to increase his efforts.

All too soon Lucian tensed, his thighs quaking and his hips bucking. A low, helpless groan heralded the spurts of hot, creamy man juice that Corey drank to his heart's content. He used his hand to wring every last drop from Lucian's balls until the man pushed him off.

As Corey climbed out from under the table, he smoothed his wrinkled clothes, ran a hand through his hair, and straightened up, even though his own dick was positively bursting inside his jeans. Corey took a moment to consider the implications of what he had done. Never before had he dreamed of a public sexual encounter. With Lucian, however, all bets were off. Corey was a live wire, exposed and ready to blow at a moment's notice.

And speaking of Lucian, he slumped against the round booth, his chest heaving as he panted roughly, almost wheezing. His forehead and neck glistened with fresh sweat, his eyes were closed, and his lips appeared plump, swollen, and redder than Corey had ever seen. Lucian must have bitten down hard to prevent the emergence of sex noises.

Corey grinned and then chuckled, the pleasure bubbling inside him.

Lucian didn't open his eyes. A breathless scolding followed nonetheless. "You sound awfully pleased with yourself. So smug."

Corey laughed and took a hungry bite of his food, letting the savory flavors of grilled chicken, sweet honey, tangy herbs, and soothing asparagus awaken his taste buds. Not that they had been asleep, *oh no*, not after Lucian's briny juices, a delectable benediction.

"I do love that ravaged look you get when I've had my way with you."

Suddenly Lucian grinned back, a wicked, dangerous gesture. "Do remember, darling, that revenge is best served... hot."

And that was when Lucian's shoeless foot landed squarely on top of Corey's bulging erection, and began a fiercely determined, unyielding rubbing.

Corey groaned and, in shock, glanced around to see if they had witnesses to their half-public game of debauchery. "Jesus, Lu...."

Lucian let out a low, alluring purr that sent frissons of pleasure cascading through each and every cell and molecule in Corey's body until he was almost doubled over the table in agony of the sensual variety. Even through the blood roaring in Corey's ears, Lucian's taunting chuckles could easily be heard.

After that it was all a blur of hectic arousal that demanded instant gratification. Lucian never let up, not once. His toes had surprising strength, and Corey could not get them to budge. The movement made him weak all over until he had no choice but to surrender to Lucian's mastery of him.

He practically ripped open his jeans, panting, and just managed to wrap a napkin over his cockhead before Lucian pushed him over the edge, headlong into the depths of orgasm. He came in heavy splashes, his tight balls achy and his cock begging to finish the release. When he had no more to give, Corey found that shoving Lucian's foot was as easy as blowing off a feather.

"Bastard," he murmured under his breath, glowing in a state of bliss. "You perfect, sweet little bastard."

Lucian snickered. With smoldering glances at each other, they cleaned up, smoothed wrinkled attire, and straightened up to appear casual and decent. Only then were they able to dig into their meals, as their other appetites were sated.

The second amazing sexual scene, definitely worthy of remembrance, came later that night when they returned to Corey's apartment and engaged in food play....

Lying on a cool platter with various dishes displayed in turn on his naked skin had been a true novelty for Corey, one he had relished with every fiber of his being. Lucian had gone all out that evening, starting with appetizers, continuing with several main courses, and topping it all off with desserts Lucian had taken his time to eat off him. It was a veritable feast for the eyes, hands, and mouth.

"Mmm, melon balls," Lucian murmured as he popped one into his mouth.

His nimble tongue captured another piece of fruit, pineapple from the looks of it, from between Corey's pecs, and he made that sweet savoring *yum-yum* sound in his throat that made Corey's toes curl, his thighs shake, and his stomach flutter.

"Oh God...."

"Ahh, forbidden fruits and carnal pleasures," Lucian whispered, his hot breath fanning over Corey's exposed skin as he nibbled on a slice of zucchini placed on Corey's rippling belly. "You are such a dish, sweetheart. I knew you would be."

By the time Lucian got to the almost runny ice cream sliding down Corey's hot and cold cock and took the whole length into his mouth, sucking so damn hard his cheeks hollowed, Corey was out of his mind, with need pulsing through his veins until he had tears streaming out of his eyes.

"Dammit, Lu. Please...." His hips jerked up of their own volition.

With a wicked, taunting laugh, Lucian popped a piece of cucumber in Corey's mouth to silence his protests at Lucian's slow advance. Crunching on the vegetable, Corey muttered a few select curses under his breath and then succumbed, letting Lucian set any pace he desired.

When his hole was pierced by a peppermint candy cane, Corey moaned and thrashed around. A sense-memory burned a hole in Corey's brain as he recalled his last bottoming session. In general, they had mostly gone the other way, with Lucian bottoming, but Corey had learned he was not averse to experiencing this role during sex. Be it with a foreign object or a real-life penis.

"Have no fear," Lucian said quietly, reassuring. "Peppermint causes natural lubrication, so you are quite safe."

The sensation that followed inside Corey's ass was less like a burning and more like a tingling. Lucian did not go in deep, but he did twirl the candy cane, sending frissons of pure pleasure through Corey.

"I hope… you're not… planning on… eating that… after you…."

Lucian giggled helplessly, his whole body shimmying. "I will not, I promise."

Then Lucian sucked on the head of Corey's dick again, and Corey's reason flew right out the window. By the time Lucian pulled out the cane, straddled Corey's hips, and slid down to impale himself on Corey's sheathed and lubed-up cock, leisurely progress and finesse were no longer an option.

Corey had already learned what it meant to be ridden, but this time Lucian went wild, bouncing up and down on Corey's dick, as if he were a cowboy fastened to a bucking stallion. His golden-red locks flung around, his nails dug into Corey's chest, and he wailed in a rising tone that had Corey wishing the encounter would never end.

"One day," Lucian murmured breathlessly, his eyes closed, his back arched, his hands braced on Corey's thighs. "We will make love tantric style. Ceremonial edging, with neither of us allowed to come. Ahh, the excruciatingly pleasurable torment that awaits us."

Corey shivered, envisioning a sensual scene unfolding, one where they lay together, tangled, rocking in rhythm, every move with an equal and opposite countermove. Delayed pleasure enhancing their delight until beginning and ending no longer mattered. Corey had heard of this sex practice, of course, but to actually engage in it? His mind whirled with the possibilities.

But for the time being, their present sexual encounter took precedence. Corey was so close to the edge he could fucking taste it. Lucian thrashed around with abandon, so he must have been dancing on the knife's edge as well.

By the time they were both coming, they were covered in food particles and smears, a bit of drink here and there, all mussed up. Fresh spunk added to the menu displayed on their skin for all to see. Not that there was anyone present to see the mess they'd made. In the end, as their jizz cooled on their skins and their labored breathing returned to normal, they were laughing and kissing and groping, as though nothing else existed in the world but the two of them.

It was one of the best times Corey ever had, and he was elated at knowing there was plenty more sexual experimentation ahead.

THE ONE thing they didn't do during the three months they spent predominantly in bed having the most amazing sex on the planet, however, was talk about the future, when their sensual collaboration would come to its inevitable end.

CHAPTER 30

COREY WAS no longer frigid. If he ever had been.

His condition could have been repression, one that required a professional touch to be awakened. Lucian certainly had the Midas touch when it came to sensuality. Coming to terms with being a grown man with the newly arisen libido of a horny teenager took some getting used to.

Returning to Heather House, however, took far more courage of conviction for Corey than engaging in new sexual acts with a willing partner. Corey ambled up and down the halls, his mind blank, but his feet knowing the right destination better than his head.

Soon Corey found himself at the doorway to the music room. Glum notes echoed into the hall, and Corey trailed after them, like a mouse dancing for the piper. The young brunet boy sat in one of the chairs, playing a gloomy, technically advanced melody. His eyes were closed as he played, swaying slightly on the chair, lost in the tune. Corey stared, as rapt as before, loving every second.

Suddenly a door banged somewhere, and the boy's eyes flew open. He stopped as if he'd hit a brick wall.

Corey awkwardly waved at the boy. "Hey."

The boy's eyes narrowed, but there was an ironic quirk on his lips. "Oh, Mr. Luxury Pimp returns. Slumming again, eh?" His gaze swept over Corey, a sarcastic grin on his face.

Corey harrumphed. "Come on. Gimme a break. I dressed down for fuck's sake." Then his cheeks flushed scarlet as he realized he had just cursed at a homeless fifteen-year-old. *Great. I'm sure batting a zero today. Again.*

But the kid chuckled, if only briefly, before tucking his instrument back in the raggedy case. "Used clothes? Nah, I don't think so. Vintage from a high-end boutique, am I right?" His tone lilted at the end as he mocked Corey.

Corey grimaced but then let out a resigned breath, slumping, and nodded. "I don't like to wear clothes other people have worn. So sue me." His clothes indeed might have appeared casual, cheap, and worn, but they weren't, not really. At least this new ensemble had cost considerably less than six hundred bucks like last time.

The kid snorted. "Snob."

"Yeah, I guess." Corey looked around but couldn't deny his interest in this boy down on his luck. "It's Dylan, right?"

The boy rolled his eyes. "Wow, the pimp remembered my name. Still not interested in any of your dirty propositions, though."

Corey let that one pass, sauntered into the room, and sat down a couple of chairs away from the boy. "Bach, huh? *Partita in A minor for solo flute*, wasn't it?"

Grudgingly, Dylan glanced at Corey, who realized the boy liked that he had known the piece. "Yeah. Third movement."

Corey nodded. "Sarabande."

"You know your concerto suites." Dylan clutched the flute case and stared at the floor, fidgeting but not getting up. "You play?"

"Nope. Tone deaf." Corey hesitated. "May I ask… where'd you learn?"

Dylan straightened up, stiffening, and scoffed. "A street kid can't know operas, is that it?"

Corey frowned, backpedaling but bristling too. "No! I didn't say that."

The boy got up, flinging his bangs out of his eyes. "Whatever, man."

Corey got up too, hating how he had failed with this boy. Again. "Hey, I didn't mean to upset—"

"This ain't your scene, Mr. Pimp. Why'd you bother? Go away." Without waiting for a response, Dylan took off.

As he stormed off, Corey noted he had new clothes. That is to say, they were cleaner and less worn, but they weren't Dylan's size or his style, so Corey assumed they were loaners or giveaways. Now he felt even worse, thinking he could come in, wearing expensive vintage and imagining them looking the same as the real thing.

I'll roll in ashes and wear a potato sack next week.

"WHY DOESN'T he like me?" Corey whined to Lucian later, feeling childish. Nearly a whole week had passed since last time, and Corey wanted to do better this time.

Lucian walked ahead of him toward the entrance to Heather House, a soft smile on his luscious lips that Corey wanted to lick, suck, and nip.

"Remember what I told you about these kids? How hard trust is for them?"

"Yeah." Corey felt depressed and completely disentitled to do so. How could he ever justify feeling glum when he had things so much better than these lost young souls? *God, could I be any more melodramatic?* He sighed and trudged up the stairs in Lucian's wake.

As usual, his feet led him to the music room. And exactly like before, Dylan sat there playing, his flute dancing in front of him, producing odd fluttering melodies with central four-note motifs that Corey did not recognize. The scales descended and ascended, expanded and diminished, a tune that echoed sighs from far away and offered images of aerial flights of fancy.

Riveted, Corey was rooted to the spot, listening till his heart hurt.

If Dylan was aware of Corey, he gave no indication of that. He played until the piece obviously finished on its own. Only then did he open his eyes and, unsurprised, look to the doorway where Corey stood.

"Again? Really?" He didn't sound bored as much as amused.

"Yeah. Guess I'm stalking you." Corey offered a poor excuse for a self-deprecating smile but didn't let it linger. "I didn't recognize that piece."

Dylan shrugged, putting his flute back in its case carefully. "Takemitsu's *Air for flute solo*. His last composition, I think."

"It's unusual."

"It has an inner dynamic, with a repetitive motif and a flutter-tongue technique."

"You're an expert." As Dylan shot him a glare, Corey put up his hands in a frustrated surrender gesture. "Forget it. I'll leave you to practice."

Dylan absentmindedly fiddled with the flute case's lock. "I've got a biology class in half an hour anyway." Then he suddenly sat down, his lips pursed in thought. "Got any requests?"

Corey smiled a little, a bit wary but seeking a connection with this musician. "Um, you know Buss's *A Day in the City?*"

Dylan nodded. "I think I have sheets for it here somewhere." He brought up a beaten backpack, unzipped it, and rummaged around until he took out a wrinkled notebook with papers stuck in between. He flipped through the sheets of music until he found the ones he was looking for and placed them on the note stand. He studied the notes while adeptly opening the flute case again and bringing up the delicate instrument. Then he wrinkled his nose. "Yeah, this is awfully upbeat. I knew there was a reason why I haven't played this in a while."

"You can pick something else," Corey said, a peace offering of sorts.

"Nah. This is fine." He brought the flute up to his lips and played. The magical, light tones cascaded out of his instrument, playful and rich and colorful, opening up visual scenes of city life, from a sunrise to a romantic interlude.

Corey listened, unable to look away or even breathe. The boy's handling of his musical instrument was absolutely heavenly. Each of the seven vignettes became alive, like buds unfolding into flowers, showcasing small sections of human life in a city, and through Dylan's music Corey saw it all in his mind.

When the last notes echoed in the room, Dylan placed the flute on his lap. "Saw you coming in with Allie. You and he hook up?"

Corey sighed, realizing these kids were no different from other teenagers who had an uncanny ability to see what adults didn't always wish them to see. "He's, uh... helping me. Kind of like he helps all of you here."

Dylan looked up, a frown marring his forehead, almost concealed by his bangs. "You homeless too?"

Corey chuckled mirthlessly and shook his head. "No. I'm, uh... frigid."

Now Dylan swiveled on the chair to fully face Corey. "Huh? You mean you can't...?" He rolled his wrist about in a vague but understandable gesture.

"Not until him. He was the first. *Is* the first. The one." Where the hell had that last part come from? Corey wondered how to take it back. Then he realized he wasn't going to.

Dylan scrunched his nose in contemplation. "You've never...? But you're, like, old."

Surprising himself, Corey laughed out loud. "Gee, thanks, kid." He sobered up quick. "I'll be thirty-four come next birthday. But yeah, I've only known Lucian for a couple of months, and he's... shown me how to be... me."

Dylan seemed to ponder this for a moment. Then he exhaled a sharp burst of air, with a chuckle. "And here I thought I had it bad!"

That comment led to them both chortling like hyenas.

Finally Corey had to ask, out of genuine curiosity. "How come you're not in a music school somewhere? 'Cause you're great, you know."

At first it seemed like Dylan was about to shut down, but then he sighed and shrugged, appearing nonchalant. Corey suspected it was false bravado. "Haven't even finished high school yet. And with my parents—" Paling, Dylan swallowed hard, and Corey wished he knew of a way to console the boy. Clearly his coming out had gone all wrong. In Corey's opinion, having a gay kid didn't make for bad parents; throwing their kid out for something beyond the kid's control *did* make for bad parents. "Anyway, those places cost money. Which I don't got."

"There are scholarships and—" Corey started to speak.

"Listen, man. Thanks but I got this. I'll figure this shit out on my own." The strength and assertiveness in Dylan impressed Corey but also depressed him a bit.

"Yeah, I get it." Corey looked down at his feet, gulping and searching for confidence to say the words without sounding condescending or as if he were offering a handout. "I just want you to know that you don't have to do everything alone, you know." He cleared his throat, feeling he was saying it all wrong. "I mean, I'm not saying you can't handle things on your own. I just, uh, I know people. And I love music. And... you know, if you ever wanted... I could, um...."

Suddenly Dylan chuckled, shaking Corey out of his speech, which sucked. "You sure you work here, Mr. Pimp? 'Cause that pep talk needs some serious work."

Corey snorted. "Little shit."

Dylan laughed again. "Dickhead." Then he looked at Corey with a mischievous glint in his eyes, reminding Corey of Lucian. "So... you'd be willing to be my...." Dylan's voice trailed off as he quirked an eyebrow— and was clearly teasing Corey for all he was worth.

"Don't fucking say it!" Corey stopped him with a grunt, certain if he heard the words *sugar daddy* from the boy he might hurl or strangle him, one or the other. "How about a sponsor?"

Dylan rolled his eyes. "Okay. Gimme twenty bucks."

Corey glared at the boy. "Why?"

Dylan flicked his tongue at Corey. "'Cause I'm sure you've got it. And *I* don't."

Corey huffed out an impatient breath. "That's not exactly how sponsorships work, but I think you damn well know that. Jackass," he murmured under his breath as a last insult.

"Whatever you say, hoss." Dylan peeked at the black storage tube Corey was carrying, slung over his shoulder. "What's that?"

Corey grabbed the storage tube and dragged it in his lap. "I carry blueprints in here."

"Blueprints of what?"

Corey was flattered by Dylan's interest, and he smiled. "I studied to be an architect. I don't work as one, but lately I've started to question a lot of things about my lifestyle."

Dylan grinned. "Days of playing rich playboy get boring, hoss?"

Corey grinned back. "You're really starting to piss me off, you know that, kid?" When Dylan said nothing, just held his flute more tightly, Corey explained. "I've been thinking about a way to contribute. Lucian's got this place and all his other… programs. I'm a bit lost." He opened the screw top of the tube and pulled out a scroll of plans he had designed over the past couple of weeks. Together, they unrolled them, and several floor plan designs became visible.

"What are these for?" Dylan asked, studying the diagrams with curiosity.

"I was thinking I could design a new, um, safe house for LGBT kids. Heather House is big, but from what I've seen, there's always a need for more. The outreach programs, even with the help of backers like Lucian, can only do so much." He examined the designs he had drawn up with great care. "I'm not a shrink or a therapist or a counselor, like most folks here. But this… this I can do."

Silence stretched until Corey realized Dylan was staring at him, dumbfounded. "You'd build a house for street kids?"

Corey nodded, resolute in his decision. "Yeah. I mean, I've still got a lot of designing to do. And that's just the start. We'll need backers, sponsors, developers, builders, electricians, and… a lot of other stuff. But…." He nodded to himself, inspecting his work. "Yeah, in a year we could have a new place. Like Heather House."

Dylan let out a half snort, half chuckle. "You're insane, dude. Just so you know."

Corey snickered, bowing his head. "Good kind of crazy." He locked gazes with Dylan. "What do you think? Could this plan work?"

Dylan got up, wary again. "You gonna ask around about this project?"

"I was planning on it, yeah."

Dylan paused everything—words and motions—an angry look replacing the earlier amusement. "Don't get their hopes up if you aren't gonna deliver."

Corey understood the responsibility he was undertaking. The moment this matter became public knowledge it would become real, and he could no longer back out, or he would risk hurting the people he wanted to help. Including himself.

"I won't." He hesitated, and then added, "I'm not gonna promise, 'cause I have a feeling you guys have heard all too many of those. But I will try my very best." He glanced down at the blueprints before rolling them up and putting them back in the tube. "I've never designed a place that actually got built. I never dreamed of doing anything like this. In fact, I never dreamed I'd dream about architecture. But now there's a goal, and I want to do this. I need to do this." Looking up, he said, "I'd love it if any of you guys wanted to help out."

The wariness still there, Dylan nodded carefully, his eyes sharp and confident. "Well, if you're gonna ask around, be prepared to replace all the schoolrooms with game rooms." He chuckled, and Corey chimed in. "Oh, and uh, if it's at all possible, lots of bathrooms. Guys hate sharing. Girls don't mind being social, I guess, but we. Fucking. Hate it."

Corey nodded, enthusiastic and smiling. "Bathrooms. Gotcha." Then he just had to ask because he valued this boy's opinion for some reason. "You gonna help me out too? Remember you're talking to a total newbie at pimping shit out."

Dylan rolled his eyes and laughed. "Guess I got no choice now. Ask me again once you've got your ducks in a row and this project started. And then, maybe... I'll be the first one to move in."

Corey smiled, relieved and happy and proud. This accomplishment, though only in its initial stages, was the first step on a new path toward a life with purpose and meaning. "It's a deal."

OVER THE next two weeks, Corey spent almost all his time with Dylan and several other kids at Heather House, going over his designs, refining and perfecting them, when they weren't in class. Everyone seemed to have an opinion, and Corey liked the youths' ideas. Before they came there, many had no homes, no money, no schooling, and no prospects, but along with a readiness and willingness to offer new insights, they had a hopeful enthusiasm Corey had come to respect and admire.

It had been a long day in the middle of the week, and Corey was looking forward to an evening spent with Lucian. Sure, he was fucking tired, but there was a good reason, other than work, for that. The night before, he had gotten precious little sleep because Lucian had decided to fulfill one of Corey's fantasies, one he'd had since the first time they had slow danced together at Boudoir.

Corey had lain in bed in his boxer briefs, waiting for Lucian to emerge from the bathroom so they could go to sleep side by side, with an hour of snuggling at first....

His yawns were interrupted by the bathroom door flinging open—and Lucian twirling to lean on the doorframe, looking ever so sexy and seductive, all naked and beautifully pale, like a jewel, except for his rainbow-colored silk and lace underwear that barely concealed his manhood. His very impressive, hardening manhood.

Then the speakers in the bedroom awakened, and the swift beat of a mambo floated in the room, filling it with a musical sensuality Corey was too stunned to react to—at first.

But the moment the intro ended and the real song began, the lyrics charged at Corey. And the marimba rhythms activated Lucian into a flurry of feverish dancing.

Lucian swirled around the room like a spinning tornado of sensuality, his hips swaying, so light on his toes he practically glided frenetically through the air.

Corey sat up on the bed, his eyes wide, staring hungrily at the scene of his lover dancing for him alone.

Lucian utilized every square inch of the room, stopping abruptly at the bedposts and doing a grind and then springing to action and using the open floor space to really let loose, dancing like a madman. Lucian was a gymnast, after all, and he could sure hit those high kicks. Some of those moves had to be illegal. He was evidently feeling the music in every sense, his body fully engaged, his arms high over his head, his butt swinging like there was no tomorrow, his feet thumping the floor and gliding as if tiptoeing on air.

His lips formed the lyrics even though no sound could be heard, silently begging Corey to dance with him, hold him close, and sway them both in unison, mimicking acts of love. With his hands and a devilish smile, he beckoned Corey to him. And Corey was powerless to resist.

Corey scrambled off the bed in a rush and joined Lucian, hugging him close with a tight arm around his waist. They clung to each other like twins joined at the hip. Then the rhythm swept them away, and they danced to their hearts' content, pressed together from lips to hips. Their legs entwined and released, as though they had danced like this a thousand times. The quick pace afforded unrestricted freedom of movement, with no need for patterns or pretenses. The hypnotic beat thudded in their bodies like a second heart, and they gyrated together, two whirlwinds joining as one.

Their hard cocks swayed along with the rest of their frames, and Corey was drowned by a tidal surge of desire, as though the trumpets and drums of the music commanded him with their primitive cadences. He kissed Lucian, his tongue plundering his lover's mouth deep with a ravenous hunger. Lucian clawed at his back and shoulders until he jumped on Corey, wrapped his legs around Corey's waist, and ground hard enough to create sparks. Unhindered by their rising passions, both men continued to dance, one welded to the other's hips, even though the music ended— only to begin anew, set in a loop.

Once they had danced their feet into mush and gotten tired of the mambo, they retired to the bed and sated their desires. Twice.

Despite the lack of sleep, Corey had loved every minute of their time together.

As a result of their activities the previous night, Corey trudged out of the elevator, yawning hard enough to dislocate his jaw. He made his way to the front door of Lucian's penthouse apartment, trying not to drag his feet too sleepily. The two of them had talked about the future only on the surface, but by a mutual, wordless agreement, it was understood that Corey would sleep in Lucian's canopy bed until further notice.

If Corey managed to keep his eyes open long enough, tonight Corey and Lucian were going to try wax play….

Amaya had given Corey a spare key, so he unlocked the door, stifled yet another jaw-cracking yawn, and entered. Usually it was quiet. But tonight piano music floated about, a blue, sorrowful tune echoing in the minimalist apartment.

Corey put his satchel and storage tube down and followed the music, a soft smile on his lips. Standing in the doorway to the wide living room, Corey watched as Lucian played the piano, his delicate fingers like butterflies dancing over the keys. Amaya was leaning against the instrument with a mournful look on her lovely, dolled-up face. Contrary to her usual attire, tonight she wore a simple, elegant black silk dress that flowed down her curves like a cascade.

Though not a classical piece of music, Corey recognized the lovely yet melancholy melody of "Mad World," the slow version from the Gary Jules cover. There were vocals, but neither Lucian nor Amaya was singing.

Then Amaya saw Corey, and she gasped, straightening up. Immediately Lucian halted his playing and swung around on his stool to stare at Corey.

Ambling toward them, Corey smiled. "I didn't know you could play the piano."

Lucian offered a rueful smile in return. "I grew up on Chopin. My mother's influence. Sadly, the piano is the only instrument I know." His smile faded, and those different-colored eyes seemed desolate somehow, haunted. "Amaya, would you please excuse us."

It wasn't a command but a request, and with a tiny bow, she left, passing by Corey with an equally joyless expression. Corey got a sudden bad feeling.

"What's wrong? What's happened?" He hurried to sit at Lucian's side and gripped his hand in his own, concerned.

Next thing Corey knew, Lucian was crying, tears streaming down his cheeks. Alarmed, Corey started to speak, to offer comfort, with a million questions plaguing his mind, but Lucian got there first, his voice hoarse and timid.

"Corey, love, I am so sorry to have to tell you this, but…." Lucian swallowed hard, obviously fighting his instinct to shed more tears. For a moment Corey only heard the unexpected endearment, but unfortunately that happy implication didn't last. "Your friend at Heather House, Dylan.... He's dead."

Corey stared, unable to absorb the bad news.

Then, as the terrible truth finally sunk in, a newborn hope within him was decimated. A precious and fragile feeling inside him—no doubt a result of Dylan's influence on him—broke, perhaps irreparably.

CHAPTER 31

"HAVE YOU ever lost someone you knew? Someone you were close to?"

Corey heard his own voice, but it sounded foreign in his ears, alien and devoid of all emotions. Lucian hugged him tighter as they lay together in bed that night, naked in every respect. Corey was tired of hiding who he was and how he felt. Lucian understood; of that Corey was sure.

But despite his sorrow at the loss of a boy who had his whole life ahead of him, suddenly he remembered an earlier talk with Lucian. "Sorry, Lu. I know you've lost loved ones. I should have recalled. Julian and Fleur. Your grandparents."

Lucian kissed Corey's temple, a soft brush over his hair, a whispering touch on his skin. "Yes. Julian…. He was important to me, as you know. Fleur…. She died when I was five. I have only the barest of memories about her. The scent of her hair, mostly. And her eyes. Julian told me they were like mine, only of different color."

"Really?" Corey propped himself up on his elbow, leaning toward Lucian, watching his face, studying him in the shadows as night had fallen. The curtains were drawn aside, and the floor-to-ceiling windows showed a nighttime city of twinkling lights. Lucian's eyes glimmered in the dark, his tears unshed.

"Yes. Only hers were green and hazel." Lucian stared up at the ceiling, a sad smile on his lips. "I wish I could remember more about her. Julian never stopped talking about Fleur. She was the love of his life." His smiled vanished, and tears ran down his cheeks as they finally spilled. "When Julian died, I was twenty-two. I was away when it happened, on a cruise in the Caribbean. I didn't get to say good-bye. I lost all sense of who I was for a long time."

That sounded horribly familiar. "I'm sorry, Lu. So sorry."

Lucian blinked, and then his focus was fixed on Corey. He caressed Corey's jaw and cheek, tracing the growing stubble, a scratching sound following. "I am sorry for your loss as well, Corey. Losing Dylan like that…. A senseless, meaningless death. I know you two were close. Friends."

Corey came back down to rest his head on the pillow, and together they lay face-to-face. "I don't know about friends. He hadn't opened up to me yet. I wish he had."

"Oh, love, you're wrong." Lucian kissed him briefly, a fleeting intimacy. "Dylan spoke more to you than he had to anyone else. Even me."

Corey frowned in disbelief, yet hopeful. "Really? But he called you Allie. I didn't…."

Lucian nodded in sympathy. "Dylan loved music, but he hated math."

Corey chuckled, but the sound was hollow. "I would've thought the two were, I don't know, connected."

"Music is a form of mathematical representation, it's true. But it is also a language of the soul, of inspiration and creation." Lucian nuzzled Corey's neck and then brushed the tips of their noses together. "He liked your architectural plans for the new house. He told me so just last week. But he made me promise I would not tell you. He had this crazy notion the flattery might go to your head."

Corey laughed, the sharp pain in his chest dulling a bit. The mirth didn't last, and he felt miserable again. This wasn't a session with Lucian. But this was about touch. Dylan's death touched Corey to the core, to his soul, a timeless connection broken. And this was about taste. The morbid taste of death, bittersweet, permeated his skin all the way to his heart, creating a sickness of longing and sorrow. He had to accept not everything always went according to plan, least of all life.

Corey could hardly breathe. "What's gonna happen to his brother?"

"He says he did not mean to kill Dylan, only beat him up and make a man out of him. An honorable, straight man. The sentencing depends on the DA, I suppose."

Corey growled. "The fucker should get the chair!" First, to turn your back on your own brother, your flesh and blood. That was one thing. But to kill…? Inconceivable.

Lucian held on to Corey tighter, threading his fingers in Corey's hair, petting. "When I saw him at the police station, he was heartbroken, inconsolable. I believe him that he did not intend for Dylan to—"

"To die?" Corey scoffed angrily, a wet sound due to his own sorrow. "Oh no. Why kill when you can just pummel and maim and—" Corey stopped himself in time. Anger was futile, and it hurt his memories of

Dylan, tarnished them. His ambivalence was making him mad. "Dylan was so good, Lu. You should've heard him play. He had a future; he had a gift; he…." His voice choked on sobs, and then he was crying again.

Lucian embraced him and kept the demons at bay. "Love is not weakness of character. But love is a source of a great many other emotions, like jealousy, rage, and sorrow. Love can be a strength or a frailty. As human beings, we are allowed to feel it all. Or burdened to feel every layer of such a complex phenomenon…." Lucian's voice trailed off, and he sighed. "I sound like a dictionary or a psychology brochure. Corey? Cry all you want. I will be here when you're done. I swear."

Corey nodded frantically and let out a wet chuckle. "Ha! You swore!" It was a silly joke, but it made Lucian purr, a kind, warm sound Corey tucked into his heart. "I'll miss him."

"As long as you do, Dylan will never really be lost."

Corey inhaled Lucian's fruity scent, letting it fill him with all the love he could get. "He was such a brat. Argumentative, brazen. He wore this kind of shield around him. A street swagger. But he played like the angels." Lucian did not speak, only held him, so Corey said, "I'm gonna finish that housing project. And I'm gonna name it after him. The Dylan Hudson House. What do you think?" Corey hadn't even known the kid's last name until after his death, when the police found his body in an alley, beaten to a bloody pulp. *No fair. Not fucking fair*.

"I think he might like that." Corey heard the smile in Lucian's voice.

"Nah. He'd probably curse me for being a sentimental dickhead. But hey, at least it'd mean I would have gotten the job done. And that… that he would like." Of that Corey was certain. Dylan had accused Corey of being a one-off, and that was the last thing Corey wanted to be.

"Did you tell your parents?"

"Yeah. They're coming with us to the funeral. They didn't know him, but Mom said it would give the right impression and give Dylan a voice in the public eye, even though he's gone, and Dad said it would be appropriate because of who he was to me." Randolph and Prudence had been saddened and furious to hear about the death of a fifteen-year-old who had come to matter a lot to Corey. They wished they had met Dylan, and Corey dreamed of the same.

Of course, now it was too late. A stupid, senseless crime that served no one.

"I hate this," Corey confessed, apparently not done with his rage against the uncaring machine called society. He knew he would have to let go of those useless emotions in order to mourn Dylan's death properly and to be able to move on in time. But a mere day later, it was fucking hard.

"I know, love. I know. I will miss him also. So much." Lucian pressed against Corey, who sensed it was his time to offer comfort as well. Lucian had spent the day at Heather House in an attempt to ensure that every kid there, whether they had known Dylan or not, got the help they needed, be it privacy to grieve or a person to talk to.

Most kids there had only known Dylan as the withdrawn flutist, and he hadn't had many friends. Corey counted himself as one, though, even if they had only known each other for a short time.

Corey thought about his own friendships. He had but a few, and not one of them was a confidant or a bosom buddy. He had an occasional beer with the guys next door, and he had some acquaintances through his social circles. But true friends? Dylan had been that more than anyone else he knew. Corey had told him about his newfound life as a gay man and his relationship with Lucian. Dylan had listened. Corey wished *he* had listened more.

But all the listening in the world would not have changed the fact that Dylan's brother had ambushed him in an alley and beaten him to death. A violent sendoff to a wonderful boy, who would never get a chance to fulfill the gift within him. What had been Dylan's dreams and hopes? Corey cursed himself for not knowing that.

In his heart he knew the kid might have shown enthusiasm but had not been ready to open up. Corey wondered if Dylan's parents would show up at the funeral. Considering they had kicked him to the curb, Corey thought it unlikely.

It was too late for Dylan.

Was it too late for Corey?

"Lu?" he asked quietly. "Do you think it's possible to love only one single person in the whole wide world?" *And get aroused by.* But he didn't finish that thought out loud.

But Lucian, as usual, was one step ahead, even if they were on the same wavelength. "To love and be turned on by, you mean? Yes." Lucian smiled at him, their gazes locked. "Yes, I do believe that. I didn't always. In fact, one could say it is a relatively new revelation for me."

Corey swallowed hard. "Y-you mean… you've fallen in love with… s-someone?"

Lucian wavered, and Corey worried. "We, that is to say you and I, have known each other for only four months." Lucian frowned, his eyes glazed over, and Corey held his breath as if his life was holding on by a thread. Then Lucian refocused on Corey, 100 percent. "But I have fallen in love with you."

Now all those hesitations of Lucian's, the hard blinking and the weird sudden silences, it all made sense. Lucian had been afraid to speak the words, just like Corey.

In his mind, Elvis crooned about fools rushing in and helplessly falling in love. The truth of those lyrics was the truth of his soul.

Corey let out a shaky breath, his heart soaring, and he couldn't help but smile, even if it was tentative. "Yeah? That's freaking awesome 'cause I love you too, Lu." He grew serious. "If you don't mind the possibility I could revert back to being frigid."

Lucian rolled his eyes—the gesture reminding him of Dylan. "We all have our quirks. Yours is no weirder than anyone else's. Besides, I think I lucked out with you." Corey wasn't exactly sure what that meant, but they would have the rest of their lives to talk things through. Then Lucian suddenly grew serious. "My only… concern is about your past."

Corey frowned, baffled. "What do you mean?"

Lucian sounded uncertain, even rueful. "You used to be an adrenaline junkie, seeking thrills from high-risk experiences when relationships with people did not fare so well. It leaves me wondering—"

"If I'll throw myself into a frenzied orgy rather than an exclusive relationship with you. That's it, isn't it?"

Lucian closed his eyes, as if in pain, and his jaw quivered. Clearly he hadn't meant to sound demanding of monogamy, but only protecting his heart. "I have my own commitment issues to deal with, so I am well aware of the hypocrisy factor of my…." He seemed to struggle to finish, and Corey could not let him dwell in the dark.

Gently Corey caressed his lover's cheek until Lucian reopened his eyes, unshed tears glistening in their blue-and-green depths. "Dylan's death showed me life is unpredictable and short and that every fleeting moment is precious and irreplaceable. Lu, I adore you. Nothing and no one makes me feel but you. Every time I've felt anything, inside or out, it's only been with you, during our sessions and our relationship. I don't know how to be any clearer with you. I love you. I guess... you need to decide whether or not you trust me."

Blinking the tears away, Lucian smiled back, a joyous glow to his expression. "I do love and trust you, Corey. Forgive me."

"There's nothing to forgive," Corey assured him. Then his own doubts surfaced. "You sure you wanna take this road with *me*? I mean, your mentoring program, and all."

Lucian studied him steadily, not unkindly but sadly. "You wish me to stop—"

"Fuck, no!" Corey all but yelled, shaking his head furiously. "I don't want you to do anything you don't want to. Plus, I want you to continue your work and help people. And I wanna help you too, any way I can. I just want to... to help." His throat clogged as the sorrow once again tried to push through, but he fended it off. "I hope I was able to give Dylan some comfort in his last days. I wanna be that for someone else too. A friend. A helping hand. I like Heather House and the kids there. I'm not as good as you, obviously, but—"

"But nothing." Lucian sounded emphatic, and Corey smiled at his decisiveness. "I am thankful for and proud of you, Corey. Thank you. I know Dylan would say the same." As Corey kept swallowing the sadness lodged in his throat, Lucian kissed him several times, soft as a breeze. "For the last couple of months, you have no longer been my client. You have been my friend, my confidant, my trusted companion, my lover, and now my partner. While before these declarations of love may have been inappropriate and even unethical, now I am able and allowed to speak of love to you. We still have to sign papers to conclude our professional relationship, but all it takes is a few signatures. Then... love. There is a saying I know: *Sing like no one is listening. Dance like no one is watching. Love like your heart has never been broken.* Blake may have been my latest love, but you, Corey, you will be my last love."

Corey smiled. "Your one true love. Yeah. That sounds good. And right." Everything now settled between them, most every teacher-novice bond between them severed, obstacles gone, the two of them were in the clear, ready to begin their new relationship. He lifted his hand, and with deliberate slowness, he trailed his fingertips over Lucian's lips. "I've dreamed of tracing your lips with my fingers so many times." He touched the tiny indentation above his upper lip. "This dip right here drives me crazy." He followed the round, plump shape of Lucian's pouty lower lip.

"This curve, so soft and ripe for me to kiss and lick and nibble on." Corey carried out his erotic description, causing Lucian to moan.

They kissed leisurely until Lucian murmured, "Any other part of me you dream about? I am more than willing to be your test subject for any kind of empirical research. Any. Kind."

Corey chuckled. "Good to know. I'll have to come up with a comprehensive, detailed research proposal. Or... I could just wing it." He winked, all concerns between them evaporated. Except for... one mundane worry he needed solved immediately. "So... *babe*... you a night owl or an early bird? 'Cause I gotta tell you, I'm *not* an early bird. Wake me up before nine, and we've got a problem." Testing the endearment came easily, like second nature.

For a moment Lucian stared, wide-eyed. Then he burst into a fit of giggles, causing Corey to fall in love with him a smidgeon more. "Oh, love. I hate to tell you this, but... I happen to be the earliest bird in town."

Corey groaned playfully. "Oh God, why me?"

Lucian grinned wickedly. "Looks like we have earned each other. Now... shut up and kiss me like you mean it."

What else could Corey do? He kissed the man he loved exactly like he meant it.

All over, to be exact.

EPILOGUE

"I HAVEN'T seen you for six months. But I hear through the grapevine you have been very active of late." Adelaide Kingsley offered the praise without reservations or guile. As usual she showed only honest appreciation. Then she quirked an eyebrow, and the hidden, mischievous part of her personality peeked out. "Well?" And there went the smug, knowing tone.

"All right. Fine. You were right. He is perfect for me. The right one. The... one." He cleared his throat. "Congratulate yourself, Ms. Kingsley. You have earned a hearty pat on the back."

Adelaide inclined her head slightly in acknowledgment of the compliment, neither her hair nor her tight dress moving an inch. "How are things faring between the two of you?"

"Very well. Corey moved in with me last week. He still retains his own apartment, for sentimental or economic reasons, I believe, but in essence everything he owns is now at my—*our*—penthouse residence. Corey still grinds his teeth in his sleep sometimes, but all other signs of stress shine in their absence. He says his stomach doesn't knot and ache so much anymore, and his cuticles look, well, cute. Anyway, we're having a family get-together this weekend, his parents meeting mine. My mother, Chastity, and his mother, Prudence, have been corresponding via phone calls, texts, and e-mails for over a month now. So this family outing will happen among friends." Lucian fixed his tie, even though it was perfectly knotted, and smoothed the imaginary wrinkles off his white slacks. He had an uncanny inkling the family dinner would end with a wedding planned for him and Corey....

Adelaide nodded. "I see. How would you characterize your progress with Corey over the past six months? Second thoughts? Regrets? Doubts?"

Lucian cocked his head to the side and then turned halfway, offering the brunette therapist his profile as he stared out the window of the skyscraper at the sunshine beaming brightly over the Manhattan skyline.

"I expected those. I waited for them. I was ready to analyze and tackle them. But none have arisen. I…." He hesitated.

Adelaide seized the window of opportunity. "Corey knows much about you, doesn't he? Instinctively."

Lucian smirked halfheartedly. "I have yet to tell him I am six years younger than him, though. I don't know how he will react to me being only twenty-seven…." He swallowed. "At first I wanted to be new and pure and shiny to Corey, instead of slutty and used and… imperfect. But even with my past—and my present as a sex mentor—for Corey, I am a dream come true. As he is to me, after a fashion. My relationship with him is… easy and effortless, as though we have been together for ages instead of six months. When we make love, it feels as if we have made love for eons." An echo of the past whisked past him but left nothing in its wake but a sigh. "As you well know, I have had commitment issues since my youth."

"Yes. That is why you first came to me three years ago."

Lucian smiled, still gazing at the outside view. Soon the heat of the city would become unbearable. Where would he take Corey to escape the heat waves? The Hamptons? Or perhaps a private island in the Caribbean?

"Now I am someone who can commit. Corey and I have talked at length about my issues with trust and his issues with sex, and I believe we have reached an understanding. We are on the same wavelength. If he wishes to try sex with another, it is something we can discuss. So far, though, he seems capable of—and willing to have—sex only with me. And I am capable of commitment to only him, willing to be with him exclusively. So…." He shrugged, but smiled, reminiscing. "Do you recall when I told you about how I had self-diagnosed myself with hypersexuality when I was young?"

"Yes." Judging from her light tone, Adelaide smiled in return, but always professional, coolly aloof.

"Well, as it turned out, I am not hypersexual. And as for my commitment issues, well, I would declare them a thing of the past too." Lucian finally looked back at the woman he trusted. "I am well aware how corny this may sound, but Corey and I, we complete each other."

"How?"

Lucian considered his response carefully. "Corey has a tendency to overanalyze, while I am more practical. He is rarely impulsive, though, not like I can be. But we share passions too, and decisive personality traits. He is as eager to help out where he can as I am."

"So you see him as a solution for your prior lack of commitment?"

"No. Yes. No." Lucian frowned, getting his thoughts in order. "In many ways Corey is an answer. But he is not an answer to my problems but to my prayers. At first he needed me. But then he began to want me. Desire me for me. And then, finally, he fell in love with me. As I with him. Are we the solutions for our individual predicaments, different but similar? Corey's frigidity and my commitment issues? Perhaps. On some level I would have to concede to that logic."

"But...?" Adelaide prompted gently, probing deeply as ever.

"But...." Lucian smiled because he was happy and unafraid to show it. "Corey and I are more than the sum of our sexual conditions. Our relationship is... emergent." Lucian giggled, and Adelaide joined with a slightly more subdued sound. "I admit I do not have all the answers, but we are each other's questions, and that is fine. It is perfect. To never run out of questions, to never want for challenges."

"Have you two spoken of love?"

Lucian nodded, beaming. "Yes. We have said the words and continue to say them. In and out of bed."

"So, in your professional opinion, Corey Paige was not and is not frigid?"

"No. If anything, it was *I* who was frigid. I melted his body, but he warmed my heart." Lucian straightened his posture on the couch. "I realize how frail and unpredictable relationships can be. Compatible partners share, not only passion and love, but personal interests and life's pursuits. I think Corey and I have all the above."

"Please, elaborate." Adelaide sounded intrigued, so Lucian updated her about Boudoir and Heather House and described the new housing project Corey was working on. Since its inception two months ago, Corey had made great headway and had found a building site plus two backers, with several others in the works. "Mr. Paige has a singular vision, it seems."

Lucian was immensely proud of his... boyfriend? Best friend? Lover? Partner? Corey was all those, and more. "He is one of a kind, I think. He has a good head on his shoulders. He makes wise decisions. He doesn't need or ask for fame or for anyone to know his name. His sole goal is to help where he can. This project of his, it was born from selflessness and, yes, sorrow too, but it has grown into something bigger. More than a monument to a lost friend. It shows a promise of a better tomorrow."

Adelaide pondered the news. "It appears you unlocked Corey's hidden potential as well as the treasure trove of his sexual capabilities."

"He did that on his own. All he required was… a nudge."

Adelaide nodded, a chuckle escaping her lips like a naughty afterthought. "Well, there are six months of events to go through and assess. Let us start from the beginning, shall we? And please, spare not a single lurid detail on my account. I am no blushing bride."

Lucian laughed at Adelaide's request. "Perish the thought. Corey and I. Our love story began six months ago, on a fine day when I was staying at my penthouse, feeding melon balls to my baby panther…."

As his voice flew effortlessly through the air, echoing around them, Lucian let his memory wander back to the first moment he laid eyes on Corey. The handsome young man with a problem he did not fully understand but wanted to deal with. His hesitance mixed with his urgency. And all the while it had been there, simmering beneath the calm surface: the need to love and be loved for who he was.

The same need that Lucian had hidden in his own heart. Same doubts, same fears. On the outside so dissimilar but inside totally alike.

Lucian might have been the key to Corey's inhibitions, but Corey had been the key to Lucian's future. As the past six months had shown, they held the keys to each other's hearts, bodies, and souls. No more were they just virgin and slut, frigid and feverish, new and old, sensualist and apprentice. During their sensual sojourn, they had exceeded those parameters and boundaries.

Lucian and Corey could now look forward to the future—without labels.

SUSAN LAINE, a multi-published author of LGBT erotic romance and a Finn through and through, was raised by the best mother in the world. She told her daughter time and again that she could be whatever she wanted to be. The spark for serious writing kindled when Susan discovered the gay erotic romance genre.

Anthropology is Susan's formal education, but she has set her long-term sights on becoming a full-time writer. Susan enjoys hanging out with her sister, two nieces and friends in movie theaters, bookstores, and parks. Her favorite pastimes include pop music, action flicks, chocolate, and doing the dishes, while a few of her dislikes are sweating hot summer days, tobacco smoke, and purposeful prejudice.

Visit Susan's website at http://www.susan-laine-author.fi/or join her newsletter or write her an e-mail at susan.laine@hotmail.com.

Falling for Rain

By Susan Laine

Matt Wetherton is just an average-looking tax attorney until he breaks up a gay bashing and unwittingly becomes a hero. He isn't looking for a date, but when he meets the man he rescued, he finds himself longing for one anyway. Rain Deveraux is a beautiful, effeminate lounge singer—and utterly unwilling to be Matt's damsel in distress, even if he does wear women's clothing for his performances. When common courtesy prompts Rain to pay Matt a thank-you call, it's the beginning of the romance of their lives.

Before long, Matt and Rain fall for each other hard and fast, but both men are stubborn: Rain clings to his right to express himself even though Matt worries for his safety. Despite their occasional clashes, the passion between them is undeniable.

When an accident compromises Rain's independence as well as his singing voice, it tests the strength of their newfound relationship. It is up to Matt to help Rain find his music again before depression sullies the brightness in Rain's soul.

http://www.dreamspinnerpress.com

Haunted Heart

By Susan Laine

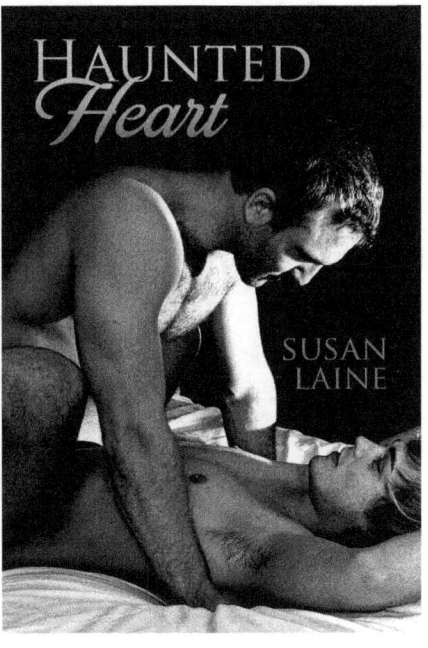

Duncan Kerr is the art director of Enamored Press, an erotic romance publisher based in Seattle. An open submissions call for new artists yields an imaginative book cover with rich details and bold colors that catches his interest. After a few more samples of work and some e-mails, Duncan is determined to hire the talented young artist on a permanent basis.

But Ruben Winterbottom isn't an average freelance artist. His agoraphobia leaves him terrified to set foot outside his secluded house in the woods by the Olympic National Park. Living alone, fear is Ruben's sole companion.

When the two men meet, Ruben has a panic attack and hides away. Although confused, Duncan sees past Ruben's anxiety to his artistic gifts and beautiful soul. So he sets out to coax the young man out of his shy shell.

http://www.dreamspinnerpress.com

Lofty Dreams of Earthbound Men

Isleshire Chronicles: Book One

By Susan Laine

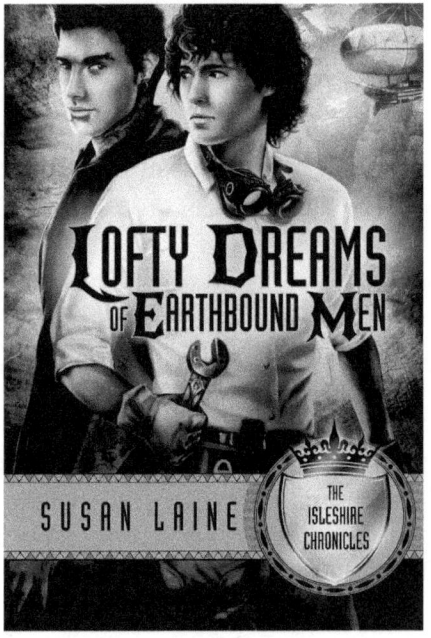

On the night of the summer solstice, Obadai Bashim encounters Jules Sterling, a young engineering sage. Jules is on the run from a ripper, an assassin of the Theocracy who has already killed his master. Open atrocities by rippers are unusual in County Isleshire, where freedom and acceptance reign over prejudice.

However, political instability between the Five Kingdoms and the Divine Theocracy has set the theocrats on a mission to crown religious doctrine over science, and the Sage's Guild is number one on their eradication list. If Obadai helps, he'll have a price on his head too, but he can't abandon Jules.

Escaping the ripper's clutches is not enough. Jules has a mission of his own: to repair a faulty airship inn about to crash into the fortified township of Dunbruth. Luckily, Obadai has a few magickal secrets up his sleeve.

http://www.dreamspinnerpress.com

Wishing Wings

Isleshire Chronicles: Book Two

By Susan Laine

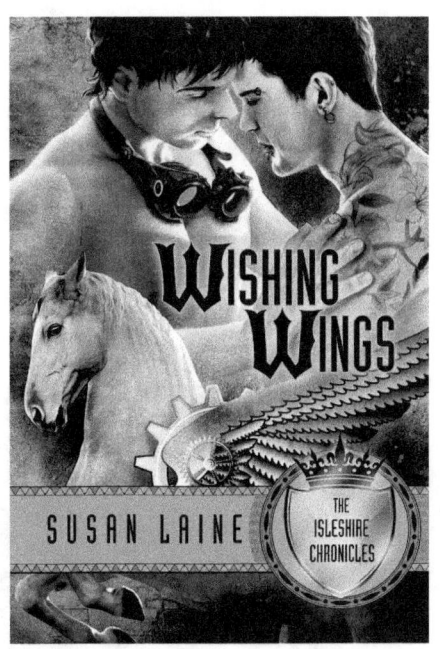

Two weeks after their encounter with a ripper, engineering sage Jules Sterling and Earth mage Obadai Bashim are surprised to learn Aelfric Fairburn, a bureaucrat from the Divine Theocracy, has arrived in County Isleshire to reward Jules for his courageous defeat of the ripper.

Fairburn's visit couldn't come at a worse time, as Jules is in the field-testing phase of his dream project—flying. But the Virtuist Church of the Spirit Gods views man's pursuit of flight as heresy and a contemptuous abomination of the ultimate ambition of the faithful—ascension.

But Fairburn's judgment is the least of Jules's problems. While he struggles to work out the kinks of his flying apparatus, a mysterious figure operates behind the scenes toward an unknown end. Once again, Jules and Obadai face a lethal foe.

http://www.dreamspinnerpress.com

http://www.dreamspinnerpress.com

The Wheel Mysteries

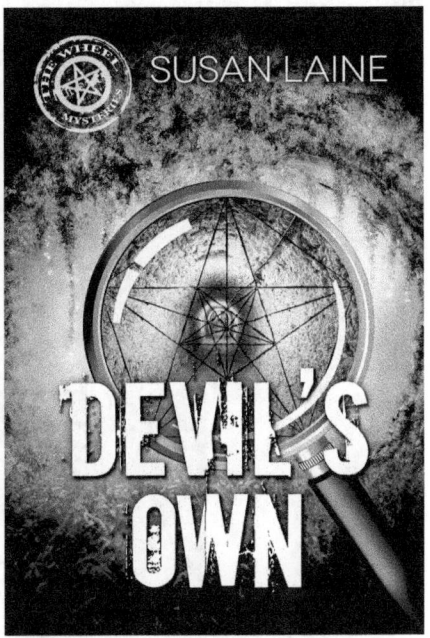

http://www.dreamspinnerpress.com

Lifting the Veil

http://www.dreamspinnerpress.com

Lifting the Veil

http://www.dreamspinnerpress.com

Senses and Sensations

Sounds of Love

Susan Laine

http://www.dreamspinnerpress.com

Love in Plain Sight

Susan Laine

http://www.dreamspinnerpress.com

A SENSES AND SENSATIONS MYSTERY: 3

A Luminous Touch

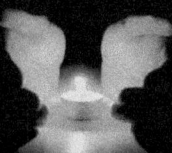

Susan Laine

http://www.dreamspinnerpress.com

Senses and Sensations

http://www.dreamspinnerpress.com

www.ingramcontent.com/pod-product-compliance
Lightning Source LLC
Chambersburg PA
CBHW070047030726
47506CB00002B/379